LADY OF QUALITY

By the same author in Pan Books

THESE OLD SHADES
THE BLACK MOTH
THE MASQUERADERS
POWDER AND PATCH
BEAUVALLET
THE CONQUEROR
DEVIL'S CUB
THE CONVENIENT MARRIAGE
REGENCY BUCK
THE TALISMAN RING
AN INFAMOUS ARMY
ROYAL ESCAPE
THE CORINTHIAN
THE SPANISH BRIDE
FARO'S DAUGHTER
FRIDAY'S CHILD
THE RELUCTANT WIDOW
THE FOUNDLING
ARABELLA
THE GRAND SOPHY
THE QUIET GENTLEMAN
COTILLION
THE TOLL-GATE
BATH TANGLE
FREDERICA
SPRIG MUSLIN
APRIL LADY
SYLVESTER
VENETIA
THE UNKNOWN AJAX
A CIVIL CONTRACT
FALSE COLOURS
BLACK SHEEP
COUSIN KATE
CHARITY GIRL

CONDITIONS OF SALE

GEORGETTE HEYER

LADY OF QUALITY

PAN BOOKS LTD

LONDON AND SYDNEY

First published 1972 by The Bodley Head Ltd.
This edition published 1973 by Pan Books Ltd,
Cavaye Place, London SW10 9PG

ISBN 0 330 23649 0

2nd Printing 1974

Made and printed in Great Britain by
Cox & Wyman Ltd, London, Reading and Fakenham

CHAPTER ONE

The elegant travelling carriage which bore Miss Wychwood from her birthplace, on the border of Somerset and Wiltshire, to her home in Bath, proceeded on its way at a decorous pace. This was dictated by her coachman, an elderly autocrat, who, having known her from the day of her birth, almost thirty years before, drove her at the pace he considered proper, and turned a deaf ear to her requests to him to 'put 'em along!' If she didn't know what was due to her consequence, as Miss Wychwood of Twynham Park, he did; and even if she was an old maid – in fact, almost an ape-leader, though he would never call her one, and had turned off the impudent stable-boy who had dared to do so, after giving him a rare box on the ear – he knew very well how his late master would have wished his only daughter to be driven about the country. He had a pretty good idea, too, of what Sir Thomas would have felt had he known that Miss Wychwood had set up her own establishment in Bath, a few months after his death, with only a squinny old Tough to lend her countenance. A mean bit, Miss Farlow, if ever he saw one: more like a skinned rabbit than a woman, and a regular gabble-grinder into the bargain. It was a marvel to him that Miss Wychwood was able to endure her bibble-babble, for *she* wasn't short of a sheet, not by any means she wasn't!

The lady thus stigmatized was seated beside Miss Wychwood in the carriage, beguiling the tedium of the journey with a stream of small talk. She was of uncertain age, but it was unkind to describe her as an old Tough; and although she was certainly very thin it was unjust to liken her to a skinned rabbit. She was a distant relation of Miss Wychwood, left by an improvident parent in indigent circumstances; and when she had received a visit from Sir Geoffrey Wychwood, and had grasped that she owed this unprecedented honour to his urgent wish to procure her services as chaperon to his sister she had seen in his unromantically stout person a Paladin sent by Providence to rescue her from a drab lodging, mean fare, and the constant dread of finding herself in debt. She was not to know that her prospective charge had fought strenuously against having her, or any other female, foisted on to her; but when she had presented herself at Twynham Park, nervously clutching her old fashioned reticule, desperately anxious to please, and staring up into Miss Wychwood's face with frightened pleading eyes, Miss Wychwood's heart had overcome her judgement, and she had had no other thought than to make the poor little creature welcome. Lady Wychwood, quite unable to picture meek little Miss Farlow as a companion, and far less as a chaperon, to the lively Miss Wychwood, took the earliest opportunity that offered to beg her sister-in-law not to accept Miss Farlow's services without careful consideration. 'I am persuaded, dearest, that you will find her a dreadful bore!' she said earnestly.

'Yes, very likely, but I should find any chaperon a dreadful bore,' said Annis. 'So, if I must have a chaperon – not that I see the least need of one, at my age! – I'd as lief have her as any other. At least she won't try to rule my house, or to dictate to me! Besides, I'm sorry for her!' She laughed suddenly, perceiving the doubtful look in Lady Wychwood's mild blue eyes. 'Ah, you are afraid she won't exercise any control over me! You are perfectly right: she won't! But nor would anyone else, you know.'

'But, Annis, Geoffrey says—'

'I know exactly what Geoffrey says,' interrupted Annis. 'I've known what he would say any time these twenty years, and I find him far more of a bore than poor Maria Farlow. No, no, don't try to look shocked! I daresay no one knows better than you that he and I *cannot* deal together. The only time when we have been in perfect agreement was when he assured me that I should love his wife!'

'Oh, Annis!' protested Lady Wychwood, blushing, and turning away her head. 'You shouldn't say such things! Besides, I can't believe you mean it, when you won't continue living with me!'

'What a rapper!' commented Annis, the laughter still dancing in her eyes. 'I could live happily with you for the rest of my days, as well you know! It's my very worthy, starched-up, and consequential brother with whom I can't and won't live. Yes, isn't it unnatural of me?'

'So *sad*!' mourned her ladyship.

'Oh, no, why? You would have cause to say so if I did remain here. You must surely own that life would be very much more peaceful without me provoking Geoffrey a dozen times a day!'

Lady Wychwood did not deny this, but she sighed and said: 'But you are far too young to be setting up your own establishment, dearest! I *quite* agree with dear Geoffrey about that!'

'You always do agree with him, Annabel: indeed, you are the perfect wife for him!' interjected Annis irrepressibly.

'I am sure I'm no such thing, though I do try to be. And as for agreeing with him, gentlemen are so much wiser than we are, and so much better able to *judge* of – of wordly matters – don't you think?'

'Emphatically, No!'

'But indeed Geoffrey is right when he says it will present a very odd appearance if you go to live in Bath all by yourself!'

'Well, I shan't be all by myself, for I shall have Maria Farlow with me.'

'Annis, I *cannot* persuade myself that she is the right person for you!'

'No, but the beauty of it is that having chosen her, and foisted her on to me, Geoffrey will never acknowledge that he was in error. Depend upon it, he will soon be discovering all manner of virtues in her, and telling you that her meek disposition will have an excellent influence over me.'

Since Sir Geoffrey had already said something very like this to her, Lady Wychwood was obliged to laugh; but she shook her head as well, and said: 'It's all very well for you to turn everything to a joke, but it won't be funny for Geoffrey – or for me either! – when we have people thinking that you left home because we were unkind to you!'

'My dear, they won't think any such thing when they see that we are on terms of perfect amity. I hope you don't mean to cut my acquaintance? I expect to entertain you frequently in Camden Place, and give you fair warning that I shall always look on Twynham as my second home, and am likely to descend upon you without ceremony for long visits. You will be wishing me at Jericho, I daresay!' She saw that Lady Wychwood was looking melancholy still, and went to sit beside her, taking her hand, and saying: 'Try to understand, Amabel! It isn't only because Geoffrey and I rub against one another that I am going to set up a home for myself. I want – I want a life of my own!'

'Oh, I do understand that!' said Lady Wychwood, in quick sympathy. 'From the moment I set eyes on you I have felt that it was positively wicked that such a lovely girl as you should be wasting her life! If only you would accept Lord Beckenham's offer, or Mr Kilbride's – well, no, perhaps not his! Geoffrey says he's a here-and-thereian, and a gamester, and I suppose that would hardly do for you, though I must confess that I thought he was excessively charming! Well, if you couldn't like Beckenham, what did you find to dislike in young Gaydon? Or—'

'Stop, stop!' begged Annis laughingly. 'I found nothing to dislike in any of them, but I couldn't discover in myself the smallest wish to marry any of them either. Indeed, I haven't any wish to marry anyone at all.'

'But, Annis, *every* woman must wish to be married!' cried Lady Wychwood, quite shocked.

'Now *that* provides the answer to what people will think when they see me living in my own house instead of at Twynham!' exclaimed Annis. 'They will think me an Eccentric! Ten to one, I shall become one of the Sights of Bath, like old General Preston or that weird creature who goes about in a hoop, and feathers! I shall be pointed out as—'

'If you don't stop talking such nonsense I shall be strongly tempted to slap you!' interrupted Lady Wychwood. 'I don't doubt you'll be pointed out, but it won't be as an Eccentric!'

In the event, both were proved to be right. Annis had acquaintances amongst the Bath residents, and several close friends living in the vicinity of Bath, with whom she had frequently stayed, so that she did not come to Bath as a stranger.

It was thought to be a trifle eccentric of her to leave the shelter of her brother's house, but she was well-known to be a very independent young woman, and as she was, at that date, six and twenty years of age, long past her girlhood, only the stiffest and most censorious persons saw anything to condemn in her conduct. She was possessed of a considerable independence, and it was not to be wondered at that she should avail herself of its advantages. The only wonder was that she hadn't been snapped up in her first London Season by some gentleman on the look out for a bride in whom birth and beauty were accompanied by a handsome fortune.

No one knew the size of her fortune, but it was obviously large: her family had owned Twynham Park for generations; and her beauty was remarkable. If there were those who considered her too tall, and others who could only see beauty in brunettes, these critics were few in number. Her admirers — and she had a host of them — declared her to be a piece of perfection, and from the top of her guinea-gold curls to the soles of her slender feet they could detect no flaw in her. Her eyes were particularly fine, being of a deep blue, and so full of light that one infatuated gentleman, of a poetic turn of mind, said that their brilliance put the stars to shame. They were smiling eyes, set under delicate, arched brows; and her generous mouth seemed to be made for laughter. For the rest, she had an elegant figure, moved gracefully, dressed herself with exquisite taste, and had charming manners, which endeared her to such elderly sticklers as old Mrs Mandeville, who pronounced her to be 'a very nice gal: none of your simpering misses! I can't think why she ain't married!'

Those who had been acquainted with her father knew that he had been dotingly fond of her, and supposed that that might have been why she had accepted none of the offers made her. No doubt, said the wiseacres, that was also why she had come to live in Bath now that he was dead: she meant to marry at last, and what chance of meeting an eligible gentleman could there be in the wilds of the country? Only one lady saw any impropriety in it, and as she was notoriously spiteful, and had two rather plain daughters of marriageable age on her hands, no one paid any heed to her. Besides, Miss Wychwood had an

9

elderly cousin living with her, and what could be more proper than that?

So Sir Geoffrey was right too, and was able to plume himself on his wisdom. He very soon became reconciled to the situation, and found himself more in charity with his sister than he had ever been before. As for Miss Farlow, she had never been so happy in all her life, or enjoyed so much comfort, and she felt that she could never be sufficiently grateful to dear Annis, who not only paid her a very generous wage, but who showered every sort of luxury on her, from a fire in her bedroom to the right to order the carriage whenever she wished to go beyond walking-distance. Not that she ever did avail herself of this permission, for that, in her opinion, would be a sadly encroaching thing to do. Unfortunately, her overflowing gratitude caused her to irritate Miss Wychwood almost beyond bearing by fussing over her incessantly, running quite unnecessary errands for her (much to the jealous wrath of Miss Jurby, Annis's devoted dresser), and entertaining her (she hoped) with an inexhaustible flow of what Annis called nothing-sayings.

She was doing that on the journey back to Bath from Twynham Park. The fact that she received only mechanical responses from Miss Wychwood did not offend her, or cause her to abate her cheerful chatter. Rather she increased it, for she could see that her dear Miss Wychwood was a trifle in the dumps, and considered it to be her duty to divert her mind. No doubt she was sad to be leaving Twynham: Miss Farlow could well understand that, for she was feeling rather sad herself: it had been such an agreeable week!

'So very kind as Lady Wychwood is!' she said brightly. 'I declare it makes one sorry to be going away, not but what home is best, isn't it? We must look forward now to Easter, when we shall have them all to stay in Camden Place. We shan't know how to make enough of those sweet children, shall we, Annis?'

'I don't think I shall find it difficult,' said Annis, with a faint smile. 'And I fancy Jurby won't either!' she added, twinkling across at her dresser, who was sitting on the forward seat, holding her mistress's jewel-box on her angular knees. 'Little

Tom's last encounter with Jurby was a very near-run thing, I promise you, Maria! Indeed, I am persuaded that had I not chanced to come into the room at that moment she'd have spanked him – as well he deserved! Wouldn't you, Jurby?'

Her dresser replied austerely: 'Tempted I may have been, Miss Annis, but the Lord gave me strength to resist the promptings of the Evil One.'

'Oh, no, was it the Lord who gave you that strength?' said Annis, quizzing her. 'I had thought it was *my* intervention that saved him!'

'Poor little fellow!' said Miss Farlow charitably. 'So high-spirited! Such quaint things as he says! I'm sure I never saw such a forward child. Your sweet little goddaughter, too, Annis!'

'I fear it's useless to ask me to go into raptures over infants in arms,' said Annis apologetically. 'I daresay I shall like both children well enough when they are older. In the meantime I must leave it to their mama, and to you, to dote on them.'

Miss Farlow realized that dear Annis had the headache, which was the only possible explanation for her want of enthusiasm over her nephew and niece. She said: 'Now, why do you let me rattle on when I am persuaded you have the headache? *That* is not treating me as you should, or as I wish you to! There is nothing so irritating to the nerves as being obliged to attend to fireside chatter – not that this is the fireside, of course, though the hot brick I have under my feet keeps me as warm as toast – when one is not feeling in good point. And it wouldn't surprise me, my love, if it is the weather which has made your head ache, for a cold wind frequently gives *me* a sort of tic, and the wind is very sharp today – not that we are conscious of it in the carriage, which I am sure is the most comfortable one imaginable, but there is bound to be a draught, and we mustn't forget that you stood talking to Sir Geoffrey for several minutes before you got into it. That was what started the mischief, depend upon it! I expect it will go off when you are safely home again, and in the meantime I shan't tease you by talking to you. Are you sure you are warm enough? Let me give you my shawl, to put round your head! Jurby will hold your hat, or I will. Now, where did I put my smelling-salts?

11

They *should* be in my reticule, for I always put them there when I go on a journey, because one never knows when one may need them, does one? But they don't seem to be— Oh, yes, here they are! They had slipped down to the bottom, and were under my handkerchief, though goodness knows how they can have *got* under it, for I distinctly recall putting them on top of everything else, so that they would be handy. I often think how extraordinary it is that things move by themselves, which no one can deny they *do*!'

She continued in this way for several minutes, and when Annis declined the shawl and the smelling-salts, wished that they had thought to bring a pillow to put behind Annis's head, or that it were possible to make her a tisane. In desperation, Annis shut her eyes, and after drawing Miss Jurby's attention to this, and telling her that they must be as quiet as mice, because Miss Annis was just dropping off to sleep, she at last subsided.

Annis had no headache, nor was she depressed at leaving Twynham Park. She was bored. Possibly the bleak weather, though it hadn't made her head ache, had affected her spirits, making her feel, most unusually, that the future was as grey and as unpromising as the sky. Lady Wychwood had tried to keep her at Twynham for a few more days, prophesying that it was going to snow, but Annis could not be persuaded to extend her visit, even if it was going to snow, which she thought extremely unlikely. Appealed to, Sir Geoffrey said: 'Snow? Pooh! Nonsense, my love! Far too much wind for that, and nothing like cold enough! Naturally we should be happy to keep Annis with us, but if she has engagements in Bath we should neither of us wish to deter her from keeping them. What's more, if it *did* snow she will be perfectly safe with Twitcham on the box.'

So Annis had been allowed to set forth without further hindrance from her anxious sister-in-law, privately thinking that if it really did snow she would be better off in her own house in Bath than immured at Twynham Park. No snow fell, but no gleam of sunlight broke through the clouds to enliven the gloom of a sodden landscape; and a north-easterly wind did nothing to alleviate the discomforts of a March day. Her spirits were understandably depressed, and she was only roused from a melancholy vision of her probable future when, some eight miles short of Bath, Miss Farlow cried: 'Oh, goodness me, has there been an accident? Ought we to stop? Do look, dear Annis!'

Jerked out of her unprofitable meditations, Miss Wychwood opened her eyes. No sooner did they alight on the cause of Miss Farlow's sudden exclamation than she tugged the check-string, and, as Twitcham pulled up his horses, said: 'Oh, poor things! Of course we must stop, Maria, and try what we can do to rescue them from such a horrid plight!'

While her footman jumped down to open the carriage-door, and to let down the steps, she had time to assimilate the details of the mishap which had befallen two fellow-travellers. A gig, with one wheel missing, was lying at a drunken angle at the side of the road, and beside it were standing two people: a female, huddled in a cloak, and a fair young man, who was feeling the knees of the sturdy cob which he had drawn out from between the shafts of the gig, and who said, just as James, the footman, pulled open the door of Miss Wychwood's carriage: 'Well, thank God, at least this bonesetter is none the worse!'

His companion, whom Miss Wychwood perceived to be a very young, and a very pretty girl, replied, with some asperity: 'I don't see much to be thankful for in that!'

'I daresay you don't!' retorted the young gentleman. '*You* won't be called upon to pay for—' He broke off, as he became aware that the slap-up equipage which had just swept round a bend in the road had come to a halt, and that its occupant, a dazzlingly lovely lady, was preparing to descend from it. He gave a gasp, pulled off his modish beaver, and stammered: 'Oh! I didn't see – I mean, I didn't think – that is to say—'

Miss Wychwood laughed, and relieved him from his embarrassment, saying, as she alighted from her carriage: 'Did you suppose anyone could be so odiously selfish as *not* to stop? Not I, I promise you! The same thing happened to me once, and I know just how helpless it makes one feel when one loses a wheel! Now, what can I do to rescue you from this horrid predicament?'

The girl, eyeing her warily, said nothing; but the gentleman bowed, and said: 'Thank you! It is excessively good of you, ma'am! I shall be very much obliged to you if you will direct them, at the next posting-house, to send a chaise here, to carry us to Bath. I am not familiar with this part of the country, so I don't know— And then there is the horse! I can't leave him here, can I? Perhaps— Only I don't like to ask you to find a wheelwright, ma'am, though I think a wheelwright is what is chiefly needed!'

At this, his companion intervened, announcing that a wheelwright was not what she needed. 'Ten to one he wouldn't come at all, and even if he did come, whoever heard of a wheelwright mending a wheel on the road? Particularly a wheel that has two broken spokes! It would be *hours* before we reached Bath, and you must *know* that it is of the first importance that I should be there not a moment later than five o'clock! I might have known how it would be when you meddled in what is quite my own affair, for of all the mutton-headed people I ever was acquainted with you are the *most* mutton-headed, Ninian!' she said indignantly.

'Let me remind you, Lucy,' retorted the gentleman, flushing up to the roots of his fair hair, 'that the accident was no fault of mine! And, further, that if I had not meddled, as you choose to call it, in your affair you would have found yourself at this moment stranded miles from Bath! And if we are to talk of *muttonheads*—!' He broke off, controlling himself with a visible effort, set his teeth, and said in the icy voice of one determined not to allow his anger to get the better of him: '*I* shall not do so, however!'

'No, don't!' said Annis, considerably amused by this interchange. 'You really have no time to indulge in recriminations at just this moment, have you? If it is a matter of importance to you to reach Bath before five o'clock, Miss—?'

She left a pause, her brows raised questioningly, but the youthful lady before her did not seem to be very willing to fill it. After hesitating for a few moments, she stammered: 'If you please, ma'am, will you just call me Lucilla? I — I have a very particular reason for not wishing anyone to know my surname — in case they come in search of me!'

14

'They?' inquired Miss Wychwood, wondering what kind of an adventure she had stumbled on.

'My aunt, and *his* father,' said Lucilla, nodding towards her escort. 'And very likely my uncle too, if he can be persuaded to bestir himself!' she added.

'Good God!' exclaimed Miss Wychwood, her eyes dancing. 'Can it be that I am assisting an elopement?'

The haste with which both the lady and the gentleman repudiated this suggestion was attended by much vehemence, and with so much loathing, that Miss Wychwood was hard put to it not to burst out laughing. She managed to keep her countenance, and said, with only a tiny tremor in her voice: 'I beg your pardon! Indeed, I can't think how I came to say anything so shatter-brained, for something seemed to tell me at the outset that it was not an elopement!'

Lucilla said, with dignity: 'I may be a sad romp, I may be a little gypsy, and my want of conduct may give people a disgust of me, but I am *not* lost to all sense of propriety, whatever my aunt says, and nothing could prevail on me to elope with *anyone*! Not even if I were madly in love, which I'm not! As for eloping with Ninian, that would be a nonsensical thing to do, because—'

'I wish you will keep your tongue, Lucy!' interrupted Ninian, looking very much vexed. 'You rattle on like a regular bagpipe, and see what comes of it!' He turned towards Annis, saying stiffly: 'I cannot wonder at it that you were misled into supposing that we are eloping. The case is far otherwise.'

'Yes, it is,' corroborated Lucilla. 'Far, *far* otherwise! The truth is that I am *escaping* from Ninian.'

'*I* see!' said Annis sympathetically. 'And he is helping you to do it!'

'Well, yes – in a way he is,' Lucilla admitted. 'Not that I wished him to help me, but – but the circumstances made it very difficult for me to stop him. It – it is all rather complicated, I'm afraid.'

'It does seem to be,' agreed Annis. 'And if you are going to explain it to me – not that I wish to be vulgarly inquisitive! – how would it be if you were to get into my carriage, and

15

allow me to convey you to wherever it is in Bath that you wish to go?'

Lucilla cast a somewhat longing look at the carriage, but shook a resolute head. 'No. It is very kind of you, but it would be too shabby of me to leave Ninian behind, and I won't do it!'

'Yes, you will!' said Ninian. 'I have been wondering how to get you to Bath before you are quite frozen, and if this lady will take you there I shall be very much obliged to her.'

'I will certainly take her there,' said Annis, smiling at him. 'My name, by the way, is Wychwood – Miss Annis Wychwood.'

'And mine, ma'am, is Elmore – Ninian Elmore, entirely at your service!' he responded, with great gallantry, 'And this is—'

'Ninian, *no!*' cried Lucilla, much flustered. 'If she were to tell my aunt where I am—'

'Oh, don't be afraid of that!' said Annis cheerfully. 'Never shall it be said of me that I'm an addle-plot, I promise you! I collect that you are going to visit a friend, or perhaps a relation?'

'Well, – well not *precisely!* In fact, I haven't met her yet!' disclosed Lucilla, in a rush of confidence. 'The thing is, ma'am, I am going to apply for the post of companion to her. She says – I have brought the notice I saw in the *Morning Post* with me, but most foolishly packed it in my portmanteau, so that I can't immediately show it to you – but she says she requires an active and genteel young lady of willing disposition, and that applicants must call at her residence in North Parade between the hours of—'

'North Parade!' exclaimed Annis. 'My poor child, can it be that you are going to visit *Mrs Nibley*?'

'Yes,' faltered Lucilla, dismayed by Miss Wychwood's very obvious pity. 'The *Honourable* Mrs Nibley, which made me think she must be a perfectly respectable person. *Isn't* she, ma'am?'

'Oh, yes! A pattern-card of respectability!' answered Annis. 'Renowned in Bath as the town's worst archwife! She has had I don't know how many active and genteel ladies to wait on her hand and foot during the three years I've been acquainted with her. Either they leave her house in strong hysterics, or she turns them off because they have not been *sufficiently* active or willing! My dear, do believe me when I tell you that the post she offers would not do for you!'

'I guessed as much!' interpolated Mr Elmore, not without satisfaction.

Lucilla bore all the appearances of having sustained a stunning blow, but at this her spirit flickered up in a brief revival, and she said: 'No, you didn't! Pray, how could you have guessed anything of the sort?'

'Well, at all events, I guessed no good would come of such a bird-witted start, and I said so at the time! You can't deny that! *Now* what do you mean to do?'

'I don't know,' said Lucilla, her lips trembling. 'I shall have to think of something.'

'There's only one thing you *can* do, and that is to return to Mrs Amber,' he said.

'Oh, no, no, no!' she cried passionately. 'I would rather hire myself out as a *cook-maid* than go back to be scolded, and reproached, and told I had made my aunt ill, and *forced* to marry you, which is what would happen, on account of my having run away with you! And it wouldn't be the least use to tell my aunt, or your papa, that I didn't run away with you, but away *from* you, because even if they believed me they would think it *worse*, and say we *must* be married!'

He blenched visibly, and ejaculated: 'Oh, my God, that's just what they would do! What a hobble we're in! It almost makes me wish I hadn't caught you creeping out of the house, and thought it my duty to see you came to no harm!'

'Forgive me!' interposed Miss Wychwood. 'May I offer a suggestion?' She smiled at Lucilla, and held out her hand. 'If you are set on being a companion, come and be a companion to me!' She heard Miss Farlow within the carriage utter a faint, outraged clucking, and made haste to add: 'It won't do, you know, to be put up at an hotel, all by yourself; and it's not to be expected that Mrs Nibley – even if she engaged you, which I think extremely unlikely – would be prepared to do

17

so immediately. She will require you to furnish her with the name and direction of some respectable person willing to vouch for you.'

'Oh, goodness!' exclaimed Lucilla, dismayed. 'I never thought of that!'

'*Most* understandable that you should not!' said Annis. 'One can't think of everything, after all! But I do feel that it is a matter which ought to be considered, and I also feel that it is quite impossible to consider anything when one is standing in the open road, with a perfectly horrid wind positively freezing one's wits! So do, pray, get into my carriage! Mr Elmore will follow us in due course, and we can discuss the matter when we have dined, and are sitting snugly beside the fire.'

'Thank you!' Lucilla said unsteadily. 'You are *very* kind, Miss Wychwood! Only – only how is Ninian to manage, when he can't leave the horse?'

'There is no need for you to fret about me,' said Mr Elmore nobly. 'I shall lead the horse to the next hostelry, and trust to being able to hire some sort of a carriage to carry me to Bath.'

'You might even ride the horse,' suggested Annis.

'But I am not dressed for riding!' he said, staring at her. 'And – and even if I were, it is not a saddle-horse!'

Annis now perceived that Mr Elmore was a very correct young gentleman. She was a good deal amused, but although the ready laughter sprang to her eyes she said, with perfect gravity: 'Very true! We must leave you to do as you think best, but I should perhaps warn you that since this is not a post-road you may find it difficult to hire a chaise at the – the "next hostelry", and may even be reduced to contenting yourself with some vehicle *quite* beneath your touch! However, I shan't despair of seeing you in Upper Camden Place in time for dinner!' She then furnished him with her exact direction, smiled benignly upon him and pushed Lucilla to the steps of her carriage.

Propelled irresistibly by a firm hand in the small of her back, Lucilla mounted them, but paused at the top, to say, over her shoulder: 'If I could be of the least use to you, Ninian, I wouldn't leave you in this fix, even though you wouldn't have been in it if you hadn't meddled in my affairs!'

'You may make yourself easy on that head!' responded Mr Elmore. 'Far from being of use to me, your presence would make everything worse! If it could be!' he added.

'Well, of all the unjust things to say!' gasped Lucilla indignantly. She would have said more, but Miss Wychwood cut short her recriminations by thrusting her into the carriage. She then directed her interested footman to transfer her unexpected guest's baggage fom the gig to the carriage, and, when this was done, herself mounted into the carriage, briskly desired Miss Farlow to make room for a third person on the back seat, pushed her own hot brick under Lucilla's feet, tucked a generous share of the fur-lined carriage-rug round her, and nodded to her footman to put up the steps. In a very few minutes the coachman had set his horses in motion, and Lucilla, snuggling between her hostess and Miss Farlow, heaved a small sigh, and stealing a cold hand into Miss Wychwood's, whispered: 'Oh, I *do* thank you, ma'am!'

Miss Wychwood chafed the little hand, saying: 'You poor child! You are quite frozen! Never mind! We shall soon be in Bath, and we shan't discuss your problems until you are warm, and have dined, and – er – have the benefit of Mr Elmore's advice!'

Lucilla gave an involuntary choke of laughter, but refrained from comment. Very little conversation was exchanged during the rest of the journey, Lucilla, worn-out by the day's adventures, being on the brink of sleep, and Miss Wychwood confining her remarks to a few commonplaces addressed to Miss Farlow. For her part, Miss Farlow's usual flow of chit-chat was dried up, because (as she would presently tell her employer) her feelings had been wounded by the imputation that her own companionship did not suffice Miss Wychwood. Miss Jurby preserved a rigid silence, as befitted her position, but she too had every intention of favouring Miss Wychwood with her opinion of her latest, ill-judged start, as soon as she was alone with her – and in far more forthright terms than would be used by Miss Farlow.

Lucilla awoke when the carriage drew up in Upper Camden

Place, and was insensibly cheered by the welcoming candlelight coming through the open door of the house, and by the benevolent aspect of the elderly butler, who beamed upon his mistress, and accepted, without a blink, the unheralded arrival of a stranger in her company.

Annis handed Lucilla over to Mrs Wardlow, her housekeeper, with instructions to bestow her in the Pink bedchamber, and to direct one of the maids to wait on her; and prepared herself to deal with her affronted companion.

Waiting only until Lucilla, meekly following Mrs Wardlow up the stairs, was out of earshot, Miss Farlow said that while she trusted it would always be far from her intention to criticize any of her dear cousin's actions she felt herself bound to say that had she known that her companionship no longer satisfied dear Annis she would instantly have resigned her post.

'Whatever the exigencies of my circumstances,' she said tearfully, 'I should prefer to live in utter penury than to remain where I am not wanted, however comfortable this house may be, which indeed it is, not to say luxurious, for *Better a dinner of herbs where love is than a stalled ox and hatred therewith*. Even though I am not at all partial to herbs, except for a little parsley in a sauce, and I have never been able to understand how anyone, even a biblical person, could possibly *live* on herbs. However, times change, and when one thinks of all the *most* peculiar things that happened in the Bible, well, it makes one positively thankful one didn't live in those days! Bushes catching fire, and ladders coming down out of the sky, and people being swallowed up by whales, and not being a penny the worse for it – well, I should find that sort of thing most disconcerting! Manna, too! I've never been able to discover what kind of food that was, but I am persuaded I shouldn't like it, even if I were starving, and it was suddenly dropped on me, which I think extremely unlikely. *But*,' she continued, fixing Miss Wychwood with a reproachful gaze, 'I would make a push to like it if you wish to set Another in my place!'

'Don't be such a goosecap, Maria!' replied Miss Wychwood, in a rallying tone. 'I haven't the least desire to set Another in your place!' Always appreciative of the ridiculous, she could not resist the impulse to say: 'I can vouch for it that there is no hatred in this house – unless Jurby hates you, but you wouldn't care for that, because you must know that she wouldn't do so if she didn't fear that you were ousting her in my regard! – but the stalled ox has me in a puzzle! Where, cousin, do you suspect me of stalling an ox?'

'I was speaking metaphorically,' answered Miss Farlow, in outraged accents. 'It is not to be supposed that you could stall an ox anywhere in Bath, for you may depend upon it that it would contravene the regulations. I daresay you wouldn't be permitted to stall a *cow*, and that would be of far more use to you!'

'So it would!' agreed Miss Wychwood, much struck.

'Oxen and cows have nothing to do with the case!' said Miss Farlow, dissolving into tears. 'My sensibilities have been deeply wounded, Annis! When I heard you invite that young woman to come here to be a companion to you, I suffered an – an electrical shock from which I fear my nerves will never recover!'

Perceiving that her elderly cousin was very much upset, Annis applied herself to the task of soothing her lacerated feelings. It took time and patience to mollify Miss Farlow, and although she succeeded in convincing her that she stood in no danger of being dismissed she failed to reconcile her to Lucilla's presence in Camden Place. 'I cannot like her, cousin,' she said impressively. 'You must forgive me if I say that I am astonished that you should have offered her the hospitality of your home, for in general you have such very superior sense! Mark my words, you will live to regret it!'

'If I do, Maria, you will have the comfort of being able to say that you told me so! But what reason could I possibly have for not rescuing that child from a very awkward predicament?'

'It's my belief,' said Miss Farlow darkly, 'that the story she told you was a take-in! A very hurly-burly young female I thought her! So coming – quite brass-faced indeed! Such a want of delicacy, running away from her home, and in the company of a *young gentleman*! No doubt I am old-fashioned, but such conduct doesn't suit *my* sense of propriety. What is more, I am very sure dear Sir Geoffrey would disapprove quite as strongly as I do!'

'Probably more strongly,' said Annis. 'But I hardly think he could be so foolish as to call her either coming or brass-faced!'

Miss Farlow quailed under the sparkling look of danger in Annis's eyes, and embarked on a confused speech which incoherently mixed an apology with a great deal of self-justification. Annis cut her short, telling her that she expected her to treat Lucilla with civility. She spoke with most unusual severity, and when the afflicted Miss Farlow sought refuge in tears was wholly unmoved, merely recommending her to go upstairs and to unpack her trunk.

CHAPTER TWO

When Miss Wychwood had changed her travelling dress for one of the simple cambric gowns she wore when she meant to spend the evening by her own fireside, and had endured a scold from Miss Jurby on the subjects of wilfulness, imprudence, and what her papa would have said had he been alive, she went to tap on the door of the Pink bedchamber, and upon being bidden to come in, found her protégée charmingly attired in sprig muslin, only slightly creased from having been packed in a portmanteau, and with her dusky curls brushed free of tangles. They clustered about her head, in the artless style known as the Sappho, which, to Miss Wychwood's appreciative eyes, was not only very becoming, but which emphasized her extreme youth. Round her neck was clasped a row of pearls. This demure necklace was the only jewellery she wore, but Miss Wychwood did not for a moment suppose that the absence of trinkets denoted poverty. The pearls were real, and just the thing for a girl newly emerged from the schoolroom. So was that sprig muslin dress, with its high waist and tiny puff sleeves, but its exquisite simplicity stamped it as the work of a high class modiste. And the shawl which Lucilla was about to drape around her shoulders was of Norwich silk, and had probably cost its purchaser every penny of fifty guineas. It was plain to be seen that Lucilla's unknown aunt had ample means and excellent taste, and grudged the expenditure of neither on the dressing of her niece. It was equally plain that such a fashionable damsel, bearing all the appearance of one born to an independence, would never find favour with Mrs Nibley.

Lucilla said apologetically that she feared her dress was sadly crumpled. 'The thing was, you see, that I haven't been in the way of packing, ma'am.'

'I shouldn't think you've ever done so before, have you?'

'Well, no! But I couldn't ask my maid to do it for me, because she would have instantly told my aunt. That,' said Lucilla bitterly, 'is the worst of servants who have known one since one was a baby!'

'Very true!' agreed Annis. 'I am afflicted with several myself, and know just how you feel. Now, tell me by what name I am to present you to people!'

'I *did* think of calling myself Smith,' said Lucilla doubtfully. 'Or – or Brown, perhaps. Some very ordinary name!'

'Oh, I shouldn't choose anything too ordinary!' said Annis, shaking her head. 'It wouldn't suit you!'

'No, and I am persuaded I should come to hate it,' said Lucilla naïvely. She hesitated for a moment. 'I think I'll keep my own name, after all, on account of not being rag-mannered, which I'm afraid I was, when I wouldn't let Ninian tell you what it is. I was in dread that you might betray me to my horrid uncle, but that was because I didn't know you, or how kind you are. So I'll tell you, ma'am. It's Carleton – with an E in the middle,' she added conscientiously.

'I will take care not to reveal the E to a living soul,' promised Annis, with perfect gravity. 'Anyone could be called Carlton without an E in the middle, but the E gives distinction to the name, and that, of course, is what you wish to avoid. So now that we have settled that problem let us go down to the drawing-room and await Mr Elmore's arrival!'

'If he does arrive!' said Lucilla unhopefully. 'Not that it signifies if he doesn't, except that my conscience will suffer a severe blow, even though it wasn't my fault that he came with

23

me. But if he gets into a hobble I shall never cease to blame myself for having left him quite stranded!'

'But why should he be stranded?' said Annis reasonably. 'We left him some eight miles short of Bath – not in the middle of a desert! Even if he can't hire a vehicle, he might easily walk the rest of the way, don't you think?'

'No,' said Lucilla, sighing. 'He wouldn't think it at all the thing. I don't care a button for such antiquated flummery, but he does. I am excessively attached to him, because I've known him all my life, but I cannot deny that he is sadly wanting in – in *dash*! In fact, he is a pudding-heart, ma'am!'

'Surely you are too severe!' objected Miss Wychwood, ushering her into the drawing-room. 'Of course, I am barely acquainted with him, but it did not seem to me that he was wanting in dash! To have aided and abetted you in your flight was not the action of a pudding-heart, you must own!'

Lucilla frowned over this, and tried, not very successfully, to explain the circumstances which had led young Mr Elmore to embark on what was probably the only adventure of his blameless career. 'He wouldn't have done it if he hadn't been sure that Lord Iverley would have thought it the right thing,' she said. 'Though I daresay Lord Iverley will blame him for not having stopped me, which is wickedly unjust, and so I shall tell him if he gives poor Ninian one of his scolds! For how could he expect Ninian to be full of pluck when he has brought him up to be a pattern-card – of – of amiable compliance? Ninian always does exactly what Lord Iverley wishes him to do – even when it comes to offering for me, which he doesn't in the least want to do! And for my part I don't believe Lord Iverley would have a fatal heart-attack if Ninian refused to obey him, but Lady Iverley does think so, and has reared Ninian to believe that it is his sacred duty not to do *anything* to put his papa out of curl. And I will say this for Ninian: he has a very kind heart, besides holding Lord Iverley in great affection, and having pretty strict notions of – of filial duty; and I daresay he would liefer do anything in the world than drive his papa into his grave.'

Surprised, Miss Wychwood said: 'But is Lord Iverley – I collect he is Ninian's father? – a very old man?'

'Oh, no, not *very* old!' replied Lucilla. 'He is the same age as my papa would have been, if Papa hadn't died when I was just seven years old. He was killed at Corunna, and Lord Iverley – well, he wasn't Lord Iverley then, but Mr William Elmore, because *old* Lord Iverley was still alive – but, in any event, he brought my papa's sword, and his watch, and his diary, and the very last letter he had scribbled to my mama, home to England, and gave them to my mama. They say he has never been the same man since Papa died. They were bosom-bows, you see, from the time when they were both at Harrow, and even joined the same regiment, and were never parted until Papa was killed! Which I *perfectly* see is a very touching story, for I am *not* hardhearted, whatever Aunt Clara may say! But what I do *not* see, and never shall see, is why Ninian and I must be married merely because our fathers, in the *milkiest* way, made an idiotish scheme that we should!'

'It does seem a trifle unreasonable,' admitted Miss Wychwood.

'Yes, and because, when he married my mama, Papa bought a house just beyond the gates of Chartley Plance, and Ninian and I were almost brought up together, and were very good friends, nothing will persuade Lord Iverley that we were *not* made for one another! And, *most* unfortunately, Ninian has fallen in love with someone whom Lord and Lady Iverley have taken in strong dislike – though why they should have done so I can't imagine, for they never stir out of Chartley Place, and have never set eyes on her! I daresay they think her rather too old for Ninian, and I must own it does seem strange that he should be dangling after a lady at least thirty years of age, and very likely more!'

This circumstance did not seem strange to Miss Wychwood, but what seemed very strange indeed to her was that the Iverleys should be taking so serious a view of what was, to her understanding, a case of calf-love, of violent but short duration. She said, smiling a little: 'I expect it does seem strange to you, Lucilla, but it is a well-known fact that young men are very apt to fall in love with women older than themselves. I fancy the Iverleys have no need to go into high fidgets over it!'

'Oh, no, of course they haven't!' Lucilla agreed. 'Good

gracious, he fell desperately in love with some girl when he was in his first year at Oxford, and even I could guess that she was *most* ineligible! Fortunately, he fell out of love with her before the Iverleys knew anything about it, so they didn't fuss and fret over it. But this time some tattling busybody wrote to tell Lord Iverley that Ninian was making up to this London-lady, so Lord Iverley taxed him with it, and Lady Iverley implored him not to – to hasten his father's end by persisting in – in his suit, and—'

'Good God!' interrupted Miss Wychwood. 'What a couple of cabbage-heads! They deserve that Ninian should marry this undesirable female out of hand!' She caught herself up on this impulsive utterance, and said: 'I shouldn't say so, but I have an unruly tongue! Forget it! Am I right in thinking that Chartley Place is somewhere to the north of Salisbury? Is that where you too live?'

'No, not now. I did live there until Mama died, three years ago, but since then I've lived at Cheltenham, with my aunt and my uncle, and the house, which belongs to me, has been leased to strangers.'

This disclosure left Miss Wychwood at a loss. The words were melancholy, but the manner in which they were uttered was not at all melancholy. She said, tentatively: 'No doubt it must have been distressing to you to see strangers in your house?'

'Oh, no, not at all!' responded Lucilla sunnily. 'They are very agreable people and pay a most handsome rent, besides keeping the grounds in excellent order. I should be happy to live in Cheltenham if my aunt would but take me to the Assemblies, and the theatre – but she won't, because she says I am too young, and it would be improper for me to go to balls and routs and drums until I have been regularly presented! But she doesn't think me too young to be married! That,' she said, her eyes kindling wrathfully, 'is why she took me to Chartley Place!' She paused, her bosom swelling with indignation. 'Miss Wychwood!' she said explosively. 'C – could you have conceived it possible that anyone could be so – so cockle-brained as to suppose that Ninian, having formed a strong attachment to another lady, would feel the least inclination to make me an offer? Or that I would be so obliging as to accept this offer? But they did! – all of them!' She stopped, deeply flushed, and it was a minute or two before she could overcome her agitation. She managed to do so, however, and continued, in a tight voice, saying: 'I thought that if I consented to visit the Iverleys I could depend on Ninian to – to stand buff, even though he lacked the – the *spunk* to tell his father he didn't wish to marry me if I wasn't there to support him! I should have known better!'

Considerably astonished, Miss Wychwood asked: 'But am I to understand that he told his father he was willing to offer for you? If that is so, isn't it possible that—'

'It isn't so!' said Lucilla flatly. 'I don't know what he said to Lord Iverley, but to me he said that it would be unwise to provoke a quarrel, and that the best thing would be for us to *seem* to be willing to become engaged, and to trust in providence to rescue us before the knot was tied between us. But I have no faith in providence, ma'am, and I felt as though – as though I was being tangled in a net! And the only thing I could think of to do was to run away. You see, there isn't anyone I can appeal to since my uncle died – and I daresay he wouldn't have been of much use, because he always let Aunt Clara have her own way in everything! He was a great dear, but *not* a man of resolution.'

Miss Wychwood blinked. 'Is he dead, then? I beg your pardon, but I thought you said that your uncle would very likely come to find you, if he could be persuaded to bestir himself!'

Lucilla stared at her, and suddenly gave a crack of scornful laughter. 'Not *that* uncle, ma'am! The other one!' she said.

'The other one? To be sure! How stupid I am to have supposed you only had one uncle! Do, pray, tell me about your *horrid* uncle, so that I shan't become confused again! Was your amiable uncle his brother?'

'Oh, no! My Uncle Abel was *Mama's* brother. My Uncle Oliver is a Carleton, and Papa's elder brother – though only three years older!' said Lucilla, in further disparagement of Mr Oliver Carleton. 'He and my Uncle Abel were appointed to be my guardians, but naturally they weren't obliged to take care of me while Mama was alive, except for managing my fortune.'

'Have you a fortune?' asked Miss Wychwood, much impressed.

'Well, I *think* I have, because Aunt Clara is for ever telling me to beware of fortune-hunters, but it seems to me that it belongs to my Uncle Oliver, and not to me at all, because I am not allowed to spend it! He sends my allowance to Aunt Clara, and she only gives me pin-money, and when I wrote to tell him that I was old enough to buy dresses *myself*, he sent me a disagreeable answer, refusing to alter the arrangement! Whenever I have appealed to him he always says that my aunt knows best, and I must do as she bids me! He is the most odiously selfish person in the world, and hasn't a particle of affection for me. Only fancy, ma'am, he has an *enormous* house in London, and has never asked me to visit him! Not once! And when I suggested that he might like me to keep house for him he answered in the rudest way that he wouldn't like it at all!'

'That was certainly uncivil, but perhaps he thought you rather too young to keep house. I collect he is not married?'

'Good gracious, no!' said Lucilla. 'Which just *shows* you, doesn't it?'

'I must own that he does sound very disagreeable,' admitted Annis.

'Yes, and what is more his manners are most disobliging – in fact, he is detestably top-lofty, never takes the least trouble to behave with civility to anyone, and – and treats one with the sort of stupid indifference which makes one *long* to hit him!'

Since it was obvious that she was fast working herself into a state of considerable agitation, it was perhaps fortunate that the entrance of Miss Farlow acted as an effectual stop to any further animadversions on the character of Mr Oliver Carleton. Miss Farlow's demeanour informed her employer that she was deeply wounded, but determined to bear the slight cast upon her with Christian resignation. Nothing could have exceeded her civility to Lucilla, which was so punctilious as almost to crush that ebullient young lady; and the manner in which she listened to whatever Annis said, and instantly agreed with it, was so servile that any impartial observer might well have supposed her to be the slave of a tyrannical mistress. But just as Annis, exasperated beyond endurance by these tactics, was on the point of losing her temper, Mr Elmore was announced, creating a welcome diversion.

He was looking decidedly out of temper, and, with only a glowering glance at Lucilla, devoted himself to the task of apologizing to his hostess for presenting himself in topboots and breeches: a social solecism which plainly lacerated all his finer feelings. In vain did Miss Wychwood beg him not to give the matter a thought, and draw his attention to her own morning-dress: nothing would do for him but to explain the circumstances which had compelled him to appear before her looking, as he termed it, like a dashed shabrag. 'Owing to the haste in which I was obliged to set out on the journey I had no time to pack up my gear, ma'am,' he said. 'I can only beg your forgiveness for being so improperly dressed! And also for being, I fear, so late in coming here! I was detained by the necessity of providing myself with additional funds, what little blunt I had in my pockets having been exhausted by the time I reached Bath!'

'I *knew* it was wrong of me to have deserted you!' cried Lucilla remorsefully. 'I am so very sorry, Ninian, but why didn't you tell me you were brought to a standstill? I have *plenty* of money, and if only you had asked me for it I would have given you my purse!'

Revolted, Mr Elmore was understood to say that he was not, he thanked God, reduced to such straits as that. He had laid his watch on the shelf, which was bad enough, but better than breaking the shins of his childhood's friend. These mysterious words left his listeners at a loss, so he was obliged to explain that he had pawned his watch, which he considered to be preferable to borrowing money from Lucilla. Miss Farlow said that such sentiments did him honour; but his childhood's friend said roundly that it was just the sort of nonsensical notion he *would* take into his head; and Miss Wychwood was obliged to intervene hastily to prevent a lively quarrel between them. Miss Farlow, who, whatever her opinion might be of girls who ran away from their homes and insinuated themselves into the good graces of complete strangers, had (like many elderly spinsters) a soft spot for a personable young man, encouraged him to unburden himself of his several grievances, and lavished so much sympathy on him that by the time the dinner-bell was heard he was in a fair way to forgetting the humiliating experiences he had undergone, and was able to make a hearty meal, washed down with the excellent claret with which Sir Geoffrey kept his sister provided. At which point Miss Wychwood ventured to ask him whether he meant to remain in Bath, or to return to his anxious parents.

'I must return, of course,' he replied, a worried expression in his eyes. 'For they won't know where I am, and I fear my father will be fretting himself into a fever. I should never forgive myself if he were to suffer one of his heart-attacks.'

'No, indeed!' said Miss Farlow. 'Poor gentleman! Your mama, too! One hardly knows which of them to pity most, though I suppose her case is the worse, because of having *double* the anxiety!' She saw that he was looking guilty, and said consolingly: 'But never mind! How happy they will be when they see you safe and sound! Are you their only offspring, sir?'

'Well, no: not precisely the *only* one,' he answered. 'I'm their only son, but I have three sisters, ma'am.'

'Four!' interpolated Lucilla.

'Yes, but I don't count Sapphira,' he explained. 'She's been married for years, and lives in another part of the country.'

'I collect your father doesn't enjoy good health,' said Miss Wychwood, 'which makes it of the first importance that you shouldn't leave him in suspense for a moment longer than is necessary.'

'That's just it, ma'am!' he said, turning eagerly towards her. 'His constitution was ruined in the Peninsula, for besides being twice wounded, and having a ball lodged in his shoulder, which the surgeons failed to extract, after subjecting him to hours of torture, he had several bouts of a particularly deadly fever, which one gets on the Portuguese border, and which he never perfectly recovered from. And although he doesn't complain, we – my mother and I – are pretty sure that his shoulder pains him a good deal.' He hesitated, and then said shyly: 'You see, when he is well he is the most amiable man imaginable, and –

and the most indulgent father anyone could wish for, but the indifferent state of his health makes him very – very irritable, and inclined to become agitated, which is very bad for him. So – so you will understand that it is of the first importance not to do anything to put him into the hips.'

'Indeed I understand!' said Miss Wychwood, regarding him with a kindly eye. 'You must certainly go home tomorrow, and by the quickest way possible. I'll furnish you with the means to pay your shot, redeem your watch, and hire a post-chaise, and you may repay me by a draft on your bank – so don't set up your bristles!'

She smiled as she spoke, and Ninian, who had stiffened, found himself smiling back at her, and stammering that he was very much obliged to her.

Lucilla, however, was frowning. 'Yes, but – Well, I see, of course, that it's your duty to go home, but what will you say when you are asked what has become of *me*?'

Nonplussed, he stared at her, saying after a pause during which he tried in vain to think of a way out of this difficulty: 'I don't know. I mean, I shall say that I can't answer that question, because I gave you my word I wouldn't betray you.'

Lucilla's opinion of this was plainly to be read in her face. 'You had as well tell them immediately where I am, because your father will make it a matter of obedience, and you'll knuckle down, just as you always do! Oh, why, *why* didn't you do as I *begged* you? I knew something like this would be bound to happen!'

He reddened, and replied hotly: 'If it comes to that, why didn't *you* do as *I* begged? I warned you that no good would come of running away! And if you mean to blame me for escorting you when I found you wouldn't listen to a word of reason it – it is beyond everything! A pretty fellow I should be if I let a silly chit of an ignorant schoolgirl wander about the country alone!'

'I am not an ignorant schoolgirl!' cried Lucilla, as flushed as he was.

'Yes, you are! Why, you didn't even know that you have to be on the waybill to get a seat on a stage-coach! Or that the

Bath coaches don't go to Amesbury! A nice fix you'd have been in if I hadn't overtaken you!'

Miss Wychwood got up from the table, saying firmly that any further discussion must be continued in the drawing-room. Miss Farlow instantly said: 'Oh, yes! So much wiser, for there is no saying when Limbury, or James, will come into this room, and one would not wish the servants to hear what you are talking about – not but what I daresay even Limbury, though a very respectable man, has been on the listen, for servants always seem to know *everything* about one, and how they should, if they don't listen at keyholes, I'm sure I don't know! Amesbury! I was never there in my life, but I am acquainted with several persons who have frequently visited it, and I fancy I know *all* about it! Stonehenge!'

On this triumphant note, she beamed upon the company, and followed Miss Wychwood out of the room. Neither of Miss Wychwood's youthful guests, both reared from birth in the strictest canons of propriety, returned any answer to this speech, but they exchanged speaking glances, and young Mr Elmore demanded of Miss Carleton, in an undervoice, what the deuce Stonehenge had to say to anything?

Having comfortably installed her guests in the drawing-room, Miss Wychwood said chattily that she had been considering their problem, and had come to the conclusion that the wisest course for Ninian to pursue would be to tell his father, his mother, and Mrs Amber the whole story of his escapade. She could not help laughing when she was confronted by two horrified faces, but said, with a good deal of authority: 'You know, my dears, there is really nothing else to be done! If the case had been different – if Lucilla had suffered ill-treatment at Mrs Amber's hands – I might have consented to keep her presence here a secret, but, as far as I can discover, she has never been ill-treated in her life!'

'Oh, no, no!' Lucilla said quickly. 'I never said that! But there is another kind of tyranny, ma'am! I can't explain what I mean, and perhaps you have never experienced it, but – but—'

'I haven't experienced it, but I do know what you mean,' Annis said. 'It is the tyranny of the weak, isn't it? The weapons being tears, reproaches, vapours, and other such unscrupulous

32

means which are employed by gentle, helpless women like your aunt!'

'Oh, you *do* understand!' Lucilla exclaimed, her face lighting up.

'Of course I do! Try, in your turn to understand what must be *my* feelings on this occasion! I couldn't reconcile it with my conscience, Lucilla, to hide you from your aunt.' She silenced, by a raised finger, the outcry which rose to Lucilla's lips. 'No, let me finish what I have to say! I am going to write to Mrs Amber asking her if she will permit you to stay with me for a few weeks. Ninian shall take my letter with him tomorrow, and I must trust that he will assure her that I am a very respectable creature, well-able to take care of you.'

'You may be sure I will, ma'am!' said Ninian enthusiastically. Doubt shook him, and his brow clouded. 'But what must I do if she won't consent? She is a very *anxious* female, you see, and almost never lets Lucy go anywhere without her, because she lives in dread of some accident befalling her, like being kidnapped, which did happen to some girl or other only last year, but not, of course, in Cheltenham, of all unlikely places!'

'Yes, and ever since Uncle Abel died she bolts all the doors and windows every evening,' corroborated Lucilla, 'and makes our butler take the silver up to bed with him, and hides her jewellery under her mattress!'

'Poor thing!' said Miss Wychwood charitably. 'If she is so nervous a good watch-dog is the thing for her!'

'She is afraid of dogs,' said Lucilla gloomily. '*And* of horses! When I was young I had a pony, and was used to ride every day of my life – oh, Ninian, do you remember what *splendid* times we had, looking for adventures, and following the Hunt, which we were not permitted to do, but the Master was a particular friend of ours, and never did more than tell us we were a couple of rapscallions, and would end up in Newgate!'

'Yes, by Jupiter!' said Ninian, kindling. 'He was a great gun! Lord, do you remember the time that pony of yours refused, and you went right over the hedge into a ploughed field? I thought we should never get the mud off your habit!'

Lucilla laughed heartily at this recollection, but her laughter soon died, and she sighed, saying in a melancholy voice that those days were long past. 'I *know* Mama would have bought a hunter for me, when I grew to be too big for dear old Punch, but Aunt Clara *utterly* refused to do so! She said she wouldn't enjoy a moment's peace of mind if she knew me to be *careering* all over the countryside, and if I was set on riding there was a very good livery-stable in Cheltenham, which provides *reliable* grooms to accompany young ladies when they wish to go for rides – on quiet old hacks! Exactly so!' she added, as Ninian uttered a derisive laugh. 'And when I appealed to my – my *insufferable* Uncle Carleton, all he did was to reply in the *vilest* of scrawls that my Aunt Clara was the best judge of what it was proper for me to do.'

'I must say, one would take him for a regular slow-top,' agreed Ninian. 'He isn't, though. It might be that he doesn't approve of females hunting.'

'A great many gentlemen don't,' said Miss Farlow. 'My own dear father would never have permitted me to hunt. Not that I wished to, even if I had been taught to ride, which I wasn't.'

There did not seem to be anything to say in answer to this, and a depressed silence fell on the company, Lucilla broke it. 'Depend upon it,' she said, 'my aunt will write to Uncle Carleton and he will order me to do as I'm bid. I don't believe there is any hope for me.'

'Oh, don't despair!' said Annis cheerfully. 'It wouldn't surprise me if your aunt were to be too thankful to learn that you are in safe hands to raise the least objection to your prolonging your visit to me. She might even be glad of a respite! And if she thinks the matter over she will surely perceive that to fetch you back immediately would give rise to just the sort of scandal-broth she must be most anxious to avoid. Ninian escorted you here because I invited you: what could be more natural? I wonder where I made your acquaintance?'

Lucilla smiled faintly at this, but it was a woebegone effort, and it took a little time to convince her that there was no other way out of her difficulties. Annis felt extremely sorry for her, since it was obvious that Mrs Amber was so morbidly conscious of the responsibility laid on her that she chafed the poor child almost to desperation by the excessive care she took of her.

Before the tea-tray was brought in, Annis took Ninian to her book-room while she there wrote the letter he was to carry to Mrs Amber, and supplied him with enough money to defray the various expenses he had incurred. She told Lucilla that she needed his help in the composition of the letter, but her real object was to discover rather more about Lucilla's flight than had so far been disclosed. She had mentally discounted much of what Lucilla had told her as the exaggeration natural to youth, but by the time Ninian had favoured her with his version of the affair she had realized that Lucilla had not exaggerated the pressure brought to bear on her, and could easily picture the effect on a sensitive girl such pressure would have. No one had ill-treated her; she had been suffocated with loving kindness, not only by her aunt, but by Lord and Lady Iverley, and by Ninian's three sisters; even Eliza, a ten-year-old, conceiving a schoolgirl passion for her, and doting on her in a very embarrassing way. Cordelia and Lavinia, both of whom Miss Wychwood judged to be two meekly insipid young women, had, apparently, told Lucilla that they looked forward to the day when they could call her sister. This, Ninian said, in a judicial way, had been a mistaken thing to have done; but it did not seem to have occurred to him that his own conduct left much to be desired. It was obvious to Miss Wychwood that his devotion to his parents was excessive; but when she asked him if he had indeed been prepared to marry Lucilla, he replied: 'No, no! That is to say – well, what I mean is – oh, I don't know, but I thought something would be bound to happen to prevent it!'

'But I collect, my dear boy,' said Miss Wychwood, 'that your parents love you very dearly, and have never denied you anything?'

'That is just it!' said Ninian eagerly. 'My – my every wish has been granted me, so – so how could I be so ungrateful as to refuse to do the only thing they have ever asked me to do? Particularly when my mother begged me, with tears in her eyes, not to shatter the one hope my father had left to him!'

This moving picture failed to impress Miss Wychwood. She said, somewhat dryly, that she was at a loss to understand why his loving parents should have set their hearts on his marriage to a girl he had no wish to marry.

'She is the daughter of Papa's dearest friend,' explained Ninian, in a reverential tone. 'When Captain Carleton bought Old Manor, it was in the hope that the two estates would be joined, in the end, by this marriage.'

'Captain Carleton, I assume, was a gentleman of substance?'

'Oh, yes! All the Carletons are full of juice!' said Ninian. 'But that has nothing to do with the case!'

Miss Wychwood thought that it probably had a great deal to do with the case, but kept this reflection to herself. After a moment, Ninian said, flushing slightly: 'My father, I daresay, has never had a mercenary thought in his head, ma'am! His only desire is to ensure my – my happiness, and he believes that because, when we were children, Lucy and I were used to play together, and – did indeed like each other very much, we should deal famously together as husband and wife. But we *shouldn't*!' declared Ninian, with unnecessary violence.

'No, I don't think you would!' agreed Miss Wychwood, amusement in her voice. 'Indeed, it has me in a puzzle to guess what made your parents think you would!'

'They believe that Lucy's wildness comes of her being young, and kept too close by Mrs Amber, and that I should be able to handle her,' said Ninian. 'But I shouldn't, ma'am! I never could keep her out of mischief, even when we were children, and – and I don't wish to be married to a headstrong girl, who thinks she knows better than I do *always*, and says I have no spirit when I try to stop her doing something outrageous! I did try to stop her running away from Chartley, but, short of taking her back by force, there was no way of doing it. And,' he added candidly, by the time I caught up with her she had reached a village, and she said if I so much as laid a finger on her she would scream for help, besides biting and scratching and kicking, and if it was pudding-hearted of me to have hung up my axe, very well, I'm a pudding-heart! Only think what a scandal it would have created, ma'am! She would have roused the whole place – and several of the farm-workers were already going to start work in the fields! I was obliged to knuckle down! Then she said that since they would none of them believe her when she said nothing would prevail upon her to marry me, the best way of proving it to them was by running away. And I'm bound to own that I did feel it might be a good thing to do. But when she tried to persuade me to go home, and pretend I knew nothing about her having left the house before dawn, I did *not* knuckle down! Well, what a miserable fellow I should be to let such a stupid chit jaunter about quite unprotected!'

'Is that what she did?' asked Miss Wychwood, unable to repress a note of appreciation in her voice.

'Yes, and if only I hadn't been woken up by the moonlight on my face I shouldn't have known a thing about it!' said Ninian bitterly. 'Of course I got up to pull the blinds closely together, and that's why I saw Lucy. She was making off down the avenue, and carrying a portmanteau. I wish I hadn't seen her, I don't mind owning, but since I did see her, what could I do but follow her?'

'I can't imagine!' confessed Miss Wychwood.

'No, well, you see how it was! I had to dress, of course, and then creep out of the house, to the stables, and by the time I'd harnessed a horse to my gig, and fobbed off Sowerby – he's one of our grooms, and what must he do but come out in his nightshirt to see who was stealing a horse and carriage! – Lucy was halfway to Amesbury. I guessed she must be going that way, for I naturally supposed her to be trying to go back to Cheltenham, and I am pretty sure there's a coach which goes to Marlborough from Amesbury, and Marlborough's on the post-road to Cheltenham. I thought that was as bird-witted as it could be, but it wasn't as bird-witted as her precious Bath-scheme! I said all I could to persuade her to abandon such a hare-brained notion, but it was to no purpose, so when it came to her saying that by hedge or by stile she would get to Bath, it seemed to me that the only thing to be done was to drive her there.'

He ended on a defensive note, and looked so sheepish that Miss Wychwood had no difficulty in realizing that Lucy, by far the stronger character, had, in fact, talked him into reluctant compliance. She said, however, that he had certainly done the right thing; and advised him to tell his father, without reserve, what were his sentiments on the subject of the marriage proposed to him. 'Depend upon it,' she said, 'he will hardly feel surprise now that Lucilla has made it abundantly clear what *her* sentiments are! I shouldn't wonder at it if he felt relief at being spared such a daughter-in-law!' She affixed a wafer to the letter she had inscribed, and rose from her desk, saying, as she handed the letter to him: 'There! That will, I trust, reassure Mrs Amber and may even convince her – though she sounds to me to be a remarkably foolish woman! – that her wisest course will be to give Lucilla permission to remain in my charge until she has had time to recover from all this agitation. Come, let us go back to the drawing-room! Limbury will be bringing in the tea-tray immediately.'

She led the way out of the room, and had reached the door into the drawing-room when a knock was heard on the front-door. Since she had no expectation of receiving any visitors, she supposed it to betoken nothing more important than a message, and went into the drawing-room. But a very few minutes later Limbury appeared on the threshold, and announced: 'My Lord Beckenham, ma'am and Mr Harry Beckenham!'

CHAPTER THREE

Miss Wychwood uttered a smothered exclamation of annoyance, but if he heard it the first of the visitors to enter the room gave no sign of having done so. He was a stockily built man, a little more than thirty years of age, with rather heavy features, and an air of considerable self-consequence. He was dressed with propriety, but it was easily to be seen that he had no modish leanings, for his neckcloth, though neatly arranged, was quite unremarkable, and the points of his shirt-collar scarcely rose above his jawbone. He first bowed, and then walked towards his hostess, as one sure of his welcome, and said, with ponderous gallantry: 'I might have guessed, when I found the sun shining over Bath this morning, that it heralded your return! And so it was, as I made it my business to discover. Dear Miss Annis, the town has been a desert without you!'

He carried the hand she held out to him to his lips, but she drew it away almost immediately, and extended it to his companion, saying, with a smile: 'Why, how is this, Harry? Have you come into Somerset on a repairing lease?'

He grinned at her. 'Shame on you, fair wit-cracker!' he retorted. 'When I have come all the way from London only to pay my respects to you—!'

She laughed. 'Palaverer! Don't try to hoax me with your flummery, for I cut my wisdoms before you were out of short coats! Miss Farlow you are both acquainted with, but I must make you known to Miss Carleton, whom I don't think you have met.' She waited until the gentlemen had made their bows, and then presented Ninian to them, and begged them to be seated.

Lord Beckenham said, with a reproving glance at his brother: 'Your vivacity carries you too far, Harry! That is not the way to speak to Miss Wychwood.'

His graceless junior paid no heed to this admonition, his attention being fully engaged by Lucilla, of whom he was taking a frankly admiring survey. He was a very elegant young gentleman, of engaging address, and fashionable appearance. His glossy brown locks were brushed into the Windswept style; the points of his collar reached his cheek-bones; his neckcloth was fearfully and wonderfully tied; he had a nice taste in waistcoats; his pantaloons were of a modish yellow; and the Hessians which encased his slim legs were so highly polished as to dazzle beholders. He looked to be the very antithesis of his brother, which indeed he was, for his character was as frivolous as his raiment, he had never showed any disposition to devote himself to his studies, and far too much disposition to squander his inheritance on revel-routs, expensive little barques of frailty, games of chance, and the adornment of his person. He also kept a string of prime hunters, and the fact that he was an accomplished horseman would never have been suspected by strangers who encountered him on the strut in Bond Street, and did not know that he had been a regular subscriber to the Heythrop since he first went up to Oxford;

and, in spite of being a neck-or-nothing rider, had never yet come to grief over the stone walls of the Cotswold country, or been thrown into one of the quarries which all too often lay beyond those walls.

Lord Beckenham was torn between secret admiration of his horsemanship and disapproval of his extravagance. He read him many lectures, but never failed to rescue him from his pecuniary embarrassments, and was always glad to welcome him to Beckenham Court. He said, and quite sincerely believed, that he held his two brothers and his three sisters in great affection, but he was not a warmhearted man, and his unremitting care of their interests sprang partly from a rigid sense of duty, and partly from a patriarchal instinct. At an early age he had succeeded to his father's dignities, and had found himself the sole support of an ailing mother, and the guardian of two sisters, and his youngest brother. His elder sister was already married to an impecunious cleric, and the mother of two infants, the forerunners of what promised to be a large family, and he instantly made it his business to find elegible husbands for Mary and Caroline. Captain James Beckenham had, at that date, risen from the position of midshipman to that of a junior officer, and his promotion thereafter had been rapid. He had had the good fortune to win a considerable amount of prize money, which, added to his handsome inheritance, put him beyond the necessity of applying to his brother for any pecuniary assistance whatsoever. He rarely visited Beckenham Court, preferring to spend his time, when on shore, in all the forms of entertainment most deprecated by his lordship. Nor were Mary and Caroline very frequent visitors, so that having arranged marriages for both to very well-inlaid gentlemen Beckenham found himself with only the eldest and the youngest members of his family still tied to what Captain Beckenham sarcastically called his apron-strings. It would have been unjust to have said that he regretted their independence; but he certainly regretted the loosening of the bonds which kept them revolving round him; and, convinced of his own worthiness, never suspected that it was his deeply ingrained habit of censuring their follies, and giving them quite unwanted advice which drove them away from the Court.

He enjoyed the advantages of a large fortune. He was the owner of an imposing estate, situated between Bath and Wells, and was a frequent visitor to Bath, where he was a prime favourite amongst those residents whom Harry irreverently called the Bath Toughs. For years he had been regarded as the biggest matrimonial catch in the district, and caps past counting had been set at him. But never, until the appearance on the Bath scene of Miss Annis Wychwood, had he shown the slightest disposition to make some lady an offer. He first encountered Annis when she was on a visit to a friend; realized, on being presented to her at one of the Assemblies, that she was the only female he had ever met who was worthy of becoming his wife; and thereafter prosecuted an unremitting assault on her defences. There were those (like Lady Wychwood) who thought that Annis would be foolish to refuse such an advantageous offer, but these provident ladies were outnumbered by those who thought it a very good joke that any man as prosy as Lord Beckenham should have set his heart on Annis Wychwood, who was as lively as he was dull.

Annis had done her best, within the dictates of propriety, to convince him that his suit was hopeless, but she had failed: partly because her recognition of his many good qualities prohibited her from treating him with Turkish brutality, and partly because he could not bring himself to believe that any female on whom he had bestowed the accolade of his approval could seriously refuse to marry him. Females were known to be capricious, and Miss Wychwood certainly enjoyed flirtations with her many admirers. This was the only fault he detected in her. It was a grave one, and every now and then he wondered whether, when under his influence, she would become more sober-minded, or whether her frivolity was incurable. But after one of these soul-searchings he would see her again, fall under the spell of her beauty, and become even more determined to add this piece of perfection to his collection of artistic treasures.

For the acquisition of pictures, and statues, and vases was his one extravagance; and since he was extremely wealthy he was able to indulge it. He employed several agents, whose business it was to inform him when and where some coveted object was coming up for sale; and frequently paid flying visits to the Continents returning usually with yet another Chinese bowl to add to his overflowing cabinets, or an Old Master to hang on his crowded walls. Miss Wychwood said that Beckenham Court was fast becoming more like a museum than a private residence; and once told her brother that she suspected his lordship of caring more for the possession of treasures which other men envied him than for the treasures themselves.

On this occasion he had come home from an expedition to The Hague, whence he had returned with a reputed Cuyp. He said he entertained doubts of the authenticity of the picture, and hoped he could persuade Miss Wychwood to drive out to Beckenham Court to see it. He described to her in exhaustive detail not only the composition of the picture, but all the circumstances which had led him to purchase it. She listened to him with half an ear, but was more interested in the comedy being enacted by the three youngest members of the party. Mr Harry Beckenham, having seated himself beside Lucilla, was making himself extremely agreeable, and she, after some initial shyness, was enjoying what Miss Wychwood guessed to be her first encounter with a personable young man who very obviously admired her, and who knew just how to set a shy damsel at her ease. On the other side of the fireplace, Mr Elmore had evidently taken Mr Beckenham in silent dislike. This might have arisen from a feeling that he was at a disadvantage beside a man not so many years his senior but possessed of far more address, and bearing all the appearance of a Man of Fashion; but as she covertly watched the trio Miss Wychwood was assailed by the sudden suspicion that Mr Elmore's hostility sprang from seeing his childhood's friend responding with the utmost readiness to Mr Beckenham's advances. This dog-in-the-manger attitude was amusing, but might easily lead to trouble. Miss Wychwood was not sorry when Lord Beckenham's meticulous adherence to the rules governing polite society led him to break up the party immediately after tea.

Nothing could more surely have confirmed her gathering belief that Lucilla had been kept in far too strict seclusion by Mrs Amber than her quite disproportionate pleasure in what had been, she confided to her hostess, her first grown-up party. 'For I don't count being civil to Aunt Clara's fusty friends, and being sent away as soon as I've said how do you do, as though I were still in the school-room.'

Had she no friends of her own? No – well, none of her own choosing! Aunt did encourage her to go for walks with two girls whose parents she knew, and approved, but as they were both models of propriety, and so stupid as to be dead bores, she never would do so. And when she had been invited to a picnic party, Aunt had refused to allow her to go, because she had once contracted the measles at a juvenile party. Aunt did not like al fresco parties: she said that nothing more surely made one catch severe chills than sitting on damp ground, and that the ground always was damp, even if the picnic wasn't spoilt by a sudden shower of rain, which, in her experience, it usually was.

Until her seventeenth birthday, a highly accomplished governess had had charge of her education, and had accompanied her wherever she went, if her aunt had succumbed (as Miss Wychwood gathered she frequently did) to one of her nervous headaches. She had been assisted by various teachers, hired at great expense, who instructed Lucilla in music, water-colour painting, and foreign languages. Aunt had chosen her as much for her rigid sense of propriety as for her learning, and she had never succeeded in winning her pupil's affection, or in inspiring her with a desire to become proficient in any of her studies. Oh, no! she hadn't been unkind! It was just that, for all her scholarship, she hadn't the least understanding of anything beyond the covers of her primers, and her lexicons.

These somewhat inarticulate revelations imbued Miss Wych-wood with a determined resolve to introduce Lucilla into a wider circle than she had been permitted to enter. Bath was no longer the fashionable resort it had once been, but it had its Assemblies, its concerts, and its theatre, and although most of its residents were elderly, there were many who had large families. These Miss Wychwood passed under rapid review, and before she went to bed that night had made out a list of suitable persons to invite to a rout-party, at which Lucilla should be presented to Bath society. Perusing this list, her ever-ready sense of the ridiculous overcame her, and sent her chuckling up to her bedchamber. It would be the dullest and most undistinguished party she had ever given in Upper Camden Place, the preponderance of the invited guests being of immature age, and the rest being made up by their parents, all of whom were eminently respectable, and very few of whom could be depended on to lend life to the party.

On the following morning, having written her invitations and given them to her footman to deliver, she took Lucilla out to do a little shopping. She had requested Mrs Amber in her very polite letter to send Lucilla's maid to Bath, bringing with her the rest of the raiment which had been taken to Chartley Place, but since it might be several days before Mrs Amber complied with this request – if she did comply with it, which was by no means certain – some additions to the scanty wardrobe Lucilla had crammed into her portmanteau were necessary. Lucilla was delighted at the prospect of visiting the Bath shops, and became rapturous when she saw the very elegant hats, mantles, and dresses displayed in Milsom Street. She made several purchases, pored over fashion plates, and was persuaded to bespeak an evening-dress, and a walking-habit from Miss Wychwood's modiste, who promised to have both made up for her as quickly as possible. Miss Wychwood wished to make her a present of them but this she resolutely refused, saying that as soon as she received her quarterly allowance of pin-money she would be so plump in the pocket as to be able to buy *dozens* of dresses.

After this agreeable session, Miss Wychwood took her down to the Pump Room, and was fortunate enough to encounter there Mrs Stinchcombe, a pleasant woman with whom she was well-acquainted, and who was the mother of two pretty girls, the elder of whom was just Lucilla's age, and one son, at present up at Cambridge. Both the girls were with their mother, and Miss Wychwood lost no time in introducing Lucilla to Mrs Stinchcombe, and soon had the satisfaction of seeing the three young ladies with their heads together, chattering away at a great rate, in a manner that showed that they were on the high road to forming bosom friendships. Mrs Stinchcombe was disposed to approve of any girl who enjoyed Miss Wychwood's patronage, and said, regarding the trio with an indulgent smile: 'What a set of little bagpipes, aren't they? Is Miss Carleton residing with you?'

'She has come to visit me, for what I hope may be a stay of several weeks,' replied Miss Wychwood. 'She is an orphan, and has been living in Cheltenham with her aunt, who has kept her in rather too strict seclusion. Not yet out, of course. But I think it of the first importance that girls should know how to go on in society before being pitchforked into the ton, and I trust I may have persuaded her aunt to permit her to try her wings in Bath before her presentation.'

Mrs Stinchcombe nodded. 'Very true, my dear! I have frequently observed how often girls being, as you aptly express it, *pitchforked* straight from the schoolroom into the ton, ruin their chances by excessive shyness, which leads them to be tongue-tied, or – worse! – disagreeably pert, in the effort to appear up to snuff, as the saying is! You must bring your protégée to a little party I am giving for my girls on Thursday: quite informal, I need hardly say!'

Miss Wychwood thanked her and accepted the invitation, reflecting, rather ruefully, that she was condemning herself to exactly the sort of party which she found intolerably boring. Another thought occurred to her, which she found peculiarly disconcerting: it flashed through her brain that she was dwindling into a duenna. It was a lowering reflection, but since she had not yet reached her thirtieth year, and had not noticed any diminution in the number of her admirers, she did not allow it to oppress her. And she had her reward when Lucilla came up to her, her eyes shining like stars, and said: 'Oh, Miss Wychwood, Corisande has invited me to a party on Thursday! May I go to it? *Pray* don't say I must not!'

'Perhaps, if you are *very* good, I shan't say that,' replied Miss Wychwood gravely. 'In fact, I have just this moment accepted Mrs Stinchcombe's kind invitation to us both.'

Lucilla laughed, but at once turned to thank Mrs Stinchcombe, and did it so prettily that Mrs Stinchcombe afterwards told Annis that the child's manners matched her lovely face.

All the way up the hill to Camden Place Lucilla bubbled

over with delight in the promised treat, and intense pleasure in having met (thanks to her dear, dear Miss Wychwood!) anyone so charming and so truly amiable as Miss Corisande Stinchcombe. Edith Stinchcombe was excessively agreeable, too, although not yet emancipated from the schoolroom; and as for Mrs Stinchcombe, could Miss Wychwood conceive of a more indulgent or more excellent parent for any girl to have? According to the testimony of her daughters, Mama always understood exactly how one felt, and was never cross! So very unlike Aunt Clara's friends! Only fancy! – she permitted Corisande to go shopping, as long as Edith, or their brother, accompanied her, without being escorted by Edith's governess! Not that Miss Frampton was in the least like the unlamented Miss Cheeseburn, who had helped Aunt to make Lucilla's life a positive burden to her! 'Corisande says Miss Frampton is the greatest dear, and so jolly that she and Edith *like* her to go out with them! Oh, and Corisande says, ma'am, that she knows of a shop in Stall Street where one may purchase reticules at half the price they charge in Milsom Street, and she says she will take me there, if you see no objection to it!'

Miss Wychwood, responding suitably to these confidences, perceived that she was doomed to be bored for the rest of Lucilla's stay by references to What Corisande Said.

On the following evening, to their surprise, Ninian walked into the drawing-room, announcing that he had brought her traps to Lucilla, and had given them into the butler's charge. He was looking bright-eyed and decidedly belligerent; and it was obvious that he was labouring under a strong sense of ill-usage.

'Oh, Ninian!' Lucilla exclaimed. 'How very kind of you! I never expected to get them so soon! But there was no need for you to have put yourself to the fag of bringing them to me yourself!'

'Oh, yes, there was!' he retorted grimly.

'No, no, Sarah could well have brought them without an escort!'

'Well, she couldn't, because she isn't there! Such a dust as I walked into! Talk of riots and rumpuses—! And why even my mother should be thrown into a taking when they must all of them have known you hadn't been murdered, or kidnapped, because they knew I'd gone away with you, had me floored!'

'Do you mean Sarah isn't there?' cried Lucilla.

'That's exactly what I mean. She and your aunt got to dagger-drawing, because your aunt worked herself into a rare passion, and rang a regular peal over her, saying it was her fault for neglecting you, and I don't know what besides, and *she* nabbed the rust, and rubbed up all manner of old sores, and the end of it was that she packed her boxes, and flounced off in a rare tantrum!' He observed, with displeasure, that Lucilla was dancing round the room in an ecstasy of delight, and added, with asperity: 'You may think that a matter for rejoicing, but I didn't, I can tell you!'

'Oh, I do, I do!' Lucilla said, executing a neat step, and clapping her hands. 'If you knew how much I was dreading Sarah's arrival—!'

Miss Wychwood intervened at this point, to ask Ninian if he had dined. He thanked her, and said yes, he had stopped to bait on the road, and must not remain for more than a few minutes, because it was growing late, and he had not yet arranged for accommodation in Bath. 'Which is something about which I need your advice, ma'am,' he disclosed. 'The thing is – well, owing to one cause and another, I'm a trifle behind the wind at the moment! Until quarter-day, in fact! As soon as my allowance is paid I shall be tolerably well up in the stirrups again, but it won't do to be getting under the hatches, so I mean to put up at one of the cheaper hotels, and I thought you would very likely be able to direct me to a – a suitable one!'

Lucilla stopped dancing round the room, and asked, in astonishment: 'Why, do you mean to remain in Bath?'

'Yes,' replied Ninian, through gritted teeth, 'I do! *That* will show them!'

Before Lucilla could ask for enlightenment on this somewhat obscure utterance, a second, and even more timely, intervention was provided by Limbury, who came in with the tea-tray. Further discussion was suspended; and when Ninian had drunk two cups of tea, and eaten several macaroons, his seething rancour had subsided enough to enable him to give the ladies a fairly coherent account of the trials he had undergone at the hands of his loving relations. 'Would you believe it?' he demanded. 'They blamed me for the whole!'

'Oh, how unjust!' cried Lucilla indignantly.

'I should rather think so! For how the devil could I have prevented you from running away, I should like to know?'

'You couldn't. No one could!' she asserted. 'They ought to have been grateful to you for coming with me!'

'Well, that's what I thought!' he said. 'What's more, if anyone was to blame for driving you out of the house it was Them, not me!'

'Did you tell them so?' asked Lucilla eagerly.

'No, not *then*, but in the end I did, when I got into a pelter myself! That was when I found that your aunt's *prostration* was being laid at my door, if you please, instead of at yours! I don't know what *she* might have said to me, because I didn't see her – thank God! She fell into hysterics when it was discovered that you had run away, and then had strong convulsions, or spasms, or whatever she calls 'em, and was laid up in bed, with our doctor in attendance, and my mother trying to restore her with burnt feathers, and sal volatile, and smelling-salts; and my father almost pushing Sarah out of the house, because the mere thought that she was still at Chartley threw your aunt into fresh spasms! Well, I did say, *What a wet-goose!* and Papa – *Papa!* – said I had much to blame myself for! And Mama said how could I have reconciled it with my conscience to have abandoned you to a total stranger, and never would she have believed that a child of hers could have behaved so heartlessly! And when it came to Cordelia and Lavinia starting to reproach me – but I precious soon put a stop to that! – I – I lost my temper, and said Very well, if they thought it was my duty to protect her from *you*, ma'am, I'd go straight back to Bath, and stay there! And – and I'm afraid I said that *any* place would be preferable to Chartley, and even though you were a *total stranger* I was sure of a welcome in your house, which was more than I had had in my own home!'

'Oh, *well done*, Ninian!' exclaimed Lucilla enthusiastically clasping his arm, and squeezing it. 'I never dreamed you were so full of pluck!'

He coloured, but said: 'I don't think it was well done of me. I ought not to have spoken so to my father. I'm sorry for it, but I meant what I said, and I'm dashed well not going to crawl back until *he* is sorry too! Even if I starve in a ditch!'

'Oh, pray don't think of doing such a thing!' said Miss Farlow, who had been listening open-mouthed to this recital. 'So embarrassing for dear Miss Wychwood, for people would be bound to say she should have rescued you! Not that I think you would be allowed to die in a ditch in Bath – at least, I never heard of anyone doing so, because they are so strict about keeping the streets clean and tidy, and destitute persons are cared for at the Stranger's Friend Society: a most excellent institution, I believe, but I *cannot* think that your worthy parents would wish you to become an inmate there, however vexed they may be with you!'

This made Lucilla giggle, but Miss Wychwood, preserving her countenance, said: 'Very true! You must hold it as a weapon in reserve, Ninian, to use only if your father threatens to cast you off entirely. In the meantime, I suggest that you put up at the Pelican. It is in Walcot Street, and I'm told its charges are very reasonable. It isn't a fashionable hotel, but I believe it is comfortable, and provides its guests with a good, plain ordinary. And if it should be *too* plain for you, you can always dine here!' She added, with a lurking twinkle in her eyes: 'I've never dined there, but *of course* I have visited it, to see the room Dr Johnson slept in!'

'Oh!' said Ninian, all at sea. 'Yes – of course! Dr Johnson! Exactly so! Was he – was he a friend of yours, ma'am? Or – or one of your relations, perhaps?'

Lucilla gave a crow of laughter. 'Stupid! He was the *dixionary*-man, and he died years ago – didn't he, ma'am?'

'Oh, a *writing* cove!' said Ninian, in disparaging accents. 'Come to think of it, I *have* heard of him – but I'm not bookish, ma'am!'

'But surely, dear Mr Elmore, they must have used his Dixionary at your school?' said Miss Farlow.

'Ah, that would be it!' nodded Ninian. 'I daresay I must have seen the name on the back of some book or other, which accounts for my having had the notion that I recognized it!'

'If recognition you could call it!' murmured Miss Wychwood.

'Never mind, Ninian! We can't all of us be bookish, can we?'

'Well, I don't scruple to say that I never had the least turn for scholarship,' Ninian somewhat unnecessarily disclosed. He added a handsome rider to this statement, saying, with a beaming smile: 'And I promise you, ma'am, no one would ever suspect *you* of being bookish!'

Overwhelmed by this tribute, Miss Wychwood uttered in a shaken voice: 'How kind of you, Ninian, to say so!'

'It's very true,' said Lucilla, adding her mite. 'No one could think she was bookish, but she reads prodigiously, and even keeps books in her bedchamber!'

'How can you be so treacherous, Lucilla, as to betray me?' demanded Miss Wychwood tragically.

'Only to Ninian!' Lucilla said, regarding her rather anxiously. 'Of course I wouldn't dream of telling anyone else, but he won't say a word about it, will you, Ninian?'

'No, never!' he responded promptly.

Miss Wychwood shook a mournful head. 'If only I may not have sunk myself beneath reproach in your eyes!'

They made such haste to reassure her that her suppressed laughter escaped her, and she said: 'You absurd babies! Oh, don't look so astonished, or you will send me into fresh whoops! I know you can't think why, and if I were to explain it to you you would believe me to be all about in my head! Tell me, Ninian, did you give my letter to Mrs Amber?'

'No, because she was too ill to receive me, but my mother gave it to her.' He hesitated, and then said, with a deprecatory grin: 'She – she wasn't well enough to write to you, but she did charge my mother with a message!'

'A message to me?' Miss Wychwood asked, her brows lifting slightly.

'Well, not precisely!' he replied. His grin widened, and he gave a chuckle. 'What she said, in fact, was that she washed her hands of Lucilla!'

'She says that every time I vex her!' said Lucilla disgustedly. 'And never does she mean it! Depend upon it, she will come to fetch me back, and all my pleasures will be at an end!'

'Oh, I don't think she'll do that!' said Ninian consolingly. 'She does seem to be quite knocked-up. What's more, when my

mother asked her if she was to direct one of the maids
up your gear and send it to you she said that if after all
done for you you preferred a stranger to her she only truste
that you wouldn't regret it, and wish her to take you back,
because she never wanted to set eyes on you again!'

Lucilla considered this, but presently shook her head, and
sighed: 'I don't set the least store by that, but it does at least
make it seem that she won't come to Bath immediately. It
always takes her *days* to recover from her hysterical turns!'

'Yes,' he agreed. 'But perhaps I ought just to mention to you
that the first thing she did, before she took to her bed, was to
send off a letter to Mr Carleton. Ten to one he won't pay any
heed to it, but I think I ought perhaps to warn you about it!'

'Oh, if that isn't just like her!' cried Lucilla, flushing with
wrath. 'She is too ill to write to Miss Wychwood, but not too ill
to write to my uncle! Oh, dear me, no! And if he means to come
here, to force me to return, I can't and I won't bear it!'

'Well, don't put yourself into a stew!' recommended Miss
Wychwood. 'If he does come here with any such intention he
will find he has me to deal with – and that is an experience
which I fancy he won't enjoy!'

CHAPTER FOUR

On the following morning, Miss Wychwood sent her groom to
Twynham Park with instructions to bring her favourite mare to
Bath. He carried with him a letter to Sir Geoffrey, in which
Miss Wychwood informed her brother that she had a young
friend staying with her whom she wished to entertain with
riding expeditions to the various places of interest in the sur-
rounding countryside.

When she had first set up her own establishment in Camden
Place, she had brought two saddle-horses with her, assuming,
rather vaguely, that she would find riding, in Bath, the everyday matter it was at Twynham. It had not taken very long to

disabuse her mind of this misapprehension. At Twynham, she had been used to ride, as a matter of course, every day of her life, whether into the village, on an errand of mercy to one of her father's tenants struck down by sickness, or on a visit to a friend living in the neighbourhood; but she soon discovered that life in town – particularly in such a town as Bath, where the steep cobbled streets made equestrian traffic rare – was very different from life in the country. In Bath, one either walked, or took a chair: one could not stroll down to the stables on a sudden impulse, and order one's groom to saddle up for one. It was necessary to appoint a time for one's horse to be brought round to the house; and it was even more necessary that the groom should accompany one. Miss Wychwood found this intolerable, and frankly owned that it was one of the disadvantages of town-life. She also owned (but only to herself) that it was one of the disadvantages of being an unattached spinster; but having decided that the advantages of living under her own roof in Bath, subject to no fraternal vetoes, outweighed the disadvantages, she indulged in no vain repinings, but within a very few weeks sent her mare back to Twynham Park, where Sir Geoffrey, to his credit, kept her, exercised and groomed, for her use whenever she came to stay with him. She kept her carriage-horses in Bath, and one neatish bay hack, which, being an old and beloved friend, she could not bring herself to sell.

Seale brought the mare to Bath, but he was accompanied by Sir Geoffrey, bristling with suspicion that his sister had taken it into her wayward head to befriend some Young Person who would prove to be an adventuress. Unfortunately, he arrived in Camden Place to find only Miss Farlow at home, and when he had learnt from her the circumstances under which Annis had made Lucilla's acquaintance he became convinced that his suspicion had been correct.

'How can you have been so caper-witted?' he demanded of his sister, an hour later. 'I had not thought it possible that you could be such a noddy! Pray, what do you know about this young woman? Upon my word, Annis—'

'Heavens, what a piece of work about nothing!' interrupted Annis. 'I collect you've been talking to Maria, who is positively green with jealousy of poor Lucilla! She is a Carleton: an orphan, living, since her mother's death, with one of her aunts; and since this Mrs Amber is in indifferent health Lucilla has come to stay with me for a few weeks, as a sort of prelude to her regular come-out. Ninian Elmore escorted her here, and—'

'Elmore? Elmore? Never heard of him!' declared Sir Geoffrey.

'Very likely you might not: he's a mere child, not long down, I fancy, from Oxford. He is the son and heir of Lord Iverley – and I daresay you haven't heard of him either, for I collect that he lives retired, at Chartley Place. A Hampshire family, and, even if you haven't heard of them, perfectly respectable, I promise you!'

'Oh!' said Sir Geoffrey, slightly daunted. Chewing the cud of this information, he made a recover. 'That's all very well!' he said. 'But how do you know this girl *is* a Carleton? Not that I like the connection any the better if she is! The only one of the family I'm acquainted with is Oliver Carleton—'

'Lucilla's uncle,' interpolated Miss Wychwood.

'Well, I can tell you this!' said Sir Geoffrey. 'He's a damned unpleasant fellow! Got no manners, never scruples to give the back to anyone he don't happen to like, thinks his birth and his wealth gives him the right to ride rough-shod over men quite as well born as himself, and – in short, the sort of ugly customer I should never dream of presenting to my sister!'

'Do you mean that he is a libertine?' asked Miss Wychwood.

'Annis!' he ejaculated.

'Oh, for heaven's sake, Geoffrey—!' she said impatiently. 'I cut my wisdoms years ago! If you wouldn't dream of presenting him to me, what else can you mean?'

He glared at her. 'You seem to me to have no delicacy of mind!' he said peevishly. 'What my poor mother would say, if she could hear you expressing yourself with such unfeminine want of refinement I shudder to think of!'

'Then don't think of it!' she recommended. 'Think instead of what Papa would say! Though I daresay that would make you shudder too! Where *did* you learn to be so mealy-mouthed,

53

Geoffrey? As for Mr Oliver Carleton, between you, you and Lucilla have inspired me with a strong desire to meet him! She has told me that he has all but one of the faults you've described to me; and you have added the one she, naturally, knows nothing about. He must be a positive monster!'

'Levity was ever your besetting sin,' he said severely. 'Let me tell you that it is not at all becoming in a female! It leads you into talking a deal of improper nonsense. A strong desire to meet a monster, indeed!'

'But I have never seen a monster!' she explained. 'Oh, well! I daresay it is nothing but a take-in, and he is much like any other man!'

'I must decline to discuss him with you. I should suppose it to be extremely unlikely that you ever will meet him, but if some unfortunate chance should bring him in your way I should be doing less than my duty if I did not warn you to have nothing to say to him, my dear sister! His reputation is *not* that of a well-conducted man. And if we are to talk of *take-ins*, what reason have you to think you are not the victim of one? I don't attempt to conceal from you that I am far from satisfied that this girl is the innocent you believe her to be. I know from Maria Farlow that she ran away from her lawful guardian, and in the company of a young man! That is not the conduct of an innocent – indeed, it is the most shocking thing I ever heard of! – and it wouldn't surprise me if she were bent on inching herself into your regard!'

'You know, Geoffrey, no one who heard you talking such skimble-skamble stuff would believe you to have any more sense than a zero! How can you be so idiotish as to pay the least heed to what Maria says? She has been convinced from the outset that Lucilla is scheming to take her place in my household, but you may rest easy on that head! Lucilla is a considerable heiress – far plumper in the pocket than I am, I daresay! She won't come into her fortune until she is of age, but she enjoys what I judge to be a pretty handsome income. Mr Carleton, who is her guardian, pays it to Mrs Amber; and it is very obvious to me that it *must* be a handsome sum, for Mrs Amber gives her what Lucilla calls *pin-money*, but which a girl in less affluent circumstances would think herself fortunate to receive as an allowance to cover the cost of all her clothing. Mrs Amber pays for every stitch the child wears – and, although she seems to be a foolish creature, I must acknowledge that her taste is impeccable. I should doubt if she ever counts the cost of anything she buys for Lucilla. None of your poplins or cheap coloured muslins for Miss Carleton!' She laughed suddenly. 'Jurby unpacked her trunk, and I may say that Lucilla has risen enormously in her estimation! She informed me, in a positively reverential voice, that Miss has everything of the best! As for her having run away with Ninian, it was no such thing: she ran away from Chartley Place, and Ninian very properly acted as her escort. Her aunt had very foolishly taken her there on a visit, and a great deal of pressure was being brought to bear on Ninian, to make her an offer, and on her to accept it. It seems that this scheme was hatched years ago between their respective fathers, who were devoted friends. Ninian believes this to be the only reason his father has for trying so hard to bring the match about, but I suspect Lucilla's fortune has a good deal to do with it. The estate she inherited from her father runs, I gather, close enough to Chartley to make its acquisition by the Elmores extremely desirable. Understandable enough, you will say, but can you conceive of anything more cocklebrained, in this day and age, than to try to force two children – for they are little more than children! – to get married when they have been on brother-and-sister terms since they were in short coats?'

He had listened to her in staring silence, and he did not immediately answer her. But after a moment or two, he pronounced in pompous accents that he was no advocate for the license granted to the modern generation. Embroidering this theme, he said: 'I hold that parents must be the best judges of such matters. They must, of necessity, know better than their children—'

'Fiddle!' said Miss Wychwood, bringing this dissertation to a summary closure. 'Did Papa arrange your marriage to Amabel?' She saw that she had discomfited him, and added, with her lovely smile: 'Trying it on too rare and thick, Geoffrey! You fell in love with Amabel, and proposed to her before Papa had ever set eyes on her! Didn't you?'

He flushed darkly, tried to meet the challenge in her eyes, looked away, and replied, with a sheepish grin: 'Well – yes! But,' he said, making another recover, 'I knew Papa would approve of my choice, and he did!'

'To be sure he did!' agreed Miss Wychwood affably. 'And if he had not approved of it, no doubt you would have cried off, and offered for a lady he did approve of!'

'I should have done no such thing!' he declared hotly. He met her laughing eyes, seethed impotently for a moment, and then capitulated, saying in the voice of one goaded to extremity: 'Oh, damn you, Annis! My case was – was different!'

'Of course it was!' she said, patting his hand. 'No one in the possession of his senses could have raised the least objection to your marriage to Amabel!'

His hand, turning under hers, grasped it warmly, and he said, with all the embarrassment of an inarticulate man: 'She – she is past price, Annis – isn't she?'

She nodded, dropped a light kiss on his brow, and said: 'Indeed she is! Now, in a little while you will see Lucilla for yourself: Maria is going to go with her, and Ninian, to the theatre this evening, which will leave us to enjoy a comfortable cose.'

He blinked at her. 'What, is the young man here too?'

'Yes, he is putting up at the Pelican, but he will be here to dine with us.'

'I don't understand any of it!' he complained.

'No, it's the most absurd situation,' she agreed mischievously. 'And the cream of the jest is that now no one is trying to prevail upon them to become engaged they are going on together perfectly harmoniously – except, of course, for a few breezes! Schoolroom stuff!'

She went away then, to change her walking habit for an evening gown, and when she returned she brought Lucilla with her. Lucilla was looking very pretty and very youthful, and when she curtsied, and said how-do-you-do, with her enchantingly shy smile, Sir Geoffrey's disapproving expression relaxed a little, and by the time Ninian presented himself he was regarding Lucilla indulgently, and drawing her out in a paternal way to talk to him. His sister was not surprised, for being himself a great stickler he was always predisposed to favour girls whose manners showed them to be well-taught and well-bred. He was at first a trifle stiff with Ninian, but Ninian's manners were very good too, so that by the time they rose from the dinner-table Sir Geoffrey had forgiven him for such signs of incipient dandyism as his uncomfortably high shirt-points, and his not entirely felicitous attempt to arrange his neckcloth in the style known as the Waterfall, and had decided that there was no harm in the boy: no doubt he would outgrow his desire to ape the dandy-set; and the deference he showed to his elders showed that he too had been strictly reared. Sir Geoffrey noted, with approval, that both he and Lucilla treated Annis with affectionate respect; but when the theatre-party had left the house, Annis saw that he was frowning. After waiting for a few moments, she said: 'Well, Geoffrey? Is she the sort of hurly-burly girl you expected?'

He did not answer immediately, and when he did speak it was to say, with a hard look at her from under his lowered brows: 'I wish you may not have got yourself into a scrape, Annis!'

'Why, how should I?' she asked, surprised.

'Good God, have you windmills in your head? That child you've chosen to befriend is no orphan lifted out of the gutter, but a member of a distinguished family, heiress to what I judge to be, from what she told me, a considerable fortune, and brought up by an aunt who may be as foolish as you say she is but who has lavished every care, attention, and luxury on her! What, I ask you, must be her sentiments upon this occasion? To all intents and purposes you have kidnapped the girl!'

'Oh, gammon, Geoffrey! I did no such thing!'

'Try if you can to persuade the Carletons to believe that!' he said grimly. 'They can hardly blame you for having taken her up into your carriage when you found her stranded on the road, but they must blame you – as I do! – for not having restored her to her aunt when you discovered what were the rights of the case! You had not even the excuse of believing that she had been ill-treated!'

She was shaken, but made a push to defend herself. 'Oh, no, but when she told me the sort of pressure Mrs Amber was bringing to bear on her – and not only Mrs Amber but the

Iverleys too! — I realized, which I daresay you don't, that she felt herself to be caught in a trap, and I pitied her from the bottom of my heart! If Ninian had had enough resolution to have told his father that he had no wish to marry Lucilla the case might have been different, but it seems that no member of Iverley's family dares thwart him, because they are all of them afraid that if he flies into a passion he will suffer a heart-attack, and very likely die of it. A contemptible form of tyr-anny, isn't it? But I fancy Ninian has begun to recognize it as such, for when he returned to Chartley, having left Lucilla in my charge, he found the whole house in an uproar, not one of his loving family, as it appears, having made the smallest at-tempt either to conceal the fact of Lucilla's flight from Lord Iverley, or to point out to him that since Ninian was with her it was extremely unlikely that she had run into any kind of danger. I collect that he had put himself into a rare passion, but so far from its having prostrated him he was in high force, and rattled Ninian off in fine style, without doing himself the least harm. So Ninian lost his temper, packed up his gear, and came back to Bath — to protect Lucilla from the machinations of "a complete stranger"! And I can't say I blame him! Poor boy! He had had the very deuce of a time with Lucilla, and to find himself the target for recriminations and abuse was rather too much for him. He had done his best to persuade her to go back with him to Chartley, but, short of taking her back by main force, there was no way of doing it. And I don't think he could have done that, for she would certainly have fought him tooth and nail, and nothing, you know, could revolt him more than the sort of public scene that would have created!'

'But this becomes even worse than I had supposed!' ex-claimed Sir Geoffrey, deeply shocked. 'Not content with having embroiled yourself with the Carletons you have created a breach between young Elmore and his parents! It was wrong of you, Annis, very wrong! I might have guessed you would do something freakish if I permitted you to leave home! Elmore, too! I had not thought it possible that such a well-mannered lad could be guilty of the impropriety of quarrelling with his father!'

'My dear Geoffrey, you're quite out!' she replied, rather

amused. 'I haven't embroiled myself with anyone, and I had nothing to do with Ninian's quarrel with Lord Iverley. Indeed, I carefully refrained from advising him not to be quite so docile a son, though I was strongly inclined to do so! To own the truth, I was astonished when I discovered that the worm had turned at last, for although he is in many respects an excellent young man I did think him lacking in pluck. I shouldn't wonder at it if this episode makes Iverley hold him in respect as well as affection. The best of it is that having accused Ninian of having "abandoned" Lucilla to a complete stranger he can't now rake him down for having come back to protect her. As for Mrs Amber, I wrote her a polite letter, explaining the circumstances of my meeting with Lucilla, and begging her to grant the child leave to stay with me for a few weeks. According to Ninian, she was enjoying a prolonged fit of spasms and hysterics, but although she has not yet done me the honour of replying to my letter she has signified consent by sending Lucilla's trunks to Bath.'

He could not be satisfied, but continued to enumerate and to discuss all the evil consequences which might result from what he termed her rash action until, in desperation, she induced him to talk instead about his children, with particular reference to little Tom's tendency to croup, and what were the best methods of dealing with it. Since he was a fond father, it was not difficult to divert his mind from matters of less importance to him, and he was still talking about his children when Lucilla and Miss Farlow came in. Lucilla was in raptures over the play she had seen. She thanked Annis over and over again for having given her such a splendid treat, and disclosed that it was the very first time she had visited a grown-up theatre. 'For I don't count the time Papa took me to Astley's, because I was only six years old, and I can only just remember it. But this I shall never forget! Oh, and Mr Beckenham was there, and he came up to our box, and made the box-attendant bring us tea and lemonade in the interval, which I thought so very kind of him! What an excessively agreeable man he is, isn't he?'

'Excessively,' said Miss Wychwood rather dryly. 'Where, by the way, is Ninian?'

'Oh, when he had handed us into the carriage he said he

would walk back to the Pelican! I fancy he had a headache, for he became stupidly mumpish, and didn't seem to be enjoying the play nearly as much as I did. But perhaps he was affected by the heat in the theatre,' she added charitably.

'I'm sure it's no wonder if he was,' said Miss Farlow. 'I was quite affected by it myself, but a cup of tea soon revived me. Nothing so refreshing as tea, is there? So very obliging of Mr Beckenham! Such a gentlemanly young man!'

Sir Geoffrey uttered a sound between a snort and a laugh, and as soon as he was alone with his sister solemnly warned her not to encourage Harry Beckenham to dangle after Lucilla. 'Another of your here-and-thereians!' he said. 'I don't like the fellow, and never did. Very different from his brother!'

'I certainly shan't encourage him to dangle after Lucilla,' she replied coolly. 'But I shall be astonished if he isn't the first of many to do so!'

'I wish to my heart you may not find yourself with the devil to pay over this business!'

'Oh, don't make yourself uneasy, Geoffrey! I promise you I am well-able to take care of myself.'

'No female is able to take care of herself,' he said positively. 'As for not making myself uneasy, I must point out to you that it is you who make me uneasy! But so it has always been! You had always a love of singularity, and how you expect to get a husband when you conduct yourself in such a headstrong, skit-terwitted fashion I'm sure I don't know!'

On this bitter speech he took himself off to bed. He was not alone with his sister again until the moment of his departure next morning, and then he contented himself with saying severely that he was far from easy about her, very far from easy. She smiled, and planted a farewell kiss on his cheek, stayed on her doorstep to see him mount the steps into his chaise, and then went back into the house, heaving a thankful sigh to be rid of him.

Her prophesy that Harry Beckenham would prove to be only the first of Lucilla's admirers was soon seen to be correct. She took Lucilla to Mrs Stinchcombe's party that evening, and had the satisfaction of seeing her protégée make a hit. She took Ninian too, knowing that no hostess would cavil at having a young and personable gentleman added to her guests. Both he and Lucilla enjoyed themselves very much, although he was at first a trifle on his dignity, feeling that such a juvenile party was rather beneath his touch. But superiority soon wore off, and before the evening was half over he was joining in all the ridiculous games with which the dancing was interspersed, and earning great applause for the skill he displayed when playing span-counters.

He accepted with obvious pleasure an invitation to join a riding-party to Farley Castle, suggested to him by the elder Miss Stinchcombe. The party was to be composed of some half-a-dozen young persons, and it was proposed that after they had inspected the ancient chapel there they should partake of a nuncheon, and ride back to Bath at their leisure. 'It's a place any visitor to Bath ought to visit, because of the chapel, which is very interesting on – on account of its relics of – of mortality and antiquity!' said Miss Stinchcombe knowledgeably.

The effect of this sudden display of erudition was spoilt by her close friend, Mr Marmaduke Hilperton, who very rudely accused her of having 'got all that stuff' out of the local guidebook. Since Corisande was known to be far from bookish, this made everyone laugh, and emboldened Ninian to confess that he himself was not much of a dab at antiquities, but would dearly love to ride. He then drew Mr Hilperton aside, to ask him which of Bath's livery stables was the best; but at this point Miss Wychwood, who had strolled over to the group, intervened, saying that she could mount him on her own hack. He coloured up to the roots of his hair, stammering: 'Oh, *thank you*, ma'am! If you think I'm to be trusted not to lame your horse, or to bring him in with a sore back! I promise you I'll take the greatest care of him! I'm *excessively* obliged to you! That is – won't you be needing him yourself?'

'No, I have other fish to fry tomorrow, and if you are joining this expedition I may do so with a quiet mind,' she answered, smiling at him. 'You will see that Lucilla doesn't come to any harm, won't you?'

'Yes, to be sure I will,' he responded promptly. 'But there's no need for you to be anxious about her, ma'am; she's a capital little horsewoman, I promise you!'

When she saw the cavalcade off on the following morning, Miss Wychwood knew at once that she need have no qualms either on Lucilla's behalf or the mare's. Lucilla had a good seat, and light hands, and easily controlled the mare's playful friskiness. It seemed too that there would be no want of solicitous escort for her, judging by the way Mr Hilperton and young Mr Forden jostled one another in the effort to be the first to throw her up into her saddle. Miss Wychwood watched them clatter off, all in the best of spirits, and obviously looking forward to a day of unrestricted pleasure – unless they regarded Seale, and Mrs Stinchcombe's elderly groom, bringing up the rear of the procession, as restrictions, which, indeed, they would be if youthful high spirits prompted their charges to indulge in any dangerous feats of horsemanship. Mrs Stinchcombe had told Annis that Tuckenhay could be trusted to look after Corisande; and Annis knew, from her own youthful experience, that Seale was more than capable of dealing with Lucilla, if excitement should lead her to show off her proficiency in the saddle to her new friends.

She herself spent the morning first writing a long overdue letter to an old friend, and next with her housekeeper. She was inspecting some linen when Limbury came upstairs to inform her that a Mr Carleton had called, and was awaiting her in the drawing-room.

CHAPTER FIVE

Five minutes later, Miss Wychwood entered the drawing-room, having paused on the way to assure herself, by a swift, critical glance at her reflection in the long looking-glass in her bed-chamber, that she was presenting just the right picture of herself to Lucilla's uncle. She was satisfied with what she saw. Her gown of soft dove-grey silk, with its demi-train, and the little lace ruff round her throat, were exactly the thing, she decided, for a lady of consequence and mature age; but what she failed to perceive (for she never gave it a thought) was that her beauty was enhanced by the subdued colour of her gown. She considered grey to be a middle-aged colour, and if it had occurred to her that her luxuriant golden locks hardly belonged to a lady past her prime she would undoubtedly have hunted through her wardrobe for a suitable cap to wear over them. Not that a cap could have dimmed the glow in her eyes, but that did not occur to her either, because familiarity with her own beauty had bred contempt of it. She would have preferred to have been a brunette, and was inclined to think her golden loveliness a trifle flashy.

On entering the drawing-room, she paused for a moment on the threshold, surveying her visitor.

He was standing before the fireplace, a powerfully built man with dark hair, and a swarthy complexion. His brows were straight and rather thick, and under them a pair of hard grey eyes stared at Miss Wychwood, their expression one of mingled surprise and disapproval. To her wrath, he raised his quizzing-glass, as though to appraise her more precisely.

Her own brows lifted; she moved forward, saying with chilling hauteur: 'Mr Carleton, I believe?'

He nodded, letting his glass fall, and replied curtly: 'Yes. Are you Miss Wychwood?'

She inclined her head, in a manner calculated to abash him.

'Good God!' he said.

It was so unexpected that it surprised an involuntary laugh out of her. She suppressed it quickly, and made another attempt to put him out of countenance, by extending her hand and saying, in a quelling tone: 'How do you do? You wish to see your niece, of course. I am sorry that she is not at home this morning.'

'No, I don't wish to see her, though I daresay I shall be obliged to,' he replied, briefly shaking her hand. 'I came to see you, Miss Wychwood – if you *are* Miss Wychwood?'

She looked amused at this. 'Certainly I am Miss Wychwood. You must forgive me if I ask why you should doubt it?'

And if that doesn't make you apologize for your incivility, nothing will! she thought, waiting expectantly.

'Because you're by far too young, of course!' he replied, disappointing her. 'I came here in the expectation of meeting an elderly woman – or, at least, one of reasonable age!'

'Let me assure you, sir, that although I don't think myself *elderly* I am of very reasonable age!'

'Nonsense!' he said. 'You're a mere child!'

'No doubt I should be grateful for the compliment – however inelegantly expressed!'

'I wasn't complimenting you.'

'Ah, no! how stupid of me! I recall, now that you have put me so forcibly in mind of it, that my brother told me that you are famed for your incivility!'

'Did he? Who is your brother?'

'Sir Geoffrey Wychwood,' she answered stiffly.

He frowned over this, in an effort of memory. After a few minutes, he said: 'Oh yes! I fancy I've met him. Has estates in Wiltshire, hasn't he? Does he own this house as well?'

'No, I own it! Though what concern that is of yours—'

'Do you mean you live here alone?' he interrupted. 'If your brother is the man I think he is, I shouldn't have thought he would have permitted it!'

'No doubt he would not had I been "a mere child",' she retorted. 'But it so happens that I have been my own mistress for many years!'

The flash of sardonic smile vanquished the frown in his eyes. 'Oh, that's doing it much too brown!' he objected. '*Many* years, ma'am? Five, at the most!'

'You are mistaken, Mr Carleton! I am nine-and-twenty years of age!'

He put up his glass again, and looked her over critically before saying: 'Yes, obviously I was mistaken, for which your youthful appearance is to blame. Your countenance belongs to a girl, but your assured manner has nothing to do with infantry. You will allow me to say, however, that being nine-and-twenty years old doesn't render you a fit guardian for my niece.'

'Again you are mistaken, Mr Carleton! I am neither Lucilla's guardian, nor have I the least ambition to supplant Mrs Amber in that post. I conclude, from your remarks, that you have come here from Chartley Place, where, I don't doubt, you have heard—'

'Well, that, Miss Wychwood, is where *you* are mistaken! What the devil should take me to Chartley Place? I've come from London – and damnably inconvenient it was!' His penetrating gaze searched her face; he said: 'Oh! Are we at dagger-drawing? What have I said to wind you up?'

'I am not accustomed, sir, to listen to the sort of language you use!' she replied frostily.

'Oh, is *that* all? A thousand pardons, ma'am! But your brother did warn you, didn't he?'

'Yes, and also that you don't hesitate to ride rough-shod over people you think beneath your touch!' she flashed.

He looked surprised. 'Oh, no! Only over people who bore me! Did you think I was trying to ride rough-shod over you? I wasn't. You do put me out of temper, but you don't bore me.'

'I am so much obliged to you!' she said, with ironic gratitude. 'You have relieved my mind of a great weight! Perhaps you will add to your goodness by explaining what you imagine I have done to put you out of temper? That, I must confess, has me in a puzzle! I had supposed that you had come to Bath to thank me for having befriended Lucilla: certainly not to pinch at me for having done so!'

'If that don't beat the Dutch!' he ejaculated. 'What the deuce have I to thank you for, ma'am? For aiding and abetting my niece to make a byword of herself? For dragging me into the business? For—'

'I didn't!' she broke in indignantly. 'I did what lay within my power to scotch the scandal that might have arisen from her flight from Chartley; and as for dragging you into the business, nothing, let me tell you, was further from my intention, or, indeed, my wish!'

'You must surely have known that that fool of a – that Clara Amber would write to demand that I should exercise my authority over Lucilla!'

'Yes, Ninian Elmore told us that she had done so,' she agreed, with false affability. 'But since nothing Lucilla has said about you led me to think that you had either fondness for her, or took the smallest interest in her, I had no expectation of

65

receiving a visit from you. To own the truth, sir, my first feeling on having your name brought up to me was one of agreeable surprise. But that was before I had had the very doubtful pleasure of making your acquaintance!'

The effect of this forthright speech was not at all what she had intended, for instead of taking instant umbrage to it he laughed, and said appreciatively: 'That's milled me down, hasn't it?'

'I sincerely hope so!'

'Oh, it has! But it's not bellows to mend with me! I warn you, I shall come about again. Now, instead of sparring with me, perhaps you, in your turn, will have the goodness to explain to me why you didn't restore Lucilla to her aunt, but kept her here, dam — dashed well encouraging her in a piece of hoydenish disobedience?'

This uncomfortable echo of what Sir Geoffrey had said to her brought a slight flush into her cheeks. She did not immediately answer him, but when, looking up, she saw the challenge in his eyes, and the satirical curl of his lips, she said, frankly: 'My brother has already asked me that question. Like you, he disapproves of my action. You may both of you be right, but I set as little store by his opinion as I do by yours. When I invited Lucilla to stay with me, I did what I believed — and still believe! — to be the right thing to do.'

'Fudge!' he said roughly. 'Your only excuse could have been that you were bamboozled into thinking that she had suffered ill-treatment at her aunt's hands, and if that is what she told you she must be an unconscionable little liar! Clara Amber has petted and cossetted her ever since she took her in charge!'

'No, she didn't tell me anything of the sort, but what she did tell me made me pity her from the bottom of my heart. Little though you may think it, Mr Carleton, there is a worse tyranny than that of ill-treatment. It is the tyranny of tears, vapours, appeals to feelings of affection, and of gratitude! This tyranny Mrs Amber seems to have exercised to the full! A girl of less strength of character might have succumbed to it, but Lucilla is no weakling, and however ill-advised it was of her to have run away I can't but respect her for having had the spirit to do it!'

He said, rather contemptuously: 'An unnecessarily dramatic way of showing her spirit. I am sufficiently well acquainted with Mrs Amber to know that she would not indulge in tears and vapours if Lucilla had not offered her a good deal of provocation. I conclude that the tiresome chit has been imposing on her aunt's good-nature yet again. Mrs Amber has frequently complained of her wilfulness to me, but what else could she expect of a girl brought up with excessive indulgence? I guessed how it would be from the outset.'

'Then I wonder at it that you should have given your *ward* into her care!' exclaimed Miss Wychwood hotly. 'One would have supposed that if you had had the smallest regard for her welfare—' She stopped, aware that she had allowed her indignation to betray her into impropriety, and said: 'I beg your pardon! I have no right, of course, to censure either your conduct, or Mrs Amber's!'

'No,' he said.

Her eyes flew to his in astonishment, a startled question in them, for she was quite taken aback by this uncompromising monosyllable.

'No right at all,' he said, explaining himself.

For a perilous moment, she hovered on the brink of losing her temper, but her ever-ready sense of the absurd came to her rescue, and instead of yielding to the impulse to come to points with him she broke into sudden laughter, and said: 'How unhandsome of you to have given me such a set-down, when I had already begged your pardon!'

'How unjust of you to accuse me of giving you a set-down when all I did was to agree with you!' he retorted.

'It is to be hoped,' said Miss Wychwood, with strong feeling, 'that we are not destined to see very much more of each other, Mr Carleton! You arouse in me an almost overmastering desire to give you the finest trimming you have ever had in your life!'

Her laughter was reflected in his eyes. 'Oh, no, you would be very unwise to do that!' he said. 'Recollect that I am famous for my incivility! I should instantly give you your own again, and since I am an ill-mannered man and you are a well-bred woman of consequence you would be bound to come off the worse from any such encounter.'

'That I can believe! Nevertheless, sir, I am determined to do what lies within my power to bring you to a sense of your obligations towards that unfortunate child. For fobbing her off on to Mrs Amber, when she was still a child, there may have been some excuse, but she is not a child now, and—'

'Permit me to correct you, ma'am!' he interrupted. 'I should undoubtedly have fobbed her off on to Mrs Amber if she had been left to my sole guardianship, but it so happens that I had no choice in the matter! My brother appointed Amber to share the guardianship with me; and it was the expressed wish of his wife that, in the event of her death, her sister should have charge of Lucilla!'

'I see,' she said, digesting this. 'But did you also delegate your authority over Lucilla's future? Were you willing to see her coerced into a distasteful marriage?'

'No, of course not!' he replied irritably. 'But as marriage doesn't come into the question I fail to see—'

'But it does!' she exclaimed, considerably astonished. 'That is why she ran away from Chartley! *Surely* you must have known what was intended? I had supposed you to be a party to the arrangement!'

He stared at her from under frowning brows. '*What* arrangement?' he demanded.

'Good gracious!' she uttered. 'Then she never told you! Oh, how – how unprincipled of her! It makes me more than ever convinced that I did the right thing when I kept Lucilla with me!'

'Very gratifying for you, ma'am! Pray gratify *me* by telling me what the devil you are talking about!'

'I have every intention of telling you, so you have no need to bite off my nose!' she snapped. 'For goodness' sake, sit down! I can't think why we are standing about in this absurd way!'

'Oh, can't you? Did you expect me to sit down before you invited me to do so? You do think me a ramshackle fellow, don't you?'

'No, I don't! I don't know anything about you!' she said crossly.

'Except that I am famed for my incivility.'

She was obliged to laugh, and to say, with engaging honesty,

68

as she sat down: 'I am afraid it is I who have been uncivil. Pray, will you not be seated, Mr Carleton?'

'Thank you!' he responded politely, and chose a chair opposite to hers. 'And now you will be kind enough to tell me what is the meaning of this farrago of nonsense about Lucilla?'

'It isn't nonsense – though I own anyone could be pardoned for thinking so! I collect that you don't know why Mrs Amber took her on a visit to Chartley Place?'

'I didn't know she had taken her there, until I received a blotched and impassioned letter from her, written from Chartley. As for the reason, I don't think she divulged it. It seemed to me a perfectly natural thing: Lucilla's own home is in the immediate vicinity, and until her mother's death she was as much a part of Iverley's household as her own, and no doubt formed friendships with his children – particularly, as I recollect, with Iverley's son, who is the nearest to her in age.'

'Are you quite positive that she didn't tell you of the scheme she and the Iverleys hatched between them?' she demanded incredulously.

'No,' he replied. 'I am not *positive* that she didn't, but I was unable to decipher more than the first page of her letter – and that with difficulty, since she had spattered it with her tears! The second sheet baffled me, for not only did she weep over it, but she crossed and recrossed her lines – no doubt with the amiable intention of sparing me extra expense.'

Her eyes had widened as she listened to him, but although she was shocked by his indifference she could not help being amused by it. Amusement quivered in her voice as she said: 'What an extraordinary man you are, Mr Carleton! You received a letter from your ward's aunt, written in extreme agitation, and you neither made any real effort, I am very sure, to decipher that second sheet, nor – if the blotches did indeed baffle you – to go down to Chartley to discover precisely what had happened!'

'Yes, it seemed at first as though that hideous necessity did lie before me,' he agreed. 'Fortunately, however, the following day brought me a letter from Iverley, which had the merit of being short, and legible. He informed me that Lucilla was in

Bath, that her aunt was prostrate, and that if I wished to rescue my ward from the clutches of what he feared was a designing female, calling herself Miss Wychwood, I must leave for Bath immediately.'

'Well, if that is not the outside of enough!' she said wrathfully. 'Calling myself Miss Wychwood, indeed! And in what way am I supposed to have *designs* on Lucilla, pray?'

'That he didn't disclose.'

'If he knew that Lucilla was staying with me, he must have written to you after Ninian's return to Chartley, for he couldn't otherwise have known where she had gone to, or what my name is! Yes, and after Ninian had given Mrs Amber the letter I had written to her, informing her of the circumstances of my meeting with Lucilla, and begging her to grant the child permission to stay with me for a few weeks! I should be glad to know why, if she thought me a designing female, she sent Lucilla's trunks to her! What a ninnyhammer she must be! But as for Iverley! How dared he write such damaging stuff about me? If he talked like that to Ninian I'm not surprised Ninian ripped up at him!'

'Your conversation, ma'am, bears a strong resemblance to Clara Amber's letter!' he said acidly. 'Both are unintelligible! What the devil has Ninian to do with this hotch-potch?'

'He has everything to do with it! Mrs Amber and the Iverleys are determined to marry him to Lucilla! *That* is why she ran away!'

'Marry him to Lucilla?' he repeated. 'What nonsense! Are you trying to tell me the boy is in love with her? I don't believe it!'

'No, I am not trying to tell you that! He wants the match as little as she does, but dared not tell his father so for fear of bringing about one of the heart-attacks with which Iverley terrorizes his family into obeying his every whim! I don't think you can have the least notion of what the situation is at Chartley!'

'Very likely not. I haven't visited the house since my sister-in-law's death. Iverley and I don't deal together, and never did.'

'Then I'll tell you!' promised Miss Wychwood, and straightway launched into a graphic description of the circumstances which had goaded Lucilla into precipitate flight.

He heard her in silence, but the expression on his face was discouraging, and when she came to the end of her recital he was so far from evincing either sympathy or understanding that he ejaculated, in exasperated accents: 'Oh, for God's sake, ma'am! Spare me any more of this Cheltenham tragedy! What a kick-up over something that might have been settled in a flea's leap!'

'Mr Carleton,' she said, holding her temper on a tight rein, 'I am aware that you, being a man, can scarcely be blamed for failing to appreciate the dilemma in which Lucilla found herself; but I assure you that to a girl just out of the schoolroom it must have seemed that she had walked into a trap from which the only escape was flight! Had Ninian had enough resolution to have told his father that he had no intention of making Lucilla an offer it must have brought the thing to an end. Unfortunately, his affection for his father, coupled with the belief – instilled into his head, I have no doubt at all, by his mother! – that to withstand Iverley's demands was tantamount to murdering him, overcame whatever resolution he may have had. As far as I have been able to discover, the only notion he had was to become engaged to Lucilla, and to trust in providence to prevent the subsequent marriage! The one good thing that has emerged from this escapade is that Ninian, finding, on his return to Chartley, that his fond father had worked himself into a rare passion, without suffering the slightest ill, began to see that Iverley's weak heart was little more than a weapon to hold over his household.'

'I am wholly uninterested in Ninian, or in any other young cub!' said Mr Carleton trenchantly. 'I accept – on your assurance! – that the pressure brought to bear on Lucilla was hard to withstand. What I do not accept, ma'am, is that her only remedy lay in flight! Why the devil didn't the little nodcock write to *me*?'

She fairly gasped at this question, and it was a full minute before she was able to command her voice sufficiently to answer it with composure. 'I fancy, sir, that her previous experiences of writing to you for support had not led her to

71

suppose that any other reply to an appeal to you for help would be forthcoming than that she must do as her aunt thought best,' she said.

She observed, with satisfaction, that she had at last succeeded in discomfiting him. He reddened, and said, in a voice of smouldering annoyance: 'Since the only *appeals* I've received from Lucilla have been concerned with matters quite outside my province—'

'Even an appeal for a horse of her own?' she interjected swiftly. 'Was that also outside your province, Mr Carleton?'

A frown entered his eyes. 'Did she ask me for one? I have no recollection of it.'

It was now her turn to be disconcerted, for she found that she could not remember whether a refusal to permit her to have a horse of her own had been one of Lucilla's accusations against him, or merely one of Mrs Amber's prohibitions against which she had not thought it worth her while to protest to her uncle. Fortunately, she was not obliged either to retract or to prevaricate, for, without waiting for a reply, he said: 'If she did, I daresay I did refuse to let her set up her own stable. I can conceive of few more foolish notions than to be keeping a horse and groom in a town – both, I have little doubt, eating their heads off!'

Having discovered the truth of this herself, she was unable to deny it, so she prudently abandoned the question, and cast back to her original accusation, saying: 'But am I not right in believing that your custom is to refer every request Lucilla has addressed to you to Mrs Amber's judgement?'

'Yes, of course you are,' he replied impatiently. 'What the devil do I know about the upbringing of schoolgirls?'

'What a miserable sop to offer your conscience!' she said.

'My conscience doesn't need a sop, ma'am!' he said harshly. 'I may be Lucilla's legal guardian, but it was never expected of me that I should be concerned in the niceties of her upbringing! Had it been suggested to me I should have had no hesitation in refusing such a charge. I've no turn for the infantry!'

'Not even for your brother's only child?' she asked. 'Don't you feel *any* affection for her?'

'No, none,' he replied. 'How should I? I scarcely know her.

72

It's useless to expect me to become sentimental because she's my brother's child: I knew almost as little about him as I know about Lucilla, and what I did know I didn't much like. I don't mean to say that there was any harm in him: no doubt there was a great deal of good, but he had less than commonsense, and too much sensibility for my tastes. I found him a dead bore.'

'Well, I find my brother a dead bore too,' she said candidly, 'but however much we rub against each other there is a bond of affection between us. I had thought that that must always exist between brothers and sisters.'

'Possibly you know him better than I ever knew my brother. There were only three years between us, but although that's a mere nothing between adults, it constitutes a wide gulf between schoolboys. At Harrow, he formed a close, and, to my mind, a pretty mawkish friendship with young Elmore. They were both army-mad, and joined the same regiment when they left Harrow. From then on I only saw him by scraps. He married a pretty little widgeon, too: she wasn't as foolish as her sister, but she had more hair than wit, and a mouth full of the sort of pap I can't stomach. I knew, of course, when he bought Chartley Manor that the bosom-bow friendship between him and Elmore was as strong as ever, and I suppose I should have guessed that such a pair of air-dreamers would have hatched a scheme to achieve a closer relationship by marrying Elmore's heir to Charles's daughter. Though why Elmore – or Iverley, as by that time he was – should have persisted in this precious scheme after Charles's death is a matter beyond my comprehension! Unless he thinks that Lucilla's property is just the thing to round off his own estate?'

'Well, that is what I suspect,' nodded Miss Wychwood, 'but it is only right that I should tell you that Ninian says it is no such thing. He says his father has never had a mercenary thought in his head.'

'On the whole,' said Mr Carleton, with considerable acerbity, 'I should think the better of him if his motive had been mercenary! This mawkish reason for trying to marry Lucilla to his son merely because he and my brother were as thick as inkle-weavers fairly turns my stomach! I never liked the fellow, you know.'

Her eyes were alive with laughter. She said perfectly gravely, however: 'For some reason or other I had suspected as much! Is there anyone whom you *do* like, Mr Carleton?'

'Yes, you!' he answered bluntly.

'*M-me?*' she gasped, wholly taken aback.

He nodded. 'Yes – but much against my will!' he said.

That made her burst out laughing. Still gurgling, she said: 'You are quite outrageous, you know! What in the world have I said or done to make you *like* me? Of all the farradiddles I ever heard that bears off the palm!'

'Oh, no! I never flummery people. I do like you, but I'm damned if I know why! It isn't your beauty, though that is remarkable; and it certainly isn't anything you have said or done. I think it must be your quality – that certain sort of something about you!'

'It's my belief,' said Miss Wychwood, with conviction, 'that you are all about in your head!'

He laughed. 'On the contrary! But don't delude yourself into thinking that my liking for you makes me think that you are a fit person to have charge of my niece.'

'How mortifying!' she retaliated. 'What do you propose to do about that, sir?'

'Give her back into her aunt's care, of course!'

'What, take her back to Chartley Place? What an addlebrained notion to take into your head! You had as well bestow your blessing on her marriage to Ninian without more ado!'

'No, not to Chartley Place! To Cheltenham, of course!'

She shook her head. 'Oh, I don't think you'll be able to do that! The last intelligence we had of *poor* Mrs Amber was that she was prostrate, with Lady Iverley's doctor in attendance on her, and since Lucilla tells me that it takes her weeks to recover from these – these hysterical seizures I should very much doubt if she will be able to return to her own home for some time to come. Now I come to think of it, she has announced that she never wants to set eyes on Lucilla again, and although I don't set much store by that I do feel that it would be unreasonable to expect her to change her mind before she is perfectly restored to health.'

'I'll soon restore her to health!' he said savagely.

'Nonsense! You'd be more likely to terrify her into strong convulsions. And even if you did succeed you could still have Lucilla to contend with.'

'There will be no difficulty about that, I promise you!'

'Oh, I don't doubt you could bully her into going with you to Cheltenham!' she said, with maddening affability. 'What I do doubt is your ability to prevail upon her to remain there.'

He regarded her with kindling eyes. 'I should not *bully* her, ma'am!'

'Well, do you know, I think that's very wise of you,' she said, in an approving tone. 'She has a great deal of spirit, and any attempt on your part to coerce her would be bound to set up her bristles. She would run away again, and it really won't do for her to spend the next four years running away! No harm has come from her *first* flight, but if she were to make a habit of it—'

'Oh, be quiet!' he interrupted, between exasperation and amusement. 'What did you call me? Outrageous, wasn't it? What's sauce for the gander, ma'am, is also sauce for the goose!'

'That's given me my own, hasn't it?' she said, with unabated cordiality.

A tell-tale muscle quivered at the corner of his mouth; he met her quizzing look, and quite suddenly laughed. 'Miss Wychwood,' he said, 'I lied when I said I liked you! I do *not* like you! I am very nearly sure that I dislike you excessively!'

'What can I say, dear sir, except that your sentiments are entirely reciprocated!' she responded.

He smiled appreciatively. 'Has anyone ever got the better of you in a verbal encounter?' he asked.

'No, but it must be remembered that I have not until today had much opportunity to engage in verbal encounters. The gentlemen I have previously been acquainted with have all been distinguished by propriety of manners and conduct!'

'That must have made 'em sad bores!' he commented.

She could not help thinking that that was one accusation which could not be levelled against him, but she did not say so. Instead, she suggested, rather coldly, that they should waste no more time pulling caps, but should turn their attention to a matter of much graver importance.

'If you mean what's to be done with Lucilla—' He broke off, frowning.

'Well, I do mean that. It would be useless to take her back to Mrs Amber – even if Mrs Amber were willing to receive her. It might be thought that you were the properest person to take charge of her—'

'Oh, my God, no!' he exclaimed.

'No,' she agreed. 'It would be quite ineligible. You would be obliged to hire some genteel lady to chaperon her, and I should doubt very much if you could find anyone suitable for the post. On the one hand she must have enough strength of mind to enable her to exercise some degree of control over Lucilla; on the other she must be meek enough to bear with your over-bearing temper, and to obey even the most idiotish of your commands without argument.' She smiled kindly at him, and added: 'An unlikely combination, I fear, Mr Carleton!'

'I am relieved! If the unpleasant picture you have drawn is with the object of inducing me to leave my ward in your care—'

'Not at all! I shall be happy to keep her with me until some more suitable arrangement has been made, but at no time have I had the smallest intention of keeping her in my permanent charge. May I suggest to you that your immediate task must be to set about the business of launching her into Society? I am astonished that this very obvious duty should not have occurred to you.'

'Are you indeed, ma'am? Then let me tell you that I have made arrangements for my cousin, Lady Trevisian, to bring her out next year!'

'Oh, that will never do!' she said quickly. 'After having had a taste of the very mild entertainments offered in Bath at this season, you cannot expect her to sink back into the school-room, which is what will happen to her if you succeed in bull-ocking Mrs Amber into resuming her guardianship.'

'In fact, ma'am,' he said, in biting accents, 'you have made her dissatisfied – which proves how very unfit you are to have even temporary charge of any girl of her age!' He saw that his words had brought a flush into her face, and fancied that he detected a hurt expression in her eyes. It was a fleeting look only, but he said, in a milder tone: 'I daresay you may have meant it for the best, but the result of your action has been to land us in a rare mess!'

'Pray don't hide your teeth, sir! You do *not* think I meant it for the best! You've as good as accused me of trying to make mischief, and I very much resent it!'

'I haven't done any such thing! And if I had it wouldn't have been as insulting as *your* accusation, that I would *bullock* Mrs Amber!' She sniffed, which had the effect of bringing the smile back into his eyes. 'What an unexpected creature you are!' he said. 'At one moment a woman of the first consequence, at the next a hornet! No, don't scowl at me! Really I've no wish to break squares!'

'Then don't provoke me!' she said crossly. 'Why don't you ask your cousin to bring Lucilla out this year?'

'Because I've no fancy for finding myself at Point Non Plus! She wouldn't do it: her eldest daughter is to be married in May, and she has her hands full already with all the ridic – with all the preparations for the wedding! I could no more persuade her to present Lucilla at such a moment than I could *bullock* her into doing it!'

'Oh, for goodness' sake!' she exclaimed, looking daggers at him, '*must* you be so – so *naggy?*'

'Alas!' he returned mournfully. 'The temptation to rouse you to fury is too great to be resisted! You can have no notion how much your beauty is enhanced by a blush of rage, and the fire in your eyes!' He watched her close her lips tightly, and his shoulders shook. 'What, lurched, Miss Wychwood?' he mocked her.

'Oh, no, there is much I could say, but having been reared – unlike yourself! – to respect the common decencies of established etiquette I am unfortunately debarred from uttering even one of the things which spring to my mind!'

'Don't give them a thought!' he begged. 'Consider under what a disadvantage you must be if you respect the common decencies which I don't!'

'If you had an ounce of – of proper feeling you would respect them!' she told him roundly. 'You are a positive rake-shame – as my brother would say!' she added, rather hastily.

His face was alive with laughter, but he said reprovingly: 'You shock me, ma'am! What an indelicate expression for a lady of quality to use!'

'Very likely! But as for its shocking you I shouldn't think anything could!'

'How well you understand me!' he said, much gratified.

'Oh, how can you be so abominable?' she demanded, laughing in spite of herself. 'Do, pray, stop trying to goad me into being as uncivil and as disagreeable as you are yourself, and let us consider what is to be done about Lucilla! I perfectly understand how awkward it would be for your cousin to be saddled with her at this moment, but have you no other relation who would be willing to bring her out?'

'No, none,' he replied. 'Nor can I think her come-out of such urgency. She can only just have reached her seventeenth birthday, and the last time I went to Almack's I found the place choke-full of callow schoolroom misses, and determined that *my* ward shouldn't swell their ranks!'

'I know exactly what you mean!' she said. 'Girls pitchforked into the ton without a notion of how to go on, and betrayed by their anxiety not to seem as innocent as they are into quite unbecoming simpering, titters, and – oh, you know as well as I do the sort of detestable *archness* which so many very young girls display! That is why I have made it my business to introduce Lucilla into Bath society! I think it of the first importance that a girl should learn how to conduct herself in company before being introduced into the ton. But you need have no fears that Lucilla would disgrace you! She is neither shy nor coming: indeed, her manners are very pretty, and do Mrs Amber the greatest credit! If you doubt me, come and see for yourself! I am holding a small rout-party here on Thursday, particularly in her honour, and shall be happy to welcome you to it. That is, if you are still in Bath then? But perhaps you don't mean to make any very long stay here?'

'I must obviously remain in Bath until I've settled what's to be done with Lucilla, and shall certainly come to your party. Accept my best thanks, ma'am!'

She said mischievously: 'I warn you, sir, it will be the most boring party imaginable! I have invited *all* the young persons of my acquaintance, *and* as many of their parents who don't care to allow their daughters to go unchaperoned to parties! I daresay you can never have attended any party even half as insipid!'

'I would hazard a guess, Miss Wychwood, that you have never before *given* such an insipid party!' he said shrewdly.

'No, very true!' she confessed. 'To own the truth, I laughed myself into stitches when I read over the list of my invited guests! However, I'm not giving it to please myself, but to introduce Lucilla into Bath society. I am confident that she will make a hit. She did so when I took her to an informal party the other day.'

'So I suppose the next confounded nuisance I shall have to face will be sending either love-lorn cubs, or gazetted fortune-hunters to the rightabout!'

'Oh, no!' she said sweetly. 'I don't number any fortune hunters amongst my acquaintances! I collect, from certain things she has said, and from her extremely costly wardrobe, that she is possessed of a considerable independence?'

'Lord, yes! She's rich enough to buy an Abbey!'

'Well, in that case I need not scruple to provide her with a good abigail.'

'I thought she had one. Indeed, I'm sure of it, for I've been paying her wages for the past three years. What has become of her?'

'She quarrelled with Mrs Amber, when Lucilla's flight was discovered, and left the house in a rage,' she responded.

'*Women!*' he uttered, with loathing. 'It's of no use to expect me to engage an abigail for her: what the devil does she imagine I know about such things? Since you have usurped Mrs Amber's place, I suggest that it is for you to engage a maid!'

'Certainly!' she replied, quite unruffled.

'Where *is* Lucilla?' he demanded abruptly.

'She has ridden out to Farley Castle with a party of young friends, and I don't expect to see her back for several hours yet.'

He looked annoyed, but before he had time to speak an

interruption occurred, in the person of Miss Farlow, who came into the room, with her bonnet askew, and words tripping off her tongue. 'Such a vexatious thing, dear Annis! I have been *all* over the town, trying to match that sarcenet, and, would you believe it, not even Thorne's were able to offer me anything like it! So that with this horrid wind, which has positively blown me to pieces, and—' She stopped, becoming suddenly aware of the presence of a stranger. 'Oh, I beg your pardon! I didn't know! What a sadly shocking thing of me to do, bursting in on you, which of course I should never have done if James had informed me that you had a visitor! But he never said a word about it – just relieved me of my parcels, you know, for it was he who opened the door, not our good Limbury, who I daresay was busy in the pantry, and I desired him to give the *large* one to Mrs Wardlow, and to have the others carried up to my bedchamber, which he said he would do, and then we exchanged a few words about the way the wind *whips* at one round every corner, and how dreadfully steep the hill is, particularly when one is burdened with parcels, as, of course, I was, and which has made me quite out of breath, besides tousling me quite abominably!'

Miss Wychwood, having observed with malicious enjoyment the effect on Mr Carleton of this tangled speech, intervened at this point, saying: 'I've no sympathy to waste on you, Maria! Indeed, I think you very well served for being so foolish as to walk home, instead of calling up a chair. As for "bursting in", I am glad you did, for I wish to make Mr Carleton known to you – Lucilla's uncle, you know! Mr Carleton, Miss Farlow – my cousin, who is kind enough to reside with me.'

He favoured Miss Farlow with a brief bow, but addressed himself to his hostess, saying, with the flicker of an impish smiled: 'Lending you countenance, ma'am?'

'Exactly so!' she said, refusing to rise to this bait.

'You astonish me! I hadn't supposed that any lady so advanced in years as yourself would be conscious of the need of chaperonage! Is your name Annis? A corruption, I believe, of Agnes, but I like it! It becomes you.'

'Well!' exclaimed Miss Farlow, bristling in defence of her patroness, 'I'm sure I don't know why you should, not that I mean to say it is not a very pretty name, for I think it *very* pretty, but if it is a *corruption* it cannot be thought to *become* dear Miss Wychwood, who is not in the least corrupt, let me assure you!'

'Thank you, Maria!' said Miss Wychwood, bubbling over with ill-suppressed mirth. 'I knew I might depend on you to establish my character!'

'Indeed you may, dearest Annis!' declared Miss Farlow, much moved. She glared through starting tears at Mr Carleton, and added, with a gasp at her own temerity: 'I shall take leave to tell you, sir, that I think it *most* ungentlemanly of you to cast aspersions on Miss Wychwood!'

'No, no, Maria!' said Miss Wychwood, trying to speak with proper sobriety, 'you wrong him! I don't *think* he meant to cast aspersions on me – though I own I wouldn't be prepared to hazard any large sum on such a doubtful chance!'

'Hornet!' said Mr Carleton appreciatively.

She twinkled at him, and awoke a reluctant smile in his hard eyes. 'Let us leave my character out of the discussion! You have come to Bath – at great personal inconvenience – to see your niece, but, most unfortunately, she is not here at the moment. So what is to be done? You will scarcely wish to sit here, kicking your heels, until she returns!'

'No, by God I wouldn't! Any more, I dare swear, than you would wish me to do so!'

'No, indeed! You would be very much in my way! Perhaps it would be best if you were to dine here tonight.'

'No,' he said decisively. 'You're very obliging, ma'am, but it would be best if you brought her to dine with me, at the York House. I'm putting up there, and they seem to keep a tolerable table. I shall expect you both at seven – unless you prefer a later hour?'

'Oh, no! But pray don't depend upon my joining you! My abigail shall escort Lucilla to York House, and I feel sure I can rely on you to bring her back later in the evening.'

'That won't do at all!' he said. 'Your presence at any discussion about Lucilla's future is indispensable, believe me! I do depend upon your joining me. Don't fail me!'

With that, he took his leave, bowing slightly to Miss Farlow, but grasping Miss Wychwood's hand for a moment, and favouring her with a rueful grin.

CHAPTER SIX

'Well!' uttered Miss Farlow, in accents of strong reprobation, as soon as Limbury had conducted Mr Carleton out of the room. 'What a *very* uncivil person, I *must* say! To be sure, Sir Geoffrey did warn us, and I do hope, dearest Annis, that you will *not* dine with him this evening! Such impertinence to have invited you – if an invitation you call it, though *I* never heard an invitation delivered so improperly! I quite thought you must have given him a heavy set-down, and was astonished that you did not!'

'Well, I did think of doing so,' admitted Miss Wychwood. 'But since he is, as you so rightly say, a very uncivil person, I couldn't be sure that he wouldn't retaliate in kind. I feel it is my duty to go with Lucilla, if only to prevent her coming to cuffs with him.'

'I make no secret of the fact that I don't consider you owe that girl any duty!' said Miss Farlow, trembling with indignation. 'But *I* have a duty towards *you*, and don't tell me I haven't, for I shan't listen to you! Sir Geoffrey and dear Lady Wychwood entrusted you to my care, and even if he didn't say so, he *meant* it, and Lady Wychwood did say so! Just as I was about to get into the carriage, or if it wasn't then, it was in the hall, or perhaps the morning-room, because she had a little chill coming on, and so didn't come out of the house, though she wished to, but I begged her not to do so, because the weather was most inclement, which you *must* remember, so we said goodbye in the hall—'

'Or perhaps in the morning-room?' interpolated Miss Wychwood.

'It may have been: I'm not perfectly sure, but it makes no difference! And she *distinctly* said, when she bade me goodbye, or perhaps just after she had said goodbye: "Take care of her, Cousin Maria!" Meaning you, of course! And I promised I would, and so I shall!'

'Thank you, Maria, I feel sure I can depend on you to come to my rescue if I should find myself in trouble. But at the moment I'm not in any sort of trouble, so do, I beg of you, put your bonnet straight, and make your hair tidy again! You look like a birch-broom in a fit!'

'Annis!' said Miss Farlow, sinking her voice impressively. 'That man is not a proper person for you to know!'

'Fiddle! I collect Geoffrey told you so, but what harm either of you expect him to do I haven't the most distant guess. Do you suspect him of having designs upon my virtue? You are quite beside the bridge if you do! He doesn't even like me!'

Miss Farlow's modesty was so much shocked by this speech that she uttered a faint shriek, and tottered away to her own room, there to write an agitated letter to Sir Geoffrey Wychwood, in which she assured him that he might depend on her to do all that lay in her power to put an end to a most undesirable friendship, and (in the same sentence) warned him that she feared there was nothing she could do to stop dear Annis in one of her headstrong moods.

When Lucilla came in, it was several minutes before Miss Wychwood was able to break the news of her uncle's arrival to her, so anxious was she to recount all the details of the day's expedition. But she did at last pause for breath, and the change that came over her countenance when she heard the dread tidings was almost ludicrous. The sparkle was quenched instantly in her eyes, the smile vanished from her lips, she turned pale, and wrung her hands together. 'He has come to drag me away! Oh, no, no, no!'

'Don't be such a goose!' said Miss Wychwood, laughing at her. 'I don't think he has any such intention, though I fancy that may well have been his original purpose. But until I told him just what the case was he had no idea that the Iverleys and Mrs Amber were trying to bring about a match between you and Ninian. You need not be afraid that he will help them to promote that precious scheme, for he most certainly will not. He was excessively vexed – partly with them, and partly with you, for not having written to tell him of it. So when you meet him don't put him out of temper by looking black at him, and getting on your high ropes! He seems to me to be as mifty as he is uncivil, and no good purpose can be served by getting into a quarrel with him, you know.'

'I don't want to meet him!' Lucilla declared, tears starting into her eyes.

'Now you are being foolish beyond permission, my dear! Of course you must see him! I am taking you to dine with him at the York House this evening, so that we may, all three of us, discuss what's to be done with you! Oh, don't look so dismayed, you ridiculous puss! I promise I won't let him bully you!'

In spite of this assurance it was a considerable time before Lucilla could be persuaded to consent to the scheme, and although she did in the end consent it was easy to see, when she took her place beside Miss Wychwood in the carriage, that she was far from being reconciled to it. Her charming little face was downcast, her eyes were full of apprehension, and it was not difficult to guess that she stood in great awe of her formidable uncle.

He received them in a private parlour, very correctly attired in the blue coat, white waistcoat, black pantaloons, and striped silk stockings which constituted the evening-dress worn by all the Smarts at private parties. Miss Wychwood noted, with slightly reluctant approval, that while he exhibited none of the exaggerated quirks of fashion which characterized the dandy-set, his coat was very well cut, his neckcloth tied with nicety, his shirt-points decently starched, and the bosom of his shirt adorned by a frill – an outmoded fashion still worn by many provincial beaux, and almost invariably by the older generation of Smarts to which he undoubtedly belonged.

He came forward to shake hands with Miss Wychwood, paying no immediate heed to Lucilla, following her into the parlour. 'You can't think how relieved I am to see that you haven't brought your cousin with you!' he said, by way of greeting. 'I have been cursing myself these three hours for not having made it plain to her that I was not including *her* in my invitation to *you*! I couldn't have endured an evening spent in the company of such an unconscionable gabble-monger!'

'Oh, but you did!' she told him. 'She took you in the greatest dislike, and can't be blamed for having done so, or for having uttered some pretty severe strictures on your total want of conduct. You must own, if there is any truth in you, that you were shockingly uncivil to her!'

'I can't tolerate chattering bores,' he said. 'If she took me in such dislike, I'm amazed that she permitted you to come here without her chaperonage.'

'She would certainly have stopped me if she could have done it, for she does not think you are a proper person for me to know!'

'Good God! Does she suspect me of trying to seduce you? She may be easy on that head: I never seduce ladies of quality!' He turned from her as he spoke, and put up his glass to cast a critical look over Lucilla. 'Well, niece?' he said. 'What a troublesome chit you are! But I'm glad to see that your appearance at least is much improved since I last saw you. I thought that you were bidding fair to grow into a Homely Joan, but I was wrong: you are no longer pudding-faced, and you've lost your freckles. Accept my felicitations!'

'I was not pudding-faced!'

'Oh, believe me, you were! You hadn't lost your puppyfat.'

Her bosom heaved with indignation, but Miss Wychwood intervened, recommending her not to rise to that, or any other fly of her uncle's casting. She added severely: 'And as for you, sir, I beg you will refrain from making any more remarks expressly designed to put Lucilla all on end, and to render me acutely uncomfortable!'

'I wouldn't do *that* for the world!' he assured her.

'Then don't be so rag-mannered!' she retorted.

'But I wasn't!' he protested. 'I didn't say Lucilla *is* pudding-faced! I said she *was*, and even complimented her on her improved looks!'

Lucilla was betrayed into a little crow of involuntary laughter, and said with engaging frankness: 'Oh, what an odiously complete hand you are, Uncle Oliver! Was I *really* such an antidote?'

'Oh, no, not an antidote! Merely a chicken that had lost its

85

down and had too few feathers to show that it might grow into a handsome bird!'

'Well!' said Lucilla, much impressed. 'I know I'm quite *pretty*, but no one has ever said I was handsome! Do you think I am, sir, or – or are you roasting me?'

'No, I don't think you handsome, but you've no need to look so downcast! Believe me, only females admire *handsome* women: men infinitely prefer pretty ones!'

She was left to digest this, while he engaged Miss Wychwood in conversation, but suddenly interrupted this exchange of elegant civilities to ask him if he thought Miss Wychwood handsome, or pretty.

Annis, torn between amusement and embarrassment, directed an admonitory frown at her, but Mr Carleton replied without hesitation: 'Neither.'

'Well, *I* think,' said Lucilla, bristling in defence of her patronness, 'that she is *beautiful*!'

'Yes, so do I,' he answered.

'I am very much obliged to you both,' said Annis, recovering from the shock, 'and I shall be even more obliged to you if you will stop putting me to the blush! I haven't come to listen to empty compliments, but to discuss with you, sir, how best to provide for Lucilla until her come-out!'

'All in good time,' he said. 'We will dine first.' He added, with that glint in his eyes which she found strangely disquieting: 'Your advanced years, ma'am, have impaired your memory! I told you, not so many hours ago, that I never try to flummery people! My years are considerably more advanced than yours, but I should warn you that my memory is still quite undamaged by senility!'

'Odious, *odious* creature!' she said softly, but allowed him to hand her to the table, where two waiters had just finished setting out the first course of a well-chosen dinner.

Lucilla was inclined to pout, but was subdued by a glance from Miss Wychwood's fine eyes, and meekly took her place at her guardian's left hand. She was young enough to regard the food set before her as a matter of indifference, but she had a schoolgirl's hearty appetite, and did full justice to the first course, partaking of every dish offered her, and allowing her elders to converse without interruption. The edge of her hunger having been taken off by the time the second course was brought in she refused the green goose, and the pigeons, but made great inroads on an orange soufflé, a Celerata cream, and a basket of pastry. Nibbling a ratafia biscuit, she stole a glance at her uncle's profile. He was smiling at something Miss Wychwood had said to him, so she ventured to ask him the question uppermost in her mind. 'Uncle Oliver!' she said imperatively.

He turned his head. 'Do rid yourself of this detestable habit you've fallen into of addressing me as *Uncle* Oliver! I find it quite repellent.'

She opened her eyes at him. 'But you *are* my uncle!' she pointed out.

'Yes, but I don't wish to be reminded of it.'

'Such a dreadfully *ageing* title, isn't it?' said Miss Wychwood, with spurious sympathy.

'Exactly so!' he replied. 'Almost worse than *aunt*!'

She shook her head sadly. 'Indeed, yes! Though it was being called aunt that drove me from my home.'

'Well, what *am* I to call you?' demanded Lucilla.

'Anything else you like,' he responded, in a voice devoid of interest.

'Now, that very generous permission opens a wide field to you, my dear,' said Miss Wychwood. 'It wouldn't do for you to call him *Bangster*, for that would be too impolite, but I see nothing amiss with you calling him *Captain Hackum*, which has the same meaning, but wrapped up in clean linen!'

Mr Carleton grinned, and kindly explained to his bewildered niece that these terms signified a bully. 'They are cant terms,' he further explained, 'and far too vulgar for you to use! Anyone hearing them on your lips would write you down as a brass-faced hussy, without conduct or delicacy.'

'Devil!' said Miss Wychwood, with feeling.

'Oh, you're quizzing me!' Lucilla exclaimed, slightly offended. 'Both of you! I wish you will not! I am not a brass-faced hussy, though I daresay people would think me one if I called you merely *Oliver*! I am sure it must be most improper!'

'It would not only be improper but it would bring down

instant retribution on your head!' he told her. 'I have no objection to your addressing me as Oliver, but Merely Oliver I'm damned if I'll tolerate!'

She gave a choke of laughter. 'I didn't meant that! You know I didn't! Of course, if you had a title it would be perfectly proper to call you by it, but only think what my aunt would say if she heard me calling you Oliver!'

'As it seems unlikely that she will hear it, that need not trouble you,' he said. 'If you have any qualms, allay them with the reflection that Princess Charlotte addresses all her uncles – and, for anything I know, her aunts too – by their Christian names, and even the youngest of them is older than I am!'

Lucilla had little interest in Royalty and dismissed the Princess Charlotte summarily. 'Oh, well, I daresay things are different for princesses!' she said. 'But you said that it's unlikely my aunt will ever hear me call you Oliver. W-what do you mean, Unc – *sir*?'

'I understand that she has washed her hands of you?'

'Yes!' breathed Lucilla, clasping her hands together, and keeping her eyes fixed on his face. 'And so—?'

'It behoves me, of course, to find some other female willing to take charge of you.'

Her face fell. 'But when am I to make my come-out?'

'Next year,' he replied.

'*Next* year? Oh, that's too bad of you!' she cried. 'I shall be past eighteen by then, and almost on the shelf! I want to come out *this* year!'

'I daresay, but it won't harm you to wait for another year,' he answered unfeelingly. 'In any event, you must, because Julia Trevisian, who is to present you at one of the Drawing-Rooms, cannot undertake the very exhausting task of chaperoning you to all the functions to which she will see to it that you are invited, until your cousin Marianne is off her hands. Marianne is to be married in May, midway through the Season, and that would be far too late for you to make your first appearance – even if Julia were not, by that time, wholly done-up, which, from her conversation when I last saw her, I gather she expects to be.'

'Is Cousin Julia going to bring me out?' she asked, brightening perceptibly. 'Well, I must say that if you arranged that, sir, it is quite the best thing you've ever done for me! In fact, it is the *only* good thing you've ever done for me, and I am truly grateful to you!'

'Handsomely said!'

'Yes, but it doesn't settle the question of where I am to live, or what I am to do for a whole year,' she pointed out. 'And I wish to make it plain to you that nothing – *nothing!* – will prevail upon me to return to Aunt Clara! If you force me to go back, I shall run away again!'

'Not if you have a particle of commonsense,' he said dryly. He looked her over, rather sardonically smiling. 'You'll do as you are bid, my girl, for if I have any more highty-tighty behaviour from you I promise you I shan't permit you to come out next Season.'

She turned white with sheer rage, and stammered: 'You – you—'

'Enough of this folly!' interposed Miss Wychwood, in blighting accents. 'You are both talking arrant nonsense! I don't know which of you is being the more childish, but I know which of you has the least excuse for behaving like a spoilt baby!'

A tinge of colour stole into Mr Carleton's cheeks, but he shrugged, and said, with a short laugh: 'I've no patience to waste on pert and disobedient schoolgirls.'

'I *hate* you!' said Lucilla, in a low and trembling voice.

'I daresay you do.'

'Oh, for heaven's sake come out of the mops, both of you!' said Miss Wychwood, quite exasperated. 'This ridiculous quarrel has sprung up for no reason at all! There can be no question of your uncle's sending you back to Mrs Amber, Lucilla, because she has made it abundantly clear that she doesn't want you back.'

'She will change her mind,' said Lucilla despairingly. 'She frequently says she washes her hands of me, but she never does so!'

'Well, it's my belief your uncle wouldn't send you to her even if she does change her mind.' She raised a quizzical eyebrow at Mr Carleton, and said: '*Would* you, sir?'

89

A reluctant smile just touched his lips. 'As a matter of fact, no: I wouldn't,' he admitted. 'She seems to me to have exercised no control over Lucilla, and is demonstrably not a fit or proper person to have charge of her. So I am now faced with the unenviable task of finding another, and, it is to be hoped, a more resolute member of the family to fill her place.'

Very little of this speech gratified Lucilla, but she was so much relieved by the discovery that he had no intention of restoring her to Mrs Amber that she decided to ignore such parts of it which had grossly offended her. She said tentatively: 'Wouldn't it be possible for me to remain in my dear Miss Wychwood's charge, sir?'

'No,' he replied uncompromisingly.

She choked back an unwise retort. 'Pray tell me why not!' she begged.

'Because, in the first place, she is even less a fit and proper person to act as your guardian than is your aunt, being far too young to chaperon you, or anyone else, and wholly unrelated to you.'

'She is not too young!' cried Lucilla indignantly. 'She is quite *old!*'

'. . . and in the second place,' he continued, betraying only by a quiver of the muscles beside his mouth that he had heard this hot interjection, 'it would be the height of impropriety for me – or, indeed, you! – to impose so outrageously on her good nature.'

It was evident that this aspect had not previously occurred to Lucilla. She took a moment or two to digest it, and said, finally: 'Oh! I hadn't thought of that.' She looked imploringly at Miss Wychwood, and said: 'I wouldn't – I wouldn't for the world impose on you, ma'am, but – but should I be an imposition? *Pray* tell me!'

Throwing a fulminating glance at Mr Carleton, Miss Wychwood replied: 'No, but *one* of the objections your uncle has raised I realize to be just. I am not related to you, and it would be thought very odd if you were to be known to have been removed from Mrs Amber's care, and put into mine. Such an extraordinary change must give rise to conjecture, and a great deal of poker-talk which I am persuaded you wouldn't relish.

Moreover, that sort of scandal-broth must inevitably reflect on Mrs Amber, and that, I know, you wouldn't wish to happen. For however many tiresome restrictions she has subjected you to, and however boring you found them, you must surely acknowledge that she has acted always – however mistakenly – with nothing but your welfare in mind.'

'Yes,' Lucilla agreed reluctantly. 'But not when she tried to make me accept an offer from Ninian!'

This, as Mr Carleton, cynically appreciative of this exchange, recognized to be (in his own phraseology) a leveller, did not prove to be a home-hit. Miss Wychwood rallied swiftly, and said: 'I shouldn't wonder at it if she thought she *was* promoting your welfare. Recollect, my love, that Ninian was quite your best friend when you were children! Mrs Amber may well have thought that you would find true happiness with him.'

'Are you – *you*, ma'am! – trying to persuade me to go back to Cheltenham?' Lucilla demanded, in a sharp suspicion.

'Oh, no!' replied Miss Wychwood calmly. 'I don't think that would answer. What I am trying to do is to point out to you that if you, by some unlikely chance, could prevail upon your uncle to appoint me to be your guardian, in preference to any of your own relations, we should all three of us come under the gravest censure. Well, I shan't attempt to conceal that I have no wish to incur such censure; and, in your case, it would be extremely damaging, for you may depend upon it that Mrs Amber would inform every one of her friends and acquaintances – and probably your paternal relatives as well – that you were quite beyond her control, and had left her to reside with a complete stranger, which—'

'. . . would have the merit of being true!' interpolated Mr Carleton.

'Which,' pursued Miss Wychwood, ignoring this unmannerly interruption, 'would have a far more damaging effect on your future than you are yet aware of. Believe me, Lucilla, *nothing* is more fatal to a girl than to have earned (however unjustly) the reputation of being a hurly-burly female, wild to a fault, and so hot-at-hand as to be ready to tie her garter in public rather than to submit to authority.'

'That would be *very* bad, wouldn't it?' said Lucilla, forcibly struck by this masterly representation of the evils attached to her situation.

'It would indeed,' Miss Wychwood assured her. 'And it is why I am strongly of the opinion that your uncle should make arrangements for you to reside, until your come-out, with some other of your relations – preferably one who lives in London, and is in a position to introduce you into the proper ways of conducting yourself in Society before you actually enter it. *He* is the only member of your father's family with whom I am acquainted, but I should suppose that he is not the only representative of it.' She turned her head, to direct a look of bland inquiry at Mr Carleton, and said: 'Tell me, sir, has Lucilla no aunts or cousins, on your side of the family, with whom it would be quite unexceptionable for her to reside?'

'Well, there is my sister, of course,' he said thoughtfully.

'My Aunt Caroline?' said Lucilla, doubtfully. 'But isn't she a great invalid, sir?'

'Yes, being burnt to the socket is her favourite pastime,' he agreed. 'She suffers from a mysterious complaint, undiscoverable, but apparently past cure. One of its strangest symptoms is to put her quite out of frame whenever she finds herself asked to do anything she doesn't wish to do. She has been known to become prostrate at the mere thought of being obliged to attend some party which promised to be a very boring function. There's no saying that she wouldn't sink into a deep decline if I were to suggest to her that she should take charge of you, so I shan't do it. I can't have her death laid at my door.'

Lucilla giggled a little at that, but expressed her profound relief as well, saying frankly that she thought life with Lady Lambourn would be even more insupportable than life with Mrs Amber. 'Besides, I am scarcely acquainted with her,' she added, as a clincher. 'Indeed, I don't think I've seen her more than once in my life, and that was years ago, when Mama took me with her to pay a morning call on her. I was only a child, but she didn't *seem* to be invalidish. I remember that she was very pretty, and *most* elegant. To be sure, she did tell Mama that she could seldom boast of being in high health, but she didn't say it in such a way as to lead anyone to suppose that she suffered from an incurable complaint.'

'Ah, that must have been before she attained the status of widowhood!' he replied. 'Lambourn had the good sense to cock up his toes when he realized which way the wind was blowing.'

'What a vast number of enemies your tongue must have made for you!' observed Miss Wychwood. 'May I suggest that instead of casting what I strongly suspect are unjust aspersions on your sister, you bend your mind to the question of which of your relations you judge to be the most proper to have charge of Lucilla until Lady Trevisian is at liberty to introduce her into the ton?'

'Certainly!' he responded, with the utmost cordiality. 'I shall make every effort to do so, but at this present I find myself at a stand, and must, reluctantly, beg you to continue in your self-appointed post as her chaperon.'

'In that case,' she said, getting up from the table, 'we have no more to do here, and will take our leave of you, sir. Come, Lucilla! Thank your uncle for his kind hospitality, and let us go home!'

He made no attempt to detain them, but murmured provocatively, as he put Miss Wychwood's shawl round her shoulders: 'Accept my compliments, ma'am! Were you obliged to put great force on yourself *not* to rise to that fly?'

'Oh, no, none at all!' she retorted, without an instant's hesitation. 'My father taught me many years ago never to pay the least attention to the ill-considered things uttered by rough diamonds!'

He gave a shout of laughter. 'A facer!' he acknowledged. He turned from her to flick Lucilla's cheek lightly with one careless finger. '*Au revoir*, niece!' he said, smiling quite kindly at her. 'Do, pray, strive to re-establish the family's reputation, which I have placed in such jeopardy!'

He then escorted them downstairs, and, while Miss Wychwood's carriage was called for, engaged her, with the utmost civility, in an exchange of very proper nothings. These were interrupted by the entrance from the street of a somewhat rakish looking gentleman whose lively eyes no sooner perceived Miss Wychwood than he came quickly forward, exclaiming: 'Ah, now, didn't I know fortune was going to smile on me today? Most dear lady, how do you do?'

She gave him her hand, which he instantly carried to his lips, and said: 'How do you do, Mr Kilbride? I collect you are in Bath on a visit to your grandmother. I trust she is well?'

'Oh, in a state of far too high preservation!' he said, with a comical look. 'Out of reason cross, too! It is most disheartening!'

She ignored this, and briefly introduced him to her companions. Her manner, which was slightly chilly, did not encourage him to linger, but he was apparently impervious to hints, and, after exchanging nods with Mr Carleton, with whom he was already acquainted, turned to address himself to Lucilla, which he did to such good purpose that she told Miss Wychwood, on the drive to Camden Place, that he was the most delightful and amusing man she had ever met.

'Is he?' said Miss Wychwood, with calculated indifference. 'Yes, I suppose he is amusing, but his wit is not always in good taste, and he is an incurable humbugger, which I find a little tedious. By the bye, your uncle has charged me with the task of engaging a new abigail for you, so will you go with me tomorrow morning to the Registry Office?'

'No, *has* he?' cried Lucilla, astonished. 'Yes, indeed I will, ma'am! And may we take a look in at the Pump Room? Corisande will be there, with her mama, and I told her I would ask you if I might join her.'

'Yes, certainly. And while we are in the town we must buy a new pair of gloves for you, to wear at our rout-party.'

'*Evening*-gloves?' Lucilla said eagerly. 'They will be the first I have ever possessed, because my aunt *will* buy mittens for me, as if I were a mere schoolgirl! Did my uncle say I might have them as well as a new maid?'

'I didn't ask him,' replied Miss Wychwood. 'From what I have seen of him, I am tolerably certain that he would have answered in a disagreeably rusty way that he knew nothing about such matters, and I must do what I thought best.'

Lucilla gave a gurgle of laughter, and said: 'Yes, but the thing

94

is, will he pay for them? For I know how expensive long gloves are, and – and I haven't very much of my pin-money left!'

'There is no need for you to tease yourself about that: of course he will do so!' replied Miss Wychwood, adding, with a good deal of mischievous satisfaction: 'His pride makes it a hard matter for him to be forced to permit *his* ward to reside with me, as my guest, and I take great credit to myself for having imbued him with enough respect to have prevented him from offering to pay me for taking charge of you! I shouldn't wonder at it if he tried to transfer the allowance he makes Mrs Amber to me. As for cutting up stiff at being required to meet the cost of whatever you may purchase – pooh! he is a great deal more likely to encourage you to be extravagant, for fear that if he refused to pay your bills I might do so!'

CHAPTER SEVEN

Just as Miss Wychwood and Lucilla were walking next morning along Upper Camden Place on their way to Gay Street, they encountered Ninian Elmore, striding towards them. It became immediately apparent that he was labouring under a strong sense of resentment, for hardly waiting to greet them he burst out with the rather unnecessary information that he was coming to visit them, adding explosively: 'What do you think has happened, ma'am?'

'I have no idea,' replied Miss Wychwood. 'Tell us!'

'I was coming to do so. You wouldn't believe it! I scarcely do myself! I mean to say, when you consider all that has taken place, and how it was *their* fault, and not mine – well, it makes me as mad as Bedlam, and so it would anyone!'

'But what *is* it?' demanded Lucilla impatiently.

'You may well ask! Not but what it will send you up into the boughs when I tell you! For of all the—'

She interrupted him, stamping her foot, and hugging her pelisse round her against the sharp wind that was blowing. 'For heaven's sake *tell* me, instead of talking in that hubble-bubble way, and keeping us standing in this detestable wind!' she almost screamed.

He glared at her, said with stiff dignity that he was just about to tell her when she had so rudely broken in on him, and, pointedly turning his shoulder towards her, addressed himself to Miss Wychwood, saying portentously: 'I have received a letter from my father, ma'am!'

'Is *that* all?' interpolated Lucilla scornfully.

'No, it is not all!' he retorted. 'But how anyone can utter more than a word with you interrupting—'

'Peace!' intervened Miss Wychwood, considerably amused. 'You cannot quarrel in the street – at least, I daresay you can, but I beg you won't! Has your father disinherited you, Ninian? And, if so, why?'

'Well, no, he hasn't done that, precisely,' he replied, 'but it wouldn't astonish me if he did do so – except that I rather fancy it isn't within his power, on account of the Settlement which was executed by my grandfather. I didn't pay much heed to it at the time, though I know that I had to sign some document or other – but he threatens to discontinue my allowance (besides repudiating any debts I may incur in Bath) if I do not instantly return to Chartley! I – I wouldn't have believed he could ever have behaved in such a manner! It has opened my eyes, I can tell you! He has always seemed to me to be the – the best of fathers, and – and the most understanding, and I don't scruple to say that *this* business has wounded me deeply! And, what's more, I'll be – dashed – if I crawl back to Chartley with my tail between my legs, as though I had done something wrong, which I have *not*!'

'It certainly seems very odd,' acknowledged Miss Wychwood. 'But perhaps there is an explanation! Will you walk with us to Gay Street, before Lucilla becomes quite frozen, and tell us why your father has issued such an ultimatum?'

He agreed to this, and, falling into step between them, disclosed that Lord Iverley (like Mrs Amber) had washed his hands of Lucilla, whose conduct had shown him that she was unworthy to be admitted into the family, being such as to convince him that she was so wholly wanting in propriety, modesty, and delicacy as to have sunk herself below reproach.

Ignoring an indignant gasp from Lucilla, he ended by saying: 'And so if you please, he forbids me to have anything more to do with her, but to return instantly to Chartley – under pain of his severest displeasure! As though the blame for her running away didn't lie at his door! Which it did! By God, Miss Wychwood, it has put me in such a rage that I have a very good mind to marry Lucilla immediately!'

Lucilla, who had listened to this speech with strong resentment, said warmly: 'He would be very well served if you did! But, for my part, I think you should ignore his letter. Because neither of us wishes to be married, and even if we did I don't think my uncle would give his consent. And I can't marry anyone without it, unless, I suppose, I eloped to the Border, which nothing would prevail upon me to do, even with someone I *wished* to marry! That *would* sink me below reproach, wouldn't it, ma'am?'

'It would indeed,' agreed Miss Wychwood. 'Besides condemning you both to a lifetime of regret!'

'Well, I know, but I didn't really mean it!' growled Ninian. 'All the same, I'd as lief be shackled to you as submit tamely to such an unreasonable order as this, and that I do mean!'

To Miss Wychwood's relief, Lucilla took this in perfectly good part. She said: 'I must say, it is enough to drive anyone to desperation. It isn't even as though you had been an undutiful son, for the case has been far otherwise. And what seems to be most extraordinary is that he never kicked up such a dust when you were trying to fix your interest with that female in London, and she was by far more improper than I am, wasn't she?'

He cast her a fulminating glance. 'I'll tell you this, Lucy! It will be well for you to learn to keep your tongue between your teeth! Besides, you know nothing about it! I was not trying to fix my interest with her! A mere flirtation! Bachelor's fare! You wouldn't understand, but you may depend upon it my father did!'

'Well, if he understood that, why doesn't he understand *this*?' Lucilla asked reasonably. 'It seems to me to be quite addlebrained!'

'It seems to *me*,' interposed Miss Wychwood, 'as though Lord Iverley wrote to you when he was in too much of a flame to consider what might be the effect of sending you such an intemperate letter, Ninian. I daresay he will be sorry for it by now; and I am very sure that it came as a shock to him when he found himself in a quarrel with you, for I fancy that had never happened before. Nor do I doubt that, however little he may acknowledge it, he knows he has been at fault in his dealings with you and Lucilla. So, having been pandered – having had his own way for a great number of years, he was naturally put into a pelter when he met with opposition – particularly from you, my dear boy! You told us yourself that you had parted from him on the worst of bad terms, and I expect he was sadly hurt—'

'Yes, I did, but I was sorry for it later, and was meaning to go back, to beg his pardon, when his letter reached me! But I shan't now! I could forgive his cutting at *me*, but the things he said about Lucy I cannot forgive – unless he withdraws them! It isn't that I approved of her running off as she did, for I didn't, but to accuse her of *wanton* behaviour, which he did, though I didn't intend to repeat that, besides having sunk herself below reproach, is unjust, and unforgiveable!'

Keeping her inevitable reflections on Lord Iverley's un-wisdom to herself, Miss Wychwood responded, with soothing tact: 'You will of course do what you feel to be best, but I cannot help feeling that you ought, in common civility, to send your father an answer to his letter – and not an angry one! If you already had the intention of going back to beg his pardon—'

'I had, but I haven't that intention now!' he declared pug-naciously.

'When you've come out of the mops,' she said, smiling at him in a disarming way, 'I am persuaded that your good sense will make you perceive the propriety of offering him an apology for having expressed yourself more forcefully than was becoming. I don't think you should mention Lucilla at all, for what purpose could be served by your defending her against accusations which Lord Iverley must know very well are unjust? As for his summons to you, it would be foolish to refuse to obey it, for that, you know, would make you seem like a naughty little boy, shouting "I won't!" Far more dignified, don't you agree, to write that you will of course return presently to Chartley, but that you have several engagements in Bath in the immediate future from which it would be grossly impolite to cry off.'

Much impressed by this worldly wisdom, he exclaimed: 'By Jove, yes! That's the dandy! I *will* write to him, exactly as you suggest! I should think it must make him ashamed, besides showing him that I am not a schoolboy but a grown man, not to be ordered about but to be treated with respect! What's more, I'll send my duty to Mama, though after the things she said to me – However, whatever *they* choose to do, I hope *I* am not one to rip up grievances!'

Miss Wychwood applauded this; and as they had reached Gay Street, took leave of him, recommending him, if he had nothing better to do, to stroll down to the Pump Room, where she and Lucilla were going as soon as they had executed some business, and done a little shopping. Since her object was to prevent his writing a reply to his father's letter until his smouldering anger had had time to die down, she was glad to see that this suggestion found favour with him. When Lucilla, adding her helpful mite, told him that he would find her dear friend, Miss Corisande Stinchcombe, there, and charged him with a message for her, his clouded brow lightened perceptibly, and he went off quite happily down the hill. 'Which,' Lucilla informed Miss Wychwood confidentially, 'I had a notion would give his thoughts another direction, because I could see yesterday that he took a marked fancy to her!'

'Then it was very well done of you,' approved Miss Wychwood. 'Which reminding him of his London-flirt was not!'

'No,' admitted Lucilla guiltily. 'I knew I had said the wrong thing as soon as the words were out of my mouth. Though why he should have taken snuff at it I haven't the least guess, for he told me all about her himself!'

Miss Wychwood was not obliged to enter into an explanation, because they had by this time mounted the flight of stairs that led to the Registry Office, recommended by Mrs Wardlow, who had engaged a highly respectable Young Person through its agency, to act as Second Housemaid in Camden Place, and was so well satisfied with the Young Person that she had no hesitation in directing her mistress to the office. Lucilla was too much overawed by the oppressive gentility of the proprietress to do more than agree with whatever Miss Wychwood suggested to her, and confided to that lady when they left the premises that the statuesque Mrs Poppleton had frightened her to death, so that she was deeply thankful her dear Miss Wychwood had been present to support her. 'And when the maids she means to send to Camden Place to be interviewed come, you *will* be there, won't you?' she said anxiously.

Reassured on this head, she tripped happily beside Miss Wychwood, and recklessly bought not one but two pairs of long kid gloves, which (she said) made her feel truly grown-up at last.

Since the Bath Season had hardly begun, the musicians who entertained the company every morning in the Pump Room during the full Season were not present, but a fair sprinkling of visitors was already in evidence. A somewhat depressingly large number of the visitors were valetudinarians, either hobbling about on sticks, being afflicted by gout or rheumatism; or elderly dyspeptics, hopefully seeking a cure for liver disorders arising from the excesses of their earlier years. There were also several dowagers, suffering from nervous disorders and from a conviction that a recital of their various ills, and the many treatments they had undergone must be of as much interest to those of their acquaintances whom they could contrive to buttonhole as they were to themselves. But as most of the confirmed invalids were attended by younger members of their families, the assembly, which at first glance appeared to consist of crippled persons, stricken in years, included quite a number of young persons wholly unafflicted by the numerous ailments for which the Bath waters were considered to be an infallible remedy. For the most part, these attendants were females, but there were some exceptions, notably the fascinating Mr Kilbride, who, whenever (for financial reasons) he came to Bath on a visit to his grandmother, dutifully escorted her to the Pump Room, tenderly settled her in a chair, brought her a glass of the hot pump water, took immense pains to discover amongst the company one of her cronies, and, having inexorably led this unfortunate up to her, and seen him (or her) safely ensconced beside her, occupied himself for the rest of his stay in the Pump Room in strolling about, greeting chance acquaintances, and flirting lightheartedly with all the prettiest girls present.

Besides these seasonal visitors there were the residents, and the first of these on whom Miss Wychwood's eyes fell, as she glanced round the Pump Room, was Lord Beckenham. He was talking to a lady in a preposterous hat, trimmed with several upstanding ostrich feathers, but as soon as he perceived Miss Wychwood he excused himself and purposefully threaded his way towards her between the several groups of people which separated them. Lucilla, having located Corisande Stinchcombe, darted away in her direction, and Miss Wychwood was left to Lord Beckenham's mercy.

He greeted her with his usual punctiliousness, but almost immediately said, with a grave look, that he was excessively sorry to learn that her young friend's visit had led to a disagreeable consequence. 'I understand that Oliver Carleton has come to Bath, and that you have been obliged to receive him,' he said heavily. 'It was inevitable, of course, that he should call in Camden Place, but I trust it was to make arrangements to remove his niece from Bath?'

'Oh, no, not immediately!' replied Miss Wychwood cheerfully. 'That would certainly be a disagreeable consequence! I hope to have her company for some time yet. She is a delightful child – positively a ray of sunshine in the house!'

'I own she appeared to be an amiable girl, and I was favourably impressed by her manners,' he conceded, with a patronizing air which she found intolerable. 'The danger attached to her visit is that you may find yourself obliged to become more closely acquainted with her uncle than can be thought desirable. You will not object to my venturing to give you a hint, I know.'

'On the contrary, sir! I object very much to it,' she said, sparks of wrath in her eyes. 'I think it is a gross impertinence – to give you the word with no bark on it! – for what right have you to give me hints on how I should conduct myself! None that I have granted you!'

He looked to be a little confounded by this forthright speech, but embarked on a ponderous explanation of the purity of his intention, in which his regard for her, his hope that he might one day have the right to guide her judgement, his conviction that the warning he had uttered would meet with her brother's warm approval, and his knowledge of the world, became entangled almost beyond unravelling. He seemed to be aware of this, for he brought his speech to an end by saying: 'In short, dear Miss Annis, you are ignorant – as indeed one would wish you to be! – of how very undesirable an acquaintance for a delicately nurtured female Carleton is! Particularly for a lady of quality such as yourself! I am persuaded that your good brother would echo my sentiments on this occasion, and that there is no need for me to say more.'

She bestowed a glittering smile upon him, and said: 'No need at all, sir! In point of fact, there was no need for you to have said as much. But since you seem to be so much concerned with my welfare let me assure you that my acquaintance with Mr Carleton is unattended by any danger either to my reputation or to my virtue! He is quite the rudest man I have ever met, and I am not so ignorant as to be unaware that he is what I believe is termed a *man of the town*, but I have it on the best of authority – his own! – that he never attempts to seduce ladies of quality! So you may be easy – and I beg you will say no more on this subject!'

An amused voice spoke at her elbow. 'I expect he will, though, and you can see he is far from easy,' said Mr Carleton. He nodded at Beckenham, who was visibly swelling with hostility, and greeted him with a careless tolerance which still further exacerbated his lordship's resentment. 'How do you do?' he said. 'They tell me it was you who bought that dubious Brueghel at Christie's last month, but I daresay rumour lied!'

'I did buy it, and I do not consider it dubious!' responded his lordship, growing almost purple in the face from his effort to suppress his spleen. 'I heard that *you* had a fancy for it, Carleton!'

'No, no! not when I had had the opportunity to inspect it

102

more closely!' replied Mr Carleton soothingly. 'I wasn't the bidder who ran you up so high – in fact, I wasn't in the bidding at all!' Observing, with satisfaction, the effect this had on the infuriated connoisseur, he added, by way of rubbing salt into the wound: 'I don't think I was told who your unsuccessful rival was: some silly gudgeon, no doubt!'

'Do I understand you to mean that I too am a gudgeon?' demanded Lord Beckenham fiercely.

Mr Carleton put up his black brows in exaggerated surprise, and said in a bewildered voice: 'Now, what in the world can I have said to put such a notion as that into your head? It cannot have escaped your notice, my dear Beckenham, that I carefully refrained from saying "some *other* silly gudgeon"!'

'I shall take leave to tell you, Carleton, that I find your – your *wit* offensive!'

'By all means!' replied Mr Carleton. 'You have my leave to tell me anything you choose! How unjust it would be in me to refuse to grant you leave to do so when it has never occurred to me that I should ask your permission to say that I find you a dead bore, which I've been doing for years.'

'If it were not for our surroundings,' said Lord Beckenham, between his teeth, 'I should be strongly tempted to land you a facer, sir!'

'It's to be hoped you would have the strength of mind to resist temptation,' said Mr Carleton, with spurious sympathy. 'Such a very gudgeon-ish thing to do, don't you agree?'

Since Beckenham was well aware that Mr Carleton was almost as famous for his punishing skill in the boxing-ring as for his rudeness this reply infuriated him so much that, with only the briefest of bows to Miss Wychwood, he turned on his heel and walked off, his brow thunderous, and his lips tightly compressed.

'I have never been able to understand,' remarked Mr Carleton, 'why it is that so many persons find it impossible to rid themselves of such pompous bores as that fellow!'

'Perhaps,' offered Miss Wychwood, 'it is because very few persons – if any at all! – are as rude as you are!'

'Ah, no doubt that is the reason!' he nodded.

'You should be ashamed of yourself!' she told him.

'No, no, how can you say so? You don't mean to tell me you didn't wish to be rid of him!'

'Well, no,' she admitted. 'I did wish it, but that was because he vexed me to death. I was going to do the thing myself if you hadn't interrupted us! And I shouldn't have been so grossly uncivil!'

'You can't be very well-acquainted with him if you imagine you would have succeeded,' he said. 'Nothing short of the *grossest* incivility has ever been known to pierce his armour of self-importance. He can empty a room quicker than any man I've ever known.'

She smiled, but said charitably: 'Poor man! One can't but feel sorry for him.'

'A waste of sympathy, believe me! He would be incredulous, I daresay, if it were disclosed to him that he was an object for pity. In his own eyes, his consequence is so great that when people smother yawns in the middle of one of his pretentious lectures *he* is sorry for *them*, because it is plain to him that they are persons of vastly inferior intellect, quite unworthy to receive instruction from him.'

Recalling very vividly the numerous occasions when she had been provoked almost to screaming point by his lordship's disquisitions, accompanied as they invariably were by kindly but intolerable attempts to enlighten her ignorance, or to correct what his superior taste assured him were her false artistic judgements, she could not suppress a little chuckle, but she atoned for this by saying that even if his lordship were a trifle prosy he had many excellent qualities.

'I should hope he had. Everyone has *some* excellent qualities. Why, even I have! Not many, of course, but some!'

She thought it wisest to ignore this bait, and continued, as though she had not heard the interpolation, to defend Lord Beckenham's character. 'He is a man of the first respectability,' she said, in a reproving tone. 'Always well-conducted, with propriety of taste, and – and delicacy of principle. He is an affectionate brother, too, and – and altogether a very worthy man!'

'I don't think you should encourage him to make such a deadset at you,' he said, shaking his head. 'You will have the poor fellow making you an offer, and if you don't accept it very likely he will be so broken-hearted that if he doesn't put a period to his life he will fall into a deep melancholy.'

The picture this conjured up was too much for Miss Wychwood's gravity. She choked, and broke into laughter, informing him, however, as soon as she was able to control her voice, that it ill-became him to poke fun at his betters.

'If it comes to that it doesn't become you to laugh at him!' he retorted.

'I know it doesn't,' she acknowledged. 'But I was not laughing at him, precisely, but at you for saying anything so absurd about him. Now, if you wish to talk to Lucilla—'

'I don't. Who is the young sprig at her elbow?'

She glanced across the room, to where Lucilla was the centre of an animated group. 'Ninian Elmore — if you mean the fair boy?'

He put up his glass. 'Oh, so that's Iverley's heir, is it? Not a bad-looking halfling, but too chitty-faced. Legs like cat-sticks too.' His glass swept round the group, and his face hardened. 'I see she has Kilbride dangling after her,' he said abruptly. 'Let me make it plain to you, ma'am, that that's a connexion I don't wish you to encourage!'

She was nettled by his suddenly autocratic tone, but replied with characteristic honesty: 'I shall certainly not do so, Mr Carleton, rest assured! To be frank with you, I was vexed that he should have come up to me last night, so that I was obliged to introduce him to Lucilla, for although I find him an agreeable companion, I am well aware that his engaging manners, coupled as they are with considerable address and a propensity for flirting desperately with almost any pretty female, make him an undesirable friend for a green girl.'

He let his glass fall, and transferred his gaze to her face. 'You have a *tendre* for him, have you? I might have guessed it! *Your* affairs are no concern of mine, Miss Wychwood, but Lucilla's are very much my concern, and I give you fair warning that I don't mean to let her fall into the clutches of Kilbride or any other loose screw of his kidney!'

She replied, in a cold voice at startling variance with the flame of anger in her eyes: 'Pray enlighten my ignorance, sir! In what way does Mr Kilbride's character differ from your own?'

Any hope she might have cherished of putting him out of countenance died stillborn: he merely looked astonished, and ejaculated: 'Good God, do you imagine I would permit her to marry any one like myself? What a bird-witted question to have asked me! And I had begun to think you a woman of superior sense!'

She found herself without a word to say, but no answer was required of her. With the briefest of bows he turned away, leaving her to regret that she had allowed her vexation to betray her into what she realized, too late, had been an impropriety. Ladies of the first consideration did not accuse even the most hardened rake-shame of being a loose screw. She told herself that the fault lay at his door: she had caught the infection of far too plain speaking from him. But it would not do; her conscience smote her; she foresaw that she would be obliged to offer him an apology; and discovered, with some surprise, that it was more mortifying to be thought by him to be bird-witted than brassily forward.

Giving herself a mental shake, she made her way to Mrs Stinchcombe's party, and greeted that lady with her usual smiling calm. But before she had time to exchange greetings with the rest of the company she suffered a set-back. Lucilla cried impulsively: 'Oh, Miss Wychwood, do pray tell Mr Kilbride that we shall be happy to see him at the party! I ventured to invite him, for you told me I might invite anyone I chose, and I know he is a friend of yours! Only he says he dare not come without an invitation from you!'

It was at this point that Miss Wychwood realized that taking charge of Lucilla was not likely to be the sinecure she had blithely expected it to be. It was impossible to repudiate the invitation so innocently given, but she did her best. She said: 'Certainly, if he cares to come, I shall be happy to include him.'

'I do care to come!' he said promptly, moving forward to bow over her hand. He raised his head, smiling wickedly at her, and added softly: 'Why don't you wish me to, most adored lady? Surely you must know that I am an excellent man to have at a party!'

'Oh, yes!' she said lightly. 'Amusing rattles always are! But I don't think mine is going to be the sort of party you enjoy. In fact, I fancy you would find it a very insipid one – almost a children's party!'

'Oh, in that case you can't possibly exclude me! I am at my best at children's parties, and will engage myself to organize any number of parlour games to keep your youthful guests entertained. Charades, for instance, or Blind Man's Buff!'

'Don't be so absurd!' she said, laughingly. 'If you come, I shall expect you to entertain the dowagers!'

'Oh, there will be no difficulty about that! I have even succeeded in entertaining my grandmother, and that, you know, calls for great skill in the art!'

'You know, you are a sad scamp!' she told him, and she moved away from him.

She found that Mr Beckenham had joined the group, and it occurred to her, as she shook hands with him, that Mr Kilbride's presence at her rout would be less marked if she invited Mr Beckenham too. He was considerably younger than Kilbride, but his easy address, and decided air of fashion made him appear to be older than his years. He was accompanied by a very dashing Tulip, whom he presented as Jonathan Hawkesbury: a friend of his who had toddled down from London to spend a few days at Beckenham Court, so Miss Wychwood promptly included him in her invitation. She did not form any very high opinion of his mental powers, but his manners were extremely polite, and his raiment so exquisite that he was bound, she thought, to lend lustre to her party. Both gentlemen accepted her invitation, Mr Hawkesbury expressing himself as being very much obliged to her, and Harry saying, with his careless grace: 'By Jave, yes! We shall be delighted to come to your party, dear Miss Annis! Will there be dancing?'

Miss Wychwood rapidly revised her plans. She had engaged a small orchestra to discourse soft music to her guests, but she now began to think that the musicians might well strike up a country dance or two, and perhaps – daring thought! – a waltz. That might shock some of the starchier dowagers, for although the waltz was becoming increasingly fashionable in London it was never danced at any of the Bath Assemblies. But it would undoubtedly raise her party from the doldrums of the dull and ordinary to the ranks of the unexpectedly modish. She said: 'Well, that will depend on circumstances! It is to be a rout-party, not a ball, but I daresay it will end as – not a ball, but an impromptu hop.'

Mr Beckenham applauded this suggestion, and added the information that his somewhat inarticulate friend sported a very pretty toe. Mr Hawkesbury disclaimed, but expressed with great gallantry the hope that he might be granted the honour of leading his hostess on to the floor. Miss Wychwood then detached herself from the group, with the intention of enlarging her party by the inclusion of Major Beverley, who had just entered the Pump Room, in attendance on his mama. He was not a dancing-man, but he was of much the same age as Denis Kilbride, and, from the circumstance of his having had the misfortune to lose an arm at the sanguinary engagement at Waterloo, was an object of awed interest to the damsels who would be present at the party. Having successfully enrolled him, she strolled round the room in search of further prey. She found two; and it suddenly occurred to her that her object was not so much to provide Lucilla with a counter-attraction, as to hide Mr Kilbride from Mr Carleton's penetrating eyes. This was so ridiculous that it made her laugh inwardly; but it was also vexing: what concern was it of his whom she chose to invite to her house? She didn't give a straw for his opinion, and wouldn't waste another thought on it.

Nothing was seen of him for the following two days, but towards evening on the third day he called in Camden Place to inform Lucilla that he had procured a well-mannered mare for her to ride. 'My groom is bringing her down, and will look after her,' he said. 'I'll tell him to come here for orders every day.'

'*Oh*!' squeaked Lucilla joyfully. '*Thank* you, sir! I am excessively obliged to you! Where does she come from? When shall I be able to ride her? What sort of a mare is she? Shall I like her?'

'I trust so. She's a grey, carries a good head, and jumps off her hocks. She comes from Lord Warrington's stables, and is accustomed to carrying a lady, but I bought her at Tattersall's, Warrington having no further use for her since his wife's death. You may ride her the day after tomorrow.'

'Oh, famous! capital!' she cried, clapping her hands. 'Was *that* why I thought you must have left Bath? Did you go all the way to London to buy me a horse of my very own? I am – I am truly grateful to you! Miss Wychwood has lent me her own favourite mare, and she is the sweetest-goer imaginable, but I don't like to be borrowing her mare, even though she says she doesn't wish to ride herself.'

'No, nor do I like it,' he said. He put up his glass, surveying through it Mr Elmore, who had risen at his entrance, but was standing bashfully in the background. 'You, I fancy, must be young Elmore,' he said. 'In which case, I have to thank you for having taken care of my niece, I believe.'

'Yes, but – but it was nothing, sir!' stammered Ninian. 'I mean, the only thing I could do was to accompany her, for I – I was unable to persuade her to return to Chartley, say what I would, which, of course, was what she should have done!'

'Heavy on hand, was she? You have my sympathy!'

Ninian grinned shyly at him. 'I should rather think she was!' he said. 'Well, she was in one of her hey-go-mad humours, you know!'

'I am thankful to say that I don't,' replied Mr Carleton caustically.

'I was not!' declared Lucilla, taking instant umbrage. 'And as for taking care of me, I was very well able to take care of myself!'

'No, you weren't!' retorted Ninian. 'You didn't even know how to get to Bath, and if I hadn't caught you—'

'If you hadn't meddled I should have hired a chaise in Amesbury,' she said grandly. 'And it wouldn't have lost a wheel, like your odious gig!'

'Oh, would you indeed? And have found yourself without a feather to fly with when you reached Bath! Don't be such a widgeon!'

Miss Wychwood, entering the room at that moment, put a stop to further hostilities, by saying in her calm way: 'How many more times am I to tell you both that I will *not* have you pulling caps in my drawing-room? How do you do, Mr Carleton?'

'Oh, Miss Wychwood, whatever do you think?' cried Lucilla eagerly. 'He has brought me a mare – a grey one, too, which is exactly what I should have chosen, because I love grey horses, don't you? And he says his own groom is to look after her, so that now you will be able to ride with us!'

'Redeeming yourself in your ward's eyes?' Miss Wychwood said quizzically, shaking hands with him.

'No: in yours, I hope!'

Startled, her eyes flew to his face, but swiftly sank again. Considerably shaken, she turned away, for there could be no mistaking the glow in his hard eyes: Mr Carleton, that noted profligate, had conceived a strange, unaccountable fancy for a maiden lady, of advanced years, who was no straw damsel, but a lady of the first consideration, and of unquestioned virtue. Her first thought, that he meant to fascinate her into accepting a *carte blanche* from him, occurred only to be dismissed: Mr Carleton might be a libertine, but he was not a fool. Perhaps he meant to get up a flirtation with her, by way of alleviating the boredom of Bath society. Hard on the heels of this thought came the realization that a flirtation with him would alleviate her own constantly growing boredom. He was so very different from any of her other flirts: in fact, she had never met anyone in the least like him.

Lucilla and Ninian were arguing about the several rides to be enjoyed outside Bath. They went into the back-drawing-room to consult the guide-book which Lucilla was almost positive she had left there. 'And if they find it,' remarked Miss Wychwood, 'they will instantly disagree on whether to go to see a Druidical monument, or a battlefield. I cannot conceive how anyone but a confirmed chucklehead could suppose that they were in the least degree suited to each other!'

'Iverley and Clara Amber are both chuckleheads,' replied Mr Carleton, dismissing them from further consideration. 'I hope you mean to join the riding-party?'

'Yes, very likely I shall. Not that I think it at all necessary to provide Lucilla with a chaperon when she goes out with Ninian!'

'No, but it is very necessary, I promise you, to provide me with a companion who won't bore me past endurance. I can

110

think of few worse fates than to be obliged to ride bodkin between that pair of bickerers.'

Surprised, she said: 'Oh, are you going with them?'

'Not unless you go too.'

'For fear that you may have to listen to bickering?' she said, smiling a little. 'You won't! They don't quarrel when they go riding together, I'm told. Corisande Stinchcombe complained that they talked of nothing but horses, hounds, and hunting!'

'Even worse!' he said.

'You are not a hunting man, Mr Carleton?'

'On the contrary! But I do not indulge myself or bore my companions by describing the great runs I've had, the tosses I've taken, the clumsiness of one of my hunters – only saved from coming to grief over a regular rasper, be it understood, by my superior horsemanship! – or the sure-footedness of another. Such anecdotes are of no interest to anyone but the teller.'

'I am afraid that's true,' she acknowledged. 'But the impulse to boast of great runs and of clever horses is almost irresistible – even though one knows one is being listened to because the other person is only waiting for the chance to do some boasting on his own account! To which, of course, one is bound to listen, for the sake of common honesty! Don't you agree?'

'Yes: it is why I learned years ago to overcome that impulse. You yourself hunt, I believe?'

'I was used to, when I lived in the country, but I was obliged to give it up when I came to Bath,' she said, with a faint sigh.

'Why did you come to Bath?' he asked.

'Oh, for several good reasons!' she responded lightly.

'If you mean that for a set-down, Miss Wychwood, I should inform you that I am not so easily set down! What good reasons?'

She looked at him rather helplessly, but, after a moment, replied with a touch of asperity: 'They concern no one but myself, sir! And if you are aware that I did give you what I hoped would be a civil set-down for asking me an – an impertinent question, you will permit me to tell you that I consider you positively rag-mannered to pursue the subject!'

'Very likely, but that's no answer!'

'It's the only one I mean to give you!'

'Which leaves me to suppose that some murky secret lies in your past,' he said provocatively. 'I find that hard to believe. With another, and very different, female, I might assume that some scandal had driven you from your home – an unfortunate *affaire* with one of the local squires, for instance!'

She curled her lip at him, and said disdainfully: 'Curb your imagination, Mr Carleton! No murky secret lies behind me, and I have had no *affaires*, fortunate or otherwise!'

'I didn't think you had,' he murmured.

'This is a most improper conversation!' she said crossly.

'Yes, isn't it?' he agreed. 'Why *did* you come to live in Bath?'

'Oh, how persistent you are!' she exclaimed. 'I came to Bath because I wished to live a life of my own – not to dwindle into a mere aunt!'

'That I can well understand. But what the devil made you choose Bath, of all places?'

'I chose it because I have many friends here, and because it is within easy reach of Twynham Park.'

'Do you never regret it? Don't you find it cursed flat?'

She shrugged. 'Why, yes, sometimes I do, but so I should, I daresay, in any place where I resided all the year round.'

'Good God, is that what you do?'

'Oh, no! That was an exaggeration! I frequently visit my brother and his wife, and sometimes I go to stay with an aunt, who lives at Lyme Regis.'

'Gay to dissipation, in fact!'

She laughed. 'No, but I am past the age of wishing for dissipation.'

'Don't talk that balderdash to me!' he said sharply. 'You have left your girlhood behind – though there are moments when I doubt that! – and have not reached your prime, so let me have no more fiddle-faddle about your advanced years, my girl!'

She gave an outraged gasp, but was prevented from flinging a retort at him by Lucilla, who came back into the front half of the room, demanding support in her contention that *somewhere* on Lansdown there were the remains of a Saxon fort which

King Arthur had besieged. 'Ninian says there isn't. He says there was no such person as King Arthur! He says he was just a legend! But he wasn't, was he? It is all here, in the guide-book, and I should like to know what makes Ninian think he knows more than the guide-book!'

'Oh, my God!' ejaculated Mr Carleton, and abruptly took his leave.

CHAPTER EIGHT

On the following day Lord Beckenham called in Camden Place to offer Miss Wychwood an apology for having offended her. Since the servants were busily employed with all the preparations for the evening's rout-party, his visit was ill-timed. Limbury, or James, the footman, would have informed his lordship that Miss Wychwood was not at home; but since Limbury was heavily engaged in the pantry, assembling all the silver and the glasses which would be needed for the entertainment of some thirty guests; and James, assisted by the page-boy and two of the maidservants, was moving various pieces of furniture out of the drawing-room, the door was opened to Lord Beckenham by a very junior housemaid whose flustered attempt to deny her mistress he had no difficulty in over-bearing. He said, with a majestic condescension which awed her very much, that he fancied Miss Wychwood would grant him a few minutes of her time, and walked past her into the house. She gave back before this determined entry, excusing herself, later, to Limbury, who took her severely to task, by saying that his lordship had walked through her as though she wasn't there. There seemed to be nothing for it but to usher him into the book-room at the back of the house, and to scurry away in search of her mistress. She found her, after an abortive tour of the upper floors, in the basement, conferring with her chef, so that Beckenham was left to kick his heels for a considerable time before Miss Wychwood appeared on the scene.

She was in no very good humour, and after the briefest of greetings, told him that she could spare him only a few minutes, having a great deal to do that morning, and begged that he would state his business with her without loss of time.

His answer disarmed her. He said, retaining her hand in a warm clasp: 'I know it: you are holding a party tonight, are you not? I shall not detain you longer than to beg you to forgive me for my part in what passed between us in the Pump Room the other day, and to believe that I was betrayed by my ardent concern for your welfare into uttering words which you thought *impertinent*! I can only assure you, dear Miss Annis, that they were not meant to be impertinent, and beg you to forgive me!'

Her resentment died. She said: 'Why, of course I forgive you, Beckenham! Don't waste another thought on it! We all of us say what we ought not sometimes.'

He pressed his lips to her hand. 'Too good, too gracious!' he said, in a deeply moved voice. 'I feared, when I learned from Harry that you had invited him and young Hawkesbury to your party this evening, but not me, that I had offended beyond forgiveness.'

'Nonsense!' she said. 'I didn't invited you, because it is a party for Lucilla, and will be entirely – *almost* entirely composed of girls not yet out, and their attendant brothers and swains, with a sprinkling of careful mamas and papas as well. You would be bored to death!'

'I could never be bored in your company,' he said simply.

She was at once assailed by a heartrending vision of him, left to endure a lonely evening, feeling himself to be unwanted while his brother went off with his friend for an evening's jollification, and yielded to a kindly impulse, saying: 'Why, by all means come, if you can face children and dowagers!'

The words were no sooner uttered than regretted. Too late did she recall that Beckenham was well-accustomed to being alone. It was seldom that Harry, during his infrequent visits, spent an evening at home. He said, when reproved, that Will didn't want him; and Theresa, Beckenham's eldest sister, complained that it was his habit to retire to his library after dinner,

114

poring over the catalogue of his possessions, or rearranging his bibelots.

She said, in an unhopeful attempt to make him refuse the invitation: 'I should warn you, sir, Lucilla's uncle will be present. You might prefer not to meet him, perhaps.'

'I trust,' he said, with a smile of superior tolerance, 'that I am sufficiently in command of myself not to embarrass you by engaging in a brangle with Carleton under your roof, dear Miss Annis!'

He then, with renewed protestations of his gratitude and devotion, took his leave. She had only to rake herself down for having been betrayed into having encouraged his pretensions.

The rest of the day passed without any other incident than the arrival of Eliza Brigham, hired to be Lucilla's abigail. Annis had been prepared to encounter criticism of this pleasant-faced woman from the older members of her domestic staff, but although Jurby said cautiously that it was early days yet to judge, she added that Miss Brigham *seemed* to know her work; and Mrs Wardlow and Limbury expressed wholehearted approval of the new inmate. 'A very genteel young woman, and such as Miss is bound to like,' said Mrs Wardlow. 'Not one to put herself forward,' said Limbury, adding confidentially: 'And no fear that she'll rub against Miss Jurby, Miss Annis!'

Miss Brigham demonstrated her quality when she dressed Lucilla for the evening's party, for she not only persuaded her to wear a muslin gown of the softest shade of rose-pink instead of the rather more sophisticated yellow one which Lucilla wished to wear, but also managed to convince her that the string of beads which Lucilla had purchased that very day was not as suitable for evening wear as her pearl necklace; brushed her dusky curls till they shone, and arranged them in a simple and charming style, which drew praise from Miss Wychwood, when she came into Lucilla's room just before dinner.

She brought with her a pretty bangle, set with pearls, and clasped it round Lucilla's wrist, saying: 'That's a small gift, with my love for your first party!'

'*Oh!*' gasped Lucilla. 'Oh, Miss Wychwood, *thank* you! Oh, how pretty it is! How *very* kind you are to me! Look, Brigham!'

'Very pretty indeed, miss. Just the thing, if I may say so,' responded Brigham, casting the eye of an expert over Miss Wychwood's attire.

She found nothing to criticize. Miss Wychwood was wearing a robe of celestial blue crape with an open front over a white satin slip. A sapphire necklace was clasped about her neck, and a sapphire spray was set in her burnished hair. She looked, Lucilla told her in awed accents, magnificent. She laughed at this, and protested at Lucilla's choice of adjective, saying that it sounded as though she were overdressed for the occasion.

'Well – well, *beautiful*!' amended Lucilla.

'Then there are a pair of us,' said Miss Wychwood. 'Let us go downstairs to dazzle Ninian! I'm told he arrived a few minutes ago.'

They found him awaiting them in the drawing-room. He had been invited to dinner, and it was evident that he had taken immense pains over his apparel. Lucilla exclaimed admiringly: 'Oh, first-rate, Ninian! You are as fine as fivepence, I do declare! Isn't he, ma'am?'

'Yes, indeed! A veritable Pink of the Ton!' said Miss Wychwood. 'I am wholly spell-bound – particularly by the elegance of his neckcloth! How long did it take you to achieve anything so beautiful, Ninian?'

'Hours!' he replied, blushing. 'It's the Oriental, you know, and I do think I've succeeded pretty well with it. Now do, pray, stop poking bogey at me, ma'am!' He turned to pick up from the table on which he had laid them two tight posies, and presented them with awkward grace, saying: 'Pray, ma'am, do me the honour to accept of these few flowers! And this one, Lucy, is for you!'

The ladies received these tributes with becoming gratitude, Lucilla being particularly struck by her posy's being composed of pink and white hyacinths, a circumstance which made her exclaim: 'How clever of you, Ninian! Did you guess that I was going to wear my pink gown?'

'Well, no!' he confessed. 'But the girl who made the posies up for me asked what you looked like, and when I told her you were dark and not yet out, she said that pink and white flowers would best become you. And I must say,' he added handsomely, looking her over, 'pink does become you, Lucy! I never saw you look so pretty before!'

Miss Wychwood, admiring her own posy, which was made up of spring blossoms ranging in colour from palest mauve to deep purple, realized with an inward chuckle that Ninian had probably described her to the helpful florist as a lady somewhat stricken in years. She refrained from quizzing him, and, with even greater nobility, refrained from telling him that posies, tied up with long ribbons, wound round stalks encased in silver paper, however proper for balls, were not commonly carried by ladies at rout-parties.

Some two hours later she had the satisfaction of knowing that not only was her party a success, but so too was her protégée. She received her guests with Lucilla beside her, and had nothing to blush for in Lucilla's manners. Not for the first time she handed a silent tribute to Mrs Amber, who, whatever her errors, had demonstrably instructed the child in all the rules governing polite behaviour. The wild rose colour that flushed her cheeks when she was embarrassed, and her occasional gaucheries did her no disservice in the eyes of Bath's most influential hostesses, even old Mrs Mandeville, that most rigid critic, who had already gratified Annis by appearing at the rout, saying to her: 'A nice gal, my dear. I don't know where you picked her up, or why you're sponsoring her, but if she's a Carleton I should say that she was born with a silver spoon in her mouth, and you'll have no difficulty in buckling her to an eligible gentleman!'

Mr Carleton was amongst the last to appear. Miss Wychwood had released Lucilla from her post at her side, but was herself still standing at the entrance to the drawing-room when he came leisurely up the stairs. Lord Beckenham, who, from the moment of his arrival, had been hovering solicitously about her, no sooner saw who was approaching than he withdrew immediately from her vicinity, muttering that it would be better if he and 'that fellow' didn't come face to face. His abrupt retreat did not escape Mr Carleton's hawklike eyes; he said as he bowed slightly, and carried Miss Wychwood's gloved hand to his lips: 'If looks could kill I should be stretched life-less on the threshold! How do you do, ma'am? Accept my felicitations on being able to hold such a brilliant Assembly thus early in the Season!' He put up his glass, and through it surveyed the crowded room. 'All the rank and fashion of Bath, I collect,' he said. 'Who, in God's name, is the formidable dame in the wig and enough feathers to furnish an ostrich with plu-mage for two of her kind?'

'That, sir,' said Miss Wychwood, controlling a quivering lip, 'is Mrs Wendlebury, one of the leaders of Bath Society. Only Mrs Mandeville's approval is more necessary than hers for a girl making her first appearance in Bath. She has brought her widowed daughter, and her granddaughter, to my party tonight – which I count amongst my triumphs!'

He lowered his glass, and directed one of his penetrating looks at her. 'I wish you will tell me why you are putting your-self to so much trouble for my tiresome niece?' he said unex-pectedly.

'I don't find her tiresome,' she replied. 'Indeed, she has provided me with a great deal of amusement! When I met her, I was feeling sadly languid and bored, but that, thanks to her, is a thing of the past. Come, I must make you known to Mrs Stinchcombe! Her eldest daughter and Lucilla have struck up a great friendship, and I am persuaded she will wish to make your acquaintance.'

She led him inexorably away to where Mrs Stinchcombe was seated beside Mrs Mandeville on an elegant settee, pushed against the wall, and performed the introductions. To her sur-prise, Mrs Mandeville said: 'No need to present him to me, child! His mama and I were bosom-bows, and I knew him when he was in his cradle! Well, Oliver, how do you do? Are you that pretty child's guardian? When Annis told me that she was a Carleton, and the ward of her uncle, it did cross my mind that you might be the uncle, but it didn't seem to me to be pos-sible!'

'It doesn't seem possible to me either, ma'am,' he said rue-fully.

She cast him a shrewd glance. 'Makes you feel older than you thought you were, does it? High time you did, if all I hear about you is true! But that's no bread-and-butter of mine! I like your little niece: not fully fledged yet, but a bud of promise. Don't you agree, ma'am?'

'Yes, I do indeed,' answered Mrs Stinchcombe. 'She casts the rest into the shade.' She smiled up at Mr Carleton, and said: 'You will certainly have enough on your hands when she comes out, driving away ineligible suitors, sir!'

'You shouldn't have invited Kilbride tonight, Annis,' said Mrs Mandeville, in her forthright fashion. 'An engaging scamp, I grant you, but dangerous.'

Avoiding Mr Carleton's eyes, Annis responded with a lightness she was far from feeling: 'I'm afraid my hand was forced, ma'am!'

'In what way, Miss Wychwood?' asked Mr Carleton, more than a hint of steel in his voice.

She was obliged to look at him, read condemnation in his face, and was goaded by vexation into making him a sharp answer. 'Lucilla forced my hand, sir, by inviting him, and begging me to endorse the invitation! As he was standing beside her at the time, what could I do but say I should be happy to see him here tonight?' She saw his brows draw together, and added quickly: 'Pray don't blame her! She knew him to be a friend of mine, and I had told her she might invite whom she liked.'

'Well, it was a pity,' said Mrs Stinchcombe, 'but I don't think any harm will come of it. From what I can see, he will find it a hard matter to get up a flirtation with her! Young Elmore is playing watch-dog, and is sticking to her as close as a court-plaster!'

Miss Wychwood soon found that this was true: Ninian was obviously standing guard over Lucilla, which would have been amusing had his hostess been in the mood to be amused. Whether he was protecting her from Kilbride, or from Harry Beckenham, each of whom was making her the object of his gallantry, was a moot point: Miss Wychwood could only be thankful that his jealously possessive instinct had prompted him to behave very much like a dog guarding a bone; and to derive a certain amount of satisfaction from the realization that Lucilla was showing no preference for either of these dashing blades, but was merely enjoying, quite innocently, the novel experience of being a Success.

A cold supper had been laid out in the dining-room. It was informal, but most of the very young gentlemen present had engaged the very young ladies of their choices to go down to it under their escorts, and just as Miss Wychwood, an accomplished hostess, had matched the dowagers with appropriate partners, she found herself being confronted by Lord Beckenham, begging for the honour of leading her down to supper. She felt that nothing more was wanting to set the seal on the most unenjoyable evening of any she had ever spent but there seemed to be no way of escaping this added scourge, and she was about to smile politely, and to lay her hand on his arm, when Mr Carleton, standing, unperceived, immediately behind her, said: 'Too late, Beckenham! Miss Wychwood is promised to me! Are you ready to go now, ma'am?'

She found herself in a quandary. If she repudiated this engagement a quarrel between the two men would be the inevitable outcome: Beckenham's face had already assumed an alarmingly purple hue. Anything, she decided, would be preferable to a brawl in her house! She forced a smile to her lips, and said, mendaciously, but placably: 'I'm afraid I did promise to let Mr Carleton take me down to supper, Beckenham! Will you oblige me very much by taking Maria down in my stead?'

Mr Carleton, having drawn her hand within his arm, and led her inexorably out of the room, said reproachfully, as they began to go downstairs: 'You know, that was quite unworthy of you, my child! To have fobbed your most distinguished suitor off on to your cousin will very likely have made him your enemy for life!'

'I know, but what else could I do, when she was the only lady left in the room, and you had claimed — falsely, as you well know! — that I had promised to go down with you? Heaven knows there is no one I wouldn't liefer be with!' she said bitterly.

'Come, come, that's trying it on much too rare and thick!' he told her. 'You can't gammon me into believing that you would prefer Beckenham's company to mine!'

'Well, I would!' she asserted. 'For I know very well you only

120

wish to be with me so that you may pinch at me for having invited Denis Kilbride to my party, and I won't endure it, and so I warn you! What right have you, pray, to dictate to me on whom I invite or do not invite to my parties?'

'Lay all those bristles!' he recommended. 'You are not going to come to cuffs with me, my girl, so don't be so ready to show hackle for no reason at all! I may deplore your taste in admirers, but I don't presume to meddle in what is no concern of mine. And when I pinch at you, it won't be in public, I promise you!'

Slightly mollified, she said, in a more moderate tone: 'Well, I will own, sir, that it was no wish of mine to include Kilbride amongst my guests. Indeed, I said all I could, within the bounds of civility, to make him think he would find the party a dead bore. And when that didn't answer I invited Harry Beckenham, and his friend, and Major Beverley, and – oh, several others as well!'

'In the belief that they might cut Kilbride out, or the hope that I might not notice him amongst so many dashers?'

This hit the nail on the head with sufficient accuracy to surprise a laugh out of her. She said: 'Oh, how detestable you are! And the worst of it is that you make me detestable too, which is quite unpardonable!'

'I don't do any such thing,' he replied, a queer twisted smile hovering at the corner of his mouth. 'I don't think I could – even if I wished to.'

They had reached the foot of the stairs by this time, and were about to enter the dining-room, so that she was not obliged to answer, which was just as well, since she could think of nothing to say. She could not even decide whether he had paid her a compliment, or whether she had misunderstood him, for although the words he had spoken were certainly complimentary the tone in which he had uttered them was coldly dispassionate. He left her side as soon as they entered the dining-room, but returned in a very few minutes with various patties for her, and a glass of champagne. She was already the centre of a group, and he did not linger, but was next to be seen exchanging a few words with Lucilla, who was eating ices under the aegis of Harry Beckenham. She greeted him with acclaim, and a demand to know whether he had ever been to a more delightful party. He looked rather amused, but assured her that he hadn't. Harry said, ' 'Evening, sir! I've been telling your niece that Miss Wychwood is famous for the first-rate refreshments she gives her guests, but all she will eat·is ices! Shall I bring you another, Miss Carleton?'

'Yes, please!' she responded promptly. 'And may I have some more lemonade? Oh, sir, should I like champagne? Mr Beckenham says I shouldn't.'

'No,' said Mr Carleton. He held out his own glass to her. 'Try it for yourself!' he bade her.

She took the glass, and sipped cautiously. The expression of distaste on her face was almost ludicrous. She gave the glass back to her uncle, saying: 'Ugh! Nasty! How *can* people drink anything so horrid? I thought Mr Beckenham was hoaxing me when he said I shouldn't like it, for he, and you, and even Miss Wychwood seem to like it very well.'

'Now you know that he wasn't hoaxing you.' He looked her over critically, and surprised her by saying: 'Remind me, when I return to London, to hand over to you your mother's turquoise set. Most of her jewels are not suitable for girls of your age, but I imagine the turquoises must be unexceptionable. As I recall, there is also a pearl brooch, and a matching ring. I'll send them to you.'

The unexpectedness of this took her breath away. She could only regain enough of it to thank him, but this she did so fervently that he laughed, flicked her cheek with one finger, and said: 'Ridiculous brat! There's no need to thank me: your mother's jewels are yours: I merely hold them in trust for you until you come of age – or until I judge you to be old enough to wear them.'

Mr Beckenham having come back by this time, Mr Carleton left Lucilla to his care, and returned to Miss Wychwood. She had been observing what had passed between him and his niece, and moved forward to meet him, saying in a conscience-stricken voice: 'I have been shockingly remiss! I ought to have told Lucilla not to drink champagne!'

'You ought indeed,' he said.

'Well, if you know that, I am astonished that you should

122

have given your glass to her!' she said, with some asperity.

'Did you like your first sip of champagne?' he asked.

'No, I don't think I did.'

'Exactly so! Young Beckenham had told her she wouldn't like it, so I proved his point for him.'

'I suppose,' she said thoughtfully, 'that that was probably more to the purpose than to have forbidden her to drink it.'

'*Certainly* more to the purpose!'

She flashed a mischievous smile at him, and murmured: 'I feel it won't be long before you become an excellent guardian!'

'God forbid!'

At this moment, Denis Kilbride, disengaging himself from a group of matrons, bore down upon his hostess and said in deeply wounded accents, belied by the laughter in his eyes: 'Now, how could you have misled me so about your party, most cruel fair one? Is it possible you can have been trying to keep me away from it! I cannot believe it!'

'Dear me, no! why should I?' she returned. 'I am glad you don't find it abominably insipid, which I feared you might.'

'No party which you grace with your exquisite presence could be insipid, believe me! I have only one fault to find with this one: I cherished the hope of being permitted to bring you down to supper, only to find myself cut out by Carleton here! But for one circumstance, Carleton, I should ask you to name your friends!'

Mr Carleton was so patently uninterested and unamused by this lively nonsense that Annis was impelled to step into the breach caused by his silence. She said smilingly: 'It's to be hoped the one circumstance was the impropriety of spoiling my party!'

'Alas, no! It was mere cowardice!' he said, mournfully shaking his head. 'He is such a devilish good shot!'

Mr Carleton accorded this sally a faint, contemptuous smile, and stepped back politely to allow Major Beverley to approach Miss Wychwood. He then strolled away, and was next seen talking to Mrs Mandeville. He left the party before the dancing began, declining unequivocally to join the whist-players for whose entertainment Miss Wychwood had had two tables set up in the book-room. Nettled by this cavalier behaviour, she raised her brows, when he took leave of her, saying sarcastically: 'But dare you leave Lucilla in such dangerous company?'

'Oh, yes!' he replied. 'From what I've seen, young Beckenham and Elmore will take good care of her. And since the only *dangerous company* seems to be bent on fixing his interest with you rather than with Lucilla there's no need for me to play the careful guardian. It's not a rôle which suits me, you know. Ah – accept my thanks for an agreeable evening, ma'am!'

He bowed, and left her. She was so much infuriated that it was long before her wrath abated sufficiently to permit the suspicion to enter her head that his outrageous conduct sprang from anger at what he no doubt considered her encouragement of Denis Kilbride's familiarities. While she continued to move amongst her guests, outwardly as serene as ever, uttering smiling nothings, her brain was seething with conjecture. She had been prepared to play the game of flirtation with Mr Carleton, but it was now plain that idle flirtation was not what he had in mind. It seemed incredible that he could have fallen in love with her, but his anger could only have been roused by jealousy, and such fierce jealousy as had led him to say the most wounding things he could think of to her had nothing to do with flirtation. It clearly behoved her to set him at a distance, but even as she resolved to do this it occurred to her that perhaps he believed her to be ready to accept an offer from Denis Kilbride, and instantly it became a matter of the first importance to disabuse his mind of this misapprehension. It was in vain that she told herself it didn't matter a button what he believed: for some inscrutable reason it did matter.

The last of her guests did not leave until eleven o'clock, a late hour by Bath standards, for which the success of the impromptu hop was responsible. Several very young ladies were too shy to waltz, or perhaps too conscious of parental eyes of disapproval on them; but although the waltz was barred from both the Assembly Rooms, even the starchiest and most old-fashioned of the dowagers knew that it would not be long before it penetrated these strongholds, and confined their objections to sighs and melancholy head-shakings over times past. As for the matrons with daughters to launch into society, few were to be found whose principles were so rigid as to make the spectacle of their daughters seated against the wall preferable to the shocking, but gratifying, sight of these dashing girls twirling round the room in the embrace of a succession of eligible young gentlemen.

Miss Wychwood confined her part in these mild revelries to keeping an eye on them, seeing to it that inexperienced girls unaccompanied by their mamas did not stand up more than twice with the same man, and finding partners for neglected damsels. Since nearly all the young people were well acquainted there was not much of this to be done: indeed, it was more important to take care that the impromptu dance did not develop into a romp, which, with so many very young persons who had known one another from the nursery onwards, was more than likely it would.

She was many times solicited to dance, but smilingly refused to stand up with even a gallant old friend, who might well have been her father. 'No, no, General!' she said, twinkling up at him. 'Chaperons don't dance!'

'Chaperon? *You*?' he said. 'Moonshine! I know to a day how old you are, puss, so don't talk flummery to me!'

'Next you will say that you dandled me when I was an infant!' she murmured.

'At all events, I might have done so. Now, come, Annis! You can't refuse to stand up with such an old friend as I am! Damme, I knew your father!'

'I should like very much to stand up with you, but you must excuse me! *You* may think it absurd, but I *am* being a chaperon tonight, and if I were to stand up with you how could I refuse to stand up with anyone else?'

'No difficulty about that!' he said. 'You have only to say that you stood up with me because you didn't care to offend an old man!'

'Yes, no doubt I could if you weren't well known to be the wickedest flirt in Bath!' she retorted.

This pleased him so much that he chuckled, threw out his chest a little, apostrophized her as a saucy minx, and went off to dally with all the best looking women in the room.

Miss Wychwood enjoyed dancing, but she was not tempted to take the floor on this occasion. There was no one with whom she wished to dance; but no sooner had she realized this truth than a question posed itself in her mind: if Mr Carleton, instead of leaving the party in something remarkably like a dudgeon, had stayed, and had invited her to dance a waltz with him, would she have been tempted to consent? She was forced to admit to herself that she would have been very strongly tempted, but she hoped (rather doubtfully) that she would have had enough strength of mind to have resisted temptation.

In the middle of these ruminations, Lord Beckenham came up, and sat down beside her, saying: 'May I bear you company, dear Miss Annis? I do not ask you to dance, for I know you don't mean to dance this evening. I cannot help being glad of it: it gives me the opportunity to enjoy a comfortable cose with you, and – to own the truth – I don't care for the waltz. I am aware that it is the height of à la modality, but it never seems to me to be quite the thing. You will say I am old-fashioned, I fear!'

'Quite Gothic!' she answered flatly. 'Excessively uncivil, too, when you must know that I delight in waltzing!'

'Oh, I intended no incivility!' he assured her. 'You lend distinction to everything you do!'

'For goodness' sake, Beckenham, stop throwing the hatchet at me!' she said tartly.

He gave an indulgent laugh. 'What an odd expression to hear on your lips! I myself am not familiar with modern slang, but I hear a great deal of it from Harry – more, indeed, than I like! – and I understand *throwing the hatchet* means to flatter a person, which, I promise you, I was not doing! Nor am I doing so when I tell you that I have rarely seen you look more beautiful than you do tonight.' He laughed again, and, laying his hand over hers, gave it a slight squeeze. 'There, don't eat me! Your dislike of receiving compliments is well known to me, and is what one so particularly likes in you, but my feelings overcame my prudence for once!'

She drew her hand away, saying: 'Excuse me! I see Mrs Wendlebury is about to take her leave.'

She got up, and moved across the room towards this form-idable dame, and, having said goodbye to her, responded to a signal from Mrs Mandeville, and went to sit beside her.

'Well, my dear, a very pleasant party!' said Mrs Mandeville. 'I congratulate you!'

'Thank you, ma'am!' Annis said gratefully. 'From you that is praise of a high order! May I also thank you for having been kind enough to honour me with your presence tonight? I assure you I appreciate it, and can only hope you haven't been bored to death!'

'On the contrary, I've been vastly amused!' replied the old lady, with a chuckle. 'What made Carleton take himself off in a rage?'

Annis coloured faintly. 'Was he in a rage? I thought him merely bored.'

'No, no, he wasn't *bored*, my dear! It looked to me as though he and you were at outs!'

'Oh, we come to cuffs whenever we meet!' Annis said lightly.

'Yes, he makes a lot of enemies with that bitter tongue of his,' nodded Mrs Mandeville. 'Spoilt, of course! Too many caps have been set at him! My second son is a friend of his, and he told me years ago that it was no wonder he's been soured, with half the mamas and their daughters on the scramble for him. That's the worst of coming into the world as rich as a Nabob: it ain't good for young men to be too full of juice. However, I don't despair of him, for there's nothing much amiss with him that marriage to the woman he falls in love with won't cure.'

'I haven't understood that *love* was lacking in his life, ma'am!'

'Lord, child, I'm not talking of his bits of muslin,' said Mrs Mandeville scornfully. 'It ain't *love* a man feels for the light-skirts he entertains! Myself, I'd always a soft corner for a rake, and it's my belief most women have! Mind you, I don't mean the sort of rabshackle who gives some gal a slip on the shoul-der, for them I can't abide! Carleton ain't one of those sneak-ing rascals. Has he put you in charge of that pretty little niece of his?'

'No, no! She is merely staying with me for a short time,

127

before going to live with one of her aunts, or cousins – I am not perfectly sure which!'

'I'm glad to hear it. You're a deal too young to be burdened with a gal of her age, my dear!'

'So Mr Carleton thinks! Only he goes further than you, ma'am, and doesn't scruple to inform me that he considers me to be quite unfit to take care of Lucilla.'

'Yes, I'm told he can be very uncivil,' nodded Mrs Mandeville.

'Uncivil! He is the rudest man I have ever met in my life!' declared Miss Wychwood roundly.

CHAPTER NINE

By the time Miss Wychwood had said goodbye to the last, lingering guests she was feeling more weary than ever before at the end of a party. Everyone except herself (and, presumably, Mr Carleton) seemed to have enjoyed it, which was, she supposed some slight consolation to her for having spent a most disagreeable evening. Lucilla was in what she considered to be exaggerated raptures over it: she wished it might have gone on for ever! Miss Wychwood, barely repressing a shudder, sent her off to bed, and was about to follow her when she found Limbury in the way, obviously awaiting an opportunity to speak to her. She paused, looking an inquiry, and he all unwittingly set the seal on a horrid evening by disclosing, with the smile of one bearing welcome tidings, that Sir Geoffrey had arrived in Bath, and wished her to give him a look-in before she retired to bed.

'Sir Geoffrey?' she repeated blankly. '*Here?* Good God, what can have happened to bring him to Bath at this hour of the night?'

'Now, don't you fret yourself, Miss Annis!' Limbury said, in a fatherly way. 'It's no worse than the toothache which Master Tom has, and which my lady thinks may be an abscess, so she

wishes to take him instantly to Mr Westcott. Sir Geoffrey arrived twenty minutes before you went down to supper, but
when he saw you was holding a rout-party he charged me not
on any account to say a word to you about it until the party
was over, him being dressed in his riding-habit, and not having
brought with him his evening attire, and not wishing to attend
the rout in all his dirt. Which is very understandable, of course.
So I directed Jane to make up the bed in the Blue chamber,
miss, and myself carried up supper to him, which is what I
knew you would wish me to do.'

Miss Farlow, who had paused in her rather ineffective attempts to restore the drawing-room to order, to listen to this
interchange, exclaimed: 'Oh, *poor* Sir Geoffrey! If only I had
known! I would have run up immediately to make sure that he
was comfortable — not that I mean to say Jane is not to be
trusted, for she is a very dependable girl, but still—! Dear little
Tom, too! His papa must be in *agonies*, for nothing is worse
than the pain one undergoes with the toothache, particularly
when an abscess forms, as well I know, for *never* shall I forget
the *torture* I suffered when I—'

'It is Tom who has the toothache, not Geoffrey!' snapped
Miss Wychwood, interrupting this monologue without ceremony.

'Well, I *know*, dearest, but the sight of one's child's suffering
cannot but cast a fond parent into agonies!' said Miss
Farlow.

'Oh, fiddle!' said Annis, and went upstairs to rap on the door
of the Blue bedchamber.

She found her brother flicking over the pages of the various
periodicals with which Limbury had thoughtfully provided
him. A decanter of brandy stood on a small table at his elbow,
and he held a glass in his hand, which, on his sister's entrance,
he drained, before setting it down on the table, and rising to
greet her. 'Well, Annis!' he said, planting a chaste salute upon
her cheek. 'I seem to have come to visit you at an awkward
moment, don't I?'

'I certainly wish you had warned me of it, so that I might
have had time to prepare for your visit.'

'Oh, no need to worry about that!' he said. 'Limbury has

looked after me very well. The thing was there was no time to warn you, because I was obliged to leave Twynham in a bang. I daresay Limbury will have told you what has brought me here?'

'Yes, I understand Tom has the toothache,' she replied.

'That's it,' he nodded. 'It became suddenly worse this afternoon, and we fear there may be an abscess forming at the root. Ten to one, it's no more than a gumboil, but nothing will do for Amabel but to bring him to Bath so that Westcott may see it, and judge what is best to be done.'

Something in his manner, which was much that of a man airily reciting a rehearsed speech, made her instantly suspicious. She said: 'It seems an unnecessarily long way to bring a child to have a tooth drawn. Surely you would be better advised to take him to Frome?'

'Ah, you are thinking of old Melling, but Amabel has no faith in him. We have been strongly recommended to take Tom to Westcott. It doesn't do, you know, to ignore advice from a trustworthy source. So I have ridden over ahead of Amabel, to arrange for Westcott to do whatever he thinks should be done tomorrow, and to ask you, my dear sister, if they may come to stay with you for a day or two.'

'They?' said Annis, filled with foreboding.

'Amabel and Tom,' he explained. 'And Nurse, of course, to look after the children.'

'Is Amabel bringing the baby too?' asked Miss Wychwood, in a voice of careful control.

'Yes – oh yes! Well, Amabel cannot manage Tom by herself, and she can't be expected to leave Baby without Nurse to take care of her, you know. But they won't be the least trouble to you, Annis! In this great house of yours there must be room for two small children and their nurse!'

'Very true! Equally true that they won't be any trouble to me! But they will make a great deal of trouble for my servants, who are none of them accustomed to working in a house which contains a nursery to be waited on! So, if you mean to saddle me with your family, I beg you will also include the maid who waits on Nurse in the party!'

'Of course if it is inconvenient for you to receive my family—'

'It is extremely inconvenient!' she interrupted. 'You know very well that I have Lucilla Carleton staying with me, Geoffrey! I am astonished that you should expect me to entertain Amabel and your children at such a moment!'

'I must say I should have thought your own family had a greater claim on you than Miss Carleton,' he said, in an offended voice.

'You haven't any claim on me at all!' she flashed. 'Nor has Lucilla! Nor anyone! That's why I left Twynham, and came to Bath, to be my own mistress, not to be accountable to you or to anyone for what I choose to do, and not to grow into a spinster aunt! Particularly not that! Like Miss Vernham, who is only valued for the help she gives her sister, can be depended on to look after the children whenever Mr and Mrs Vernham wish to go junketing to London! but at other times is very much in the way. She can't escape, because she hasn't a penny to fly with. But I have a great many pennies, and I *did* escape!'

'You are talking wildly!' he said. 'I should like to know what demands have ever been made of you when you lived with us!'

'Oh, none! But if one lives in another person's house one is bound to share in the tasks which arise, and who can tell how long it would have been before you and Amabel fell into the way of saying: "Oh, Annis will look after it! She has nothing else to do!"'

'I really believe your senses are disordered!' he exclaimed. 'All this scolding merely because I have ventured to ask you to shelter my wife and children for a few days! Upon my word, Annis—'

'You didn't ask me, Geoffrey! You made it impossible for me to refuse by arranging for Amabel to set out for Bath tomorrow morning, knowing that I should be forced to let them stay here.'

'Well, I was obliged to make all possible haste, when Tom was crying with pain,' he said sulkily. 'He was awake all last night, let me tell you, and here are you expecting me to write you a letter through the post, and wait for you to answer it!'

'Not at all! What I should have expected you to do, had I known anything about it, would have been to have taken Tom to Melling immediately he complained of the toothache – whatever Amabel's opinion of his skill may be! Good God, how much skill is required to pull out a milk-tooth? Why, I daresay Dr Tarporley would have whisked it out in a trice, and spared Tom his sleepless night!'

This left Sir Geoffrey with nothing to say. He looked discomfited, and sought refuge in wounded dignity. 'No doubt it will be best for me to hire a suitable lodging in the town!'

'Much best – except that it would set all the Bath quizzes' tongues wagging! I will give orders in the morning for rooms to be prepared, but I am afraid I shan't be able to entertain Amabel as I should wish: I have a great many engagements which I must keep, in addition to accompanying Lucilla when she goes out. That, since her uncle has entrusted her to my care, is, you will agree, an inescapable duty!'

On this Parthian shot, she left the room. She was still seething with anger, for her brother's demeanour and lame excuses for his descent on her had confirmed her suspicion that his real reason was an obstinate determination to prevent any intimacy between her and Oliver Carleton. Amabel was to be planted in her house as a duenna – though what Geoffrey imagined Amabel (poor little goose!) could do to prevent her doing precisely as she chose only he knew! She was too angry to consider whether what seemed to her to be unwarrantable interference might not be a clumsy but well-meaning attempt to protect her from one whom he believed to be a dangerous rake; and the sight of Miss Farlow, hovering on the threshold of her bedchamber did nothing to assuage her wrath. She had no roubt that Miss Farlow was responsible for Geoffrey's sudden arrival, and it would have afforded her great pleasure to have shaken the iritating titter out of that meddlesome old Tabby, and have boxed her ears into the bargain. Suppressing this most unladylike impulse, she said coldly: 'Well, Maria? What is it you want?'

'Oh!' said Miss Farlow, in a flutter. 'Nothing in the world, dear Annis! I was just wondering whether dear Sir Geoffrey has everything he needs! If only Limbury had told me of his arrival I should have slipped away from the party, and attended to his comfort, as I hope I need not assure you, for it is my business to provide for your visitors, is it not? And even such excellent servants as our good Limbury, you know—'

'Limbury is far more capable than you, cousin, to provide for Sir Geoffrey's needs,' interposed Miss Wychwood, putting considerable force on herself to hold her temper in check. 'If anything should be wanting, Sir Geoffrey will ring his bell! I advise you to go to bed, to recruit your strength for the task that lies before you tomorrow! I shall require you to provide for several more visitors! Goodnight!'

A night's repose restored much of Miss Wychwood's shaken equilibrium, and she was able to confront her brother over the breakfast cups with tolerable composure. She asked him, quite pleasantly, whether he wished her to provide accommodation for him during Amabel's stay, and accepted, without betraying the relief she felt, his prosy explanation of why circumstances prevented him from staying beyond the time of Amabel's arrival. This instantly made Miss Farlow break into a flood of protestations, in which (she said) she knew well dear Annis would join her. 'I am persuaded dear Lady Wychwood must need your support through the approaching ordeal!' she said. 'Such a time as it is, too, since you last came to stay in Bath, for I don't count the scrap of a visit you paid us the other day! And if you are thinking that there is no room for you, there can be no difficulty about *that*, for you and dear Lady Wychwood can be perfectly comfortable in the Green room, which can be made ready for you in a trice. You have only to say the word!'

'If he can edge one in!' said Miss Wychwood dryly.

Sir Geoffrey gave a snort of laughter, and exchanged a glance pregnant with meaning with her. As little as any man did he welcome conversation at the breakfast-table, and it was probable that he had never liked Miss Farlow less than when he came under the full fire of her inconsequent chatter.

'When am I to expect Amabel to arrive?' asked Miss Wychwood smoothly.

'Well, as to that, I can't precisely answer you,' he replied, looking harassed. 'She has the intention of starting out betimes, but with all the business of packing, and seeing to it that Nurse hasn't forgotten anything – which very likely she

133

will, because excellent though she is in her management of the children she has no head – none at all! When we took Tom to visit his grandparents last year, we had to turn back *three* times! I can tell you it tried my patience sadly, and I was provoked into declaring that I would never undertake a journey in her company again! Or in Tom's!' he added, with a reluctant grin. 'The thing is, you know, that he is a bad traveller! Feels sick before one has gone a mile, and after that one has to be for ever pulling up, to lift him down from the chaise to be sick in the road – poor little fellow!'

This perfunctory rider made Miss Wychwood break into laughter, in which he somewhat sheepishly joined her. 'Now I know what the circumstances are which make your immediate return to Twynham quite imperative!' she said.

'Well, I hope I am not an unfeeling parent, but – well, you know how it is, Annis!'

'I can hazard a guess at all events! It has not yet been my fate to travel with a child afflicted with carriage-sickness, I thank God!'

'Oh, it quite wrings my heart to think of that sweet little boy being sick, for there is nothing more miserable!' broke in Miss Farlow. 'Not that I am myself a bad traveller, for I daresay I could drive from one end of the country to the other without experiencing the least discomfort, but I well remember how ill my particular friend, Miss Aston, always felt, even in hackney carriages. She is dead now, poor dear soul, though not in a hackney carriage, of course.'

Judging from her brother's expression that he was on the brink of delivering himself of a hasty snub, Miss Wychwood intervened, to suggest to her garrulous companion that if she had finished her breakfast she should go to talk to Mrs Wardlow about the arrangements to be made for Lady Wychwood, her children, her nurse, her dresser, and the nurse's maid. Miss Farlow expressed the utmost willingness to do so, and instantly plunged into a minute description of the plans she had already formulated. Miss Wychwood checked her by saying: 'Later, Maria, if you please! Domestic details are not interesting to Geoffrey!'

'No, indeed! Gentlemen never take an interest in them, do

they? My own dear father was always used to say—'

She was interrupted by the impetuous entrance of Lucilla, so they never learned what the late Mr Farlow was always used to say. Lucilla was full of apologies for being so late. 'I can't think how I came to oversleep, except that I wasn't called! Oh, how do you do, Sir Geoffrey! My maid told me you arrived in the middle of the party: were you too tired to join it? I wish you might have done so, for it was a truly *splendid* party, wasn't it, ma'am?'

Miss Wychwood laughed, told her to pull the bell for a fresh pot of tea, and said that she had given orders she was not to be disturbed. 'Indeed, I meant to have your breakfast carried up to you as soon as you woke,' she said.

'Oh, yes, Brigham told me so, but I am not in the least fagged, and I can't *bear* having my breakfast in bed! The crumbs get into it, and the tea gets spilt over the sheet. Besides, I am to ride my mare this morning, and how dreadful it would be if I were late! Did my uncle tell you when he means to bring the horses round, ma'am?'

'No,' replied Miss Wychwood, aware that Sir Geoffrey had stiffened alarmingly. 'To own the truth, I had forgotten we were to ride out today. I have had other things to think of. My sister-in-law is bringing her children to stay with me, and I am not very sure when they will arrive.'

'Oh!' Lucilla said blankly. 'I didn't know. Does it mean that you can't go with us? *Pray* don't cry off, ma'am!'

His evil genious prompted Sir Geoffrey to utter unwise words. 'My dear young lady,' he said kindly, 'you must not expect my sister to jaunter off on an expedition of pleasure, leaving no one to receive Lady Wychwood!'

'No. Of course not,' Lucilla agreed politely, but in a disappointed tone.

Now, Miss Wychwood had decided, many hours before, not to ride out in Mr Carleton's company, not even to see him. She had had the intention of charging Lucilla with a formal message of regret. That, she thought, would teach him a salutary lesson. But no sooner had Sir Geoffrey spoken than her hackles rose, and she said: 'As to that, Mrs Wardlow will be only too happy to receive Amabel, and to be granted an opportunity to

135

dote on the children, besides discussing with Amabel all the nursery details which they both find so absorbing, and in which I take no interest.' She rose as she spoke, saying: 'I must go and tell Miss Farlow what I wish her to do for me this morning.'

'You *will* ride with us?' Lucilla cried eagerly.

Miss Wychwood nodded smilingly, and left the room. She was almost immediately followed by Sir Geoffrey, who caught her up as she was about to mount the stairs. 'Annis!' he said commandingly.

She paused, and looked over her shoulder at him. 'Well, Geoffrey?'

'Come into the library! I can't talk to you here!'

'There is no need for you to talk to me anywhere. I know what you wish to say, and I have no time to waste in listening to it.'

'Annis, I must insist—'

'Good God, will you never learn wisdom?' she exclaimed.

'Wisdom! I have more of that than you, I promise you!' he said angrily. 'I will not stand by and watch my sister compromising herself!'

'Doing *what?*' she gasped, taken-aback. 'Don't be such a dummy, Geoffrey! Compromise myself indeed! By going for a morning's ride with Lucilla, her uncle, and Ninian Elmore? You must have windmills in your head!'

She began to go upstairs, but he halted her, stretching up an arm to grasp her wrist. 'Wait!' he ordered. 'I warned you to have nothing to do with Carleton, but so far from paying any heed you have positively encouraged him to pursue you! He has dined here, and you have even dined with him at his hotel – and in a private parlour! I had not thought it possible you could behave with such impropriety! Ah, you wonder, I daresay, how I should know that!'

'I know exactly how you know it,' she said, with a disdainful curl of her lip. 'I don't doubt Maria has kept you informed of everything I do! That is why you are here today, and why you have bullocked Amabel into coming to keep an eye on me! Before you accuse me of impropriety, I recommend you to consider your own conduct! I can conceive of few more improper things than to have permitted Maria to report to you on my actions, and few things more addlebrained than to have believed them when anyone but a gudgeon must have realized that they sprang from the jealousy of a very stupid woman!'

She wrenched herself free from his hold on her wrist, and went swiftly upstairs, only pausing when he said weakly that Maria had only done what she thought to be her duty, to say dangerously: 'I would remind you, brother, that it is I who am Maria's employer, not you! I will add that I keep no disloyal servants in my house!'

Five minutes later she was giving Miss Farlow precise instructions about the shopping she wished her to undertake. As these included a command to obtain from Mrs Wardlow a list of the various items of infant diet which would be needed, Miss Farlow showed signs of taking umbrage, and said, bridling, that she fancied she was quite as well qualified as the housekeeper to decide what were the best things to give children to eat.

'Please do as you are told!' said Miss Wychwood coldly. 'You need not trouble yourself to prepare the necessary bed-chambers: Mrs Wardlow and my sister will settle that between them. Now, if there is anything you wish to know that I've not told you, pray tell me what it is immediately! I am going out, and shall be away all the morning.'

'Going out?' exclaimed Miss Farlow incredulously. 'You cannot mean that you are going on this riding expedition when dear Lady Wychwood may arrive at any moment!'

If anything had been needed to strengthen Miss Wychwood's resolve, that tactless speech supplied the necessary goad. She said: 'Certainly I mean it.'

'Oh, I am persuaded Sir Geoffrey won't permit it! Dear Miss Annis—' She broke off, quailing before the fiery glance cast at her.

'Let me advise you, cousin, not to meddle in what in no way concerns you!' said Miss Wychwood. 'You have worn my patience very thin already! I shall have a good deal to say to you later, but I've no time now to waste. Will you be kind enough to send Jurby up to me?'

Considerably alarmed by this unprecedented severity, Miss Farlow became flustered, and plunged into an incoherent speech, partly apologetic, partly self-exculpatory, but she did not get very far with it, for Lucilla came running up the stairs, to inform Miss Wychwood that Mr Carleton's groom had just called with a message from his master: if it was convenient to the ladies, he would bring the horses to Camden Place at eleven o'clock.

'So I said it was convenient! That was right, wasn't it?'

'Quite right, but we shall have to make haste into our riding-habits.'

Miss Farlow uttered a sound between a hen-like cluck and a moan, and wrung her hands together, which had the effect of making Annis turn on her, and to say, in an exasperated voice: 'Maria, will you have the goodness to send Jurby to me at once? Pray don't make it necessary for me to ask you a third time!'

Miss Farlow scuttled away. Lucilla, wide-eyed with surprise, asked: 'Are you vexed with her, ma'am? I never heard you speak so crossly to her before!'

'Yes, I am a trifle vexed: she is the most tiresome creature! Her tongue has been running on wheels ever since we sat down to breakfast. But never mind that! Run and change your dress!'

Lucilla, having assured her that she could scramble into her habit in the twinkling of a bedpost, darted off to her own chamber, and if (thanks to Brigham) she did not actually scramble into her habit she was ready before her hostess. By the time Miss Wychwood came downstairs, Mr Carleton and Ninian had arrived, and Lucilla was cooing over a pretty grey mare, patting and stroking her, and feeding her with sugar-lumps. Ninian, who had borrowed a well ribbed-up hack from one of his new acquaintances, was pointing out all the mare's good points to her; and Mr Carleton, who had dismounted from his chestnut, was holding his own and Miss Wychwood's bridles, and when Miss Wychwood came out of the house he handed both to his groom, making it plain that he meant to put her up into the saddle himself. She went forward, greeting him with a good deal of reserve, and without her usual delightful smile. He took her hand, and surprised her by saying quietly: 'Don't look so sternly at me! Did I offend you very much last night?'

She said, rather stiffly: 'I must suppose you meant to do so, sir.'

'Yes,' he answered. 'I did mean to. But afterwards I wished I had cut out my tongue before I said such things to you. Forgive me!'

She was not proof against this blunt apology. She had not expected it; and when she answered him her voice was a little unsteady. 'Yes – of course I forgive you! Pray say no more about it! What a – a *prime 'un* you have bought for Lucilla! You will be first-oars with her hereafter!'

She gathered her bridle, and allowed him to take her foot between his hands. He threw her up into the saddle where she quickly settled herself, while the mare danced on impatient hooves.

'Bit fresh, ma'am!' warned the groom.

'Yes, because she hasn't been out for three days, poor darling! She'll settle down when the saddle has had time to get warm to her back. Stand away, if you please! Now, steady, Bess! Steady! You can't gallop through the town!'

'By Jupiter, you're a regular out-and-outer, ma'am!' exclaimed Ninian, watching the mare's playful and unavailing attempts to unseat her. 'I'll go bail you set a splitting pace in the hunting-field!'

'That sounds as though you take me for a thruster!' she retorted. 'Have you decided which way we are to go?'

'Yes, up on to Lansdown – unless you had liefer go somewhere else, ma'am?'

'No, not at all: Lansdown let it be! Well, Lucilla? How do you like her?'

'Oh, beyond anything great!' Lucilla said ecstatically. The groom had mounted her, and she was groping for her stirrup-leather under her skirt. 'Oh, botheration!'

'Here, I'll do that for you!' Ninian said. 'Do you want it shortened or lengthened?'

'Shortened, please. Just one hole, I think. Yes, that is exactly right! Thank you!'

He tested the girths, tightened them, told her sternly to remember that her hand was strange to the mare, and to be careful what she was about, and swung himself into his own saddle. They then set forward, Lucilla and Ninian leading the way, and Mr Carleton, following close on their heels with Miss Wychwood beside him, keeping a critical eye on his ward. He seemed soon to be satisfied that a perfect understanding between the grey mare and her rider was in a fair way to becoming established, for he withdrew his gaze from them, and turned his head to speak to Miss Wychwood, saying: 'No need to follow so closely: she seems to know how to handle strange horses.'

'Yes,' she agreed. 'Ninian assured me that I had no need to worry about her for she was a capital horsewoman.'

'She should be,' he responded. 'My brother threw her into the saddle when she was hardly out of leading-strings.'

'Yes,' she said again. 'She told me that.'

Silence fell between them. It was not broken until they had drawn clear of the town, and Ninian and Lucilla, once off the stones, were trotting some way ahead. Mr Carleton said then, in his direct fashion: 'Are you still angry with me?'

She started a little, for she had been lost in her own thoughts, and replied, with an uncertain laugh: 'Oh, no! I'm afraid I was wool-gathering!'

'If you are no longer angry with me, who, or what, has put you all on end?'

'I – I'm not all on end!' she stammered. 'Why – why should you think I am, merely because I let my thoughts wander for a minute or two?'

He appeared to give this question consideration. A slight frown drew his brows together, and a searching look between narrowed eyes, staring between his horse's ears into the middle distance, failed to provide him with an answer, for, after a short pause, he smiled wryly, and said: 'I don't know. But I do know that something has happened to put you in a passion, which you are trying to bottle up.'

'Oh, dear!' she sighed. 'Is it so obvious?'

'To me, yes,' he replied curtly. 'I wish you will tell me what has destroyed your tranquillity, but if you don't choose to do so I won't press you. What would you wish to talk about?'

She turned her head to look at him wonderingly, a smile

wavering on her lips, and in her mind the thought that he was strangely incalculable. At one moment, he could be brusque, and unfeeling; and then, when he had made her blazingly angry, his mood seemed to change, and her resentment was dispelled by the sympathy, however roughly expressed, which she heard in his voice, and detected in the softened look in his eyes. Now, as she met those penetrating eyes, she saw the hint of a smile in them, and was conscious of an impulse to admit him, at least a little way, into her confidence. There was no one else to whom she could unburden herself, and she badly needed a safe confidant, for the more she kept her rancour to herself the greater it grew. Why she should consider Mr Carleton a safe confidant was a question it never occurred to her to ask herself: she felt it, and that was enough.

She hesitated, and after a moment he said in a matter-of-fact way: 'You had better open the budget, you know, before all that seething wrath in you forces off the lid you've clamped down on it, and scalds everything within sight.'

That made her laugh. She said: 'Like a pot of boiling water? That would be very shocking! It's true that I *am* out of temper, but it's no great matter. My brother arrived in Camden Place last night, to inform me that he was planting his wife, his two children, their nurse, and – I conjecture! – my sister-in-law's abigail, upon me today, for – according to himself! – a few days! Without warning, if you please! I am very fond of my sister-in-law, but it vexed me very much!'

'I imagine it might. Why are you to be subjected to this invasion?'

Her eyes kindled. 'Because he—' She stopped, realizing suddenly that it was impossible to disclose to Mr Carleton, of all people, Sir Geoffrey's true reason. 'Because Tom – my small nephew – has the toothache!' she said.

'You must think of something better than that!' he objected. 'I daresay you believe me to be a cabbage-head, but you are mistaken: I'm not! And swallow that clanker I can't!'

'I don't think anything of the sort,' she retorted. 'If you want the truth, I believe you to be a most complete hand, awake upon every suit!'

'Then you should know better than to try to tip me the

double,' he said. 'Bring his entire family to Bath because Tom has the toothache? What a Banbury story!'

'Well, I must own it does sound like one, but it isn't. My sister-in-law is – is set on taking Tom to the best dentist possible, and has had Westcott recommended to her. If you think that ridiculous, so do I!'

'I think it is a damned imposition!' he said roundly. 'Oh, you are not accustomed to the language I use, are you? Accept my apologies, ma'am!'

'Willingly! You have exactly expressed my feelings! To overset all my arrangements without so much as a by your leave makes me so out of reason cross that I want to rip and tear! You need not tell me that I am building a mountain out of a molehill, for I know I am!'

'Oh, no, I shan't! You are far too well-bred to vent your wrath on Wychwood, so rip and tear at me instead!'

'Don't be so absurd! *You* are not – in this instance – the cause of my vexation!'

'Oh, don't let that weigh with you! I will confidently engage myself to offer you enough provocation to rattle me off in fine style! Don't hesitate to make use of me!'

'Mr Carleton,' she said, with a quivering lip, 'I have already requested you not to be absurd!'

'But didn't I promise to offer you provocation?'

'One of the things I most dislike in you, sir, is your disagreeable habit of *always* having an answer!' she told him, with considerable acerbity. 'And, in general,' she added, 'a rude one!'

'Come, this is much better!' he said encouragingly. 'You have already rid yourself of some of your spleen! Now tell me exactly what you think of me for having said an unjust thing to you last night, and for having, with such abominable rudeness, left your rout-party! If that doesn't rid you of the rest of your spleen, you can animadvert, more forcefully than you did in the Pump Room that day, on the obliquity of my life and character! And if that doesn't take the trick—'

She interrupted him, the colour flaming into her cheeks. 'I beg you to say no more! I should not have said – what I did say – and I regretted it as soon as the words were out of my mouth,

142

and – and have wished to beg your pardon ever since. But somehow the opportunity to do so never arose. It has arisen now, and – and I do beg your pardon!'

He did not immediately answer her, and, stealing a glance at his face, she saw that that queer smile had twisted in his mouth. He said: 'One of the things I most dislike in you, my entrancing hornet, is your unfailing ability to put me at Point Non Plus! I'm damned if I know why I like you so much!'

She was powerfully affected by these words, but made a gallant attempt to pass them off lightly. 'Indeed, I can't think why you should like me, for we have come to points whenever we have met! And I have a melancholy suspicion that we should continue to do so, however many times we were condemned to meet each other!'

'Have you?' he said, a harsh note in his voice. 'With me it is otherwise!' He saw the instinctive gesture of repulsion she made, and said, with a short, sardonic laugh: 'Oh, don't be afraid! I shall say no more until I have contrived by hedge or by stile to overcome your dislike of me! In the meantime, let us push on to overtake Lucilla and young Elmore!'

'Yes, do let us!' she said, not knowing whether to be glad or sorry for this abrupt change of subject. In an effort to bridge an awkward gap, she said, as she encouraged her mare to break into a canter: 'I must tell you that I shouldn't – I trust! – have allowed my vexation to take such strong possession of me if my cousin Maria had not chosen that most unlucky moment to talk me almost to the gates of Bedlam!'

'That doesn't surprise me at all!' he replied. 'If I were forced to endure more than five minutes of her vapid gibble-gabbling there would be nothing for it but to cut my throat! Or hers,' he added, apparently giving this alternative his consideration. 'No, I think not: the jury, not having been acquainted with her, would probably find me guilty of murder. What shocking injustices are perpetrated in the name of the law! How the case of your cousin brings that home to one! She ought, of course, to have been strangled at birth, but I daresay her parents were wanting in foresight.'

This drew a positive peal of laughter out of Miss Wychwood. She turned her head towards him, her eyes brimful of merriment, and said: 'Oh, how often I have felt the same! She is the most tactless, tedious bore imaginable! When I left Twynham, my brother prevailed on me to employ her as my companion, to lend me countenance, and I have seldom ceased to wonder at myself for having been so want-witted as to have agreed to do it! How horrid I am to say so! Poor Maria! she means so well!'

'Worse you could not say of her! Why don't you send her packing?'

She sighed and shook her head. 'I own, I am often tempted to do so, but I am afraid it isn't possible. Her father, according to what Geoffrey tells me, was sadly improvident, and left her very ill provided for, poor thing. So I couldn't turn her off, could I?'

'You might *pension* her off,' he suggested.

'And have Geoffrey plaguing my life out to hire another in her place? No, I thank you!'

'Does he do that? Do you permit him to plague you?'

'I can't prevent him! I don't permit him to dictate to me — which is why we are so frequently at outs! He is older than I am, you see, and nothing will ever disabuse his mind of its belief that I am a green and headstrong little sister whom it is his duty to guide, admonish, and protect! Which is, I acknowledge, very admirable, but as vexatious as it is misjudged, and seldom fails to send me up into the boughs!'

'Ah! I thought there was more to his descent on you than his little boy's toothache! He came, in fact, to warn you to have nothing to say to me, didn't he? Does he suspect me of having designs on your virtue? Shall I tell him that his suspicion is groundless?'

'No, certainly not!' she said emphatically. 'I am very well able to deal with Geoffrey myself. Ah, there are the children! Indulge me with a race to overtake them, Mr Carleton! I have been pining these many weeks for a good gallop!'

'Very well, but 'ware rabbit holes.'

'Pooh!' she threw at him, over her shoulder, as the mare lengthened her stride.

She had the start of him, but he overtook her, and they reached the two winning posts neck and neck, and were greeted, by Lucilla with applause, and by Ninian with mock reproach, for having, he said, set Lucilla such a bad example.

'Don't you mean a good example?' inquired Mr Carleton.

'No, sir, I don't, for how the deuce am I to stop her galloping hell-for-leather when she has seen Miss Wychwood doing it?'

'As though you could *ever* stop me if I choose to gallop!' said Lucilla scornfully. 'You couldn't catch me!'

'Oh, couldn't I? If I had my Blue Devil between my legs we'd soon see that!'

'Blue Devil would never come within *lengths* of my Lovely Lady! Oh, sir, that is the name I've given her! I thought at first that I would call her Carleton's Choice, but Ninian said he didn't think you would care for that!'

'Then I am very much obliged to him! I should *not* have cared for it!'

'Well, I meant it as a compliment!' said Lucilla, slightly aggrieved.

'Good God!' he said.

Ninian chuckled, and said: 'I told you so! I don't like Lovely Lady either: a sickly name to give a horse! But at least it's better than the other!'

'Shall we ride on to visit the Saxon fortifications, or would you prefer to remain here abusing one another?' intervened Miss Wychwood.

Thus called to order the combatants hastily begged pardon, and the whole party moved forward.

CHAPTER TEN

It was considerably past noon when Miss Wychwood re-entered her house, and there were unmistakable signs that her uninvited guests had arrived, and were partaking of a late nuncheon in the breakfast parlour. James was halfway up the stairs, lugging, with the assistance of one of the maids, a large trunk; the page-boy was collecting as many of the smaller articles of luggage as he could conveniently carry; Lady Wychwood's abigail was sharply admonishing him, and warning James to be careful not to let the trunk fall; and Limbury had just come out of the parlour with a tray. He was looking somewhat harassed, as well he might, for the hall was littered with portmanteaux, valises, and bandboxes, amongst which he was forced to pick his way. At sight of his mistress, he looked even more harassed, and begged her to excuse the disorder, in a voice which gave her to understand that it was no fault of his that the luggage was still in the hall. 'The coach in which it was packed, ma'am, arrived barely a quarter of an hour ago, and since Nurse wanted something out of one of the trunks, and insisted on searching for it immediately, and was unable to recall in which of the trunks she had packed it, we have been, as you might say, slightly impeded.' He added, in an expressionless tone: 'It happened to be in one of the valises, ma'am.'

The abigail took up the tale, bobbing a curtsy, and saying that she was sure she was excessively sorry that Miss should have come home to find her house in such a pickle, which would not have happened if the second-coachman had not fallen so far behind on the road, and if Nurse had not been so foolish as to have packed at the bottom of a trunk what one would have supposed she must have known she would need on the journey.

'Well, never mind,' said Miss Wychwood. 'Are Sir Geoffrey and her ladyship eating a nuncheon, Limbury?'

Lucilla, who was looking at the impedimenta in round-eyed astonishment, whispered: 'Good gracious, ma'am! What an extraordinary amount of baggage for just a few days! One would think they had come to spend *months* with you!'

'They probably have,' replied Miss Wychwood bitterly. 'Run up and change your dress, my love! I must greet my sister-in-law, I suppose, before I do the same.'

'I will bring a fresh pot of tea for you directly, Miss Annis. Would you care for a baked egg, or a bowl of soup?'

'No, nothing, thank you: I'm not hungry!'

Limbury bowed, set his tray down on one of the trunks, and

opened the door for Miss Wychwood to pass into the parlour.

Her brother, his wife, and Miss Farlow were seated at the table, but they all rose, and Amabel tottered towards her, and almost fell into her arms, saying faintly: 'Oh, Annis, dearest one, how glad I am to see you at last! How good you are to me! You cannot imagine how much I have longed for you through this dreadfully agitating time! I can't describe to you what I have been through! Now I can be comfortable again!'

'Of course you can!' said Annis, returning her fond embrace, and gently pushing her back to her chair. 'Sit down, and tell me how Tom is!'

Lady Wychwood shuddered. 'Oh, my poor, precious little son! He was so brave through it all, even though he was screaming with pain most of the night! Nothing eased it until I ventured to give him a few drops of laudanum, in a teaspoon, which did send him to sleep for a very little while, but, alas, not for long, and I dared not give him any more, for I am convinced it is unwise to dose children with laudanum. And this morning the pain was so much worse that if the trunks had not been packed, and the horses harnessed, I think I *must* have gone against Geoffrey's wishes, and taken the poor little love to Melling after all!'

Miss Wychwood cast a satirical glance at her brother. He was obviously discomposed, but he returned the glance with a defiant glare, and said, in minatory accents: 'You forget, my love, that it was you who wished Westcott to see Tom!'

'Oh, I am persuaded you were right, dear Lady Wychwood!' exclaimed Miss Farlow, for once in her life stepping opportunely into an awkward breach. 'My dear father always said it was a false economy to consult any but the *best* medical practitioners in such cases! I daresay this Melling you speak of would have bungled the extraction, but once Westcott had coaxed dear little Tom to open his mouth he whisked the tooth out in the shake of a lamb's tail!'

'Well, that's good news, at all events!' said Miss Wychwood. 'I collect he is now relieved of his pain, for I heard no screams of anguish when I entered the house.'

'He is asleep,' said Lady Wychwood, sinking her voice as

though she feared to disturb the rest of her son, tucked into a crib three floors above her. She directed a wan smile at Miss Farlow, and said: 'Cousin Maria sang lullabies to him until he dropped off. I don't think I can ever be grateful enough to her for all she has done this morning! She even accompanied us to Westcott's, and was of the greatest support to me through the ordeal. She had the strength of mind to hold Tom's hands down at the Fatal Moment, which I could not bring myself to do!'

'But where was Geoffrey at the Fatal Moment?' inquired Annis, in seeming bewilderment.

Lady Wychwood began to explain that Geoffrey had been unable to go to the dentist because he had a business engagement in the town, but he broke in on this, well-aware that his loving sister was not one to be so easily bamboozled. 'No use trying to come crab over Annis, my love!' he said, laughing. 'She's far too needle-witted! Well, you are right, Annis, and I don't mind owning that I cut my stick when I saw what a state Tom had worked himself into, kicking, and screaming, and saying he wouldn't have his tooth drawn! Well, what could *I* do in such a situation, I ask you?'

'Spanked him!' said Annis.

He grinned, and admitted that he had been strongly tempted to do so, but Amabel uttered a shocked protest, and Miss Farlow said that she knew he was only funning, and that it would have been the height of brutality to have spanked dear little Tom when he was demented with the agony he was suffering.

Annis then withdrew, saying that she must put off her riding habit, and recommending Amabel to lie down on her bed for an hour or two, to recover from so many sleepless nights. As she left the room, she heard Miss Farlow eagerly endorsing this piece of advice, assuring dear Lady Wychwood that she had no need to be anxious about poor little Tom, and telling her that a hot brick had already been put into her bed. 'For I gave orders for that to be done before we drove to Westcott's, knowing that you would be quite exhausted, after all the trials you have been forced to undergo!'

Sir Geoffrey, following his sister out of the room, caught up with her at the head of the stairs. 'Stay a moment, Annis!' he said. 'Something I wish to consult with you about! These new vapour-baths which I hear so much about: do you agree with me that they would be of benefit to Amabel? The state of her health has been causing me grave concern — very grave concern! She insists that she is in perfectly good point, but you must have noticed how pulled she looks! It's my belief she never *has* been in high health since her confinement, and this unfortunate business of Tom's abscess has put her quite out of curl. You would be doing me a great favour if you would prevail upon her to take a course of the baths, which, I'm told, are excellent in such cases.'

She regarded him steadily, and with a disquieting smile in her eyes, which had a discomposing effect on him, but all she said was: 'I am sorry you should feel so anxious about her. She is certainly tired, and overwrought, but that was to be expected, wasn't it, after so many sleepless nights? She seemed, when I was visiting you, to be in a capital way!'

He shook his head. 'Ah, she is never one to complain of feeling out of sorts, and, I daresay, would be laid by the wall before she would admit to being fagged to death when *you* were visiting us! But so it was — not that she will own it!'

'I've no doubt she won't,' said Miss Wychwood. 'I have heard, of course, of the new baths in Abbey Street, but I know nothing of them, except that they are under the management of a Dr Wilkinson. And I cannot suppose, dear brother, that if *you* have failed to persuade Amabel to try a course of them she would yield to any persuasion of mine.'

'Oh, I think she might!' he said. 'She sets great store by your opinion, I promise you! You have great influence over her, you know.'

'Have I? Well, I should think it most impertinent to exert it in a matter of which she can be the only judge. But you may be easy! Amabel may remain with me for as long as she chooses to do so.'

'I knew I might depend on you!' he said heartily. 'You are wishful to change your dress, so I won't detain you another minute! I must make haste to be off myself, so I'll take my leave of you now. I daresay I shall be riding over to see how

Amabel goes on in a day or two, but I know I can rely on you to take good care of her!'

'But surely you have brought her here so that *she* may take good care of *me*?'

He thought it prudent to ignore this, but halfway down the stairs he bethought him of something he had forgotten to tell her. He paused, and looked back at her, saying: 'Oh, by the bye, Annis! You asked me to send the nursery-maid, didn't you? There was no time for me to send a message to Amabel, so I have arranged to hire a suitable girl to wait on the nursery here.'

'You shouldn't have put yourself to the trouble of doing that,' she answered, rather touched.

'No trouble at all!' he said gallantly. 'I wouldn't for the world upset your servants! Maria has promised to attend to the matter this very day.'

He waved an airy hand, and went off down the stairs, feeling that he had done all that could have been expected of him.

By the time Miss Wychwood descended to the drawing-room he had left the house, and Amabel, as Miss Farlow informed her in an audible aside, was laid down on her bed, with the blinds drawn, and a hot brick at her feet. She would have described all the arrangements she had made for Amabel's comfort, had Miss Wychwood not checked her, and moved past her to greet Lord Beckenham, who had called to return thanks for the previous evening's party, and was making ponderous conversation to Lucilla. He kissed her hand, and told her that his intention had been to have left his card, but that hearing from Limbury that she was at home he had ventured to come in, just to see how she did.

'Miss Carleton has been telling me that you went out riding this morning. You are inexhaustible, dear Miss Annis! And now I hear that Lady Wychwood has come to stay with you, which must have meant that you were obliged to go to a great deal of trouble! I wish – indeed, we must all of us wish! that you would take more care of yourself!'

'My dear Beckenham, you speak as though I were one of these invalidish females for ever hovering on the brink of a decline! You should know better! I don't think I've suffered a day's illness since I came to Bath! As for being knocked-up by a small rout – what a poor thing you must think me!' She turned to Lucilla, and said: 'My dear, did you tell me that you were going to go for a walk in the Sydney Garden with Corisande and Edith and Miss Frampton this afternoon? I had meant to have accompanied you to Laura Place, and to have had a chat with Mrs Stinchcombe, but I'm afraid I must cry off, now that Lady Wychwood has come to visit me. Oh, don't look so downcast! Brigham can go with you to Laura Place, and I will send the carriage to bring you back again in time for dinner. You will make my excuses to Mrs Stinchcombe, and explain the circumstances, won't you?'

'Oh, yes, indeed I will, ma'am!' said Lucilla, her clouded brow clearing as if by magic. 'I will run up to put on my bonnet immediately! Unless – unless there is anything you would wish me to do for you here?'

'Not a thing!' said Miss Wychwood, smiling affectionately at her. 'Say goodbye to Lord Beckenham, and be off with you, or you will keep them waiting!' When the door was shut behind Lucilla, she addressed herself to Miss Farlow, speaking with cool friendliness. 'You too should be off, Maria, if you have pledged yourself to hire a suitable maid to wait on the nursery, which I understand is the case.'

'Oh, yes! I was persuaded it was what you would wish me to do! If I had known one would be needed I would have popped into the Registry Office this morning, on my way home from Milsom Street, only if I had done so I should have been too late to welcome dear Lady Wychwood, for, as it was, I had so much shopping to do that I almost *was* too late. Not that I mean to complain! That would be a very odd thing for me to do! But so it was, and I saw a chaise drawn up outside the house just as I was passing that house with the green shutters, so I ran the rest of the way, and reached *our* house at the very moment James was helping Nurse to get down from the chaise. So I gave all my parcels to Limbury, and told him to take them down to the kitchen, and was able – though sadly out of breath! – to welcome dear Lady Wychwood, and explain to her how it came about that you were obliged to depute the agreeable task to me. And then, you know—'

'Yes, Maria, I do know, so you need not tell me any more! These details are of no possible interest to Lord Beckenham.'

'Oh, no! Gentlemen never care for domestic matters, do they? I well remember my dear father saying that I was a regular *bagpipe* when I recounted some little happening to him which I quite thought would entertain him! Well, I mustn't run on, must I? You and his lordship will be wanting to talk about the party, and although I should like very much to stay I see that it wants only two minutes to the hour, and I must tear myself away!'

Lord Beckenham showed no disposition to follow her example; he remained for more than an hour, and might have stayed for another hour had not Amabel come into the room. This gave Miss Wychwood an opportunity to get rid of him, which she did quite simply by telling him that Amabel ought to be in her bed, for she was quite worn-out, and in no fit state to have come down to the drawing-room. He said at once that he would go away, and pausing only to express his concern to Lady Wychwood, and his hope that Bath air, and the tender care which he knew well she would receive in her sister-in-law's house, would soon restore her to the enjoyment of her usual health, he did go away.

Lady Wychwood said, when she was alone with Annis: 'How devoted he is to you, dearest! You shouldn't have sent him away on my account!'

'Yes, I know you have a *tendre* for him,' said Annis, gravely shaking her head. 'I am very sorry to be so disobliging, but I feel it my duty to Geoffrey to keep such a dashing blade away from you.'

'For shame, Annis! It's very naughty of you to poke fun at the poor man! Keep him away from me indeed! How ridiculous you are!'

'No more ridiculous than you, my dear.'

Lady Wychwood's eyes flew to her face. 'Why -- why what can you mean?' she faltered.

'Haven't you come here to keep Oliver Carleton away from me?' Annis asked her, a little satirical smile lilting on her lips.

Colour flooded Lady Wychwood's cheeks. 'Oh, Annis!'

Annis laughed. 'Don't sound so tragical, you goose! I'm well aware that this absurd notion is Geoffrey's, and not yours.'

'Oh, Annis, pray don't be vexed!' Lady Wychwood said imploringly. 'I would never have ventured to presume — I was perfectly sure you would never do anything imprudent! I begged Geoffrey not to meddle! Indeed, I went so far as to say that nothing would prevail on me to come to stay with you! I was never nearer falling into a quarrel with him, for I *knew* how bitterly you would resent such interference!'

'I do resent it, and wish very much you hadn't yielded to Geoffrey,' Annis replied. 'But that's past praying for, I collect! Oh, don't cry! I am not angry with *you*, love!'

Lady Wychwood wiped away her starting tears, and said, with a sob in her voice: 'But you are angry with Geoffrey, and I cannot bear you to be!'

'Well, that too is past praying for!'

'No, no, don't say so! If you knew how anxious he has been! how fond he is of you!'

'I don't doubt it. Each of us has a good deal of fondness for the other, but we are never so fond as when we are apart, as you know well! *His* fondness doesn't lead to the smallest understanding of my character. He persists in believing me to be a sort of bouncing, flouncing girl, with no more rumgumption than a moonling, who is so caper-witted as to stand in constant need of guidance, admonition, prohibition, and censure from an elder brother who thinks himself far wiser than she is, but — if you will forgive me for saying so — very much mistakes the matter!'

These forceful words made the gentle Amabel quail, but she tried, bravely, to defend her adored husband from his sister's strictures. 'You wrong him, dearest! indeed, you do! He is for ever telling people how clever you are — needle-witted, he calls it! He is excessively proud of your wit, and your beauty, but — but he knows — as how should he not? — that in *worldly* matters you are not as experienced as he is, and — and his dread is that you may be taken-in by — by a *man of the town*, which he tells me this Mr Carleton is!'

'I wonder what it was that gave poor Geoffrey such a dislike of Mr Carleton?' said Annis, considerably amused. 'I would hazard a guess that he received from him, at some time or another, one of his ruthless set-downs. I remember that Geoffrey told me he was the rudest man in London, which I don't find it difficult to believe! He is certainly the rudest man *I* ever encountered!'

'Annis,' said Lady Wychwood, impressively sinking her voice, 'Geoffrey has informed me that he is a libertine!'

'Oh, no! Has he sullied your ears with *that* word?' Annis exclaimed, her eyes and her voice brimming over with laughter. 'He didn't sully *my* virgin ears with it! It was what he meant, of course, when he said that Mr Carleton was an ugly customer whom he would not dream of presenting to me, but when I asked him if it *was* what he meant all the answer he made was to deplore my want of *delicacy of mind!* Well! You and I, Amabel, cut our eye-teeth years ago, so let us, for God's sake, have the word with no bark on it! I should be amazed if a bachelor of Mr Carleton's age had had no dealings with straw damsels, but I am still more amazed at his apparent success in that line! It must, I conjecture, be due to his wealth, for it cannot have been due to his address, for he has none! From the moment of our first meeting, he has neglected very few opportunities to be unpardonably uncivil to me, even going to the length of informing me that Maria had no need to fear he was trying to seduce me, because he had no such intention.'

'Annis!' gasped her ladyship. 'You must be funning! He *could* not have said anything so – so abominably rude to you!'

She obviously was more shocked by this evidence of Mr Carleton's crude manners than by Sir Geoffrey's allegation that he was a profligate. Miss Wychwood's eyes began to dance; but all she said was: 'Wait until you have met him!'

'I hope never to be compelled to meet him!' retorted Amabel, the picture of affronted virtue.

'But you will be bound to meet him!' Annis said reasonably. 'Recollect that his niece – and ward – is in my charge! He comes frequently to this house, to assure himself that I am not permitting her to encourage the advances of such gazetted fortune-hunters as Denis Kilbride, or to overstep the bounds of the strictest propriety. He does not, if you please, consider me a fit and proper person to have charge of Lucilla, and doesn't scruple to say so! I'm told it is always so with loose-screws: they become downright prudes where the females of their own families are concerned! I imagine that must be because they know too much about the wiles of seducers – from their own experiences! Besides, my dear, how can you possibly protect me from him if you run out of the room the instant he is ushered into it?'

Lady Wychwood could find no answer to this, except to say, weakly, that she had told Geoffrey that no good could come of his insisting on her going to stay in Camden Place.

'None at all!' agreed Annis. 'But don't let that cast you in the mops, love! I hope I have no need to assure you that I am always happy to welcome you to my house!'

'Dear, dear, Annis!' uttered Lady Wychwood, powerfully affected, and wiping away a fresh flow of tears from her brimming eyes. 'Always so kind! So much kinder to me than my own sisters! Believe me, one of the wishes nearest to my heart is to see you happily married, to a man *worthy* of you!'

'Beckenham?' inquired Annis. 'I don't think I'm acquainted with anyone worthier than he is!'

'Alas, no! I wish very much that he had been able to fix his interest with you, but I know there is no chance of that: you think him a bore, and a bobbing-block, and – I sometimes think – are blind to all his excellent qualities.'

'Oh, no! He is stuffed with good qualities, but the melancholy truth is that however much I may respect a man's good qualities they don't inspire me with a particle of love for him! I shall either marry a man stuffed with bad qualities, or remain a spinster – which is the likeliest fate to befall me! Don't let us talk any more about my future! Tell me about yourself!'

But Lady Wychwood said that there was nothing to tell. Annis asked her whether she indeed meant to take a course of Russian vapour-baths. This made her giggle. 'Oh, no, and so I told Geoffrey!'

'Well, he depends on me to persuade you to do so! I told him that I should deem it an impertinence to do any such thing. Is it true that you have been out of sorts?'

'No, no! That is to say, I had a slight cold, but it was nothing! And then, of course, I had all the anxiety about Tom, which has made me look horridly hagged. I daresay that was what made Geoffrey get into one of his ways. Perhaps I might drink the waters, just – just to satisfy him! After all, that can't do me any harm!'

'Unless they make you feel as sick as I did, the only time I ever took a glass! We shall soon see! Since Lucilla came to stay with me I have visited the Pump Room almost every day, so that she can meet her new friend, who accompanies her mother to the Pump Room. I fancy you have met Mrs Stinchcombe: did she not come to dinner here when you and Geoffrey visited me last year?'

'Oh, yes! A most agreeable woman! I remember her very well, and shall be happy to renew my acquaintance with her. But this Lucilla of yours! Where is she?'

'You will see her presently. She has gone to take a walk in the Sydney Garden, with Corisande and Edith Stinchcombe. She and Corisande have become almost inseparable, for which I am truly thankful! I am extremely attached to the child, but I own I find it more than a little boring to be obliged to go everywhere with her! Chaperonage is no light task, I promise you!'

'No, indeed! I was shocked when I heard that you had taken it upon yourself to look after Miss Carleton. You are much too young to be *any* girl's duenna, no matter who she may be. Geoffrey thought you should have restored her to her aunt, and I must own I cannot but feel he was quite right. I don't mean to say that she is not an agreeable girl: Geoffrey was pleasantly surprised by her manners, which he tells me are very pretty – but what a responsibility to have assumed, dearest! I cannot like it for you.'

'Well, if she were to be with me permanently I shouldn't like it either,' admitted Miss Wychwood. 'She is a lovely little innocent, had never been in Society – what she calls "grown-up" parties – until she came to Bath, and made an instant hit! Already she has I know not how many young men dangling after her, which makes it necessary for me to keep a strict watch over her. To make matters worse, she is a considerable heiress: a sure bait for fortune-hunters! Fortunately, the Stinchcombes have a governess to whom the girls are devoted

– even Lucilla likes her, having previously taken the whole race of governesses in detestation! – and so I am able to relinquish Lucilla into her care when it is a question of going for walks, or buying 'fripperies in the town. I only wish the Stinchcombes lived in Camden Place, but they don't! They have a house in Laura Place, so that I am obliged to provide Lucilla with an escort when she visits them. However, Mr Carleton gave me leave to engage a maid for her, who, I judge, is to be trusted to fill my place at need.'

'But, Annis, is it so necessary to chaperon girls in *Bath*? Why, even in London my sisters tell me that nowadays it is quite unremarkable to see two girls walking together without even a footman coming behind them!'

'*Two* girls, yes!' said Miss Wychwood. 'But not one girl alone, I think! Mrs Stinchcombe is an indulgent parent but I am very sure she would not permit Corisande to come up to Camden Place unattended. And in Lucilla's case – no, no! Out of the question! Mr Carleton has, however reluctantly, confided her to my care until he has made other arrangements for her, and what a *horrid* fix I should be in if I let her come to harm!'

'He had no right to lay such a charge upon you!'

'He didn't. He had no alternative but to leave her with me, having himself, as he so gracelessly told me, no turn for the infantry, and not the smallest intention of taking Lucilla into his own charge. I will allow that he has enough sense of his duty to his ward to place her in the temporary guardianship of a – a lady of unquestioned respectability, which I flatter myself I am! But it went sadly against the grain with him to do it, and I fancy nothing would afford him more satisfaction than a failure on my part to guard Lucilla from all the hazards threatening a green young heiress on her first emergence from the schoolroom!' She checked herself, and, after a moment's consideration, said: 'No! Perhaps I am wronging him! He would certainly derive satisfaction from the knowledge that he had been right to doubt my ability to take proper care of Lucilla; but I do him the justice to think that he would be seriously displeased if Lucilla were to come to harm.'

'I wish you had never met her!' sighed Lady Wychwood.

But when Annis presented Lucilla to her that evening she was quite as pleasantly surprised as her husband had been, talked very kindly to her, and later told Annis that it was difficult to believe that such a sweet and pretty-behaved child could be the ward of a man of Carleton's reputation. She was rather puzzled by Ninian's presence at dinner, still more by the familiar terms he stood on with Annis, her house, and her servants. He behaved as if he had been a favoured nephew, or, at any rate, a boy who had known Annis all his life and it was evident that he ran tame in the house, and more often than not dined there. She wondered if he was perhaps related to Lucilla, and when Annis disclosed his identity she was at first incredulous, and then so forcibly struck by the absurdity of the situation that she went into paroxysms of laughter.

'Oh, I haven't been so much diverted since Mrs Preston's hat was carried off by the wind, and took her wig with it!' she gurgled. 'The end of it will be, of course, that they will marry one another!'

'God forbid! What a cat-and-dog life they would lead!'

'I don't know that. You say they disagree on every subject, but it didn't seem like that to me, listening to them at dinner. I think they have a great deal in common. Only wait for a year or two, when they will both be wiser, and see if I am not right! They are still only a pair of bickering children, but when they are a little older they won't bicker, any more than I bicker with my sisters – though when we were all in the schoolroom we were used to bicker incessantly!'

'I can't conceive of your bickering with anyone!' smiled Annis. 'As for Lucilla and Ninian, the Iverleys no longer wish for that marriage, and would – if they are to be believed – strongly oppose it. It wouldn't astonish me if Mr Carleton opposed it too, for he doesn't like Iverley.'

'Oh, that settles it!' said Lady Wychwood, laughing. 'Opposition is all that is wanting in the case!'

Annis could not help thinking that opposition from Mr Carleton would probably take a ruthless form, impossible to withstand, but she kept this reflection to herself.

She was destined, a few hours later, to be confronted by a dilemma. Lucilla, peeping into her bedchamber on her return from Laura Place, to thank her for having sent the carriage to bring her home, and to tell her how much she had enjoyed her first visit to the Sydney Garden, with its shady groves, its grottoes, labyrinths, and waterfalls, said, her eyes and cheeks aglow: 'And Mr Kilbride says that during the summer they have illuminations, and gala nights, and public breakfasts! Oh, *dear* Miss Wychwood, will you take me to a gala night? Pray say you will!'

'Yes, certainly I will, if your heart is set on it,' replied Miss Wychwood. 'Did Mr Kilbride tell you of the galas and the illuminations last night?'

'Oh, no! It was this afternoon, when I told him that I was going to explore the Garden with Corisande. We walked smash into him, Brigham and I, not two minutes after we left the house. He said he was coming to visit you, but he *very* obligingly turned back, to escort me to Laura Place. Wasn't that kind of him, ma'am? He was so amusing, too! He had me in whoops with the droll things he said! I do think he is a delightful creature, don't you?'

Miss Wychwood took a full minute to respond to this, covering her silence by pretending that her attention was concentrated on the pinning of a brooch to her corsage. In truth, she knew not what to say. On the one hand, she felt it to be incumbent on her to warn Lucilla against the wiles of a charming, but impecunious man on the look-out for a rich wife; on the other, she neither wished to destroy Lucilla's innocence, nor – which would be worse – to arouse in the child a rebellious spirit which might, too easily, lead her to flout the authority of her elders, and to encourage Kilbride's advances.

She compromised. She said, with an indulgent little laugh: 'Kilbride's ingratiating manners and lively wit are his stock-in-trade. Pray do not you, my dear, administer to his vanity by adding yourself to the list of his victims! He is an irreclaimable here-and-thereian, and cannot see a personable female without making up to her! I long since lost count of the silly girls left languishing on his account.'

Her words brought a crease between Lucilla's brows. She said hesitantly: 'Perhaps he found that he didn't truly love any of them, ma'am?'

'Or that they were none of them as well-endowed as he had supposed!'

No sooner had she uttered these acid words than she regretted them. Lucilla's eyes flashed, and she said hotly: 'How can you say anything so – so detestable about him, ma'am? I thought he was a friend of yours!'

She ran out of the room, leaving Miss Wychwood with nothing to do but to blame herself bitterly for having been betrayed into saying precisely what she had determined not to say. She could only hope that no malicious tongue had informed Mr Carleton that his ward had been escorted through the town by a man whom he knew to be a gazetted fortune-hunter.

It was an empty hope. On the following morning, she went with Lady Wychwood and Lucilla to the Pump Room. Mrs Stinchcombe, who was seeking a cure for her rheumatism by drinking a glass of the famous water every morning, was there, with both her daughters, and Annis led Lady Wychwood up to her at once, and had the satisfaction of seeing the two ladies fall instantly into very friendly conversation. She left them together while she went across the room to procure a glass of the water from the pumper, and was wending her way back with it to Lady Wychwood's side when she saw Mr Carleton advancing purposefully towards her. She braced herself, but the first words he spoke were quite unalarming. 'Well met, Miss Wychwood!' he said cheerfully. 'Ought I to condole with you? Are you too a martyr to rheumatism?'

'No, indeed, I'm not!' she replied lightly. 'This is for my sister-in-law, not for me! What brings you here this morning, sir?'

'The hope of finding you here, of course. There is something I wish to say to you.'

Her heart sank, but she replied coolly enough: 'Well, you may do so, but first I must give this horrid drink to my sister-in-law. I should like, besides, to present you to her.' Another two steps brought her to Lady Wychwood's side, and she handed the glass to her saying: 'Here you are, my dear! I believe it should be drunk hot, so take hold of your courage and gulp it down immediately!'

160

Lady Wychwood eyed the potion doubtfully, but obediently took, not a gulp, but a cautious sip. She then took a larger sip, and declared that it was not by half as nasty as Annis had led her to expect.

'By which I collect you to mean that it is not as nasty as they tell me the Harrogate water is! You must let me present Mr Carleton to you: he is Lucilla's uncle, you know!'

Mr Carleton, who had exchanged a brief greeting with Mrs Stinchcombe, bowed, and said that he was happy to make her ladyship's acquaintance. He sounded indifferent rather than happy, and Lady Wychwood, somewhat coldly acknowledging his bow, was much inclined to suspect that her dear Geoffrey had been mistaken in believing Annis stood in danger of succumbing to this libertine's fascinating arts. It did not appear to Lady Wychwood that he had any fascinating arts at all: why, he wasn't even a handsome man! Recalling Annis's past suitors, all of whom had been blessed with good-looks and distinguished manners, she began to suspect that Annis had been making a May-game of her brother, as (regrettably) she too often did. She could perceive nothing in Mr Carleton that could appeal to any female as critical and fastidious as Annis, and consequently unbent towards him, complimenting him on his charming niece, and saying how much she liked Lucilla.

He bowed again, and said: 'You are too kind, ma'am. Are you making a long stay in Bath?'

'Oh, no! That is to say, I hardly know, but not more than a week or two, I think. Are you making a long stay, sir?'

'Like you, I hardly know. It depends on circumstances.' He glanced round, and addressed himself to Annis, saying: 'Spare me a moment, Miss Wychwood! I wish to consult you – about Lucilla.'

'Certainly! I am quite at your disposal,' said Annis.

He took civil but unsmiling leave of the two other ladies, and moved apart with Miss Wychwood. No sooner were they out of tongue-shot of her companions than he said abruptly: 'How came it about that you permitted Kilbride to escort Lucilla through the town yesterday, ma'am? I thought I had made my wishes plain to you!'

'My permission was not sought,' she replied frigidly. 'Mr

Kilbride met Lucilla, and her maid, on their way to Laura Place, and turned back to accompany Lucilla.'

'It hardly seems that the maid was an adequate chaperon.'

'I don't know what you would have had her do,' she said. nettled. 'It was not as though Kilbride were a stranger! Lucilla greeted him with pleasure, believing him to be a friend of mine, and I have no doubt Brigham accepted him as such.'

'In which she was justified!'

She heaved an exasperated sigh. 'Very well! he is a friend of mine, but I am as well aware as you are, Mr Carleton, that he is not a fit friend for an impressionable and quite inexperienced girl, and I shall do my best to keep him at arm's length. In future, when I am unable to accompany her myself I will send her out in the carriage! And when she objects, as object she will, I shall tell her that I am merely obeying your orders!'

'But I haven't given such an unreasonable order!' he said. 'I haven't, in fact, given any order at all.'

'You said that you thought you had made your wishes plain to me, and you might as well have said orders, instead of wishes, for that was what you meant! So detestably top-lofty that you apparently think I must obey your *wishes*, as though I had no mind or will of my own!'

'Well, where Lucilla is concerned I do think you must,' he said. 'Recollect that you took it upon yourself to assume control over her, and not, let me remind you, by any wish of mine! I said then, and I will say again, that I do not think you a fit person to have charge of her.'

'Then I suggest, sir, that you take charge of her yourself!' she said tartly.

'I might have known you would be quick to seize the opportunity to throw me in the close,' he murmured.

She was obliged to laugh. 'I collect that is a piece of pugilistic slang, and I suppose I can guess what it means! I only wish it might prove to be true! It would, I daresay, be useless to tell you that it is not at all the thing to employ cant terms when you are talking to a female!'

'Oh, quite!' he said affably.

'You know, you are perfectly abominable!' she said. 'And far less a fit and proper person to have charge of Lucilla than I am!'

'You can't think how relieved I am that you've realized *that*!' he said.

She cast her eyes despairingly. 'I had as well level at the moon as try to get a point the better of you!'

'You are mistaken. You tipped me a settler at our very first meeting, my dear!'

'Did I?' she said, wrinkling her brow. 'I can't imagine how I contrived to do so!'

'No. I am unhappily aware of that,' he replied, with a wry smile. 'And this is not the place in which to tell you what I mean!'

Colour rushed into her cheeks, for these words had made his meaning very plain to her. She said hurriedly: 'We seem to have strayed a long way from the point, sir. We were discussing Lucilla's somewhat unfortunate meeting with Denis Kilbride. I shan't attempt to deny that I regret it, but is it, after all, such a great matter that she should have accepted his escort to Mrs Stinchcombe's house? What harm could come of it?'

'More than you think!' he answered. 'I haven't sojourned in Bath for long, but for long enough to have arrived at a pretty fair estimate of the amount of tale-pitching that goes on amongst those known, I believe, as the Bath quizzes! Kilbride's reputation is well-known to them, and I think it of the first importance that Lucilla should not be seen in his company. Tongues are wagging already, and who can say how many of the scandalmongers have friends or relations living in London whom they regale with tit-bits of the local *on dits*? Don't think that it was one of these who dropped a word of warning in my ear! It was Mrs Mandeville, with whom I dined last night!'

'Oh, heavens!' exclaimed Miss Wychwood, dismayed. 'I wouldn't for the world have Mrs Mandeville, of all people, think Lucilla to be a *coming* girl!'

'You have no need to be afraid of that. She doesn't think it, but she knows as well as I do that nothing can do a pretty innocent more harm than to be seen to encourage the attentions of such men as Kilbride.'

'Oh, nothing! nothing!' said Miss Wychwood fervently. 'I can assure you that I shall take good care that it doesn't happen again!' A rather rueful smile touched her lips. She said, not without difficulty: 'I am afraid she is not – not impervious to his charm, and I ought perhaps to tell you that I find it very difficult to know how best to combat this. I think – no, I am *sure* that I took a false step yesterday, when she was telling me about his escorting her to Laura Place, and how kind and amusing she thought him: I said – funningly, of course! – that I had lost count of the silly girls who had lost their hearts to him, and had been left languishing. If I had said no more than that, it might have given her pause, but when she replied that perhaps he hadn't truly loved any of them I was betrayed into suggesting that perhaps none of them had been as well-endowed as he had believed them to be. She – she flew out at me, asked me how I could say anything so detestable about him, and fairly ran out of the room. Pray don't rake me down for having said anything so ill-judged! I have been raking myself down ever since I said it!'

'Then stop raking yourself down!' he replied. 'I am not concerned with the possibility that Lucilla might fall in love with him: one doesn't form a lasting passion at her age, and the experience won't harm her. All that concerns me is that she should not be beguiled into indiscretion.'

'You don't feel – it has occurred to me that *you* might perhaps say something to Kilbride?'

'My dear girl, it is not in the least necessary that I should do so. He may flirt with her, but he won't go beyond flirtation, believe me! He is no coward, but he is as little anxious to risk a meeting with me, as I am to force one on him. You may rest assured that I shan't do so, for nothing could be more prejudicial to Lucilla's reputation than the scandal *that* would create! Take that anxious frown off your face! It doesn't become you! I perceive that Lady Wychwood is about to descend on you, so we had better part: she clearly feels it to be her duty to come between us! I wonder what harm she thinks I could do you in such a public place as this?'

CHAPTER ELEVEN

In assuming that Lady Wychwood was coming towards them to protect Annis, Mr Carleton wronged her. She had swallowed the glass of hot water, had enjoyed a comfortable chat with Mrs Stinchcombe, and she now wished to go back to Camden Place, to take Tom for a gentle airing in the crescent-shaped garden which lay between Upper and Lower Camden Place. Not being in the habit of indulging ridiculous fancies, the fear that Mr Carleton could do Annis a particle of bodily harm in the Pump Room never entered her head; and as for the danger of his ingratiating himself with her to her undoing, she thought this equally ridiculous. While she talked to Mrs Stinchcombe, she had contrived to watch, from the tail of her eye, the brief tête-à-tête between Annis and this reputed profligate, and she was perfectly assured that her lord had allowed his brotherly anxiety to overcome his good sense. She was going to occupy herself during the afternoon by writing a soothing letter to him, and she said, as she and Annis left the Pump Room: 'I can't for the life of me conceive, dearest, what can have made Geoffrey take such a maggot into his head as to suppose that there was the least fear of that disagreeable man's making you the object of his gallantry – if gallantry it can be called! I promise you, I mean to give him a *severe* scold, for supposing that you, of all people, could possibly develop a tendre for such a brusque, and extremely *un*gallant man!'

'Deplorably rag-mannered, isn't he?' agreed Annis.

'Oh, shockingly! I could see that he had made you as cross as crabs, and positively *quaked* for fear that you would fly up into the boughs, which wouldn't have astonished me, but which would have been a very improper thing to have done in the Pump Room. How unfortunate it is that you are obliged to be on terms with him! Forgive me if I say that I think the sooner he removes Lucilla from your house the better it will be for you! What was he looking so black about?'

'Denis Kilbride,' replied Miss Wychwood, calmly, but with a gleam in her eyes hard to interpret.

'Denis Kilbride?' echoed Lady Wychwood, too much surprised to notice either the gleam, or the little smile that hovered at the corners of Miss Wychwood's mouth. 'Why, what has he to say to anything?'

'Too much!' said Miss Wychwood, with a wry grimace. 'I fear he may be in a fair way towards capturing Lucilla's silly heart, and although that possibility doesn't seen to worry Mr Carleton much, what does worry him, and made try to ring a peal over me just now, is the circumstance of Kilbride's having escorted Lucilla yesterday all the way from Camden Place to Laura Place. It was unfortunate, for several people saw them, and if you had ever lived in Bath, Amabel, you would know that it is a veritable hotbed of gossip!'

'But surely, Annis, it is perfectly permissible for a gentleman to accompany a girl through the town, in the daytime, and with her maid walking behind, as I don't doubt Lucilla's maid did!' expostulated Lady Wychwood. 'Why, it is quite the thing for a gentleman to take up some young female beside him in his curricle, or his phaeton, or whatever sporting vehicle he happens to be driving! And *without* her maid!'

'Perfectly permissible, my dear, but not if the gentleman is Denis Kilbride! At the best, he is recognized as a dangerous flirt, and at the worst, a confirmed fortune-hunter.'

'Oh, dear!' said Lady Wychwood, sadly shocked. 'I know Geoffrey didn't at all like it when Kilbride was courting you, when we were all three of us in London. He said he was a here-and-thereian; and I do recall that he once said he suspected him of hanging out for a rich wife. I didn't set much store by that, for Geoffrey does sometimes say things he doesn't really mean, when he takes anyone in dislike, and he never desired me not to receive him, or to invite him to my parties. And when, last year, he had been visiting his grandmother, and had ridden over to Twynham to pay his respects to us, Geoffrey received him with perfect complaisance.'

'By that time, Geoffrey knew that there was no fear of my succumbing to Kilbride's wiles,' said Annis, with a touch of cynicism. 'He is everywhere received, even in Bath! In part, this is due to the respect in which old Lady Kilbride is held; and in part because he is regarded as an amusing rattle, whose presence can be depended on to enliven the dullest party. For myself, though I can imagine few worse fates than to be leg-shackled to him, I like him, I invite him to my own parties, I frequently dance with him at the Assemblies. But although – in Geoffrey's opinion – I set too little store by the conventions! – I take care not to see so much of him as to give even the most censorious critic reason to say that I live in his pocket! Because I was well-acquainted with him before I came to reside in Bath, he is thought to be an old friend of mine, and as such his presence at my parties, the free-and-easy terms on which we stand are looked on with indulgence. But although I am no girl, and might be supposed to be past the age of looking for a husband, I should hesitate very much to drive with him, ride with him, or even walk with him. No because I am not very well able to check his familiarites, but because I know just how many malicious tongues would start to wag if I were to be seen tête-á-tête with him! So, with the best will in the world to do so, I cannot blame Mr Carleton for having raked me down!'

'I consider it to have been excessively impertinent of him, and I hope you gave him a set-down!' said Lady Wychwood roundly.

Annis made no reply to this, but it occurred to her that giving Mr Carleton a set-down was something she had never yet succeeded in doing. She thought that it would perhaps be as well if she didn't discuss his character with her sister-in-law, for she had made the disconcerting discovery that however much she herself criticized his faults an almost overmastering impulse to defend them arose in her when anyone else did so. So she turned the subject by directing Lady Wychwood's attention to a very pretty bonnet displayed in a milliner's window. The rest of the walk was beguiled by an animated discussion of all the latest quirks of fashion, which lasted until they reached Upper Camden Place, and Lady Wychwood caught sight of her small son, playing ball in the garden with Miss Farlow. This made her exclaim: 'Oh, look! Maria has taken Tom into the garden! What a good, kind creature she is, Annis!'

'I wish I were rid of her!' replied Annis, with considerable feeling.

Lady Wychwood was shocked. 'Wish you were rid of her? Oh, no, how can you say so, dearest? I am sure there was never anyone more amiable, and obliging! You cannot be serious!'

'I am very serious. I find her a dead bore.'

Lady Wychwood thought this over for a moment, and then said slowly: 'She isn't bookish, of course, and not *clever*, as you are. And she does talk a great deal, I own. Geoffrey calls her a gabble-grinder, but gentlemen, you know, don't seem to like *chatty* females, and even he recognizes her many excellent qualities.'

'Are you trying to hoax me into thinking that you don't find her a bore?' demanded Annis incredulously.

'No, indeed! I mean, I truly don't. Oh, sometimes she does chatter rather too much, but, in general, I enjoy talking with her because she is interested in the things which don't interest you. *Little* things, such as household matters, and the children, and – and new recipes, and a host of things of that nature!' She hesitated, and then said simply: 'You see, dearest, I'm not clever, as you are! Indeed, I often wonder whether you don't find *me* a dead bore!'

Annis instantly disclaimed, and warmly enough to win a grateful smile from Lady Wychwood; but in her secret heart she knew that fond though she was of her gentle sister-in-law she did find most of their conversation insipid.

'What I like in her so much,' pursued Lady Wychwood, in a thoughtful tone, 'is the way she enters into all one's *chiefest* concerns, as one couldn't expect even Geoffrey to do, gentlemen not being able to share one's anxieties about household matters, and croup, and the red gum. And the way she busies herself with any small difficulty that arises, without having been asked to do so – which I hope I should never do! I cannot tell you what a support she was to me when I arrived here, with poor little Tom frantic with the toothache! She went with us to Mr Westcott's, and actually held Tom's hands down – which I, alas, had not the resolution to do – when he pulled out the offending tooth.'

'Sister,' said Annis, solemnly, but with wickedly dancing

eyes, 'I have long wanted to make you a present of real value, and you have now shown me how I may do it! I will bestow Maria upon you!'

'How can you be so absurd!' said Lady Wychwood laughingly. 'As though I would dream of taking her away from you!'

No more was said, Tom, by this time, having seen his mother, and run to the railings to greet her. She entered the garden, and Annis went on by herself to the house. Lucilla was spending the rest of the day with the Stinchcombes, and as Mrs Stinchcombe had promised to have her escorted back to Camden Place in time for dinner she felt herself relieved of responsibility. She could not help feeling glad of it, for not only was the entertainment of a lively seventeen-year-old a more onerous charge than she had foreseen, but what Mr Carleton had said to her had made her realize that a period of quiet reflection was her most immediate need. Unless she had been wholly mistaken in the meaning of his cryptic utterance in the Pump Room, she could not doubt that he had the intention of making her an offer of marriage. It would have been false to have said that such a notion had never occurred to her: it had occurred, but only as a suspicion, which she had been able, without very much difficulty, to banish from her mind. Now that the suspicion had been confirmed she felt that she had been taken by surprise, and was vexed by the realization that she was shaken quite out of her calm self-possession, and was suffering all the fluttering uncertainties of a girl in her first Season. She had been for so long a single woman that it had become a habit with her to think herself beyond marriageable age, and even more beyond the age of falling in love. It was a shock to discover that this had suddenly become a question open to doubt, and that it was a matter for doubt made her out of reason cross with herself, for she ought, surely, to be old enough and wise enough to know her own mind. But the melancholy truth was that she didn't know it. She told herself, in a scolding way, that it ought to be obvious to her that Mr Carleton possessed none of the attributes (except fortune, which was of no interest to her) which could be supposed to make him an acceptable suitor to a lady who had had many suitors, nearly all of whom had been blessed with good-looks, excellent address, polished manners, and a considerable degree of charm. To none of these attributes could Mr Carleton lay claim: it made her smile to think of setting even one of them to his credit; and as she smiled the thought darted through her mind that perhaps it was his lack of social grace which attracted her. It seemed absurd that this should be so, but it was undeniable that not the most charming of her suitors had so much as scratched her heart. She thought that if she had been left without the means to support herself she might have accepted an offer from that particular man, for she liked him very well, and felt reasonably sure that he would be an amiable husband; but when he did make her an offer she unhesitatingly declined it; and, far from regretting her decision, was thankful that her circumstances did not compel her to accept it. She had been sorry for him, because he had been desperately in love with her, and had exerted himself in every imaginable way to win her regard. The only effect her snubs had seemed to have on him had been to make him redouble his efforts to please her. She thought, recollecting his courtship, that he had been quite her most assiduous suitor; and as she remembered the attentions he had lavished on her she instantly contrasted him with Mr Carleton, and gave an involuntary chuckle. No two men could be more unlike. The one had employed every art known to him to bring his courtship to a successful conclusion; the other employed no arts at all. In fact, thought Miss Wychwood judicially, he seemed to lose no opportunity to alienate her. He was ruthlessly blunt, too often brusque to the point of incivility, paid her no extravagant compliments, and showed no disposition to go out of his way to please her. A very odd courtship – if courtship it was – and why he should have seriously disturbed her tranquillity, which, since she was to honest to deceive herself, she owned that he had done, was a problem to which she could discover no answer, the only solution which presented itself to her, that her well-regulated mind had become disordered, being wholly unacceptable to her. She wondered if she was refining too much on the few signs he had given of having fallen in love with her, whether they betokened nothing more than a wish to engage her in a flirtation. This idea no sooner occurred to her than she dismissed it: he had never tried to flirt with her, and the indifference of manner which characterized him did not belong to a man bent on idle dalliance. She thought that the best thing for her peace of mind would be for him to go back to London; and instantly realized that she did not wish him to do so. But she found herself unable to decide whether she wished to become his wife, or what she was to say if he did propose to her. She had always supposed that if ever she had the good fortune to meet the man destined to reach her heart she would recognize him immediately, but it seemed that either she had been mistaken in this belief, or that he was not that man.

It was with these tangled thoughts jostling against each other in her head that she joined Lady Wychwood and Miss Farlow to partake of a light luncheon, but she was too well-bred to allow the least sign of her mental perturbation to appear either in her face or in her manner. To invite anxious questions which she had no intention of answering would be to show a lamentable want of conduct: no woman of consideration wore her heart on her sleeve, or made her guests uncomfortable by behaving in such a way as to lead them to think she was blue-devilled, or suffering from a severe headache. So neither Lady Wychwood nor Miss Farlow suspected that she was not in spirits. She listened to their everyday chit-chat, responded to such remarks as were addressed to her, made such comments as occurred to her, all with her lovely smile which hid from them her entire lack of interest in what they were discussing. It was second-nature to her to maintain a boring conversation with the better part of her mind other-where, but she would have been hard put to it when she rose from the table to tell an inquirer what had been the subjects under discussion.

It was Lady Wychwood's custom to retire to her own bed-chamber for an hour's repose in the early afternoon before spending the next hour with her much loved offspring; Miss Farlow, for reasons which she frequently gave at tedious length, never rested during the daytime, and brightly detailed the several tasks which awaited her. They ranged from mending a broken toy for Tom to darning a sad rent in the flounce

171

of one of her dresses. 'How I came to tear it I cannot for the life of me conjecture!' she said. 'I haven't the smallest recollection of having caught it on anything, and I am persuaded I couldn't have done so without noticing it, and I am always careful to raise my skirt when I go upstairs so I cannot have trodden on it, for even if I did I should very likely have fallen, which I did once, when I was young and thoughtless. And I must have noticed *that*, for I daresay I should have bruised myself. Yes, and talking of bruises,' she added earnestly, 'it has me in a puzzle to know how it comes about that one can bruise oneself without having the least recollection of having done so! It seems to me to be most extraordinary that this should be so, for one would suppose it *must* have hurt one when it happened, but it is so. I well remember—'

But what it was she well remembered Miss Wychwood never knew, for she slipped away at this point, and sought refuge in her book-room, with the intention of dealing with her accounts. She did indeed make a determined effort to do so, but she made slow progress, because her mind wandered in an exasperating way which put her out of all patience with herself. Mr Carleton's swarthy countenance, and his trenchant voice kept on obtruding themselves so that she continually lost count in the middle of a column of figures, and was obliged to start adding it up again. After she had arrived at three different answers to the sum, she was so cross that she uttered in a far from ladylike manner: 'Oh, the devil fly away with you! You needn't think I like you, for I don't! I hate you!'

She bent again to her task, but ten minutes late Mr Carleton again intruded upon her, this time in person. Limbury came into the room, carefully shutting the door behind him, and informed her that Mr Carleton had called, and begged the favour of a few words with her. She was immediately torn between conflicting emotions: she did not wish to see him; there was no one whom she wished to see more. She hesitated, and Limbury said, in deprecating accents: 'Knowing that you was busy, Miss Annis, I informed him of the circumstance, and ventured to say that I doubted if you was at home to visitors. But Mr Carleton, miss, is regrettably not one to take a hint, and instead of leaving his card with me, and going away, he desired me to convey to you the tidings that he had come to see you on a matter of considerable importance. So I agreed to do so, thinking that it was on some question concerning Miss Lucilla.'

'Yes, it must be, of course,' replied Miss Wychwood, with all her usual calm. 'I will join him immediately.'

Limbury coughed in a still more deprecating manner, and disclosed that he had been obliged to leave Mr Carleton in the hall. Encountering an astonished stare from Miss Wychwood, he explained this extraordinary lapse by saying: 'I was on the point, Miss Annis, of conducting him upstairs to the drawing-room, as I hope I have no need to tell you, when he stopped me by asking me in his – his forthright way if there was any danger of his finding Miss Farlow there.' He paused, and a slight quiver disturbed the schooled impassivity of his countenance, which Miss Wychwood had no difficulty in interpreting as barely repressed sympathy for a fellow-man faced with the prospect of encountering her garrulous cousin. He continued smoothly: 'I was obliged to tell him, Miss Annis, that I believed Miss Farlow to be occupied with some stitchery there. Upon which, he desired me to carry his message to you, and said that he would await your answer in the hall. What would you wish me to tell him, miss?'

'Well, I am very busy, but no doubt you are right in thinking he has come to consult with me on some business connected with Miss Lucilla,' she replied. 'I had better see him, I suppose. Pray show him in!'

Limbury bowed and withdrew, reappearing a minute later to usher Mr Carleton into the room. Miss Wychwood rose from the chair behind her desk, and came forward, holding out her hand, and with a faint questioning lift to her brows. Nothing in her demeanour or in her voice could have given the most acute observer reason to suspect that her pulses had quickened alarmingly, and that she was feeling strangely breathless. 'For the second time today, how do you do, sir?' she said, with a faintly mocking smile. 'Have you come to issue some further instructions on how I am to treat Lucilla? Ought I to have asked your permission before permitting her to spend the day with the Stinchcombes? If that is the case, I *do* beg your pardon, and must hasten to assure you that Mrs Stinchcombe has promised to see her safely restored to me!'

'No, my sweet hornet,' he retorted, 'that is not the case! I've no wish to see her, and I don't care a straw for her present whereabouts, so don't try to stir coals, I beg of you!' He shook hands with her as he spoke, and continued to hold hers in a strong grasp for a moment or two, while his hard, penetrating eyes scanned her countenance. They narrowed as he looked, and he said quickly: 'Did I hurt you this morning? I didn't mean to! It was the fault of my unfortunate tongue: pay no heed to it!'

She drew her hand away, saying as lightly as she could: 'Good God, no! I hope I have too much sense to be hurt by the rough things you say!'

'I hope so, too,' he said. 'If my tongue is not to blame, what has happened to cast you into the doldrums?'

'What in the world makes you think I have been cast into the doldrums, Mr Carleton?' she asked, in apparent amusement, sitting down, and inviting him with a slight gesture to follow her example.

He ignored this, but stood looking down at her frowningly, in a way which she found disagreeably disconcerting. After a short pause, he said: 'I can't tell that. Suffice it that I know something or someone has thrown a damp on your spirits.'

'Well, you are mistaken,' she said. 'I am not in the doldrums, but I own I am somewhat out of temper, because I can't make my wretched accounts tally!'

His rare smile dawned. 'Let me see whether I can do so!'

'Certainly not! That would be to acknowledge defeat! I wish you will sit down, and tell me what has brought you here!'

'First, to inform you that I am returning to London tomorrow,' he replied.

Her eyes lifted swiftly to his face, and as swiftly sank again. She could only hope that they had not betrayed the dismay she felt, and said at once: 'Ah, you have come to take leave of us! Lucilla will be very sorry to have missed you. If only you had told us that you were going back to London she would certainly have stayed at home to say goodbye to you!'

'Unnecessary! I don't expect to be absent from Bath for very many days.'

'Oh! She will be glad of that, I expect.'

'Doubtful, I think! Lucilla's sentiments upon this occasion don't interest me, however. Will you be glad of it?'

Something between panic and indignation seized her: panic because a proposal was clearly imminent, and she was as far as ever from knowing how she was to respond to it; indignation because she was unaccustomed to dealing with sledge-hammer tactics, and strongly resented them. He was an impossible creature, and the only fit place for any female crazy enough to consider becoming his wife for as much as a second was Bedlam. Indignation made it possible for her to say, with a tiny shrug, and in a voice whose indifference matched his own: 'Why, certainly, Mr Carleton! I am sure we shall both of us be happy to see you again.'

'Oh, for God's sake—!' he uttered exposively. 'What the devil has Lucilla to do with it?'

She raised her brows. 'I imagine she has everything to do with it,' she said coldly.

He apparently managed to get the better of his spleen, for he gave a short laugh, and replied: 'No, not everything, but certainly a good deal. I am going to London to try if I can discover amongst my numerous cousins one who will be willing to take charge of her until her come-out next year.'

Her eyes flashed, colour flooded her cheeks, and she said, in a shaking voice: 'I see! To be sure, it is stupid of me to feel surprise, for you have repeatedly informed me that you consider me to be totally unfit to take care of Lucilla. Alas, I had flattered myself into thinking that your opinion of my fitness had undergone a change! But that, of course, was before you flew up into the boughs when you learned that Denis Kilbride had accompanied Lucilla to Laura Place! I perfectly understand you!'

'No, you do not understand me, and I shall be grateful to you if you will stop ripping up grievances and flinging them in my teeth!' he said savagely. 'My decision to remove Lucilla from your charge has nothing whatsoever to do with *that* episode! I don't deny that I thought, at the outset, that you were not a fit person to act as her chaperon. I thought it, and I said it, and I still think it, and I still say it, but not for the same reason! I find it intolerable that anyone as young and as beautiful as you are should set up as a duenna, behaving as though you were a dowager when you should be going to balls and assemblies for the pleasure of dancing till dawn, not to spend the night talking to the real dowangers and keeping a watchful eye on a silly chit of a girl only a few years younger than you are yourself!'

'Lucilla is twelve years younger than I am, and I *frequently* dance the night through—'

'Don't try to humbug me, my girl!' he interrupted. 'I was cutting my wisdoms when you were sewing samplers! I know very well when dancing comes to an end at the New Assembly Rooms. Eleven o'clock!'

'Not at the Lower Rooms!' she protested. 'They – they keep it up till midnight there! Besides, there are private balls, and – and picnic parties, and – and all manner of entertainments!' She perceived by the curl of his lip that he was not impressed by this list of Bath gaieties, and said defiantly: 'And in any event if I choose to chaperon Lucilla it is quite my own concern!'

'On the contrary! It is mine!' he said.

'I acknowledge that you have the right to do as you think best for Lucilla, but you have no right to dictate to me, sir! And, what is more,' she added wrathfully, 'you need not try to ride rough-shod over me, so don't think it!'

That made him laugh. 'I am more likely to box your ears!'

She was spared the necessity of answering by the appearance on the scene of Miss Farlow, who peeped into the room at that moment, saying: 'Are you here, dear Annis? I just looked in to tell you that I am obliged to – Oh! I didn't know you had a visitor! I do trust I don't intrude! If I had had the least suspicion that you were not alone I shouldn't have dreamt of disturbing you, for it is of no consequence, only that I find myself obliged to run into the town to purchase some more thread, and so I just popped in to ask you if you happen to need anything yourself. Oh, how do you do, Mr Carleton? I daresay you are wishing me at Jericho so I won't stay another moment! I shall just look into the nursery before I go out, Annis, because we think poor Baby is cutting another tooth, and I mean to ask dear Lady Wychwood if she would wish me to purchase some teething-powder, though I daresay she has some by her, or, if she hasn't, you may depend upon it Nurse will have brought some from Twynham. Well! I mustn't interrupt you for another instant, must I? Of course, I shouldn't have come in if I had known that Mr Carleton was with you, no doubt to consult with you about Lucilla. So, if you are quite sure there is nothing I can do for you in Gay Street — not that I am not perfectly ready to go further, as I hope I need not assure you!'

Miss Wychwood stemmed the flow at this point by saying firmly: 'No, Maria, there is nothing you can do for me, thank you. Mr Carleton has come to talk privately to me about Lucilla's affairs, and I am afraid you *are* interrupting us! So pray go away to do your shopping without any more ado!'

She had been in a state of seething fury when Miss Farlow had come into the room, but the expression on Mr Carleton's face had turned fury into amusement. He looked as though it would have afforded him the maximum amount of pleasure to have wrung Miss Farlow's neck, and this struck Miss Wychwood as being so funny that a bubble of laughter grew in her which she had the greatest difficulty in suppressing.

The door was hardly shut behind Miss Farlow when he demanded, in the voice of one driven to the extreme limit of his patience: 'How you can endure to have that prattle-bag living with you is beyond my comprehension!'

'Well, I must confess that it is beyond mine too,' she answered, allowing her mirth to escape her.

'What the devil possessed her to come in babbling about thread and teething-powder when she must have known you were not alone?'

'Rampant curiosity,' she replied. 'She must always discover whatever may be going on in the house.'

'Good God! Send her packing!' he said peremptorily.

'I wish I might! But since the world thinks that I should sink myself beneath reproach if I didn't employ a respectable female to act as my chaperon I fear I can't. It would be too brutal to dismiss her, for she *means* well, and what possible reason could I give for getting rid of her?'

'That you are about to be married!'

She was growing accustomed to his abrupt utterances, but this one came as a shock to her. She stared at him with startled eyes, and only managed to say faintly: 'Pray don't be absurd!'

'I am not being absurd. Marry me! I'll engage myself to keep you safe from all such pernicious bores as your cousin.'

'You *are* being absurd!' she declared, in a much stronger voice. 'Marry you to escape from poor Maria? I never heard anything to equal it! You must be out of your mind!'

'No – unless to be deep in love is to be out of one's mind! I am, you see. After all these years, to have found the woman I had come to think didn't exist—!' He saw that she was looking at him in considerable astonishment, and exclaimed, with a rueful crack of laughter: 'Oh, my God, what a mull I'm making of it! I deserve that you should refuse ever to speak to me again, don't I?'

'Yes,' she said candidly.

'I can't make elegant speeches. I wish I could! If I could find the words to tell you what's in my heart—!' He broke off, and took a quick turn about the room.

'Do you always find it impossible to make elegant speeches?' she asked. 'I can't bring myself to believe that, sir. You must have made many pretty speeches in your time – unless report has wronged you.'

'To the incognitas? That's a very different matter!' he said impatiently. 'A man don't form a connexion with a convenient with the same feeling as he has when he forms a lasting passion for the one woman in the world he wishes to make his wife!' He came to a sudden stop in his agitated perambulation, and directed a look of fierce inquiry at her, saying incredulously: 'Good God, are you holding it against me that I have frequently had some high-flyer in keeping?'

This blunt reference to his checkered career, coupled as it was with his cool acceptance of her understanding of the meaning of such terms as he had used to describe his mistresses, pleased rather than shocked her, and certainly did him no harm in her eyes. Contrasting his attitude with her brother's, she thought it was as refreshing as it was unusual, and, insensibly, she warmed to him. The abominable Mr Carleton was not one either to credit unmarried ladies with an innocence very few of them possessed, or to subscribe to the convention that prohibited a gentleman from mentioning in their presence any subject that could bring a blush to their cheeks. She liked this, but saw no reason why she should say so. Instead, she said, with unruffled composure: 'By no means, sir! Your past life concerns no one but yourself. But if I were to accept your extremely obliging offer your future life would also concern me, and, at the risk of offending you, I must tell you that I have no ambition to marry a rake.'

He did not seem to be at all offended; rather, he seemed to be amused. He heard her out in appreciative silence, but when she came to an end, he adjured her not talk like a ninny-hammer. 'Which, dear love, I know well you are not! You should know better than to suppose I should continue in that way of life if I were married to you. I shouldn't even wish to! No man who had the inestimable good fortune to call you his wife would ever desire any other woman. If you don't know that, there is nothing I can do or say to convince you!'

She felt her cheeks growing hot, and instinctively pressed her hands to them. 'You are very obliging, sir, but – but sadly mistaken, I fear! I am not the – the paragon you seem to think me!' she stammered. 'I – I know that I am generally held to be quite pretty, but—'

'If ever I heard such a whisker!' he interjected. 'Generally held to be *quite pretty*? You are generally held to be a diamond of the first water, my girl! And don't tell me you don't know it, for I am a hard man to bridge, and I give you fair warning that you'll catch cold if you try to gammon me!'

She smiled. 'That I can well believe! Try, in your turn, to believe me when I say that I don't admire any kind of – oh, beauty, for want of a better word!'

'There isn't one,' he said. 'I have a wide experience of beauties, but during the course of a misspent career I have never set eyes on a woman as beautiful as you are.'

She tried to laugh, and said: 'It is clearly midsummer moon with you! I think you have fallen in love with my face, Mr Carleton!'

'Oh, no!' he responded, without hesitation. 'Not with your face, or with your elegant figure, or your graceful carriage, or with any of your obvious attributes! Those I certainly admire, but I didn't fall in love with any of them, any more than I fell in love with Botticelli's Venus, greatly though I admire her beauty!'

She knit her brows, in honest bewilderment. 'But you know nothing about me, Mr Carleton! How could you, on so short an acquaintance?'

'I don't know *how* I could: I only know that I do. Don't ask me *why* I love you, for I don't know that either! You may be sure, however, that I don't regard you as a valuable piece to be added to my collection!'

This acid reference to Lord Beckenham's determined courtship drew a smile from her, but she said: 'You have paid me so many extravagant compliments, that I need not scruple to tell you that yours is not the first offer I have received.'

'I imagine you must have received many.'

'Not many, but several. I refused them all, because I preferred my – my independence to marriage. I think I still do. Indeed, I am almost sure of it.'

'But not quite sure?'

'No, not quite sure,' she said, in a troubled tone. 'And when I ask myself what you could give me in exchange for my liberty, which is very dear to me, I – oh, I don't know, I don't know!'

'Nothing but my love. I have wealth, but that's of no consequence. If it were – if you were purse-pinched – I would never offer you any of my possessions as inducements. If you marry me, it must be because you wish to spend your life at my side, not for any other reason! There are many things I can give you, but I don't mean to dangle them before you, in the hope that you might be bribed into marrying me.' His eyes gleamed. 'You would send me to the rightabout in two shakes of a lamb's tail if I did, wouldn't you, my dear hornet? And I wouldn't blame you!'

'It would certainly be carrying incivility to the verge of insult!' she said, trying for a lighter note. 'There's no saying, however, that you might be able to bribe me by promising never to snap my nose off!'

He smiled, and shook his head. 'I never make empty promises!'

She could not help laughing, but she said: 'A grim warning, in fact! I begin to suspect, sir, that you already wish you hadn't made me an offer, and are now trying to frighten me into refusing it!'

'You know better!' he said. '*Could* I frighten you? I doubt it! It would be an easy matter to promise never to be out of temper, but I mean you to find me as good as my word, and the deuce is in it that I have an untoward disposition, and a hasty temper!'

'Yes, I have noticed that!'

'You could hardly have failed to!' He hesitated, and then said roughly: 'I've several times hurt you – snapping your nose off, as you say – but never without wishing that I hadn't done so. But when I'm put out my tongue utters cutting things before I can check it!'

'What an admission to make!'

'Shocking, ain't it? It cost me something to make it, but I like pound dealing, and I won't attempt to fob myself off on to you with court-promises.' She did not reply to this, and, after a moment, he said: 'Have I made you take me in dislike? Be frank with me, my dear!'

'No – oh, no!' she said. 'I too like pound dealing, and I *will* be frank with you. I don't know if you can understand – or think that I must be indulging a distempered freak – but the truth is that my mind is all chaos!' She got up jerkily, and again pressed her hands to her cheeks, saying with an uncertain little laugh: 'I beg your pardon! I must sound detestably missish!'

'I think I do understand. You have persuaded yourself into the belief that you prefer to live alone – and that, if the alternative was to live with your brother and sister-in-law, is perfectly understandable. You have grown so much accustomed to your single state that to change it seems to you unthinkable. But you are thinking of it! That's why your mind is all chaos. If you felt that to continue to live alone would be infinitely preferable to living with me, you would have refused to marry me without an instant's hesitation. Was your mind thrown into chaos when Beckenham proposed to you? Of course it wasn't!

181

You regard him with indifference. But you don't regard me with indifference! I've taken you by surprise, and I am threatening to turn your beautifully ordered life upside-down, and you don't know whether you would like it or loathe it.'

'Yes,' she said gratefully. 'You do understand! It's true that I don't regard you with indifference, but it is such a big step to take – such an important step – that you must grant me a little time to think it over carefully before I answer you. Don't – don't press me to answer you now! Pray do not!'

'No, I won't press you,' he said, unexpectedly gentle. He took her hands, and smiled into her eyes. 'Don't look so fussed and bewildered, you absurd child! And don't turn me into a Bluebeard while I am away! I have a damnably quick temper, I have no agreeable talents, and very little regard for the proprieties, but I'm not an ogre, I assure you!' His clasp on her hands tightened; he raised them to his lips, kissed them, and released them, and went out of the room without another word.

CHAPTER TWELVE

It was long before Miss Wychwood was able to regain some measure of composure, and longer still before she could try to unravel the tangle of her thoughts. Never before had she been confronted with any question concerned with her life which she had experienced the least difficulty in answering, and it vexed her beyond bearing that a proposal from Mr Carleton should have so disastrously overset the balance of her mind as to have made it impossible for her to consider it with the calm judgement on which she had hitherto prided herself. The hardest question which had confronted her had been whether or not to remove from Twynham, and to carve a life for herself; but when she recalled what had been her sentiments on this occasion she knew that the only difficulty which had then made her hesitate had been a natural reluctance either to offend her brother, or to wound his gentle spouse. She had never had a doubt of her own sentiments, nor of the wisdom of her ultimate decision. Nor had she experienced the slightest heartburning when she had refused the many offers of marriage which had been made to her, though several of them had been (as she remembered, with an inward but reprehensibly saucy smile) extremely flattering. Endowed as she was with beauty, an impeccable lineage, and a handsome fortune, she had taken the ton by storm in her very first Season, and might, at this moment, have been married to the heir to a dukedom had she been content to marry for the sake of a great position, and to have let love go by the board. But she had not been so content, and she had never regretted her decision to refuse the young Marquis' proposal. Geoffrey, of course, had been shocked beyond measure, and had prophesied that she would end her days an old maid. That dismal prospect had not at all dismayed her: she was very sure that, comfortably circumstanced as she was, it would be far better to remain single than to marry a man for whom she felt nothing more than a mild liking. She was still sure of it, but she was well aware that there was nothing mild about her feeling for Mr Carleton. No man had ever before held such power to sway her emotions from one extreme to another, making her feel at one moment that she hated him, and at the next that she liked him much too well for her peace of mind. It was easy enough to understand why she should so often hate him; nearly impossible to know what it was in him that made her feel that if he were to go out of it her life would become a blank. Trying to solve this mystery, she recalled that he had told her not to ask him why he loved her, because he didn't know; and she wondered if that was the meaning of love: one might fall in love with a beautiful face, but that was a fleeting emotion: something more was needed to inspire one with an enduring love, some mysterious force which forged a strong link between two kindred spirits. She was conscious of feeling such a link, and could not doubt that Mr Carleton felt it too, but why it should exist between them she was wholly unable to discover. They were for ever coming to cuffs, and surely kindred spirits didn't quarrel? Surely there ought never to be any differences of opinion between them? No sooner had she put this question to herself than she thought, involuntarily: 'How very dull it would be!' It made her laugh softly to picture herself and Mr Carleton living together in perfect agreement, and suddenly it occurred to her that it would make him laugh too – if it didn't make him say *how mawkish!* which, in all probability it would.

She had begged him not to demand an answer from her until she had had time to think the matter over; she had told him that the step he was asking her to take was too big a one to be taken without careful consideration. It was true, but even as she had said it the realization had darted into her head that it was not the nature of her sentiments which required consideration, but other and more worldly matters which would arise if she married Mr Carleton. They might be relatively unimportant, but they were, in their degree, of some importance. Foremost amongst them was the knowledge that her brother would be most violently opposed to such a marriage. He would do all that lay within his power to dissuade her from marrying a man whom he not only disliked, but of whom he unequivocally disapproved. He would not succeed, but it was possible that he might sever all connexion between his household and hers; and that was a prospect she found it hard to face. She had set up for herself because she had found that he and she were continually chafing one another, but she had been careful to do so without wounding him by betraying the real cause of her removal from Twynham. They were unable to live in amity together, but they were bound by ties of family affection, and although these might be loose they existed, and she knew that it would give her great pain if they were to be broken. One could not lightly cut oneself off from one's home and one's family. And if Geoffrey did cast her off, it must inevitably redound to Mr Carleton's discredit, and that was a consequence she would find it very hard to bear.

Then there was the question of being obliged to give up her freedom, to turn her life upside-down, as he had himself said, to submit to his judgement, and how was she to know that he would not prove to be a domestic tyrant? He was certainly of an autocratic disposition. But then she remembered how well (and how unexpectedly) he had understood her jumbled thoughts, and with what sympathetic compassion he had refrained from pressing her to give him an answer, and she decided that however autocratically he might express himself he was no tyrant.

By this time she had reached the point where she was forced to own that she was in love with Mr Carleton, but for no discoverable reason. She thought, disgustedly, that she was behaving like a silly schoolgirl, and that it was a very good thing that he was going away. Probably she would find that she went on quite happily without him, in which case it would be a sure sign that she was not in love, but merely infatuated. So the wisest thing she could do would be to put him out of her mind. After which, she continued to think about him until Jurby came in to tell her severely that it wanted only ten minutes till dinner-time, and if she didn't come up to change her dress immediately she would be late. 'Which is not like you, Miss Annis! A full half-hour have I been waiting for you!'

Miss Wychwood said guiltily that she had been too busy to notice the time, thrust her accounts, on which she had done no work at all, into a drawer, and meekly went upstairs with her stern hench-woman. An attempt to dissuade Jurby from brushing her glowing locks, and pinning them up afresh, failed. 'I have my pride to consider, miss, and permit you to go down with your hair looking as though you had come backwards through a bush I will not do!' said Jurby.

So it was ten minutes after the dinner-bell had sounded before Miss Wychwood hurried down to the drawing-room, where she found her guests patiently awaiting her. She apologized, saying, with her lovely smile: 'I *do* beg your pardon, Amabel! So rag-mannered of me to have kept you waiting! I have been busy all the afternoon, and never noticed how the time was slipping by. I've been making up my accounts, and an errant shilling persisted in going astray!'

'Oh, and I interrupted you, didn't I, dear Annis?' exclaimed Miss Farlow remorsefully. 'I am sure it is no wonder that you should have lost count of your shillings! The only wonder is that you should be able to count them up at all, for *I* can never do so! I daresay it would divert you excessively if I were to tell you of the ridiculous mistakes I make in my addition. Not but what you had already been interrupted when I burst on you, which, I hope you know me well enough to believe, I would never have done if I had known you had a visitor with you!'

'Yes, Mr Carleton called,' replied Miss Wychwood smoothly. 'Good-evening, Ninian!'

Young Mr Elmore was wearing for the first time a new and beautiful pair of Hessians which had been made for him by the first bootmaker in Bath, and he could not resist the urge to draw attention to their shining magnificence, which he did by begging his hostess to forgive him for coming to dine with her in boots. 'Which is not at all the thing, of course, but I thought you would excuse it, because I am engaged with a party of friends this evening, and it is not a *dress*-party. No ladies, I mean, or dancing, or anything of that sort!'

'*I* see!' said Miss Wychwood, twinkling at him. 'Just a few choice spirits! Well, don't get taken up by the Watch!'

He grinned, and blushed. 'No, no, nothing of that nature!' he assured her. 'Only a – a small jollification, ma'am!'

'Whatever brought my uncle here?' wondered Lucilla. 'I thought I saw you talking to him in the Pump Room, ma'am!'

'Very true: you did!' responded Miss Wychwood. 'But as he didn't then know that he would be obliged to go up to London tomorrow, for a few days, he came to inform us of it. He was sorry not to find you at home, but I promised to make his apologies to you!'

Lucilla's eyes widened in amazement. '*Well!*' she gasped. 'Whoever heard of his being so civil?' She added shrewdly, and with a mischievous look: 'If he really did say he was sorry not to find me at home, it was a great fib, for he never shows the least wish to see me, and *I* think it is you he always wished to see!'

'For the pleasure of picking quarrels with me, no doubt!' retorted Miss Wychwood, laughing. 'Shall we go down to dinner now, Amabel?'

Lady Wychwood had looked up quickly at Lucilla's saucy speech, as though struck by a sudden and by no means agreeable suspicion, and Annis was aware that her eyes were fixed on her face. For perhaps the only time in her life she was thankful to Miss Farlow for interrupting, even though Miss Farlow did so merely because she seldom missed an opportunity to give Lucilla a set-down. She said sharply: 'A very odd thing it would be in your uncle if he were to leave Bath without taking leave of dear Miss Wychwood, to whom he has so *much* cause to be grateful! I am sure it isn't wonderful that he should wish rather to see her than you, Miss Carleton, for gentlemen find girls only just out of the schoolroom excessively boring! Indeed, at your age I should never have expected a gentleman to *wish* to see me!'

Lucilla's eyes flashed, and she replied swiftly: 'How fortunate!'

Ninian uttered a choking sound, which he turned into a very unconvincing cough; and Lady Wychwood rose, and said with gentle dignity: 'Yes, do let us go down, dearest, or we shall be in disgrace with your cook. Cooks *always* look black if one keeps dinner waiting, and one cannot blame them, for it must be dreadfully provoking to have one's work spoilt!'

She then recounted a mildly amusing story about a French cook she had once employed, and Annis, grateful to her for bridging the awkward gap, laughed, and led her on to tell a few more anecdotes. Behind them, on the staircase, came Miss Farlow, muttering to herself. Not much of what she said reached Annis' ears, but such overheard scraps as 'pert minx ... grossly indulged ... shocking manners' were enough to give her fair warning that she would be forced to listen to Miss Farlow's outraged complaints before the evening was out.

Lucilla and Ninian brought up the rear. Ninian whispered: 'You abominable little gypsy! You dashed nearly had me in whoops!'

Lucilla jerked up an impatient shoulder, saying under her breath that she didn't care; but at the foot of the stairs she caught up with Annis, who was standing aside to allow Lady Wychwood to precede her into the dining-room, and detained her by tugging a fold of her dress, and said in her ear, as Miss Farlow, in obedience to a sign from Annis, followed Lady Wychwood: 'I'm sorry! I know I ought not to have said it! Don't say I must beg her pardon, because I won't!'

Annis smiled, but held up an admonitory finger, murmuring: 'No, very well, but don't do it again!'

Lucilla followed her into the room in a chastened mood, and for the better part of the meal remained largely silent. But by the time the second course was placed on the table a chance remark made by Ninian put her in mind of something she wanted to ask Annis, and she said impetuously: 'Oh, Miss Wychwood, will you take me to the Dress Ball at the Lower Rooms on Friday?'

'Not without your uncle's permission, my dear – and I doubt very much if he would give it.'

'But he isn't here, so how can I ask him if I may go?' objected Lucilla. 'Besides, even if he was here he would be bound to say that you must be the only judge of what is proper for me to do!'

'Oh, no, not a bit of it! He keeps a stricter watch over you than you think!'

'Well, he needn't know anything about it!' said Lucilla, with something very like a pout.

'I hope you are not suggesting that I should try to conceal from him that I had allowed you to do anything of which I am very certain he would disapprove!' said Miss Wychwood. 'You must remember that he has entrusted you to my care! How very shocking it would be if I were to prove myself unworthy of his trust! You are trying to get me into a scrape, and I beg you won't!'

'No, but I don't see why I shouldn't go to the Dress Ball,' argued Lucilla. 'I have been to *several* private balls, so why may I not attend a public one?'

'I daresay it does seem rather hard to you,' said Miss Wychwood sympathetically, 'but there is a difference between the private parties you've been to and a public ball, believe me! The private parties you've attended have been informal hops, not *balls*; and have been got up for the entertainment of girls, like yourself, who are not yet out. Don't eat me! but I am afraid that if your uncle asked me if it would be proper for you to go to the Friday Dress Ball I should be obliged to say that I didn't think it would be at all the thing for a girl not yet out.'

'No, indeed!' struck in Miss Farlow. 'A very off appearance it would present! In *my* young days—'

Miss Wychwood flickered a warning glance at Lucilla, and silenced her cousin by saying: 'You sound just like my Aunt Augusta, Maria! That is what she was used to say whenever I wanted to do something she disapproved of. And I strongly suspect that it was said to her, and to you too, in *your* young days, and that you found it quite as provoking as I did!'

Miss Farlow opened her mouth to argue this point, but shut it again as she encounted a quelling look from Miss Wychwood which she dared not ignore. Lucilla was not so easily silenced, and continued to harp on the subject until Miss Wychwood lost patience, and said: 'That's enough, child! I daresay Harry Beckenham will be disappointed not to see you at the ball, but he will certainly not be surprised.'

'Yes, he will be!' Lucilla said, firing up. 'I told him I should be there, when he asked me, because I never *dreamed* you wouldn't take me—'

'Oh, do cut line!' interrupted Ninian impatiently. 'You're getting to be a regular jaw-me-dead, Lucy!'

Flushing scarlet, Lucilla prepared to give battle, but Miss Wychwood applied an effective damper by saying that if they wished to quarrel they might do so in the breakfast-parlour, but not at the dinner-table. Ninian, conscience-stricken, instantly begged pardon; but Lucilla was too angry to follow his example. However, she did not venture to pursue the quarrel, so Miss Wychwood was satisfied.

Ninian took his leave as soon as dinner came to an end; and Lucilla, having maintained what she believed to be a dignified silence, but which bore a strong resemblance to a fit of childish sulks, until she found that no one was paying the least attention to her, took herself off to bed before the tea-tray was brought in.

'Very pretty behaviour, upon my word!' said Miss Farlow, with an irritating titter. 'Of course, I knew how it would be from the moment I set eyes on her! I said at the start—'

'You have said more than enough already, Maria!' interrupted Miss Wychwood. 'I hold you entirely to blame for Lucilla's miftiness, and wasn't surprised that she lost her temper, and gave you a back-answer! No, don't start again, for I haven't the patience to listen to you!'

Miss Farlow began to cry, and to explain between sobs that it was her sincere affection for her dear Annis which had led her to offend her. 'Not that I meant to offend you, but to see you being imposed on is more than flesh and blood can bear!'

Perceiving that Annis was far from being mollified, Lady Wychwood intervened, and applied herself to the task of soothing Miss Farlow's injured feelings and succeeded so well that Miss Farlow soon stopped crying, accepted a cup of tea, agreed that she had a headache, and allowed herself to be persuaded to retire to bed.

'What a conjuror you are, love!' said Annis, as soon as Miss Farlow had departed. 'You can't think how grateful I am to you! I was within ames-ace of giving her such a rake down as I daresay she has never had in her life!'

'Yes, I could see you were,' replied Lady Wychwood, smiling a little. 'Of course she shouldn't have said what she did to Lucilla, but one can't help feeling sorry for her!'

'I can very easily help it!'

'No, you only say that because she vexed you. Poor Maria! She is so dreadfully jealous of Lucilla! I think she feels that Lucilla has put her nose quite out of joint, and she is one of those who wants to be held in affection – to know that she is valued. And when she thinks you value Lucilla far more highly than you value her it makes her miserably jealous, and then she says foolish things which she doesn't really mean.'

'Such as saying that Lucilla imposes on me!'

'Yes. Nonsensical, of course: Lucilla is just a spoilt child.' She paused, hesitating for a moment or two, and then said apologetically: 'Will you be cross with me if I say that I do think you have indulged her rather too much?'

'No, how should I be?' said Annis, sighing. 'I have come to realize it myself. You see, she had been kept so close by her aunt, never being allowed to go to parties, or to make friends of her own choosing, and never out of her governess's sight that I made up my mind that I would do what I could to make up for the dreary time she had had ever since her mother died. You can't think what satisfaction it gave me when I watched her huge enjoyment of things other girls think the merest commonplace amusements! I suppose I ought to have foreseen that it would go to her head a little. You'll say I ought also to have foreseen that chaperoning a high-spirited and very pretty girl is not an easy task to undertake! I have a melancholy suspicion that Mr Carleton is odiously right when he says I am not a fit person to have charge of his niece!'

'It was uncivil and ungrateful of him to have said it, but I must own that I think it was the truth. I wish very much that he would place her in somebody else's care.'

'Well, you may be easy, for that is what he is going to do. His purpose in coming here today was to inform me of it. I haven't told Lucilla. I am afraid she will violently object to being taken away from me, so I am leaving her uncle to break the news to her. If she runs away, as it is quite likely she will – indeed, she might even elope with Kilbride! – it is Mr Carleton who will bear the responsibility, and not me!'

'Oh, I hope she won't do anything so foolish!' said Lady Wychwood, in a voice of comfortable conviction. 'I understand that you don't wish to give her up, but you should reflect, dearest, that you would be bound to lose her when she comes out next spring, and the longer she lives with you the harder you would find it to part with her. So don't let yourself be thrown into gloom, will you?'

'Good God, no! I shall certainly miss her, for she is a very engaging girl, and I have become attached to her; but to tell you the truth, Amabel, I do find the task of taking care of her rather more irksome than I had thought it would be. If Mr Carleton can discover, amongst his relations, one who is not only willing to receive her into her household, but one whom Lucilla will be happy to live with until her come-out, I shall be perfectly content to relinquish the child into her charge.'

Lady Wychwood said no more, and it was not long before she went away to bed, saying that she didn't know how it was but that Bath air always made her sleepy. Annis soon followed her, but it was some time before she was able to get into bed, because while Jurby was still brushing her hair a knock on the door heralded the entrance of Lucilla, who stood hesitating on the threshold, and stammering: 'I came – I wanted to say something to you – I will come back later!'

She had obviously been crying, and little though Annis wished for any emotional scenes that day she could not bring herself to repulse the girl. She smiled, and held out her hand, saying: 'No, don't do that! Jurby has just finished making me ready for bed. Thank you, Jurby! I shan't need you any more, so I'll bid you goodnight.'

Jurby went away, sharply adjuring Lucilla not to keep Miss Annis up until all hours: 'For she's fagged to death, as anyone can see! And no wonder! Racketting all over at her age!'

'At my age?' exclaimed Annis, with a comical look of dismay. 'Jurby, you wretch, I'm not in my *dotage*!'

'You're old enough to know better than to be on the jaunter from morning till night, miss,' replied Jurby implacably. 'The next thing will be that we shall have people saying you're a regular gadabout!'

This made Miss Wychwood burst out laughing, which had the effect of sending her sternest critic out of the room, saying darkly: 'Mark my words!'

'I wonder which of her words I am to mark?' said Miss Wychwood, still laughing.

'She means that you are quite worn out with taking me about, and oh, *dear* Miss Wychwood, I never meant to wear you out!' declared Lucilla, on a convulsive sob.

'Lucilla, you goose! How *can* you be so absurd? Pray, how old do you think I am? Take care how you answer, for between you, you and Jurby have made me feel that I am dwindling into the grave, and if anyone else dares to tell me that I'm looking hagged I shall go into strong hysterics!'

But it would not do. Lucilla, having passed from the sulks into remorse and indulged in a flood of tears, was in no mood to deny herself the relief of pouring out her contrition into Miss Wychwood's unwilling ears. It was long before she could be persuaded that her momentary lapse had been quite as much Miss Farlow's fault as hers; and when she had at last been brought to accept the assurance that her regrettable, but very understandable breach of the canons of propriety in which she had been reared had not put her beyond pardon, it was

192

only to fall into an orgy of self-blame for having been so forget-
ful of all she owed Miss Wychwood as to have teased her to
take her to the Dress Ball, and to have behaved thereafter as
though she had been born in a back-slum.

By the time Miss Wychwood had succeeded in sending her to
bed in a more cheerful frame of mind, it was nearly an hour
later, and she herself was feeling quite exhausted and was
much inclined to crawl into bed without putting on her night-
cap. That, of course, would not do at all, and she was tying the
strings under her chin when another knock fell on her door, to
be immediately followed by Miss Farlow, also in a lachrymose
condition, and more than ordinarily garrulous. She had come,
she said, to explain to her dear cousin how it had come about
that she had allowed her feelings to overcome her. Annis said
wearily: 'Pray don't, Maria! I am too tired to listen, and can
think of nothing but my bed. It was an unfortunate con-
tretemps, but too much has been said about it already. Let us
forget it!'

But this Miss Farlow declared herself unable to do. She
would not for the world keep dear Annis from her bed. 'I shan't
stay above a minute,' she said, 'But I shouldn't be able to close
my eyes all night if I didn't tell you what my feelings are upon
this occasion!'

In fact, she stayed for twenty minutes, saying: 'Just one
word more!' every time Annis tried to get rid of her; and might
have stayed for twenty more minutes had Jurby not stalked in,
and informed her, in forbidding accents, that it was high time
she went to bed, instead of talking Miss Annis into a headache.
Miss Farlow bridled, but she was no match for Jurby, and pausing only to press Annis to take a few drops of laudanum if she
found herself unable to sleep, she bade her a fond goodnight
and at last went away.

'There's one that has more hair than wit, and a mouthful of
pap besides,' Jurby said grimly. 'It's a good thing I didn't go to
bed myself, which I never meant to do, not for a moment, for I
guessed she'd come fretting you to death! As though you
hadn't had enough trouble this day!'

'Oh, Jurby, hush! You shouldn't speak of her like that!' said
Annis weakly.

'Nor I wouldn't to anyone but you, miss, but it's coming to something, after all the years I've looked after you, if I can't speak my mind to you. Next you'll be telling me I'd no right to send her packing!'

'No, I shan't,' sighed Annis. 'I'm too thankful to you for having rescued me! I haven't had anything to *trouble* me, but from some cause or another I'm out of temper – probably because my accounts wouldn't come right!'

'And probably for quite another reason, miss!' said Jurby. 'I haven't said anything, and nor I don't mean to, for you know your own business best.' She tucked in the blankets, and began to draw the curtains round the bed. 'Which isn't to say I don't know which way the wind is blowing, for *I'm* not a cabbage-head, and I haven't lived next and nigh you ever since the day you came out of the nursery without getting to know you better than you think, Miss Annis! Now, you shut your eyes, and go to sleep!'

Miss Wychwood was left wondering how many members of her domestic staff also knew which way the wind was blowing; and fell asleep wishing that she did know her own business best.

The night brought no counsel, but it did restore her to something not too far removed from her usual cheerful calm, and enabled her to support with creditable equanimity the spate of conversation which enlivened (or made hideous) the breakfast-table. For this, Lucilla and Miss Farlow were responsible, Miss Farlow being determined to show that she bore Lucilla no ill-will by chatting to her in a very sprightly way, and Lucilla being anxious to atone for her pert back-answer, by responding to these amiable overtures with equal amiability and the appearance of great interest.

In the middle of one of Miss Farlow's reminiscent anecdotes, a note addressed to Lucilla was brought in by James, who told her that Mrs Stinchcombe's man had been instructed to wait for an answer. It had been written in haste by Corisande, and no sooner had Lucilla read it than she gave a squeak of delight, and turned eagerly to Miss Wychwood. Oh, ma'am, Corisande invites me to join a riding-party to Badminton! May I do so? *Pray* don't say I mustn't! I won't tease you – but I want to visit

Badminton above all places, and Mrs Stinchcombe sees no objection to the scheme, and it is *such* a fine day—'

'Stop, stop!' begged Miss Wychwood, laughing at her. 'Who am I to object to what Mrs Stinchcombe approves of? Of course you may go, goose! Who is to be of your party?'

Lucilla jumped up, and ran round the table to embrace her. 'Oh, *thank* you, dear, dear Miss Wychwood!' she said ecstatically. 'And will you send someone down to the stables to desire them to bring Lovely Lady up to the house immediately? Corisande writes that if I am permitted to join the party they will pick me up here, on the way, you know! It is Mr Beckenham's party, and Corisande says there will be no more than six of us: just her, and me, and Miss Tenbury, and Ninian, and Mr Hawkesbury! Besides Mr Beckenham himself, of course.'

'Unexceptionable!' said Miss Wychwood, with becoming gravity.

'I made sure you would say so! And I think Mr Beckenham is one of the most obliging people imaginable! Only fancy, ma'am! He arranged this expedition merely because he heard me telling someone in the Pump Room yesterday – I forgot who it was, and it doesn't signify! – that I had *not* visited Badminton, but hoped very much to do so. And the best of it is,' she added exultantly, 'that he will be able to take us inside the house, even if this doesn't chance to be a day when it is open to visitors, because he has frequently been staying there, being a friend of Lord Worcester's, Corisande says!'

She then sped away to hurry into her riding-habit, and before she reappeared Ninian arrived in Camden Place, and, leaving James to take charge of his borrowed hack, came in to tell Miss Wychwood that although he did not above half wish to join Mr Beckenham's party he had consented to do so because he thought it his duty to see that Lucilla came to no harm. 'Which I thought you would wish to be assured of, ma'am!' he said grandly.

It was difficult to imagine what possible harm could threaten Lucilla in such elegant company, but Miss Wychwood thanked him, said that she could now be easy, and that she hoped he would contrive to derive *some* enjoyment from the expedition. She was perfectly aware that he regarded Harry Beckenham

195

with a jealous eye; and guessed, shrewdly, that seeing Lucilla came to no harm was his excuse for accepting an invitation too tempting to be refused. The guess became a certainty when he said, in an off-hand way: 'Oh, well, yes! I daresay I shall! I own, I *should* like to get a glimpse of the Heythrop country! And it isn't everyone who gets the chance to see the house in a *private* way, so it would be a pity to miss it. I believe it is very well worth a visit!'

Miss Wychwood agreed to this, without the glimmer of a smile to betray her amusement at the instant picture this airy speech conjured up of young Mr Elmore's dazzling his family and his acquaintances with casual references to the elegance and the various amenities of a ducal seat, which he had happened to visit, quite privately, of course, during his sojourn at Bath.

She saw the party off, a few minutes later, confident that Mr Carleton in his most censorious mood would be hard put to it to find fault with her for having done so. And if he did find fault with her, she would take great pleasure in reminding him that when he had so abruptly left her rout-party he had said that since Ninian and Harry Beckenham were taking good care of Lucilla there was no need for him to keep an eye on on her.

The rest of the morning passed without incident, but shortly after Lady Wychwood had retired for her customary rest, Miss Wychwood, again wrestling with accounts in her book-room, received a most unexpected visitor.

'A Lady Iverley has called to see you, miss,' said Limbury, proffering a salver, on which lay a visiting-card. 'I understand she is Mr Elmore's respected parent, so I have conducted her to the drawing-room, feeling that you would not wish me to say you was not at home.'

'Lady Iverley?' exclaimed Miss Wychwood. 'What in the world – No, of course I don't wish you to tell her I'm not at home! I will come up directly!'

She thrust her accounts aside, satisfied herself, by a brief glance at the antique mirror which hung above the fireplace that her hair was perfectly tidy, and mounted the stairs to the drawing-room.

Here she was confronted by a willowy lady dressed in a

clinging robe of lavender silk, and a heavily veiled hat. The gown had a demi-train, a shawl drooped from Lady Iverley's shoulders, and a reticule from her hand. Even the ostrich plumes in her hat drooped, and there was a strong suggestion of drooping in her carriage.

Miss Wychwood came towards her, saying, with a friendly smile: 'Lady Iverley? How do you do?'

Lady Iverley put back her veil, and revealed to her hostess the face of a haggard beauty, dominated by a pair of huge, deeply sunken eyes. 'Are you Miss Wychwood?' she asked, anxiously staring at Annis.

'Yes, ma'am,' replied Annis. 'And you, I fancy, are Ninian's mama. I am very happy to make your acquaintance.'

'I knew it!' declared her ladyship throbbingly. 'Alas, alas!'

'I beg your pardon?' said Annis, considerably startled.

'You are so beautiful!' said Lady Iverley, covering her face with her gloved hands.

An alarming suspicion that she was entertaining a lunatic crossed Miss Wychwood's mind. She said, in what she hoped was a soothing voice: 'I am afraid you are not quite well, ma'am; pray won't you be seated? Can I do anything for you? A – a glass of water, perhaps, or – or some tea?'

Lady Iverley reared up her head, and straightened her sagging shoulders. Her hands fell, her eyes flashed, and she uttered, in impassioned accents: 'Yes, Miss Wychwood! You may give me back my son!'

'*Give you back your son?*' said Miss Wychwood blankly.

'You cannot be expected to enter into a mother's feelings, but surely, surely you cannot be so heartless as to remain deaf to her pleadings!'

Miss Wychwood now realized that she was not entertaining a lunatic, but a lady of exaggerated sensibility, and a marked predilection for melodrama. She had never any sympathy for persons who indulged in such ridiculous displays: she considered Lady Iverley to be both stupid and lacking in conduct; but she tried to conceal her contempt, and said kindly: 'I collect that you are labouring under a misapprehension, ma'am. Let me hasten to assure you that Ninian isn't in Bath on my account! Do you imagine him to be in love with me? He would stare to hear you say so! Good God, he regards me in the light of an aunt!'

'Do you take me for a fool?' demanded her ladyship. 'If I had not seen you, I might have been deceived into believing you, but I have seen you, and it is very plain to me that you have ensnared him with your fatal beauty!'

'Oh, fiddle! 'said Miss Wychwood, exasperated. 'Ensnared him, indeed! I make all allowances for a parent's partiality, but of what interest do you imagine a green boy of Ninian's age can possibly be to me? As for his having fallen a victim to my *fatal beauty*, as you choose to call it, such a notion has never, I am very sure, entered his head! Now, do, pray, sit down, and try to calm yourself!'

Lady Iverley sank into a chair, but shook her head, and said mournfully: 'I don't accuse you of *wantonly* ensnaring him. Perhaps you didn't realize how susceptible he is.'

'On the contrary!' said Miss Wychwood, laughing. 'I think him very susceptible – but not to the charms of a woman of my age! At the moment I believe him to be dangling after the daughter of one of my closest friends, but there's no saying that by tomorrow he won't be fancying himself in love with some other girl. I think it will be some few years yet before he outgrows the youthful gallantries which he is now enjoying.'

Lady Iverley looked to be unconvinced, but the calm good sense of what had been said had had its effect, and she said far less dramatically: 'Are you telling me that he has cut himself off from his home and his family for the sake of a girl he never laid eyes on until he came to Bath? It isn't possible!'

'No, of course it isn't! Nor do I believe that he has the slightest intention of cutting himself off! Forgive me if I say that if you, and his father, had not set up his bristles by raking him down – really very unjustly! – when he returned to you, he would in all probability be with you today.'

Lady Iverley paid little heed to this, but said tragically: 'I would never have believed he would have behaved so undutifully! He was always such a good, affectionate boy, so considerate, and so devoted to us both! And he hadn't any excuse for leaving us, for his papa granted him *every* indulgence, and never uttered a word of censure when he was obliged to settle his debts! I am persuaded he has fallen under an evil influence.'

'My dear ma'am, it's no such thing! He is merely enjoying a spell of freedom! He is extremely attached to his father, and to you too, of course, but perhaps you have kept him in lamb's wool for rather too long.' She smiled. 'I think he and Lucilla are suffering from the same complaint! Too much anxious care, and too little liberty!'

'Do not speak to me of that wicked girl!' begged Lady Iverley, shuddering. 'I was never so deceived in anyone! And if it is *her* influence which has made my deluded child turn against us I shall not be surprised. A girl who could bring her poor aunt to death's door would be capable of anything!'

'Indeed? I had no notion that things were as serious as that!' said Miss Wychwood, with a satirical smile.

'I fancy you do not understand what it means to have shattered nerves, Miss Wychwood.'

'No, I am happy to say that I don't. But we must trust that the damage done to Mrs Amber's nerves won't prove to be past mending. I daresay she will feel very much better when she is assured that there is no danger of having Lucilla restored to her care.'

'How can you be so unfeeling?' said Lady Iverley, gazing reproachfully at her. 'Have you no sympathy for the agonizing anxiety suffered by Mrs Amber, knowing that the niece to whose well-being she has devoted her life has left her to live with a stranger?'

'I am afraid I haven't, ma'am. To own the truth, I feel that if Mrs Amber had been so excessively anxious she would have come to Bath to discover for herself whether or not I was a proper person to take care of Lucilla.'

'I see that it is useless to say any more to you, Miss Wychwood,' replied Lady Iverley, rising to her feet. 'I shall only beg you to prove your sincerity by sending Ninian back to me.'

'I am sorry to be disobliging,' said Miss Wychwood, 'but I shall do nothing of the sort! A most impertinent piece of meddling that would be! Ninian's concerns are no bread-and-butter of mine. May I suggest that you speak to him yourself? And I think you would be wise not to mention this visit to him, for he would, I am certain, very much resent your having discussed his business with anyone other than his father!'

CHAPTER THIRTEEN

The riding-party did not return until close on six o'clock, by which time Miss Farlow was begging Miss Wychwood to prepare herself to meet the news of a disaster's having befallen the company, and saying that she had known how it would be from the start, if dear Annis permitted Lucilla to go off with a set of heedless young people. As two middle-aged and far from heedless grooms had accompanied the party, this description of it was singularly inept; but when Lady Wychwood placidly reminded her of this circumstance she only shook her head and demanded of what use two grooms could be? She was very sure that dear Annis must be excessively anxious, however bravely she tried to hide it.

Miss Wychwood was not at all anxious; she was not even surprised, for she had never expected to see Lucilla as early as had been promised, and had, in fact, told her chef, as soon as she had seen the party off, not to serve dinner until a later hour than was usual. 'For you may depend upon it they will find so much to interest them at Badminton that they will never notice the time!' she said.

She was perfectly right, of course. Just after seven o'clock, Lucilla and Ninian burst into the drawing-room, both full of apologies, and disjointed attempts to describe the glories of Badminton, and the splendid time they had had, which had included – only fancy! – a delicious cold nuncheon, especially provided by his Grace's housekeeper for their delectation. Nothing had ever been like it!

It seemed that careless Harry Beckenham had gone to considerable trouble to ensure the success of the expedition. 'I must own,' said Ninian honestly, 'I didn't expect him to have done the thing in such bang-up style! He actually sent a message to Badminton yesterday, warning the housekeeper that it was very likely he would be bringing a few friends to visit the house today! Or perhaps he wrote to the steward, for it was the steward who led us over the place, and told us all about everything. And I must say it was amazingly interesting!'

'Oh, I never enjoyed anything as much in all my life!' said Lucilla, with an ecstatic sigh. 'Corisande and I were in raptures, and neither of us had a notion how late it was until Miss Tenbury chanced to catch sight of a clock in one of the saloons, and drew our attention to it. And so we were obliged to hurry away immediately, and I do hope, ma'am, that you aren't vexed!'

'Not in the least!' Miss Wychwood assured her. 'I am famous for my foresight, and had set dinner back before you were all out of sight!'

Ninian then disclosed that (if she did not think him very uncivil) he had accepted an invitation from Harry Beckenham to join him and Mr Hawkesbury at the White Hart for dinner. 'Oh, and he told me to present his compliments to you, ma'am, and to explain why he was unable to come in to beg you, in person, to forgive him for having made us all so late! The thing is, you see, that he was obliged to escort Miss Stinchcombe and Miss Tenbury to their homes. He said that he knew you would understand.'

Miss Wychwood said that she perfectly understood, and that she would have thought Ninian quite muttonheaded if he had refused Mr Beckenham's invitation. What she did not tell him was that she was considerably relieved to learn that he would not be dining in Camden Place that evening. The foresight for which she had said she was famous had several hours earlier warned her that an awkward situation might arise, if it came to Lady Iverley's ears that Ninian, according to his usual custom, had dined with her, instead of hastening to his doting parent's side. It seemed improbable that he would return to the Pelican before going to the White Hart, since he would think it unnecessary to change his riding clothes for evening attire – indeed, quite improper for him to do so, when he knew that it was impossible for his host, or the amiable Mr Hawkesbury, to change their raiment. That meant that whatever message Lady

Iverley might have left for him at the Pelican he would not receive until an advanced hour of the evening, which was, she acknowledged, regrettable, but not as regrettable as it would have been if Lady Iverley had been able to lay the blame of his failure to respond instantly to the summons at her door. So she sped Ninian on his way, adjured Lucilla to make haste to put off her riding-habit, and left whatever tomorrow's problems might be to take care of themselves.

On the following morning, Lucilla, who was eager to discuss the previous day's entertainment with Corisande, volunteered to accompany Lady Wychwood to the Pump Room. Annis excused herself from going with them, for she felt reasonably certain that she would receive a visit from Ninian. Nor was she mistaken; but it was nearly midday before he arrived on the doorstep, hot and out of breath from having walked at breakneck speed up the steep hill from the Christopher. She received him in the book-room, because it seemed likely that her sister-in-law and Lucilla would return at any minute; and he said impetuously as he crossed the threshold: 'Oh, I am so glad to find you at home, ma'am! I was afraid you might have gone down to the Pump Room, where I couldn't have talked privately to you! And that I must do!'

'Then it is as well that I didn't go to the Pump Room this morning,' she replied. 'Sit down, and tell me all about it!'

He did sit down, and dragged his handkerchief from his pocket to wipe the sweat from his brow. Recovering his breath, he said in a tight, rigidly controlled voice: 'I've come to take my leave of you, ma'am!'

'Have you decided to go back to Chartley?' she asked. 'We shall miss you, but I think perhaps you should go back.'

'I suppose so,' he said dejectedly. 'I said at first – but I see it won't do! It seems that my father is quite knocked-up, and – and all through my having left Chartley in a huff, though I wrote to him, just as I told you I should, so why he should have taken it into his head that I meant never to return I can't conceive! It makes me afraid that he must be in very, very queer stirrups, and – and I could never forgive myself if – if anything happened to him! There seems to be nothing for it

202

but for me to go back. You see, my mother arrived here yesterday morning, Miss Wychwood. She is putting up at the Christopher.'

'I see,' she replied sympathetically.

'And my sister Cordelia as well,' he added, on a gloomy note. 'If she *had* to bring one of my sisters with her she might at least have brought Lavinia, for she has *some* sense, and she ain't a watering-pot, and she don't wind me up anything like as often as Cordelia does! I can tell you, ma'am, it made me as mad as fire when the silly wet-goose flung her arms round my neck before I could stop her, and wept all over me!'

'I – I expect it did!' said Miss Wychwood, a trifle unsteadily.

'Well, of course it did, and it would have made any man feel just as I did! I told Mama – *perfectly* politely! that it was enough to make me jump on the Bristol coach, and ship aboard the first packet bound for America, or anywhere else that the Bristol boats sail to, because I had rather live in the *Antipodes* than have Cordelia hanging round my neck, and dashed well ruining my neck-tie, besides calling me her beloved brother, which was the biggest hum I ever heard, for she don't like me any better than I like her! So then Cordelia asked me, as though she had been acting in some tragedy or another, if I wished to drive my sainted parents into their graves! Well, that did make me lose my temper, and I told her to her head that I had come to talk to Mama, and not to listen to fustian rubbish from *her*!'

Miss Wychwood, hugely enjoying this recital, perceived that the eldest Miss Elmore was a daughter after Lady Iverley's heart. She also perceived that his sojourn in Bath had done Ninian (to her way of thinking) a great deal of good; and she hoped that Lady Iverley had realized that he was no longer the adored and dutiful son who did as he was bid, but a young gentleman who had crossed the threshold of adolescence, and had become a man.

Apparently she had. She had sent Cordelia out of the room. According to Ninian, she had done this because she had recognized the justice of his complaint; Miss Wychwood thought that she had done it because she had been frightened. But this

203

she did not say. She merely said: 'Oh, dear! What a sad ending to the day!'

'I should rather think it was!' said Ninian fervently. 'Except that it wasn't the end of the day, but the beginning of it! Of *this* day, I mean! Well, I didn't get back to the Pelican till past midnight, so I didn't see the note my mother wrote me until then, when it was far too late to visit her, even if I hadn't been—' He stopped, in a good deal of embarrassment.

'Foxed?' suggested Miss Wychwood helpfully.

He grinned at her. 'No, no, not *foxed*, ma'am! Just a little bit on the go! If you know what I mean!'

'Oh, I know exactly what you mean!' she assured him, the smile dancing in her eyes. 'You had been dipping rather deep, but you were not too bosky to perceive the unwisdom of presenting yourself to your mama until you had slept off your potations! Have I that right?'

He burst out laughing. 'Yes, by Jupiter you have! You're a great gun, ma'am! Well, I went up to bed, but I told the boots to wake me not a moment later than eight this morning, which he did, and though I must say I felt pretty devilish at first, a cup of strong coffee more or less set me to rights, and I went off to the Christopher.' He paused; the laughter vanished from his voice, a frown descended on to his brow, and his mouth hardened. It was a full minute before he spoke again, and when he did speak it was with a little difficulty. He said: 'Do you think it chicken-hearted of me to have knuckled down, Miss Wychwood?'

'By no means! You owe a duty to your father, remember!'

'Yes, I know. But – but I have begun to wonder if he is so very ill as Mama believes him to be. Or even if she does believe it, or if she says it to compel me to go home, and stay at home, because she is – well, much more deeply attached to me than to my sisters!'

'I daresay she might *exaggerate* a little, but from what you have told me I collect that Lord Iverley's constitution was seriously impaired by his service in the Peninsula.'

'Yes, it was: there can be no doubt about that!' said Ninian, brightening. He thought it over for a moment, and then said: 'And he did have a bad heart-attack some years ago. But – but

Mama seems to live in dread of his having another, which might prove fatal, if he is put into a passion, or if one doesn't do exactly as he bids one!'

'That is very natural, Ninian.'

'Yes, but it isn't true! He was in the devil of a passion when Lucy ran away, and I helped her to do it; and when I lost my temper, and we quarrelled, and I said I should go straight back to Bath, he flew into such a rage that he *shook* with anger, and could hardly speak. But he didn't suffer a heart-attack! What's more, he went *on* being in a rage, for it was several days later that he wrote me that thundering scold, so that it is absurd to expect me to believe that he was exhausted. But when I tried to point this out to Mama, all she would say was that she couldn't blame me for turning against my parents because she knew well that I had fallen under an evil influence! I couldn't think what had put such a crackbrained notion into her head! It took me an age to get it out of her, but she did tell me in the end, and what do you think it was? *Your* influence, ma'am! Lord, I nearly laughed myself into stitches! Well, did you ever hear of anything so ridiculous?'

'Never!' said Miss Wychwood. 'I trust you were able to convince her that she was mistaken?'

'Yes, but it was deuced hard work! Someone seems to have told her that you were the most beautiful woman in Bath – described you pretty thoroughly to her, too, for she talked of your eyes, and your hair, and your figure as though she had actually seen you! So I said Yes, you were very beautiful, and very clever too, and I'm dashed if she didn't accuse me of having *fallen a victim to your beauty*!'

'I can almost hear her saying it!' murmured Miss Wychwood appreciatively.

'I daresay it would have made you laugh, but it didn't make me laugh, though I suppose it was funny. The thing was that it made me very angry, and I told Mama that it was a great piece of impertinence to talk in that outrageous style about a lady whom everyone holds in respect, and who has been as kind to me as though I had been her nephew. Which you have been, ma'am, and I couldn't leave Bath without telling you how very grateful I am to you for all the things you've done to make my stay in Bath so agreeable! Letting me run tame in your house, inviting me to go with you and Lucy to the theatre, making me known to your friends – oh, hosts of things!'

'My dear boy, I wish you won't talk nonsense!' she protested. 'It is I who am grateful to you! Indeed, I have made shameless use of you, and am wondering what I should have done without you, to take Lucilla about, and to stand guard over her! And another thing I wish you won't do is to talk as though we were never to meet again! I hope you will often visit Bath, and promise you will always be a welcome guest in Camden Place.'

'Th–thank you, ma'am!' he stammered, blushing. 'I mean to be a frequent visitor, I can tell you! I have made it plain to Mama that if I go home with her today it must be on the strict understanding that I am at liberty to come and go as I choose, and without having to coax Papa into giving his consent every time I wish to do something he doesn't approve of!'

'Ah, that was very wise of you!' she said. 'I daresay he may not like it at first, but depend upon it he will very soon grow accustomed to having a sensible man for his son and not a mere boy!'

'Do you think he will, ma'am?' he asked, rather doubtfully.

'I am very sure of it,' she smiled, getting up. 'You will take some nuncheon with us before you go, will you not?'

'Oh, thank you, ma'am, but no! I mustn't stay. My mother is anxious to reach Chartley today, because she fears my father will be fretting over the chance that she may have met with an accident. Which is very possible, for she *never* goes away without him. It would be much wiser, of course, if we postponed our departure until tomorrow morning, but when I suggested this to her, I saw at once that it would not do. I don't mean that she tried to – to *persuade* me – in fact, she said I must be the only judge of what was best – but I could see that she wouldn't get a wink of sleep tonight for worrying about Papa, so even if we don't reach Chartley before *midnight* it will be better for her to go home today than to be worrying herself into a fever. And it don't really signify if we do have to drive after dark, because it won't *be* dark, the moon being at the full, and no fear that I can see of the sky's becoming overcast.' He added imploringly, as though he had detected in Miss Wychwood's expression what were her feelings on the subject: 'You see, ma'am, Mama is not robust, and her disposition is nervous, and – and I know what trials she has to undergo – and – and—'

'You love her very much,' supplied Miss Wychwood, patting his flushed cheek, and smiling at him warmly. 'She is a fortunate woman! Now you will wish to say goodbye to Lucilla, so we will go up to the drawing-room. I think I heard her come in, with my sister, a minute or two ago.'

'Yes – well, I must do so, though ten to one she will abuse me for not having any resolution!' he said resentfully.

However, Lucilla behaved with perfect propriety. She exclaimed, when he told her that he was obliged to return to Chartley: 'Oh, no, Ninian! Must you do so? Pray don't go away!' but when he explained the circumstances she made no further demur, but looked thoughtful, and said that she supposed he would be obliged to go. It was not until he had left the house that, emerging from a brown study, she said earnestly to Miss Wychwood: 'It makes me almost *glad* I am an orphan, ma'am!'

Lady Wychwood uttered a slightly shocked protest, and said: 'Good gracious, child, whatever can you mean?'

'The way the Iverleys bullock Ninian into doing what they want him to do in – in an infamous way!' Lucilla explained. 'Lady Iverley appeals to his *better self*, and the pity of it is that he *has* a better self! I quite see that it is very creditable to have a better self, but it does make him rather milky.'

'Oh, no! I should never say he was milky,' responded Miss Wychwood. 'You must remember that he is very much attached to his mama, and is, I believe, fully aware of the anxious life she leads. I rather fancy she is inclined to cling to him—'

'Yes, indeed she does, and in the most *cloying* way!' said Lucilla. 'So do Cordelia and Lavinia! I wonder that he can bear it! I could not.'

'No, but you haven't a better nature, have you?' said Miss Wychwood, quizzing her.

Lucilla laughed, but said: 'Very true! And thank goodness I haven't, for it must be excessively uncomfortable!'

Miss Wychwood was amused, but Lady Wychwood shook her head over it, and later told her sister-in-law that she thought the remark a melancholy illustration of the evils attached to growing up without a mother.

'Well, they could scarcely be worse than the evils of growing up with such a mother as Lady Iverley!' said Annis caustically.

Ninian's absence was felt to have created a sad gap in the household; and even outside the household a surprising number of people told Annis how sorry they were that he had left Bath, and how much they hoped it would not be long before he revisited the town. He seemed to have made many friends, which circumstance increased Annis's respect for him: very few young men would have sacrificed their pleasures to so lachrymose and unreasonable a parent as Lady Iverley. She hoped that he was not moped to death at Chartley, but feared that he must be finding life very flat.

However, some few days later she received a letter from him, and gathered from its closely written pages that although he thought wistfully of Bath and its inhabitants conditions at Chartley had improved. He had had a long talk with his father, the outcome of which was that he was now occupying himself with the management of the estate, and spent the better part of his time going about with the bailiff. Miss Wychwood would stare if she knew how much he was learning. His quarrel with Lord Iverley had been quite made up. He had found his lordship looking dragged and weary, but was happy to say that he was plucking up wonderfully, and had even said that if Ninian wished to invite any of his friends to visit him he should be glad to welcome them to Chartley.

Miss Wychwood concluded that his lordship had learnt a valuable lesson, and that there was no need to worry about Ninian's future.

There was no need to worry about anything, of course: Lucilla was well, and behaving with great docility; little Tom's toothache was remembered by no one but his mama and Nurse; Miss Farlow had won Nurse's approval and had begun to spend a large part of the days either in the nursery or taking Tom for walks; and if Mr Carleton had thought better of his intention to return to Bath it was a very good thing, for they went on perfectly happily without him.

But when, one morning, she received a letter from him her heart jumped, and she hardly dared to break the seal, for fear that she might read that he had indeed changed his mind.

It did not seem as though he had done so, but although it was a relief to know that he still meant to come back his letter was not really very satisfactory. Mr Carleton had written it in haste, and merely to inform her that he had been obliged to postpone his return. He was much occupied with some tiresome business which made it necessary for him to visit his estates. He was on the point of setting out on the journey, and begged her to excuse his sending only a short scrawl to apprise her of his immediate intentions. He had no time for more, but remained hers, as ever, Oliver Carleton.

Not a model of the epistolary art; still less the letter of a man in love, she thought. The only part of it which encouraged to hope that he did still love her was its ending. But very likely he signed all his letters *Yours, as ever,* and it would be nonsensical to read more into these simple words than mere friendliness.

She found herself in low spirits, and tried very hard to shake off this silly fit of the dismals, and not to allow herself to think about Mr Carleton, or his letter, or how much she was missing him. She thought that even if she didn't succeed in carrying out this admirable resolution she had at least succeeded in hiding her depression from Lady Wychwood, but soon discovered that she was mistaken. 'I wish you will tell me, dearest, what is making you so – so down pin,' said her ladyship coaxingly.

'Why, nothing! Do I seem to be down pin? I wasn't aware of it – except wet streets, dripping trees, and nothing else to be seen but umbrellas and puddles, always does put me into the hips. I hate being shut up in the house, you know!'

'Well, it is sad that the weather should have turned off, but you were never used to care a straw for the weather. How often have I begged you not to venture out, when it was raining pitchforks and shovels! But you never paid any heed! You said you liked to feel the rain on your face.'

'Oh, that was in the country, Amabel! It is a very different matter in town, where one can't tie a shawl round one's head, find a pair of stout list shoes and go for a tramp! You wouldn't have me make such a figure of myself in Bath!'

'Of course not,' said Lady Wychwood quietly, and bent her head again over the robe she was making for her infant daughter.

'The truth is, I expect, that I need occupation,' offered Annis. 'Now, if only I didn't find sewing a dead bore, or if I had Lucilla's talent for water-colour drawing — have you seen any of her sketches? They are infinitely superior the generality of young-lady-drawings!'

'Oh, I don't think sewing or sketching would answer the purpose! They don't divert one's mind, do they? I don't know about sketching, for I was never at all fond of it, but I should think it is much the same as sewing, and that I find doesn't divert one's mind in the least – in fact, quite the reverse!'

'I think I shall embark on a course of serious reading,' said Annis, bent on leading Lady Wychwood down a less dangerous conversational avenue.

'Well, dearest, I daresay that might answer the purpose, but you have been sitting with a book open in front of you for the past twenty minutes, and I could not but notice that you haven't yet turned the page,' replied Lady Wychwood. She looked up, and smiled faintly at Annis. 'I don't mean to tease you with prying questions, so I'll say no more. Only that I hope so much that you won't do anything you might live to regret. I couldn't bear you to be made unhappy, my dear one. Tell me, do you think I have made this bodice large enough for Baby?'

CHAPTER FOURTEEN

The weather remained unsettled for several days, and it became obvious that the various al fresco entertainments which had been planned by Corisande and her many friends would have to be postponed. This was naturally a disappointment to Lucilla; and after a very short space of time, even Lady Wychwood's patience wore thin, and upon Lucilla's asking, for the twentieth time, if she didn't think the sky was growing lighter, and if it might not still be possible for the morrow's party at the Sydney Garden to take place, she addressed mild but measured words of reproof to her, saying: 'Dear child, the weather won't improve because you keep running to the window, and asking us if we don't believe it to be clearing up. Neither my sister nor I have the least notion whether it will be a fine day tomorrow, so of what use is it to expect us to answer you? You would do much better to stop pressing your nose against the window every few minutes and to occupy yourself with your drawing, or your music, instead.' She smiled kindly, and added: 'You know, my dear, however fond people may be of you they will soon begin to think you a sad bore if you fall into the way of harping on every little thing that puts you out, as though you were still only a spoilt baby.'

Lucilla reddened, and it seemed for a moment as though she was going to retort; but after a moment's inward struggle she said, in a subdued voice: 'I'm sorry, ma'am!' and ran out of the room.

It was soon seen that Lady Wychwood's words had gone home, for although Lucilla frequently cast wistful glances at the rain-drops chasing one another down the window-panes she only now and then complained of the perversity of the weather, and really made a praiseworthy effort to bear her disappointment with cheerful composure.

Just as the weather at last showed signs of improvement,

Miss Farlow created a most unwelcome diversion by succumbing to an attack of influenza. She dragged herself about the house, wrapped in a shawl, saying that she had contracted a slight cold in the head, and not until she fainted one morning when she got out of bed could she be induced either to remain in bed or to allow Annis to send for the doctor. There was nothing the matter with her; she was a trifle out of sorts, but would very soon be better; it was quite unnecessary for dear Annis to send for Dr Tidmarsh, not that she knew anything against him, for she was sure he was very amiable and gentleman-like, but dear papa hadn't believed in doctors; and, besides, very strange behaviour it would be for her to fall ill when the house was full of guests, and it was her duty to remain on her feet, even if it killed her. However, she was clearly feverish, and in spite of being flushed, and complaining of feeling too hot, she shivered convulsively; so Annis took matters into her own hands, and despatched the page-boy with a message for Dr Tidmarsh. By the time he arrived, Miss Farlow was feeling so poorly that instead of repulsing him she greeted him as a saviour, wept bitterly, and described to him, with a wealth of detail, every one of her many symptoms. She ended by imploring him not to say that she had scarlet fever.

'No, no, ma'am!' he said soothingly. 'Merely a touch of influenza! I shall send you a saline draught, and you will very soon be more comfortable. I'll look in tomorrow, to see how you go on. Meanwhile, you must stay quietly in your bed, and do as Miss Wychwood bids you.'

He then went out of the room with Annis, told her that there was no reason for her to be anxious, gave her some instructions, and, when he took his leave, looked rather narrowly at her, and said: 'Now, don't wear yourself out, ma'am, will you? You don't look to be in such good point as when I saw you last: I suspect you have been trotting too hard!'

When Annis returned to the sickroom, she found Miss Farlow in a state of tearful agitation, the reason for this fresh flow of tears being her fear that poor little Tom might have taken the disease from her, for which she would never, never forgive herself.

'My dear Maria, it will be time enough to cry about it if he *does* contract influenza, which very likely he won't,' said Annis cheerfully. 'Betty will be bringing you some lemonade directly, and perhaps when you have drunk a little of it you will be able to go to sleep.'

But it soon became plain that Miss Farlow was not going to be an easy patient. She begged Miss Wychwood not to give her a thought, but to go away and on no account to feel she must stay at her side, because she had everything she wanted, and she couldn't bear to be giving her so much trouble; but if Miss Wychwood absented herself for more than half-an-hour she fell into sad woe, because this showed her that nobody cared what became of her, least of all her dear Annis.

Lady Wychwood and Lucilla were both anxious to share the task of nursing Miss Farlow, but Annis would not permit either of them to go into the sickroom. Lucilla looked decidedly relieved, for she had never nursed anyone in her life, and was secretly scared that she might do the wrong things; and Lady Wychwood, when it was pointed out to her that she had her children to consider and owed it to them not to expose herself to the risk of infection, agreed reluctantly to stay away from Poor Maria. 'But you must promise me to take care of yourself, Annis! You must let Jurby help you, and you mustn't linger in the room, or approach Maria too closely! How shocking it would be if *you* were to become ill!'

'Very shocking — and very surprising too!' said Annis. 'You know I am never ill! You can't have forgotten all the occasions when an epidemic cold has laid everyone at Twynham low, except Nurse and me! If you will look after Lucilla for me I shall be very much obliged to you!'

Jurby, when asked if she would help to nurse Miss Farlow, said that Miss Annis might leave it entirely to her, and not bother her head any more; but as she apparently believed that Miss Farlow had contracted influenza on purpose to set them all by the ears Annis took care always to be at hand when she stalked into the room to measure out a dose of medicine, wash Miss Farlow's face and hands, or shake up her pillows. Jurby disliked Miss Farlow, thought that she could be better if she wished, and in general behaved as if she had been a gaoler in charge of a troublesome prisoner. Miss Wychwood remonstrated with her in vain. 'I've no patience with her, miss, making such a rout about nothing more than the influenza! Anyone would think she was in a confirmed consumption to hear the way she talks about her aches and ills! What's more Miss Annis, it puts me all on end when she says she don't want you to be troubled with her, or to sit with her, and the next minute wonders what's become of you, and why you haven't been next or nigh her for hours!'

'Oh, Jurby, pray hush!' begged Miss Wychwood. 'I know she – she is being tiresome, but one must remember that influenza does make people feel very ill so that it is no wonder she should be in – in rather bad skin! But you won't have to bear with her for much longer, I hope: Dr Tidmarsh has told me that he sees no reason why she should not get out of her bed for a little while tomorrow, and I think it will vastly improve her spirits if she does so, because it is what she has been wanting to do from the outset.'

Jurby gave a snort of disbelief, and said darkly: 'That's what she *says*, Miss Annis, but it's my belief we shan't see her out of her bed for a sennight!'

But in this prophecy she wronged Miss Farlow. Permitted to sit up in an armchair for an hour or two on the following day, her spirits revived; she began to enumerate all the tasks which she had been obliged to leave undone; and announced her conviction that by the next day she would be stout enough to resume all her duties; so that Miss Wychwood had difficulty in dissuading her from setting to work immediately on the careful darning of a damaged sheet. Fortunately, she discovered herself to be so sadly weakened by her brief but severe attack that after the exertion of dressing her hair she was glad to sit quietly in her armchair, with one shawl round her shoulders and another spread over her legs, and to engage in no more strenuous occupation than that of reading the Court News in the Morning Post.

However, she was certainly on the mend, and Miss Wychwood, in spite of feeling unaccountably exhausted, was looking forward to a period of calm when she received from Jurby, as that stern hand-maid drew back the curtains from round her

bed on the following morning, the sinister tidings that Nurse
wished to have Dr Tidmarsh summoned to take a look at
Master Tom.

Thus rudely awakened, Miss Wychwood sat up with a jerk,
and said in horrified accents: 'Oh, Jurby, *no*! You can't mean
that *he* has got the influenza?'

'There isn't a doubt of it, miss,' said Jurby implacably. 'Nurse
suspicioned he was sickening for it last night, but she had the
sense to take the baby's crib into the dressing-room, so we
must hope the poor little innocent won't have caught the infection from Master Tom.'

'Indeed we must!' said Annis, flinging back the blankets, and
sliding out of bed. 'Help me to dress quickly, Jurby! I must send
a message to Dr Tidmarsh at once, and warn Wardlow to lay in
a stock of lemons, and some more pearl barley, and chickens
for broth, and – oh, I don't know, but no doubt she will!'

'You may be sure she will, miss; and as for the doctor, her
ladyship sent down a message to him the instant Nurse told her
Master Tom was taken ill. Of course,' she added gloomily, as
she handed her stockings to Miss Wychwood, 'the next thing
we shall know is that her ladyship has caught the infection.
Then we *shall* be in the suds!'

'Oh, pray don't say so, Jurby!' begged Miss Wychwood.

'I shouldn't be doing my duty by you, miss, if I didn't warn
you. In my experience, if you get one trouble coming on you
which you didn't expect you may look to get two more.'

Miss Wychwood might smile at this oracular pro-
nouncement, but it was in a mood of considerable dismay that
she went down, some minutes later, to the breakfast-parlour.
Here she found Lady Wychwood eating bread-and-butter, with
her infant daughter in her lap, and Lucilla watching this domestic picture with a kind of awed fascination. Miss Wychwood,
knowing how anxious her sister-in-law was inclined to be
whenever anything ailed her children, was much relieved to see
her looking so calm. She said, as she bent to kiss her: 'I am so
sorry, Amabel, to hear that Tom is now a victim of this horrid
influenza!'

'Yes, it is most unfortunate,' agreed her ladyship, sighing
faintly. 'But not unexpected! I thought he would be bound to

215

take it from Maria, for she had been playing with him the very day she began to feel unwell. But Nurse doesn't think it will prove to be a bad attack, and I am persuaded I may have complete faith in Dr Tidmarsh. I formed the opinion, when I was talking to him the other day, that he is a *perfectly* competent person, which, of course, one would expect a *Bath* doctor to be. The worst of it is,' she added, her eyes filling with tears, and her lips trembling a little, 'that I must not take care of Tom myself. Whenever he has been ill he has always called for *Mama*, and *never* have I left him for more than a minute! However, I do see that it's my duty to keep Baby out of the way of the infection, and I don't mean to be silly about it. I have talked it over with Nurse, and we are agreed that she is to look after Tom, and I am to have sole charge of Baby. Which I shall like very much, shan't I, my precious?'

Miss Susan Wychwood, who had been chortling to herself, responded to this by uttering a series of unintelligible remarks, which her mama interpreted as signifying agreement; and blew several bubbles.

'*What* a clever girl!' said Lady Wychwood, in a voice of doting fondness.

When the doctor arrived, he confirmed Nurse's diagnosis; warned Lady Wychwood that Tom was unlikely to make such a quick recovery as Miss Farlow's had been; and told her that she must not worry if he was still inclined to be feverish at the end of a sennight, because it was often so with obstreperous little boys whom it was almost impossible to keep quietly in their beds, since the instant their aches and pains subsided it was one person's work – or, perhaps it would be more accurate to say *two* persons' work, to prevent them from bouncing about, and even getting out of bed the instant one took one's eyes off them. 'I have two little rascals of my own, my lady!' he told her, with ill-concealed pride. 'Just such bits of quicksilver as your boy is, so you may believe I don't speak without personal experience!' He then told her that she was very wise to preserve her baby from any risk of infection; complimented her on Miss Susan Wychwood's sturdy limbs and powerful lungs; and went off leaving her to inform Annis that he was quite the most agreeable and sympathetic doctor she had ever known.

On Miss Farlow the news that Tom was ill acted like a tonic. She did indeed burst into tears, and say that she would never dare to look dear Lady Wychwood in the face again, but this threatened relapse into gloom was not of long duration. An opportunity to prove herself to be of real value had presented itself, and she seized it. She cast off her shawls, dressed herself, and emerged from her bedchamber, rather shakily, but determined to share with Nurse the task of keeping Tom quiescent. Nurse accepted her services graciously. 'For there is no denying, Miss Jurby,' said Nurse, 'that though she may be a hubble-bubble female with a tongue that runs like a fiddlestick, she does know how to handle children, and will sit for hours telling them fairy-tales, and the like, which makes it possible for me to get a bit of rest.'

It began to seem as though Jurby's bleak prophecy was going to be falsified, but two days later Betty, the young housemaid who had waited on Miss Farlow throughout her indisposition, also took to her bed, a circumstance of which Jurby informed her mistress with somewhat heartless satisfaction. 'Which all goes to show how right I was, miss!' she said, opening the doors of the big wardrobe which housed Miss Wychwood's dresses. 'I told you troubles come in threes, and if it's only Betty who's got this dratted influenza there's no harm done. Now, will you wear your blue cambric today, or shall I put out the French muslin, with the striped spencer?'

'Jurby,' said Miss Wychwood, in an uncertain voice, 'I think – I am afraid – that I too have the influenza!'

Jurby turned quickly. Miss Wychwood was sitting on the edge of her bed, still wearing her nightgown, and although the rainy spell had given way to a hot, sunny day she was shivering so violently that the teeth chattered in her head. Jurby took one look at her, and then cast the French muslin aside, and hurried towards her, muttering: 'Oh, my goodness me! I might have known this would happen!' She grasped Miss Wychwood's hands, and instantly thrust her back into bed. 'And there you'll stay, Miss Annis!' she said, in a threatening tone. 'It's to be hoped you've nothing worse the matter with you than influenza!'

'Oh, no, I don't think so!' Annis said faintly. 'It came on me during the night. I woke up, feeling as though I had been beaten all over with cudgels, and with *such* a headache—! I hoped it would pass off, if I kept my eyes shut, but it didn't, and I feel quite dreadfully ill. Don't tell her ladyship!'

'Now, don't start fretting and fussing, Miss Annis!' said Jurby, laying a hand on Miss Wychwood's brow. 'I'm bound to tell her ladyship that you're out of curl today, and mean to stay in bed, but I won't let her come into the room, I promise you!'

'Don't let Miss Lucilla come near me either!'

'The only person who'll come into this room is the doctor!' said Jurby grimly, stumping over to the window and drawing the blinds across it. 'Do you lie quiet now till I come back, and don't get into the high fidgets, fancying the house will fall down just because you're knocked up with all the trouble you've had, and mean to recruit your strength by staying in bed today, because it won't!' She sprinkled lavender-water lavishly over the pillow, drenched a handkerchief with it, which she tenderly wiped across Miss Wychwood's burning forehead, assured her that she would be as right as a trivet before the cat had time to lick her ear, and hurried away, first to send the page-boy scurrying down the hill with an urgent message for Dr Tidmarsh, and then to inform Lady Wychwood, who had not yet left her room, that Miss Annis was laid up, and that she had sent for the doctor. 'I don't doubt it's nothing worse than the influenza, my lady, but she's in a raging fever!' she said bluntly.

Lady Wychwood started up instinctively, saying: 'I'll come at once!'

'No, that you won't, my lady!' said Jurby, barring her passage to the door. 'There's nothing you can do for her, and you've got the baby to consider. Miss Annis has laid it on me not to let you, or Miss Lucilla, come near her. Very agitated she is, for fear you should insist on seeing her and get ill in consequence. If you don't want her to get into a stew, which I'm sure you don't, you'll do as she asks you.'

'Alas, I *must*!' said Lady Wychwood, much distressed. 'Why, oh, *why* didn't I send the children home with Nurse the instant Miss Farlow took ill? Why didn't I persuade Miss Annis to go to bed yesterday, and send for Dr Tidmarsh immediately? I could see she wasn't quite well, but I never dreamed she was sickening for anything, because she is so very rarely ill! I might have guessed, though! *Fool* that I was!'

'Well, my lady, I don't see that it would have done a bit of good if the doctor had come to see her yesterday, because if she had the influenza on her there was nothing he nor anyone else could have done to drive it off. And as for not guessing she was ill, I don't see that you've any call to blame yourself, for *I* didn't guess it, and – if you'll pardon me for saying so, my lady! – there's no one who knows her as well as I do! I knew she wasn't in very plump currant but I thought she was out of sorts, on account of having to dance attendance on Miss Farlow, on top of—' She checked herself, and ended her sentence by saying, at her most forbidding: 'Other things!'

They looked at one another. After a moment, Lady Wychwood said simply: 'I know.' She then turned away to pick up her rings from the dressing-table, and said, as she slid them on to her fingers: 'Give her my dear love, Jurby, and tell her that she mustn't worry about the house, or about Miss Lucilla, because she knows she can trust me to see that everything goes on just as it ought. And tell her that I shan't attempt to see her until Dr Tidmarsh says it is safe for me to do so.'

'Thank you, my lady! You can be sure I will! It will do her good to have *that* worry at least taken off her mind!' said Jurby, with real gratitude. She lingered, on the pretext of picking up a hairpin, and said: 'I shall take the liberty of saying, my lady – being as I have been Miss Annis's personal maid since she came out of the nursery – that I can't help hoping that Mr Carleton will make some other arrangement for Miss Lucilla. Not that I have anything against her, for I am sure she is a sweetly behaved young lady, but I have always felt that Miss Annis was taking too much on her shoulders when she adopted her, as one might say. Particularly now, when Miss Annis is ill, and will be in a tender state, I daresay, for some weeks. I suppose you don't know when Mr Carleton means to return to Bath? Or if he has gone away for good?'

'No,' answered Lady Wychwood. 'I am afraid I don't know, Jurby.'

Nothing more was said between them, but much that was unspoken was understood.

Dr Tidmarsh, when he arrived less than an hour later, spent much longer with Miss Wychwood than he had found it necessary to spend either with Miss Farlow or with Tom, and when he came downstairs again, he told Lady Wychwood that while Miss Wychwood was suffering from no more serious disorder than influenza the attack was a severe one. He had found her pulse tumultuous; she was extremely feverish; and although he was confident that the medicine he had prescribed for her would soon reduce the fever, he warned her ladyship that it was possible – even, he was sorry to say, probable – that she might become a trifle delirious as the day wore on. 'I tell you this, my lady, because I don't wish you be alarmed if she should wander a little in her mind. I assure you there is no cause for alarm! I hope that she will sleep, but if she should be restless you may give her a few drops of laudanum. Rather, I should say, her maid may do so, for you will, I trust, abide by your wise determination to stay out of the way of infection. I must add that the fear that you, or Miss Carleton, should run the slightest risk of taking influenza from her is preying on her mind, which is very undesirable, as I am persuaded you must recognize. In short, I consider it to be of the first importance that she should be kept as quiet as may be possible. The fewer people to enter her room the better it will be for her, while she is so feverish.'

'No one shall enter it without your permission, doctor,' said Lady Wychwood.

She was agreeably surprised, when she reported the doctor's words to Lucilla, to see a look of chagrin in Lucilla's face, for she had been inclined to think that for all her engaging ways and pretty manners she wanted heart. She had certainly not expected tears to spring to Lucilla's eyes when she was told that she must not enter Miss Wychwood's room until all danger of infection was over, and she was a good deal touched when Lucilla said forlornly: 'May I not nurse her, ma'am?'

'No, my dear, I am afraid not. Jurby is going to nurse her.'

'Oh, yes, but I could help her, couldn't I? I promise I would do just as she bade me, and even if she doesn't think I'm old enough to nurse people I could at least sit with Miss Wychwood while Jurby rests, or goes down to eat her dinner, couldn't I? I can't bear it if I am not allowed to do *anything*, because I do love her so much, and she does *everything* for me!'

Lady Wychwood was moved to put an arm round her, and to give her a slight hug. 'I know how hard it is for you, dear child,' she said sympathetically. 'I'm in the same case, you know. I would give anything to be able to look after my sister, but I must not.'

'But you have your baby to look after, ma'am, which makes it quite different!' Lucilla said urgently. 'I haven't got a baby, or *anyone* who would be a penny the worse for it if I caught influenza!'

'I can tell you of *one* who would be the worse for it, and that is my sister,' said Lady Wychwood. 'Jurby tells me that she is in a great worry about us, and has made Jurby promise not to permit either of us to go near her. I know you wouldn't wish to distress her – and to tell you the truth I think she is feeling too poorly even to *wish* to see anyone but Jurby. Wait until she is rather better! The instant Dr Tidmarsh tells us that she is no longer infectious I promise you shan't be kept out of her room. As for sitting with her now, she isn't ill enough to make it necessary for someone to be always with her, you know. Indeed, from what I know of her, I am very sure she would find it very irksome never to be left alone!'

Lucilla heaved a doleful sigh, but submitted, saying humbly that she didn't mean to be troublesome. Lady Wychwood then had the happy notion that she might like to go out with Mrs Wardlow, who had shopping to do, and buy some flowers to put in Miss Wychwood's room. The suggestion took well. Lucilla's face brightened, and she exclaimed: 'Oh, yes! I should like that of all things, ma'am! Thank you!' But when Lady Wychwood further suggested that she should write a note to Corisande to ask her to ride with her on the following morning, she shook her head, and said decidedly that nothing would prevail upon her to go pleasuring while Miss Wychwood was ill.

It was not to be expected that Miss Farlow would submit as meekly to the doctor's decree, and nor did she. Hardly had

Lucilla tripped out with the housekeeper than she subjected Lady Wychwood to an extremely trying half-hour, during which she complained passionately of Jurby's insolence in daring to shut her out of Annis's room; declared her intention of taking care of Annis herself, whatever the doctor said; delivered herself of a moving but muddled speech in support of her claims to be the only proper person to have charge of the sick-room, in which she several times begged Lady Wychwood to agree that whatever *anyone* said blood was thicker than water; and ended an agitated monologue by pointing out, in triumph, that it was of no use for her ladyship to talk of the danger of infection, because she had already had the influenza.

It was some little time before Lady Wychwood was able to bring her to reason, and a great deal of tact was necessary; but she managed it at last, and without wounding Miss Farlow's sensibilities. She said that she did not know how she and Nurse were to go on, if Maria felt she must devote herself to Annis. That was quite enough. Miss Farlow, in a gush of affection, said that she was ready to do anything in the world to ease the burdens under which she knew well dear, dear Lady Wychwood was labouring, and went off, happy in the knowledge that her services were indispensable.

Unlike Tom, or Miss Farlow, Miss Wychwood was a very good patient. She obeyed the doctor's directions, swallowed the nastiest of drugs without protest; made few demands, and still fewer complaints; and resolutely refrained from tossing and turning in what she knew to be an unavailing attempt to get into a more comfortable position. As Dr Tidmarsh had prophesied, her fever mounted, and though it was too much to say that she became delirious, her mind did wander a little, and once she started out of an uneasy doze, exclaiming: 'Oh, why doesn't he come?' in an anguished voice; but she almost immediately came to herself, and after staring for a moment in bewilderment at Jurby's face, bent over her, she murmured: 'Oh, it's you, Jurby! I thought – I must have been dreaming, I suppose.'

Jurby saw no reason to report this incident to Lady Wychwood.

The fever began to abate on the second day, but it still remained high enough to make Dr Tidmarsh shake his head; and it was not until the third day that it burnt itself out, and did not recur. Miss Wychwood emerged from this shattering attack so much exhausted that for the next twenty-four hours she had no energy to do more than swallow, with an effort, a little liquid nourishment, or to rouse herself to take more than a vague interest in whatever events were taking place in her household. For the most part of the day she slept, conscious of a feeling of profound relief that her bones were no longer being racked, and that the catherine wheel in her head was no longer making her life hideous.

The fourth day saw the arrival in Camden Place of Sir Geoffrey. He had borne with equanimity the news, conveyed to him by his dutiful wife, that Miss Farlow was in bed with influenza; a second letter, informing him that Tom had caught the infection disturbed him a little, but not enough to make him disregard Amabel's assurance that there was not the smallest need for him to be anxious; but the third letter (though she still begged him not to come to Bath), containing the news that Annis too had succumbed to the prevailing epidemic, set him on the road to Bath within an hour of his receiving it. He couldn't remember any occasion since her childhood when Annis had contracted anything more serious than a slight cold in the head, and it seemed to him that if she could fall ill there was no saying when his Amabel would also be laid low.

Lady Wychwood received him with mixed feelings. On the one hand she was overjoyed to have his strong arms round her again; on the other, she could not help feeling that his presence in the house would be an added burden in an establishment already overburdened by three invalids, one of whom was the second housemaid. She was a devoted wife, but she knew well that he did not shine in a sickroom: in fact, he was more of a liability than an asset, for, enjoying excellent health himself, he had very little experience of illness, and either caused the invalid to suffer a relapse by talking in heartily invigorating tones; or (if warned that the invalid was extremely weak) by tiptoeing into the room, addressing the patient in an awed and hushed voice, and bearing all the appearance of a man who had come to take a last farewell of one past hope of recovery.

He was considerably relieved to find that his Amabel, instead of being on a bed of sickness, was looking remarkably well, but he could not like it that she had been tied to a cradle ever since Tom had developed influenza. He thought it extraordinary that there should be no one in the household able to look after a mere infant, and could not be convinced that Amabel was neither tired nor bored. She laughed at him, and said: 'No, no, of course I'm not! Do you realize, my love, that it is the first time I have ever had Baby all to myself? Except for being unable to go to Tom, and being very anxious about Annis, I have enjoyed every minute, and shall be sorry to give her back to Nurse tomorrow. Dr Tidmarsh considers it to be perfectly safe now, but I am keeping Baby with me for one more night, for she is cutting another tooth, and is rather fretful, and I want Nurse to have a peaceful night before she takes charge of her again. You shall see Tom presently: he is laid down for his rest at the moment. Say something kind to Maria, won't you? She has been most helpful, looking after Tom.'

'Yes, very well, but tell me about Annis! I was never more shocked in my life than when I read that she was in such very queer stirrups! I could hardly believe my eyes, for I don't recall that I've ever known her to *collapse* before. It must have been a pretty violent catching?'

At this moment they were interrupted by Miss Susan Wychwood, who had been laid down to sleep on the sofa in the back drawing-room, and who now awoke, querulously demanding attention. Lady Wychwood glided into this half of the room, and was just about to pick Miss Susan up when Miss Farlow came hurrying in, and begged to be allowed to take the little darling. 'For I saw Sir Geoffrey drive up, and so, of course, I knew he would wish to talk to you, which is why I have been on the listen, thinking that very likely Baby would wake – Oh, how do you do, Cousin Geoffrey? Such a happiness to have you with us again, though I feel you will be quite alarmed, when you see our dear Annis – if Jurby permits you to see her!' She gave vent to a shrill titter. 'I daresay it will astonish you to know that Jurby has become the Queen of Camden Place: none of us dares to move hand or foot without her leave! Even *I* have not been permitted to see dear Annis until today! I promise you, I was excessively diverted, but I couldn't help pitying poor Annis, compelled to accept the services of her abigail when those of a blood-relation would have been more acceptable. However I made no demur, because I knew that, tyrant though she is, I could depend upon Jurby to take almost as good care of her mistress as I should have done, besides that there was dear Lady Wychwood to be thought of, so worn-down as she was, which made me realize that *her* need of me was greater than Annis's!'

She began to rock the infant in her arms, and Sir Geoffrey, who had listened to her with growing disfavour, beat a retreat, almost dragging his wife with him. As they mounted the stairs he said: 'Upon my word, Amabel, I begin to wish I hadn't prevailed upon Annis to engage that woman! But I don't remember that she talked us silly when she and Annis have visited us!'

'No, dear, but at home you never saw very much of her. That is what I dislike about town-houses: however commodious they may be one can never get away from the other people living in the house! And goodnatured and obliging though poor Maria is I own I have frequently been forced to shut myself into my bedchamber to escape from her. I think,' she added reflectively, 'if ever she came to live at Twynham I should give her a sitting-room of her own.'

'Came to live at Twynham?' he ejaculated. 'You don't mean that Annis means to turn her off?'

'Oh, no! But one never knows what circumstances might arise to make her chaperonage unnecessary. Annis might be married, for instance.'

He laughed at this, and said, with comfortable conviction: 'Not she! Why, she's nine-and-twenty, and a confirmed old maid!'

She said nothing, but he apparently turned her words over in his mind, for he asked her, a few minutes later, if that fellow Carleton was still in Bath.

'He went to London some ten days ago,' she replied. 'His niece, however, is still here, so I imagine he must mean to return.'

'Ay, you wrote to me that she was here, and I wish to my heart she were not! Mind you, she's a taking little thing, and I don't wish to say a word against her, but I've never approved of Annis's conduct over that business, and I never shall!'

'Mr Carleton doesn't approve of it either. He says Annis is not a fit person to take charge of Lucilla.'

'Damned impudence!' growled Sir Geoffrey. 'Not but what she ain't a fit person, and so I've said all along!'

'No, I am persuaded you are right,' she agreed. 'But I fancy – indeed, I *know* – that Mr Carleton has every intention of removing her from Annis's charge. That is why he has gone to London. You must not mention this, Geoffrey, for Lucilla knows nothing about it, and Annis told me in confidence.'

'You told me in the first letter you wrote after I left you here that you thought there was no danger of Annis's losing her heart to him. The Lord only knows why so many women do lose their hearts to him, for a more disagreeable, top-lofty fellow I wish I may never meet!'

'I own I don't like him, but I think he could make himself very agreeable to anyone he wished to please.'

'Good God, you don't mean to tell me he's been making up to Annis?' he exclaimed, in patent horror.

'You wouldn't think so, but – I don't know, Geoffrey! He doesn't flirt with her, and he seems to say detestably uncivil things to her, but if he isn't trying to fix his interests with her, I cannot help wondering why he has remained in Bath for so long.'

'Does she *like* him?' he demanded.

'I don't know that either,' she confessed. 'One wouldn't think so, because they seem to rip each other every time they meet; but I have lately suspected that Annis is not as indifferent to him as she would have me believe.'

'You must be mistaken! Annis, of all people, to have a tendre for a fellow like Carleton? It isn't possible! Why, they call him the rudest man in London! I am not surprised that he should be trying to attach her: he is notorious for his philandering, and I was very uneasy as soon as I discovered that Lucilla was his niece, for it seemed likely that he would come here, and Annis is a devilish goodlooking woman! But that *she* should be in love with *him* – no, no Amabel, you *must* be mistaken!'

'Perhaps I am, dearest. But if I am not – if she accepts an offer from him – we must learn to like him!'

'*Like him?*' echoed Sir Geoffrey, in a stupefied voice. 'I can tell you this, Amabel: nothing will ever prevail upon me to consent to such a marriage!'

'But Geoffrey—!' she expostulated. 'Your consent isn't needed! Annis isn't a minor! If she decides to marry Mr Carleton she will do so, and you will be obliged to accept him with a good grace – unless you wish to become estranged from her, which I am very sure you don't.'

He looked to be somewhat disconcerted, but said: 'If she chooses to marry Carleton, she will have to bear the consequences. But I shall warn her most solemnly that they may be more disgreeable than she foresees!'

'You will do as you think proper, dearest, but you must promise me that you won't mention this matter to her until she herself speaks of it. Recollect that it is all conjecture at present! And on no account must you say anything to distress her! But when you see her you won't wish to!'

He was not to see her, however, until the following day, a visit from Miss Farlow having left her with a headache, and a disinclination to receive any more visitors. Once the doctor had said that there was no longer any danger of infection to be feared, Lady Wychwood had found it to be impossible to exclude Miss Farlow from her room, for Annis had asked to see Lucilla, and Miss Farlow had, most unfortunately, encountered Lucilla coming out of the sickroom. A painful scene had been the outcome, for, accused of having gone slyly in to see Miss Wychwood when Jurby's back had been turned, Lucilla said indignantly that she had done nothing of the sort: Miss Wychwood had asked for her, and as for Jurby's back having been turned, Jurby had been in the room and was still there. This sent Miss Farlow scurrying away in search of Lady Wychwood, demanding hysterically to know why Lucilla had been permitted to see Miss Wychwood while *she*, her own cousin, was kept out. The end of it was Lady Wychwood, feeling that there was a certain amount of justification for Miss Farlow's threatened attack of the vapours, had said that no one was trying to keep her away from Annis: of course she might visit her! She added that she knew Maria might be trusted not to stay with her too long, or to talk too much. Miss Farlow, still convulsively sobbing, had replied that she hoped she knew better than to talk too much to persons in dear Annis's tender condition. So too did Lady Wychwood, but she doubted it, and put an end to the visit twenty minutes after Miss Farlow had entered the room, by which time Annis looked as if she was in danger of suffering a relapse.

'I think I must turn you out now, Maria,' Lady Wychwood said, smiling kindly. 'The doctor said only a quarter of an hour, you know!'

'Oh, yes, indeed! So right of him! Poor Annis is sadly pulled! I declare I was quite shocked to find her so pale and unlike herself, but, as I have been telling her, we shall soon have her to rights again. Now I shall leave her, and she must try to go to sleep, must she not? I will just draw the blinds across the window, for nothing is more disagreeable than having the light glaring at one. Not that it is not very pleasant to see the sun again after so many dull days, and they say that it is very beneficial, though I myself rather doubt that. I remember my dear mama saying that it was injurious to the female complexion, and she never went out into the open air without a veil over her face. Well, I must leave you now, dear Annis, but you may be sure I shall be always popping in to see how you go on!'

'Amabel,' said Miss Wychwood faintly, as Miss Farlow at last got herself out of the room, 'if you love me, murder our dear cousin! The first thing she said when she came in was that she wasn't going to talk to me, and she hasn't ceased talking from that moment to this.'

'I am so sorry, dearest, but there was no way of keeping her out without giving grave offence,' responded Lady Wychwood, drawing the blinds back. 'I shan't let her visit you again today, so you may be easy.'

Miss Farlow succeeded in exasperating Sir Geoffrey at the dinner-table, first by uttering a series of singularly foolish observations, and then by trying to argue with Lady Wychwood. As dinner came to an end, she got up, saying: 'Now you must excuse me, if you please! I am going up to sit with our dear invalid for a little while.'

'No, Maria,' said Lady Wychwood, 'Annis is extremely tired, and must have no more visitors today.'

'Oh,' said Miss Farlow, with an angry little titter. 'I do not rank myself as a visitor, Lady Wychwood! *You* have several times gone into Annis's room, and *some* might think *I* had a better claim to do so, being a *blood* relation! Not that I mean to say that you are not a *welcome* visitor, for I am sure she must always be pleased to see you!'

Sir Geoffrey took instant umbrage at this, told her sharply that Lady Wychwood must be the only judge of who should, and who should not be permitted to visit Annis; and added, for good measure, that if she took his advice she would not allow her to go near Annis again, since he had no doubt that it was her ceaseless bibble-babbling that had tired her.

Realizing that she had gone too far, Miss Farlow hastened to say that she had no intention of casting the least slight on dear Lady Wychwood, but she was unable to resist the temptation to add, with another of her irritating titters: 'But as for my visit having tired dear Annis, I venture to suggest that it was Lucilla who did the mischief! A great mistake, if I may say so, to have permitted her to visit—'

'Shall we go up to the drawing-room?' interposed Lady Wychwood, in a voice of quiet authority. 'I think you are rather tired yourself, Maria. Perhaps you would prefer to retire to bed. We must not forget that it is only a very few days since you too were ill.'

Finally quelled, Miss Farlow did retire, but in so reluctant and lingering a way that she was still within tongue-shot when Sir Geoffrey said: 'Well done, Amabel! Lord, what a gabster! Ay, and worse! The idea of her having the brass to say that it was Lucilla who exhausted Annis! A bigger piece of spite I never heard! More likely your visit did my sister a great deal of good, my dear!'

'Of course it did,' said Lady Wychwood. 'Don't look so downcast, child! You must surely be aware that poor Maria is eaten up with jealousy. And allowances must be made for people who are convalescent from the influenza: it often makes them cantankersome! Pray let us put her out of our minds! I was wondering whether it would entertain you to play a game of backgammon with Sir Geoffrey until Limbury brings in the tea-tray?'

But hardly had the board been set out than it had to be put away again, for a late caller arrived, in the person of Lord Beckenham. He had come to inquire after Miss Wychwood. He had only that very afternoon heard of her indisposition, for he had been obliged to visit the Metropolis at the beginning of the week. He explained at somewhat tedious length that he had stopped to eat his dinner at the Ship before continuing his journey, why he had done so, how he had come by the distressing news, and how he had been unable to wait until the next day before coming to discover how Miss Wychwood was going on. He did not know what she, and her ladyship, must have been thinking of him for not having called days ago.

He stayed to drink tea with them, and by the time he left Sir Geoffrey was heartily sick of him, and having seen him off the premises, informed his wife that if he had to listen to any more forty-jawed persons that day he would go straight off to bed.

CHAPTER FIFTEEN

Miss Wychwood, next morning, declared herself to be so much better as to be in a capital way. Jurby did not think that she looked to be in a capital way at all, and strenuously opposed her determination to get up. 'I *must* get up!' said Miss Wychwood, rather crossly. 'How am I ever to be myself again, if you keep me in bed, which of all things I most detest? Besides, my brother is coming to see me this morning, and I will *not* allow him to find me languishing in my bed, looking as if I were on the point of cocking up my toes!'

'We'll see what the doctor says, miss!' said Jurby.

But when Dr Tidmarsh came to visit his patient, just as her almost untouched breakfast had been removed, he annoyed

Jurby by saying that it would do Miss Wychwood good to leave her bed for an hour or two, and lie on the sofa. 'I don't think she should dress herself, but her pulse has been normal now since yesterday, and it won't harm her to slip on a dressing-gown, and sit up for a little while.'

'Heaven bless you, doctor!' said Miss Wychwood.

'Ah, that sounds more like yourself, ma'am!' he said laughingly.

'Begging your pardon, sir,' said Jurby. 'Miss Wychwood is not at all like herself! And it is my duty to inform you, sir, that she swallowed only three spoonfuls of the pork jelly she had for her dinner last night, and has had nothing for her breakfast but some tea, and a few scraps of toast!'

'Well, well, we must tempt her appetite, mustn't we! I have no objection to her having a little chicken, say, or even a slice of boiled lamb, if she should fancy it.'

'The truth is that I don't fancy anything,' confessed Annis. 'I have quite lost my appetite! But I will try to eat some chicken, I promise!'

'That's right!' he said. 'Spoken like the sensible woman I know you to be, ma'am!'

Miss Wychwood might be a sensible woman, but the attack of influenza had left her feeling much more like one of the foolish, tearful creatures whom she profoundly despised, for ever lying on sofas, with smelling-salts clutched in their feeble hands, and always dependent on some stronger character to advise and support them. She had heard that influenza often left its victims subject to deep dejection, and she now knew that this was true. Never before had she been so blue-devilled that she felt it was a pity she had ever been born, or that it was too much trouble to try to rouse herself from her listless depression. She told herself that this contemptible state really did arise from her late illness; and that to lie in bed, with nothing better to do than to think how weak and miserable she felt, was merely to encourage her blue-devils. So she refused to yield to the temptation to remain in bed, but got up presently, found that her legs had become inexplicably wayward ('as though the bones had been taken out of them!' she told Jurby, trying to laugh), and was glad to accept the support of Jurby's strong arm on her somewhat tottery progress to her dressing-table. A glance at her reflection in the mirror did nothing to improve her spirits. 'Heavens, Jurby!' she exclaimed. 'What a fright I am! I have a good mind to send you out to buy a pot of rouge for me!'

'Well, I wouldn't buy you any such thing, Miss Annis! Nor you don't look a fright. Just a trifle hagged, which is only to be expected after such a nasty turn as you've had. When I've given your hair a good brushing, and pinned it up under the pretty lace cap you bought only last week, you won't know your-self!'

'I don't know myself now,' said Miss Wychwood. 'Oh, well! I suppose it doesn't signify: Sir Geoffrey never notices whether one is looking one's best or one's worst – but I do wish I had asked you to paper my hair last night!'

'Well, your hair don't signify either, miss, for I shall tuck it into your cap,' replied her unsympathetic handmaid. 'And it's such a warm day there's no reason why you shouldn't wear that lovely dressing-gown you had made for you, and haven't worn above two or three times – the satin one, with the blue posies embroidered all over it, and the lace fichu. That will make you feel much more like yourself, won't it?'

'I hope so, but I doubt it,' said Miss Wychwood.

However, when she had been arrayed in the expensive dress-ing-gown, and had herself tied the strings of the lace cap under her chin, she admitted that she didn't look *quite* such a mean bit.

Sir Geoffrey was admitted shortly after eleven o'clock, and so far from not noticing that she was not looking her best he was so much shocked by her white face, and heavy eyes that he forgot the injunctions laid upon him and ejaculated: 'Good God, Annis! Dashed if I've ever seen you look so knocked-up! Poor old lady, what a devil of a time you've been having! And when I think that it was that infernal bagpipe who gave it you I could – Well, never mind!' he added, belatedly remembering his instructions. 'No use working ourselves up! Now, I'll tell you what Amabel and I wish you to do, and that is to come to Twynham as soon as you're well enough to travel, and pay us a long visit. How would that be?'

'Delightful! Thank you: how kind of you both! But tell me, how do you find Tom?'

He never needed much encouragement to talk about his children, and spent the rest of his brief stay thus innocuously employed. When he got up to go, he kissed her cheek, gave her an encouraging pat on the shoulder, and said: 'There, no one can accuse *me* of having stayed too long, or talked you to death, can they?'

'Certainly not! It has done me a great deal of good to have a chat with you, and I hope you'll give me a look in later on.'

'Ay, to be sure I will! Ah, is that you, Jurby? Come to turn me out, have you? What a dragon you are! Well, Annis, be a good girl, and see how fast you can get back into high force! I am going to take Amabel for an airing now: just a gentle walk, you know; but I'll look in on you when we come back.'

He then went off, and Jurby removed one of the cushions which was propping her mistress up, and adjured her to close her eyes, and have a nap before her nuncheon was brought up to her.

Lady Wychwood, having reluctantly handed her daughter over to Nurse, was very well pleased to go for an ambling walk with Sir Geoffrey, and not sorry when Lucilla refused an invitation to accompany them. She set off in the direction of the London Road, leaning on her husband's arm, and saying: 'How agreeable it is to be with you again, dearest! Now we can have a comfortable cose, without poor Maria's breaking in on us!'

'Yes, that's what I thought, when I coaxed you to come for a walk with me,' he said. 'Devilish good notion of mine, wasn't it?'

But he would not have thought it a good notion had he known that little more than ten minutes later Mr Carleton would be seeking admittance to Miss Wychwood's house.

Limbury, opening the door to Mr Carleton, said that Miss Wychwood was not at home to visitors. Miss Wychwood, he said, had been unwell, and had not yet left her room.

'So I have already been informed,' said Mr Carleton. 'Take my card up to her, if you please!'

Limbury received the card from him, and said, with a slight bow: 'I will have it conveyed to Miss's room, sir.'

'Well, don't keep me standing on the doorstep!' said Mr Carleton impatiently.

Limbury, an excellent butler, found himself at a loss, for he had never before encountered a morning caller of Mr Carleton's calibre. Vulgar persons he could deal with; no other of Miss Wychwood's friends would have demanded admittance when told that Miss Wychwood was not at home; and Sir Geoffrey, who disliked Mr Carleton, as Limbury was well aware, would certainly wish him to be excluded.

'I regret, sir, that it is not possible for you to see Miss Wychwood. Today is the first time she has been well enough to sit up for an hour or two, and her maid informs me that she had hardly enough strength to walk across the floor to the sofa. So I am persuaded you will understand that you cannot see her today.'

'No, I shan't,' said Mr Carleton, rudely brushing past him into the hall. 'Shut the door! Now take my card up to your mistress immediately, and tell her that I wish to see her!'

Limbury was affronted by Mr Carleton's unceremonious entrance, and he by no means relished being given peremptory commands. He was about to reply with freezing dignity when a suspicion entered his head (he described it later to Mrs Wardlow as a blinding light) that he was confronting a man who was violently in love. To gentlemen in that condition much had to be forgiven, so he forgave Mr Carleton, and said in the fatherly way he spoke to Master Tom: 'Now you know I can't do that, sir! I'll tell Miss you called, but you can't expect to see her when she has only just got up out of her bed!'

'I not only expect to see her, but I am going to see her!' replied Mr Carleton.

Fortunately for Limbury, he was rescued from his predicament by the appearance on the scene of Jurby, who came down the stairs, dropped the hint of a curtsy, and said: 'Were you wishful to see Miss Annis, sir?'

'Not only wishful, but determined to see her! Are you her abigail?'

'Yes, sir, I am.'

'Good! I have heard her speak of you, and I think your name

is Jurby, and that you have been with Miss Wychwood for many years. Am I right?'

'I have been with her ever since she was a child, sir.'

'Good again! You must know her very well, and can tell me whether it will harm her to see me.'

'I don't think it would *harm* her, sir, but I cannot take it upon myself to say whether she will be willing to receive you.'

'Ask her!'

She seemed to consider him dispassionately for a moment; and then said: 'Certainly, sir. If you will be pleased to wait in the drawing-room, I will do so.'

She turned and went majestically up the stairs again; and Limbury, recovering from the shock of seeing the most formidable member of the household yield without a sign of disapproval to Mr Carleton's outrageous demand, conducted him to the drawing-room. He was immensely interested in the unprecedented situation, and his enjoyment of it was no longer marred by fear of Sir Geoffrey's wrath, because if Sir Geoffrey came the ugly he could now foist the blame of Mr Carleton's intrusion on to Jurby.

Mr Carleton had not long to wait before Jurby came into the drawing-room, saying: 'Miss Annis will be happy to receive you, sir. Please to come with me!' She conducted him up the second pair of stairs, and paused on the landing, and said: 'I must warn you, sir, that Miss Annis is by no means fully restored to health. You will find her very pulled by the fever, and I hope you won't agitate her.'

'I hope so too,' he replied.

She seemed to be satisfied with this reply, for she opened the door into Miss Wychwood's bedroom, and ushered him in, saying in a voice wholly devoid of interest: 'Mr Carleton, miss.'

She stayed, holding the door open, for a few moments because when she had carried the news of Mr Carleton's arrival to her mistress Miss Wychwood had behaved in an extremely agitated way, and had seemed not to know whether she wished to see him or not. She had started up from her recumbent position, uttering distractedly: 'Mr Carleton? Oh, no, I cannot

– Jurby, are you hoaxing me? Is he indeed here? Oh, why must he come back just when I am so hagged and miserably unwell? I won't see him! He is the most detestable – Oh, whatever am I to do?'

'Well, miss, if you wish me to send him away, I'll try my best to do it, but from the looks of him it's likely he'll order me to get out of the way, and come charging up the stairs, and the next thing you'll know he'll be knocking at your door – if he don't walk in without knocking, which wouldn't surprise me!'

Miss Wychwood gave an uncertain laugh. '*Odious* man! Take this horrid shawl away! If I *must* see him, I will *not* do so lying on the sofa as though I were dying of a deep decline!'

So, when Mr Carleton entered, he found Miss Wychwood seated at one end of the sofa, the train of her dressing-gown lying in soft folds at her feet and her glorious hair hidden under a lace cap. She had managed to regain a measure of composure, and said, in a tolerably steady voice: 'How do you do? You must forgive me for receiving you like this: Jurby will have told you, I daresay, that I have been unwell, and am not yet permitted to leave my room.'

As she spoke, she tried to rise, but her knees shook so much that she was obliged to clutch at the arm of the sofa to save herself from falling. But even as she tottered Mr Carleton, crossing the room in two strides, caught her in his arms, and held her close, breast to breast, and fiercely kissed her.

'Oh!' gasped Miss Wychwood, making a feeble attempt to thrust him off. 'How *dare* you? Let me go at once!'

'You'd tumble over if I did,' he said, and kissed her again.

'No, no, you must not! Oh, what an abominable person you are! I wish I had never met you!' declared Miss Wychwood, abandoning the unequal struggle to free herself, and subsiding limply within his powerful arms, and shedding tears into his shoulder.

At this point, Jurby, smiling dourly, withdrew, apparently feeling that Mr Carleton was very well able to deal with Miss Wychwood without her assistance.

'Don't cry, my precious wet-goose!' said Mr Carleton, planting a third kiss under Miss Wychwood's ear, which, as her head was resting on his shoulder, was the only place available to him.

A watery chuckle showed that Miss Wychwood's sense of humour had survived the ravages of influenza. 'I am not a wet-goose!'

'You can't expect me to believe you if you don't stop crying at once!' he said severely. He swept her off her feet as he spoke, and set her down again on the sofa, himself sitting beside her, taking her hands in his, and pressing a kiss into each pink palm. 'Poor Honey!' he said. 'What a wretched time you've been having, haven't you?'

'Yes, but it is very unhandsome of you to call me a poor Honey!' she said, trying for a rallying note. 'You had as well tell me that I've become a positive antidote! My glass has told me so already, so it won't come as a shock to me!'

'Your glass lies. I see no change in you, except that you are paler than I like, and are wearing a cap, which I've not known you to do before.' He surveyed it critically. 'Very fetching!' he approved. 'But I think I prefer to see your guinea-curls. Will you feel obliged to wear caps when we are married?'

'But – *are* we going to be married?' she said.

'Well, of course we are! You don't suppose I'm offering you a *carte blanche*, do you?'

That made her laugh. 'I shouldn't be surprised if you were, for you are quite abominable, you know!'

'Wouldn't you be surprised?' he demanded.

Her eyes sank before the hard, questioning look in his. She said: 'You needn't glare at me! I only meant it for a joke! Of course it would surprise me!'

'Unamusing! Are you afraid I should be unfaithful to you? Is that why you said "*are* we to be married?" as though you still had doubts?'

'No, I'm not afraid of that. After all, if you did become unfaithful I should only have myself to blame, shouldn't I?'

The hard look vanished; he smiled. 'I don't think you would find many people to agree that *you* were to blame for *my* sins!'

'Anyone with a particle of commonsense would agree with

me, because if you were to set up a mistress it would be because you had become bored with me.'

'Oh, if that's the case we need not worry! But you do still have doubts, don't you?'

'Not when you are with me,' she said shyly. 'Only when I'm alone, and think of all the difficulties – what a very big step it would be – how much my brother would dislike it – I wonder if perhaps it wouldn't be a mistake to marry you. And then I think that it would be a much greater mistake *not* to marry you, and I end by not knowing *what* I want to do! Mr Carleton, are you *sure* you want to marry me, and – and that I'm not a mere passing fancy?'

'What you are trying to ask me is whether I am sure we shall be happy, isn't it?'

'Yes, I suppose that is what I mean,' she sighed.

'Well, I can't answer you. How can I be *sure* that we shall be happy when neither of us has had any experience of marriage? All I can tell you is that I am perfectly sure I want to marry you, and equally sure that you are not a "mere passing fancy" of mine – what a damned silly question to ask me! If I had ever been such a shuttlehead as to have asked one of many passing fancies to marry me, I shouldn't be a bachelor today! – and there are two other things I am *sure* of! One is that I have never cared for any of the charmers with whom I've had agreeable connexions as I care for you; and another is that I have never in my life wanted anything more than I want to win you for my *own* – to love, and to cherish, and to guard – Oh, damn it, Annis, how can I make you believe that I love you with my whole heart and body, and mind?' He broke off, and said sharply: 'What have I said to make you cry? Tell me!'

'Nothing! I d-don't know why I began to cry. I think it must be because I'm so happy, and I've been feeling so dreadfully miserable!' she replied, wiping her tears away, and trying to smile.

Mr Carleton took her back into his arms. 'You're thoroughly knocked-up, sweetheart. *Damn* that woman for having foisted her influenza on to you! Kiss me!'

'I won't!' said Miss Wychwood, between tears and laughter. 'It would be a most improper thing for me to do, and you have *no* right to fling orders at me as though I were one of your bits of muslin, and I won't submit to being ridden over rough-shod!'

'Hornet!' said Mr Carleton, and put an end to further re-criminations by fastening his lips to hers.

Not the most daring of her previous suitors had ventured even to slide an arm round her waist, for although she enjoyed light-hearted flirtation, she never gave her flirts any cause to think she would welcome more intimate approaches. She had supposed that she must have a cold, celibate disposition, for she had always found the mere thought of being kissed, and (as she phrased it) mauled by any gentleman of her acquaintance shudderingly distasteful. She had once confessed this to Amabel, and had privately thought Amabel's response to be so foolishly sentimental as to be unworthy of consideration. Amabel had said: 'When you fall in love, dearest, you won't find it at all distasteful, I promise you.' And sweet, silly little Amabel had been right! When Mr Carleton had caught Miss Wychwood into his arms, and had so ruthlessly kissed her, she had not found it at all distasteful; and when he did it again it seemed the most natural thing in the world to return his embrace. He felt the responsive quiver that ran through her, and his arms tightened round her, just as someone knocked on the door. Miss Wychwood tore herself free, uttering: 'Take care! This may well be my sister, or Maria!'

It was neither. The youngest of her three housemaids came in, bearing a jug and a glass on a tray. At sight of Mr Carleton this damsel stopped on the threshold, and stood goggling at him, with her eyes starting from their sockets.

'What the devil do you want?' demanded Mr Carleton, pardonably annoyed.

'Please, sir, I don't want anything!' said the intruder, trembling with terror. 'I didn't know Miss had a visitor! Mrs Wardlow told me to bring the fresh barley-water up to Miss, being as Betty is sick!'

'*Barley-water?*' ejaculated Mr Carleton, in revolted accents. 'Good God! No wonder that you are in low spirits if that's what they give you to drink!'

'It has lemon in it, sir!' offered the maid.

'So much the worse! Take it away, and tell Limbury to send up some burgundy! *My* orders!'

'Yes, sir, b-but what will I say to Mrs Wardlow, if you p-please, sir?'

Miss Wychwood intervened. 'You need say nothing to her, Lizzy. Just set the barley-water on that table, and desire Limbury to send up a bottle of burgundy for Mr Carleton ... And when it comes *you* will drink it,' she informed her visitor, as soon as Lizzy had scurried away. '*I* don't want it!'

'You may think you don't, but it is exactly what you *do* want!' he retorted. 'Next they will be bringing you a bowl of gruel!'

'Oh, no!' said Miss Wychwood demurely. 'Dr Tidmarsh says that I may have a little chicken now that I am so much better. Or even a slice of boiled mutton.'

'That ought to tempt you!' he said sardonically.

She smiled. 'Well, to tell you the truth, I haven't any appetite, so it doesn't much signify what they bring me to eat!'

'Oh, how much I wish I had you under my own roof!'

'So that you could bullock me into eating my dinner, Mr Carleton? I shouldn't like that at all!' she said, shaking her head.

'If you don't stop calling me *Mr Carleton*, my girl, we shall very soon find ourselves at dagger-drawing!'

'Oh, that terrifies me into obedience – Oliver! What a shocking thing it would be if we were to fall out!'

He smiled, and raised her hand to his lips. 'Shocking indeed! And so unprecedented!'

'It's all very well for you to kiss my hand,' said Miss Wychwood austerely, 'but what you *ought* to do is to promise that you will never quarrel with me again! But as I have known ever since I made your acquaintance that you haven't the least notion of conducting yourself with elegance or propriety, I imagine it is ridiculous of me to expect that of you!'

'Quite ridiculous! I never promise what I know I can't perform!'

'*Odious* creature!'

He grinned at her. 'Should I be less odious if I humbugged you with court-promises? Of course we shall quarrel, for I have a naggy temper, and you, I thank God, are not one of those meek women who say yes and amen to everything! Which reminds me that I have hit on a solution to the problem of what to do with Lucilla to which I do expect you to say yes and amen!'

'But when we are married she will naturally live with us!'

'Oh, no, she will not!' he said. 'If you imagine, my loved one, that I am prepared to stand by complacently while my bride devotes herself to my niece, rid yourself of that idiotic notion! Think for a moment! Do you really wish to include a third person – and one who must be chaperoned wherever she goes! – into our household? If you do, I do not! I want a *wife*, not a chaperon for my niece!' He took her hands, and held them in a compelling grasp. 'A companion, Annis! Someone who may say, if I suggest to her that we should jaunt over to Paris, that she doesn't feel inclined to go to Paris, but who won't say: "But how can I leave Lucilla?" Do you understand what I mean?'

'Oh, my dear, of course I do! I don't wish to include a third person in our household, and I must own that fond though I am of Lucilla I do find that the task of looking after her is heavier than I had supposed it would be. But how unkind it would be to send her to live with someone else, for no fault of hers, but merely because we didn't wish to be bothered with her! If she knew, and liked, any of her paternal aunts, or cousins, the case would be different, but she doesn't, and thanks to that miserable aunt the only friends the poor child has are those she has made here, in Bath!'

'Yes, exactly so! What do you say to giving her into Mrs Stinchcombe's charge until it is time for her to make her come-out?'

Miss Wychwood sat up with a jerk. 'Oliver! Of course it would be the very thing for her, and what she would like best, I am very sure. But would Mrs Stinchcombe be willing to take her?'

'Perfectly willing. In fact, it was settled between us this morning! I came here straight from Laura Place. It was Mrs Stinchcombe who told me that you had been ill, and – Oh, lord, *now* what?'

But the timid tap on the door merely heralded the reappearance of Lizzy, who came in carrying a silver salver, on which stood a decanter, two of Miss Wychwood's best Waterford wineglasses, and a wooden biscuit-tub with a silver lid. Mr Carleton, perceiving that the decanter was in imminent danger of sliding off the salver, got up quickly, and went to take the tray into his own hands, saying: 'That's a good girl! Run along now!'

'Yes, sir! Thank you, sir!' said Lizzy, and slid out of the room in a manner strongly suggestive of one escaping from a tiger's cage.

Miss Wychwood, observing with some surprise her cherished Waterford glasses, said: 'What in the world possessed Limbury to send up the best glasses? I only use them for parties! I collect you frightened him out of his wits, just as you frightened poor Lizzy!'

'No such thing!' said Mr Carleton, pouring burgundy into one of the best glasses. 'Limbury is doing justice to this occasion. Good butlers are always awake upon every suit! Here you are, love: see if my prescription doesn't pluck you up!'

Miss Wychwood took the glass, but refused to drink the burgundy unless Mr Carleton joined her. So he poured out a glass for himself, and was just raising it to toast her when Miss Farlow burst into the room, powerfully agitated, stopped dead on the threshold, and exclaimed: '*Well!*'

Miss Wychwood was startled into spilling some of the burgundy. She set her glass down, and tried to rub away the stains from the skirt of her gown with her handkerchief, saying crossly: 'Really, Maria, it is too bad of you! *Look* what you have made me do! What do you want?'

'I am here, Annis, to preserve you from the consequences of your own folly!' said Miss Farlow. 'How *could* you receive a member of the Male Sex in your bedchamber, and in your *dressing-gown?* Sir, I must request you to leave immediately!'

'You don't mean to tell me that's a dressing-gown?' interrupted Mr Carleton, a dangerous gleam in his eyes. 'Well, it's by far the most elegant one I've ever been privileged to see, and

242

I suppose I must have seen scores of 'em in my time – paid for them too!'

'For goodness' sake, Oliver—!' Miss Wychwood said, in an imploring whisper.

Trembling with outraged propriety, Miss Farlow uttered a terrible indictment of Mr Carleton's manners, morals, and shameless disregard of the rules of conduct governing any man venturing to call himself a *gentleman*. A shattering retort rose to his lips, but he bit it back, because he saw that Miss Wychwood was by no means enjoying this encounter, and merely said: 'Well, now that you have convinced me, ma'am, that I am so far sunk in moral turpitude as to be past praying for, may I suggest that you withdraw from this scene of vice?'

'Nothing,' declared Miss Farlow, 'will prevail upon me to leave this room while you remain in it, sir! I do not know by what means you forced yourself into it—'

'Oh, do, pray, Maria, stop talking such fustian nonsense, and go away!' begged Miss Wychwood. 'Mr Carleton did not force his way into my room! He came at my invitation, and if I have to listen to any more ranting from you I shall go into strong hysterics!'

'Sir Geoffrey entrusted you to my care, Annis, and never shall it be said of me that I betrayed the confidence he reposed in me! Since Jurby has been so unmindful of her duty – not that that surprises me, for I have always considered that you permitted her *far* too much license, so that she has grown to be so big in her own esteem that—'

'Oh, cut line, woman!' said Mr Carleton, striding to the door, and opening it. 'Miss Wychwood has asked you to go away, and I have every intention of seeing to it that you do go away! Don't keep me waiting!'

'And leave my sacred charge unprotected? Never!' declared Miss Farlow heroically.

'Oh, for God's sake—!' snapped Mr Carleton, at the end of his patience. 'What the devil do you suppose I'm going to do to her? Rape her? I will give you thirty seconds to leave this room, and if you are not on the other side of the door by that time I shall eject you forcibly!'

'Brute!' ejaculated Miss Farlow, bursting into tears. 'Offering violence to a defenceless female! Only wait until Sir Geoffrey knows of this!'

He paid no heed, but kept his eyes on his watch. Miss Farlow hesitated between heroism and fright. He shut his watch with a snap, restored it to his pocket, and advanced purposefully towards her. Miss Farlow's courage failed. She uttered a shriek, and ran out of the room.

Mr Carleton shut the door, and applied himself to the more agreeable task of soothing Miss Wychwood's lacerated nerves, in which he succeeded so well that in a very short space of time her racing pulses had steadied to a normal rate, and she not only allowed herself to be coaxed to swallow the rest of the burgundy in her glass, but even to nibble a biscuit.

Miss Farlow's state was less happy. The intelligence, conveyed to her by Jurby, who was hovering on the landing, that Miss Wychwood had a visitor with her, and did not wish to be disturbed, had aroused all her smouldering jealousy. She had told Jurby that she had had no business to introduce a visitor into Miss Wychwood's room, and was unwise enough to say: 'You should have asked leave to do so from me, or from her ladyship! Who is this visitor?'

'One that will do her more good than you ever will, miss!' had said Jurby, goaded into retort. 'It is Mr Carleton!'

Miss Farlow had been at first incredulous, and then sincerely shocked. In her chaste mind, every man – except, of course, doctors, fathers, and brothers – figured as a potential menace to a maiden's virtue. Even had it been Lord Beckenham who was closeted with Miss Wychwood she would have felt it to be her duty to have pointed out to him the impropriety of his visiting a lady in her bedchamber, who was wearing nothing but a dressing-gown over her nightdress. But Lord Beckenham – such a perfect gentleman! – would never have dreamt of compromising a lady in such a scandalous fashion. As for Annis, not only tolerating, but actually *encouraging* Mr Carleton in his nefarious conduct, she could only suppose that her poor dear cousin had taken leave of her senses. Since she (a defenceless female) had been unable to prevail upon this Brute to withdraw from Miss Wychwood's room, there was only one thing to be done, and that was to pour the whole story into Sir

Geoffrey's ears the instant he returned from his walk with Lady Wychwood. With this intention, she hurried downstairs, mentally rehearsing her role in the forthcoming drama, and working herself up into a hysterical state. She encountered Sir Geoffrey just as he was about to enter the drawing-room.

He and Lady Wychwood had returned to the house some minutes earlier. Fortunately for Lady Wychwood, she had gone up immediately to the nursery, to assure herself that Tom had taken no harm from his first expedition, since his illness, into the garden, so she was spared the horrid news Miss Farlow was only too anxious to recount to her.

Sir Geoffrey was not so fortunate. Having regaled himself with a glass of sherry, he mounted the stairs to the first floor, and was instantly assailed by Miss Farlow, who came stumbling down the stairs, uttering in a hysterical voice: 'Cousin Geoffrey! Oh, Cousin Geoffrey! Thank God you are come!'

Sir Geoffrey eyed her with disfavour. He was unaccustomed to females who flew into distempered freaks, and he had already taken Miss Farlow in dislike. He said: 'What the deuce is the matter with you, Maria?'

'Oh, nothing, nothing – except that I have never been so shocked in my life! It is Annis! You must go up to her room immediately!'

'Eh?' said Sir Geoffrey, startled. 'Annis? Why, what's amiss with her?'

'I do not know how to tell you! If it were not my duty to do so, I could not bring myself to disclose to you what will curl your liver!' said Miss Farlow, extracting the last ounce of drama from the situation.

Sir Geoffrey was incensed. 'For God's sake, Maria, stop talking as if you were taking part in a Cheltenham tragedy, and tell me what has put you into this taking! Curl my liver indeed! Without any more ado, answer me this! – Is there anything wrong with my sister?'

'Everything!' declared Miss Farlow, clinging to the most important role of her life.

'Balderdash!' said Sir Geoffrey. 'It's my belief you're getting to be queer in your attic, Maria! Never mind my liver! *What has happened to my sister?*'

245

'That Man,' disclosed Miss Farlow, 'has been closeted with her since you and dear Lady Wychwood left the house! And he is still with her! Had I known that he had forced his way into the house, and that Jurby was so lost to all sense of her duty as to admit him into Annis' bedchamber – but no doubt he bribed her to do it! – I should have summoned James to cast him out of the house! But I was with Tom, in the garden, and I knew nothing until I came in, and was just about to pop into Annis's room, when Jurby stopped me, saying that Annis was engaged. "Engaged?" I said. "She has a visitor with her, and she don't wish to be disturbed," she said. You may depend upon it that I insisted on her telling me who had come to visit Annis without so much as a by your leave! And then Jurby told me that it was That Man!'

'*What* man?' demanded Sir Geoffrey.

'Mr Carleton!' said Miss Farlow, shuddering.

'Carleton? What the devil is he doing in my sister's room?'

'Carousing!' said Miss Farlow, reaching her grand climax.

It fell sadly flat. Sir Geoffrey said testily: 'I wish to God you wouldn't talk such nonsense, Maria! Next I suppose you'll tell me my sister was *carousing* too!'

'Alas, yes!'

'It seems to me that it's you who have been carousing!' said Sir Geoffrey severely. 'You had best go and sleep it off!'

With this he went on up the stairs to the second floor, paying no heed whatsoever to the protests, the assurances that she never touched strong liquor; or the impassioned entreaties to listen to her, which Miss Farlow addressed to him.

He entered Miss Wychwood's room without ceremony, and was confronted by the spectacle of his sister seated beside Mr Carleton on the sofa, supported by his arm, and with her head on his shoulder.

'Upon my word!' he ejaculated thunderously. 'What the devil does this mean?'

'Oh, pray don't shout!' said Miss Wychwood, straightening herself.

Mr Carleton rose. 'How do you do, Wychwood? I've been waiting for you! I imagine you must know what the devil it

246

means, but before we go into that, I want to know what the devil *you* mean by planting that atrocious woman on your sister! Never in the whole of my existence have I encountered anyone who talked more infernal twaddle, or who had less notion of how to look after sick persons! She burst in on us, just as I had succeeded in getting Annis to drink a glass of burgundy – which, if I may say so, will do her far more good than barley-water! See to it that she has a glass with her dinner, will you? – and had the damned impudence to say that nothing would prevail upon her to leave the room while I remained in it! I can only assume that she thought Annis was in danger of being raped! If I hadn't threatened to throw her out, she'd be here still, upsetting Annis with all her ravings and rantings, and I-will-not permit her, or anyone else, to upset Annis!'

Sir Geoffrey disliked Mr Carleton, but he found himself so much in sympathy with him that instead of requesting him, with cold dignity, to leave the house, which he had meant to do, he said: 'I didn't plant her on Annis! All I did was to *suggest* to Annis that she would be a suitable person to act as her companion!'

'*Suitable?*' interpolated Mr Carleton scathingly.

Sir Geoffrey glared at him, but being a just man he felt himself obliged to say: 'No, of course she's not suitable, but I didn't know *then* that she was such an infernal gabster, and I didn't know until today that she's touched in her upper works! I shall certainly take care she don't come near Annis again – though what right *you* have to interfere I'm quite at a loss to understand! What's more, I'll thank you to leave *me* to look after my sister!'

'That,' said Mr Carleton, 'brings us back to the start of our conversation. Your sister, Wychwood, has done me the honour to accept my hand in marriage. That's what the devil this means, and it also explains the right I have to concern myself with her welfare!'

'Well, I won't have it!' said Sir Geoffrey. 'I refuse to give my consent to a marriage of which I utterly disapprove!'

'Oh, Geoffrey, don't! *Pray* don't get into a quarrel!' begged Miss Wychwood, pressing her hands against her throbbing temples. 'You are making my head ache again, *both* of you! I am very sorry to displease you, Geoffrey, but I am not a silly schoolgirl, and I haven't decided to marry Oliver on an impulse! And as for giving your consent, your consent isn't necessary! I'm not under age, I'm not your ward, and never was your ward, and there is nothing you can do to stop me marrying Oliver!'

'We'll see that!' he said ominously. 'Let me make it plain to you—'

'No, don't try to do that!' intervened Mr Carleton. 'She's far too exhausted to talk any more! Make it plain to me instead! I suggest we go down to the book-room, and discuss the matter in private. We shall do much better without female interference, you know!'

This made Miss Wychwood lift her head from between her hands, and say indignantly: 'This has nothing to do with Geoffrey! And if you think I am going to sit meekly here while you and he—'

'Come, come!' said Mr Carleton. 'Where is your sense of decorum? Your brother, very properly, wishes to discover what my circumstances are, what settlement I mean to make on you—'

'No, I do not!' interrupted Sir Geoffrey angrily. 'Everyone knows you're swimming in lard, and settlements don't come into it, because if I have anything to say to it there will be no marriage!'

'You have nothing to say to it, Geoffrey, and no right to meddle in my affairs!'

'Oh, that's going too far!' said Mr Carleton. 'He may not have the right to *meddle*, but he has every right to try to dissuade you from making what he believes would be a disastrous marriage. A poor sort of brother he would be if he didn't!'

Taken aback, Sir Geoffrey blinked at him. 'Well – well, I'm glad that you at least realize that!' he said lamely.

'Well, I do not realize it!' struck in Miss Wychwood.

'Of course you don't!' said Mr Carleton soothingly. 'In another moment you'll be saying that the marriage has nothing to do with me either, my lovely wet-goose! So we will postpone this discussion until tomorrow. Oh, no! don't look daggers at me! I never come to cuffs with females who are too knocked-up to be a match for me!'

She gave a choke of laughter. 'Oh, how detestable you are!' she sighed.

'That sounds more like you,' he approved. He bent over her, and kissed her. 'You are worn out, and must go back to bed, my sweet. Promise me you won't get up again today!'

'I doubt if I could,' she said ruefully. 'But if you and Geoffrey mean to quarrel over me—'

'It takes two to make a quarrel. I can't answer for Wychwood, but I have no intention of quarrelling, so you may be easy on that head!'

'*Easy?* When you spend your life quarrelling, and being disagreeable to people for no reason at all? I am not in the least easy!'

'Hornet!' he said, and went out of the room, thrusting Sir Geoffrey before him. 'I don't think much of your strategy, Wychwood,' he said, as they began to descend the stairs, 'Abusing me won't answer your purpose: it will merely set up her bristles.'

Sir Geoffrey said stiffly: 'I must make it plain to you, Carleton, that the thought of my sister's marriage to a man of your reputation is – is wholly repugnant to me!'

'You've done so already.'

'Well, I have no wish to offend you, but I don't consider you a fit and proper person to be my sister's husband!'

'Oh, that doesn't offend me! I have every sympathy with you, and should feel just as you do, if I were in your place.'

'Well, upon my word!' gasped Sir Geoffrey. 'You are the most extraordinary fellow I've ever met in all my life!'

'No, am I?' said Mr Carleton, grinning at him. 'Because I agree with you?'

'If you agree with me I wonder that you should have proposed to Annis!'

'Ah, that's a different matter!'

'Well, I think it only right to warn you that I think it is my duty – distasteful though it is to speak of such things to delicately nurtured females – to tell Annis frankly *why* I consider you to be unfit to be her husband!'

Mr Carleton gave a crack of laughter. 'Lord, Wychwood, don't be such a gudgeon!' he said. 'She knows all about my reputation! Tell her anything you like, but don't do so today, will you? I don't want her to be upset again, and she would be. Goodbye! My regards to Lady Wychwood!'

A nod, and he was gone, leaving Sir Geoffrey at a loss to know what to make of him. He went gloomily up to the drawing-room, and when Lady Wychwood joined him a little later, disclosed to her that she had been right in her forecast, adding, with a heavy sigh, that he didn't know what was to be done to prevent the match.

'I'm afraid there's nothing to be done, dearest. I know it isn't what you like. It isn't what I like for her either, but when I saw the *difference* in her! I have just come from her room, and though she is tired, she looks much better, and so happy that I knew it would be useless, and even *wrong* to try to make her cry off! So we must make the best of it, and *pray* that he won't continue in his – his present way of life!'

Sir Geoffrey shook his head. 'A man don't change his habits,' he said. 'I don't believe in reformed rakes, Amabel.'

'I don't mean to set up my opinion against your judgement, for naturally you must know best, but has it occurred to you, dearest, that although we have heard a great deal about his mistresses, and the shameless way he flaunts them abroad, and the money he squanders on them, we have never heard of his attaching himself particularly to any girl of quality? Indeed, I believe Annis is the only woman to whom he has offered marriage, though lures past counting have been thrown out to him, because even the highest sticklers think that his wealth is enough to make him acceptable. So don't you think, Geoffrey, that perhaps he never *truly* loved anyone until he met Annis? Which makes me feel that they were *destined* for each other, for it has been the same with her. I don't mean, of course, *exactly* the same, but only think of the offers she has received, and refused! Such brilliant ones, too! Never, until she met Mr Carleton, has she been in love! Not even with Lord Sedgeley, though one would have said he was the very man for her! You will think me fanciful, I daresay, but it seems to me as if – as if each of them has been waiting for the other for years, and when they at last met they – they fell in love, as though it had been ordained that they should!'

Sir Geoffrey, listening to this speech in frowning silence, was secretly impressed by it, but all he said was: 'Well, you may be right, my love, but I do think that you're being fanciful! All I can say is that if you *are* right, I wish to God they never had met!'

'It is very natural that you should,' responded the perfect wife. 'But don't let us talk about it any more until you have had time to weigh the matter in your mind! Mrs Wardlow asked me this morning if she should instruct the chef to send up baked eggs for our nuncheon, and, knowing how partial you are to baked eggs. I said it was the very thing. So let us go down to the breakfast-parlour now, before the eggs grow cold!'

Sir Geoffrey got up, but before he had reached the door stopped in his tracks like a jibbing horse, and said: 'Is Maria there? Because if she is nothing would prevail upon me—'

'No, no, dearest!' Lady Wychwood hastened to assure him. 'Mrs Wardlow and I have put her to bed, and have compelled her to drink a glass of laudanum and water, as a sedative, you understand. She fell into a fit of the vapours when you went up to see Annis, and what it was that you said to her to overset her so completely, I haven't a notion, for you cannot possibly have accused her of being *inebriated*, which is what she said you did! But I am sorry to say that when Maria becomes hysterical, one cannot place the least dependence on the ridiculous things she says. She even said that Mr Carleton offered her *violence*!'

'No, did he?' exclaimed Sir Geoffrey, brightening perceptibly. 'Well, damme if I don't think he's not by half as black as he's been painted! But mind this, Amabel! I may not have the power to stop him marrying my sister, but if he thinks he's going to foist Maria on to us, he will very soon learn that he is mistaken! And so I shall tell him!'

'Yes, dearest,' said Lady Wychwood, gently propelling him

towards the door. 'You will of course do what you think is right, but do, pray, come and eat your baked egg before it is quite spoilt!'

Elizabeth Byrd

THE FAMISHED LAND   40p

'A vivid and moving re-creation' – Susan Howatch, author of *Penmarric*

A memorable novel of Ireland in the 1840s when the flower-soft days of Ballyfearna became a hunger-ridden nightmare as blight turned the blossoming potato fields to vile, black decay . . .

. . . and young Moira McFlaherty must cope with family, fever, passions, jealousies, threats of eviction and the roving eye of the man she loves.

'Splendidly readable . . . Moira, the red-haired heroine, is not too good to be true – she existed then, I'm sure, and still does' – *Daily Telegraph*

'Wonderful flashes of Irish humour and compassion' – *American Publishers' Weekly*

Also available by this author in PAN:

IMMORTAL QUEEN   40p
THE FLOWERS OF THE FOREST 35p

HOW TO BE YOUR OWN BEST FRIEND 35p

Mildred Newman and Bernard Berkowitz with Jean Owen

The Number One American Bestseller

'Are you for yourself or against yourself?'

'What most people mean when they say
"I *couldn't* help myself" is
"I *didn't* help myself".'

This remarkable book, written with warmth, understanding and wisdom by two practising psychoanalysts, provides simple guidelines for you to become the person it is in you to be.

You *can* learn to become your own best friend.

'There is no pill made that is as simple, effective and fast-working as *How To Be Your Own Best Friend* ... positively inspirational' – Neil Simon

'On a remote movie location the cast and crew called it, simply, *the book*. Appropriate title, I'd say' – Anthony Perkins

Constance Heaven

The glitter of Tsarist Russia – the glamorous balls, skating parties, all the extravagance of fashionable society. Here is the setting for two sparkling novels from Constance Heaven, winner of *The Romantic Novelist of the Year Award*.

THE HOUSE OF KURAGIN	30p
THE ASTROV INHERITANCE	35p

Constance Heaven also writes under her maiden name of CONSTANCE FECHER.

LION OF TREVARROCK	40p
QUEEN'S DELIGHT	40p
TRAITOR'S SON	40p
KING'S LEGACY	40p

THE GEORGE BERNARD SHAW VEGETARIAN COOK BOOK 35p

Mrs Alice Laden
Edited by R. J. Minney

'It is beneficial to one's health not to be carnivorous. The strongest animals, such as the bull, are vegetarians. Look at me. I have ten times as much good health and energy as a meat eater.'

So said George Bernard Shaw, a vegetarian and also a man much concerned about his weight; the calories in each of his meals had to be carefully weighed and the total accurately calculated.

His cook-housekeeper, Mrs Laden, looked after him for the sixteen years before his death in 1943 at the age of ninety-four. These are the recipes that made up the menus she devised for him – all delicious, satisfying, and all conforming to his standards of vegetarianism, low calory count and economy.

'An intelligent man's practical guide (the recipes are for four persons) to the vegetarian kitchen' – Brigid Brophy, *Listener*

These and other PAN Books are obtainable from all booksellers and newsagents. If you have any difficulty please send purchase price plus 7p postage to PO Box 11, Falmouth, Cornwall.

While every effort is made to keep prices low, it is sometimes necessary to increase prices at short notice. PAN Books reserve the right to show new retail prices on covers which may differ from those advertised in the text or elsewhere.